Living with the Single Dad

The Single Dads of Seattle

Book 4

Whitley Cox

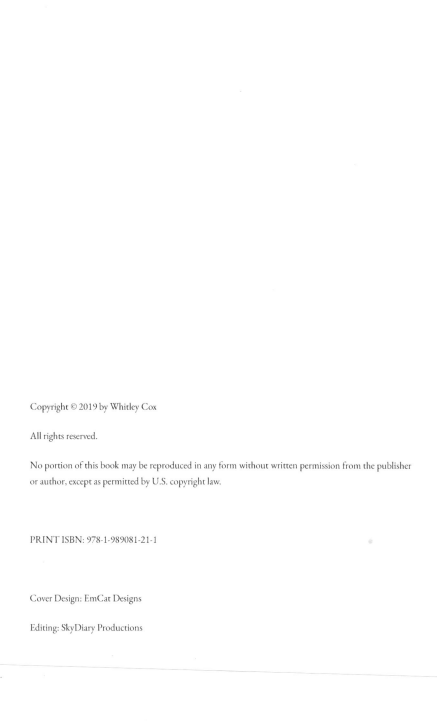

PRINT ISBN: 978-1-989081-21-1

Cover Design: EmCat Designs

Editing: SkyDiary Productions

♥

For Author Jeanne St. James.

A friend, a mentor, a sounding-board, my alpha-reader, and a fucking phenomenal writer.

You are an inspiration and I am so thankful to have you in my life.

xoxo

Contents

Chapter 1

His feet were made of fucking concrete.

His heart the same.

People visiting babies in the NICU shouldn't have to pay for fucking parking. They shouldn't have to pay for squat. A human that weighed less than a fucking house cat was fighting for her life in a plastic box, hooked up to only God knows how many electrodes and monitors, and they were charging him to go and see her. They would also charge him to keep her there, to keep her alive.

And if he couldn't pay?

Would they pull the plug on a one-month-old?

This country was so fucked up.

Pay to live. Pay to be kept alive.

Hippocratic oath, his fucking left nut.

You were only worth saving if you could afford it.

Thank Christ he could pay.

Dina made good money as a lawyer. She'd made sure Sophie would want for nothing.

Except her mother.

She'd want her mother.

She'd need her mother.

Fuck.

Aaron needed his sister.

Grief ensnared him, digging its razor-sharp claws into every cell of his body and shaking him like a rag doll. He pounded his fists on the steering wheel, hollering at the top of his lungs until tears rolled down his cheeks and his throat was raw.

How?

How could this have happened?

He'd spoken to Dina on the phone not two days ago. He was on his way back from a wedding in the South Pacific and couldn't wait to go see Sophie. Dina said that they were getting ready to take her off the ventilators and that if her glucose stayed steady and she could breathe on her own, then they might be able to bring her home soon.

Home.

To Dina's condo.

To the nursery his sister had spent hours decorating. Where the crib he'd built for his niece sat waiting for her to sleep in.

The home his sister had created for a child she'd longed for her entire life, and then finally decided to go it alone when she knew her clock was ticking and she hadn't found the right man yet.

They were going to raise Sophie together.

She would be the mother, the world's best mother, and he would the cool uncle who spoiled his niece rotten. He would be the one to buy her her first tutu, her first horseback riding lessons, her first phone, her first car. He'd also be the tattooed muscle at the front door to intimidate the shit out of any boy that tried to mess with his precious Sophie.

From the first moment he laid eyes on her after Dina had her, he'd fallen in love and had vowed to protect her with everything that he was, everything that he had. He would gladly lay down his life for his niece.

He'd also said all that when he knew Dina would be doing the majority of the child-raising. When he knew she'd be doing all the hard stuff, like diapers and discipline.

But now, he was all Sophie had.

He was her everything. Mother, father. Uncle, aunt.

There was no *cool* uncle status anymore. Just the overwhelming responsibility of being everything she needed.

Sophie wouldn't be running to him when her mother brought down the hammer, pissed her off and she needed somebody to talk to. Now he was going to have to be the one to bring down the hammer. Who would she run to?

Two days.

Two days ago, his sister had been alive. She'd been happy, madly in love with her daughter and both excited and scared to embark on her new role as a mom.

"Give her a kiss for me," Aaron had said as he stood in line with his boarding pass in his hand. He'd been out of town for ten days at his buddy Rob's wedding in French Polynesia and was just heading back to the States. "I can't wait to see how much she's grown and changed."

"She's doing so well. Gained nearly a pound and half, her jaundice is gone, and she's starting to nurse a bit. Which is amazing, because I fucking hate pumping, and my boobs are constantly sore. I look like a porn star."

"Not an image I want to conjure up about my sister, thanks."

Dina chuckled into the phone. Aaron had always loved his sister's laugh. It was so big and loud and full. You knew she put her whole soul into her laugh. "Whatever. One day you'll have a wife or whatever, and she'll be complaining of the same shit."

Aaron made a noise in his throat that said he wasn't sure he agreed. He couldn't see himself settling down anytime soon—if ever. "We'll see." He approached the desk before the jet bridge and handed the attendant his boarding pass and passport. "But listen, sis, I'm about to board. I can't wait to see the little monkey ... and Sophie too."

3

"Ha. Ha." He could practically see her eye roll from across the globe.

Then they'd said they loved each other, like they always did before they said goodbye on the phone, and they hung up. And that was the last time he spoke to his baby sister before she was gunned down during a mass shooting in a mall as she was busy picking out preemie baby clothes for Sophie.

His baby sister, the only person he'd ever loved, his best friend in the entire fucking world, was gunned down in a goddamn shopping mall while buying baby clothes for her premature daughter, who was back at the hospital breathing via machine.

It would never sink in.

Never.

How did shit like this happen?

How?

Still unable to move from behind the driver's seat of his black Chevy pickup truck, Aaron Steele, retired Navy SEAL and special operative, stared straight ahead at the sign for hospital parking and how much it would cost him an hour to go and sit with his one-month-old niece, who'd been born one month premature. To stare at her little body as it struggled to live, knowing that she would never see her mother again. Knowing that she would never know the sound of her mother's voice, the feel of her mother's lips on her soft baby cheeks, her arms around her.

Sophie was in there fighting for her life, and in the blink of an eye, her mother's life had ended.

How in the fuck did this make any goddamn sense at all?

How was Aaron supposed to get out of the truck, walk into the hospital and go be a father to Sophie? He had no idea how to be a father. He'd never had a father to know how to be one, let alone a good one. He could hardly take care of himself. He wasn't even sure he ever wanted kids.

Cool uncle had been fine with him.

Love them until they're annoying and then pass them back to their parents.

Win-win for everyone. Mainly him.

But all that changed in a fucking instant, and now he was a dad. He was a single dad with a one-month-old daughter who would never know her mother, and he had no fucking clue where to start.

A knock on his window had him reaching for the gun on his hip. Only he wasn't carrying a gun today. He hadn't carried a gun in two days, and he wasn't sure he ever would again.

The only thing that stops a bad guy with a gun is a good guy with a gun.

Yeah, fucking right. He called bullshit. Where the hell had the good guy with the gun been when his sister was in the baby boutique bleeding out?

The only person who should have a gun is a fucking sane person with proper training and a fucking permit.

You needed a license to own a dog, to drive a car, to catch a fish. Why the fuck didn't you need one to own a goddamn weapon?

Another knock on the window, and a confused face brought his thoughts back to the present.

Liam stared at him through the window, his brown eyes as hollow as Aaron's heart. He'd been one of Dina's closest friends and colleagues. He was Dina's *in case of emergency* person because Aaron had been a SEAL for so long and not always around. It was Liam who'd called Aaron with the news about Dina.

Aaron rolled down the window.

Liam's throat undulated on a hard swallow. The man looked like complete shit. Dark bags under his eyes, messy dark blond hair, days and days' worth of scruff.

He looked how Aaron felt.

"Hey."

Aaron nodded a hello.

"Going in?"

"Hoping to."

Liam scanned the parking lot. It was late August and hot as fuck. You could probably fry an egg on the blacktop. "I just left."

Aaron lifted his head and narrowed his eyes at Liam. "You saw Sophie?"

Liam nodded. "Yeah. I've been going as much as I can since she was born. Whenever Dina had to leave, she always made sure someone else was with Soph. Someone besides a nurse or doctor. Like a friend."

Aaron's heart ripped in two. His sister was the best fucking mom in the whole fucking world. And of course she would be. She knew what a shitty mother was like. They both did. Having grown up in foster care their entire lives, Aaron and Dina had bounced around the system for years. They never found a home or family they could really call *theirs*. But at least they had each other.

When Aaron turned eighteen, he left the system, or more accurately was *kicked out* of the system, left to his own devices to either flounder or flourish in the big cruel world.

Thankfully, he flourished. The day he graduated high school, he got a job in construction. Walked right onto the site and refused to leave until the foreman gave him a job. And at 4:58 p.m, right before quitting time, he was handed his very first hard hat.

Over the next six months, he proved himself, and his boss at the construction company offered to pay for Aaron to go to carpentry school while he worked. He earned his journeyman ticket in carpentry and obtained all of his necessary apprenticeship hours by the time he was twenty-one.

Shortly after Aaron got hired, his boss—who became more of a father figure than anything else—helped him petition the courts to get legal custody of Dina—and he won. She was fifteen and he was eighteen, and he was happy to get her out of the shit show house they'd been living in before that. Eight foster kids, one foster mother, one bathroom and barely enough food to feed a family of rabbits.

Though he and Dina didn't live like royalty, at least they were together. He found them a modest little two-bedroom apartment in a questionable part of

Seattle, but it was clean, it was safe, and most importantly, it was theirs, and they were together.

He worked and went to night school for his journeyman ticket. She went to high school and worked a part-time job at a movie theater on the weekends. They made ends meet—just barely, but they did. They never went to bed hungry, were never late on a rent or utility bill. Somehow, by grace and by God, Aaron even managed to save a small sum by the time Dina's senior prom came around, and he surprised her with the dress she'd been dreaming of for over six months.

She was his person, and he was hers.

Because they were all the other ever had.

Sure, he had his brothers in arms. He had Rob and Colt, Wark and Ash. They were his brothers.

They were his team.

But they weren't blood.

Dina was his blood.

She was the only blood he had. His only connection to his past.

They didn't know their parents, their grandparents or whether they had more siblings out there. It was just the two of them. Aaron and Dina Steele, taking on the world.

When she graduated high school, he made sure she got into college before he enlisted in the Navy. He knew she'd be safe and make friends at college. She wouldn't be alone. He put her through four years of school and then law school, sending her money whenever he could. Even if they went months without seeing each other, he wanted her to know that he was always there for her. Always supporting her.

He'd never cried so much in his life—up until recently—than he did the day his sister accepted her diploma at her law school graduation. And he didn't give a flying fuck who saw him bawling his eyes out. His baby sister was a motherfucking lawyer, and he would shout it from the rooftops and sob until his eyes were empty, he was so damn proud.

"I can go back in with you." Liam's voice drew Aaron out of his thoughts. He'd been spacing out a lot over the last two days. Jet lag and grief will do that to a person. "If you're not ready to go face Sophie alone, I can go back in. She knows me. Seems to like me."

Aaron pursed his lips together before rolling the window back up in his truck, turning off the ignition and opening the door. "Thanks, man. Right now I'm not sure how to face her alone."

He locked the truck and dug into his pocket to grab his wallet so he could pay for parking.

Liam's hand slapped his shoulder. "Don't worry about it, man. I got ya. I'll go enter your license plate number and get your parking. Go see your niece."

Swallowing down the razor blade that had lodged in his throat, Aaron did nothing but nod, murmur a thanks and then head in the direction of the hospital main entrance, the ache in his heart feeling more like an anvil on his chest as he approached the main doors.

He wasn't cut out to be a dad.

He was going to fail Sophie, fail Dina, fail them all.

Just like he'd failed in Colombia.

Chapter 2

♥

"Zucchini noodles with parmesan, prawns and sun-dried tomatoes," Isobel Jones sang as she set the dinner plate down in front of her sister and roommate, Tori. She set a plate with the same food down in her spot and thanked her sister for pouring the wine.

"Ooh," her sister cooed. "Did you try out that new spiralizer I bought?"

Isobel nodded. "Works slick. I'm trying to decide what to spiralize next. Sweet potato? Cucumbers?"

"Cucumbers could be good for a salad," Tori offered.

They sat across from each other at the small bistro table in their shared apartment. It was a rare occasion that they ate together, as Isobel was normally working and Tori was either working or off with her sexy new boyfriend, *Dr. Mark.*

"How's the new commission coming?" Tori asked, diving into her zucchini noodles.

Isobel nodded, taking a sip of her wine. "Going great. Paige is a peach. So easy to work with. She's liked all my mock-ups so far. Thanks again for singing my praises."

Tori winked. "I've got your back, Jack."

Isobel was about to delve further into an explanation about her new graphic design commission, designing the new logo and signage for The Lilac and Lavender Bistro, when Tori's phone started to ring.

Her sister squinted her bright blue eyes at the caller ID. "Liam?"

Isobel had only met Liam once. He was one of The Single Dads of Seattle that Mark played poker with on Saturdays. The guy seemed nice enough. A lawyer with a potty mouth was how she'd best describe him, which only made her think he was probably a shark in the courtroom and a tiger in the sack. Most men who were professional by day were dirty at night.

"Answer it," Isobel said, nodding at her sister's phone.

Tori twisted her lips. "I'm sure it's nothing. I can call him back after dinner."

Isobel rolled her eyes. "Answer it."

Tori huffed out a breath. "Fine." She punched the *on* button. "Hey Liam, what's up?"

Isobel twirled her zucchini noodles around on her fork, speared a prawn and popped the whole thing into her mouth, watching as her sister's facial expressions changed from sad to curious to understanding to excited. What could Liam possibly be telling her?

"Okay, here she is," Tori said, thrusting her arm over the table and handing the phone to Isobel. "He wants to talk to you."

"To me?" She pointed at herself in the chest for some stupid reason.

"Is there another Isobel Priscilla Jones in the house I don't know about?" her sister asked with a smirk.

"How does he know my whole name?"

"Just take the damn thing," Tori said. "I'm hungry."

Frowning in confusion, Isobel took the phone from her goofy big sister and put it to her ear. "Hello?"

"Hi, Isobel. It's Liam Dixon. We met at one of Mark and Tori's barbecues a while back."

"That's right. How are you?"

Was he calling to ask her out?

Liam was good-looking. She just wasn't sure he was her type. He was also like forty or something. Was that too old? She hadn't dated an older guy in a while. Last time had been when she was twenty and the guy was thirty. And even then, they struggled to find something in common besides how much they both liked having sex while watching *The Office* on Netflix.

But maybe that had just been him.

He'd been weird.

Sexy but weird.

Crap, she was getting off track. Had Liam replied? She'd stopped listening and was now thinking about Devon and his rippling six pack, his long tongue, his thick ...

"Isobel, you still there?"

Whoops.

"Yep, still here. Sorry, Liam. It's been a long day. Had a mini power nap there."

His chuckle was forced. "Sorry I'm not more exciting for you. So, what do you think? Are you interested in the job?"

Job?

She looked across the table to her sister, who was rolling her eyes and mouthing the words "nanny job."

Oh!

"A nanny job for your son?" If she remembered correctly, Liam's son was named Jordan, and he was a sweet little boy, albeit a touch wild. But what little boy wasn't at the age of five?

"Uh, no," he said slowly. "It's for a friend of mine. Mark mentioned that you're a nanny and looking for a new family." He cleared his throat. The next words he spoke were filled with pain. "He just lost his sister in that mass shooting at the Emerald City Mall."

"Oh no!" She clapped her hand over her mouth. She'd read about that. Twelve dead, fifteen more injured. A SWAT team sniper had taken out the lone gunman, but only after he'd terrorized hundreds of people for a solid ten minutes.

"Yeah." He grunted. "She was a very dear friend of mine." Was that a hiccup or a sob? "My best friend. And she'd just had a baby a month ago. Sophie was a month early too and is still in the NICU."

"Oh my God." Isobel's eyes welled up with hot tears that stung like a bitch. "No. Liam, no. That's terrible."

"Dina had no partner. She went through a sperm bank, so now Dina's brother is Sophie's guardian. But he doesn't have any children of his own, and he's really taking Dina's death hard. He might need some help for a bit." She could tell he was struggling to get each and every word out, that it physically pained him to speak about his friend in the past tense. Isobel could feel his heartache through the phone and across the miles. Her own heart shattered at the thought of this tiny baby never getting to know her mother, all because of some psychopath with access to an automatic rifle.

Fuck, the gun laws needed to change.

"I'll do it," she blurted out, not even sure if she was cutting Liam off or not. Hell, she'd do it for free.

Tori's eyes narrowed across the table at her. She mouthed, "Think this through."

Isobel rolled her eyes. Her sister was such a worry-wart. An overthinker.

Liam let out a sigh of relief. "Thanks, Isobel. I don't know how long the job will be for, or how long until Aaron finds his footing, but just know that if he can't cover your wages, I will."

She used her napkin to wipe up the tears streaming down her face and sniffled before answering. "We'll figure it out, Liam. Don't worry about that. I have other jobs too, so it's not like I'm destitute."

"Well, if you wouldn't mind sending me your resume and credentials, like CPR et cetera, I'd really appreciate it. That way I can show Aaron I'm not just hiring him some random person off the street or some website. That you're qualified and experienced. I mean, *I* would hire you right now without needing that shit, because Mark and Tori have vouched for you, but Aaron might need to see some qualifications."

"No problem. I totally understand. I can do that this evening."

"Cool. Thank you. I'll text Tori my email address when we hang up here and you can send me your info."

"Okay."

He blew out a breath. "Thanks so much, Isobel. Just let me know if you need anything. Sophie is still in the NICU, but we were there to see her earlier today, and they think she'll be ready to go home in about five days. I'll pass along your information to Aaron, and he can let you know when you start."

All she could do at this point was nod.

"Still there?"

"Mhmm."

Liam's voice was hoarse and full of emotion. "Okay, thanks, Isobel. I really appreciate it. Sophie's going to need as many people in her family as we can manage. That little girl needs an army at her disposal. A village to raise her."

Isobel swallowed and nodded again. "Right. Army. Village. Got it."

"'Kay, I'll talk to you later." Then he hung up.

Tori passed Isobel her napkin, since Isobel's own napkin was now soaking wet. "I had no idea Liam's friend was a victim of the mall shooting," Tori started. "He left abruptly Saturday night from Mitch's photography studio opening when he got the call. That's terrible. Poor baby."

Isobel's eyes teemed with tears as she hung her head and covered her face with her hands, letting the sobs take over her body and the grief for these people she didn't even know consume her.

A protective arm wrapped around her shoulders, and Tori's lips landed gently on her temple. "Your empathy is your greatest strength, as well as your biggest weakness," her sister murmured, rocking them to a gentle sway. "You sure you're up for it?"

Isobel lifted her head from her hands, focusing her gaze on her sister. "I have to do this, Tor. That baby …" She shuddered on an inhale. "Oh my God, that poor baby."

Her sister squeezed her tighter. "You're going to have your hands full with a newborn. Have you thought this through? Like *really* thought it through. It's going to be a really demanding job. Newborns are tough. And a grieving brother who thought he was going to be an uncle but is now a father—you've got your work cut out for you."

Isobel shook her head. "I don't mind. I like work."

Tori chuckled, squeezing her sister tighter. "I've never met a harder working person in my life, Iz."

Isobel pushed her plate away. She was no longer hungry. She hung her head and stared at the tops of her bare knees, peeking out from beneath her soft cotton gray shorts. She lifted her head. "Do you think I can help them?"

Tori smiled. "If anybody can, you can. Remember the Trammell family? They were a mess before you stepped in. You got Keegan eating vegetables, Spencer stopped hitting kids at school, and little Melinda was speaking in sentences by the time you left them. You did all of that. You not only saved that family, you saved their freaking marriage." Her lips flattened into a thin line in thought. "Are you having second thoughts? Do you want to call Liam back and say no? I'm sure he can find a nanny for this Aaron guy somewhere else. There are websites and agencies for this kind of thing."

Isobel shook her head. "No. I want to be there for her."

Tori blew out a breath before leaning her head on Isobel's shoulder. "Is being an empath exhausting? It seems like it would be exhausting. Feeling everybody's feelings like they're your own, having this constant need to save the world."

Isobel knew her sister was trying to lighten the mood. Her tone held a tinge of teasing to it, but Tori wasn't wrong. Isobel had always been a sensitive person, almost to a fault and often to her own detriment.

A bleeding heart.

14

A sucker for a sob story.

An-always-see-the-best-in-people-no-matter-how-many-times-they've-burned-her-before soft-hearted fool.

Or as her mother called her, *a marshmallow but not a doormat.*

Because she wasn't a doormat, but she was a softy.

She'd nearly been abducted as a child when she believed the man at the park needed help finding his puppy. Thank God her older sister was a skeptic and an overthinker who told the man to "fuck off" or she would call the cops.

You'd think Isobel would have learned from that, but no. She never got abducted or anything, but she'd certainly been burned over the years, putting her faith and trust in people who didn't deserve an ounce of it.

She'd also met some amazing people along the way. Helped some truly wonderful souls and in turn, they helped her. Helped her find her passion, and although she loved art and had gone to graphic design school, ultimately, her biggest passion was helping people. Particularly children. Which was why she was now a twenty-six-year-old graphic design graduate that preferred to be a nanny than get a full-time job with a design firm.

She exhaled a shaky breath. She needed to get ahold of herself. She'd felt Liam's heartache through the phone as he told her about Sophie and Aaron, felt the physical pain talking about his dead friend and her infant daughter was putting him through. What would she do when she finally came face to face with them? When she finally saw tiny Sophie, completely innocent and desperate for her mother?

"I don't envy you," Tori whispered. "I admire you and am crazy proud of you, but I don't envy you. I'll take my overthinking, analytical, cynical brain any day of the week."

Isobel half-choked, half-laughed. "Sometimes I wish I was like you. I'd probably have been burned a hell of a lot less if I cut my losses before they hurt me."

Tori grabbed Isobel's wineglass and handed it to her before getting up from where she'd been kneeling on the floor. She circled around the table to her own chair, sitting down and taking a sip of her wine. "Yeah, but we are who we are for a reason. I'm the hardened cynic who overanalyzes things, takes forever to pick a restaurant to eat at and researches even the most mundane of things to death before I do them. And you're the free spirit who follows her heart, always sees the good in people and picks the restaurants for us by closing her eyes, spinning in a circle and pointing."

"You're saying we balance each other out?"

Tori nodded. "We do. You're the yin to my yang. I'm ruled by gravity, you're ruled by air, and together we both float just inches from earth. Without each other, you'd be off floating in the stratosphere, and I'd be unable to lift one foot in front of the other."

New tears pricked the corners of Isobel's eyes, but unlike earlier, these were tears of joy. How did she get so lucky to get such an amazing sister?

Tori lifted her wineglass in the air. "To balance."

Isobel clinked Tori's class with her own. "To balance."

"I don't know what I'd do without you, Iz." Their eyes locked, blue to blue. She could see right into her sister's soul, past the tough exterior and down into the big, welcoming heart Isobel knew Tori hid deep inside.

"I don't know what I'd do without you either."

Tori dug into her meal, but Isobel simply stared at her full plate. She had her sister, her parents, her health, her life. But in the blink of an eye, the speed of a bullet, someone's world can flip upside down. Someone's world can be destroyed.

Aaron was without his sister, and Sophie was without a mother.

Isobel's life was full.

Aaron and Sophie's lives were empty.

Where was the justice there?

How was that fair?

And more than anything, how could she help?

16

Chapter 3

Aaron slammed the back door of his truck after hauling out the bucket car seat, where a tiny, sleeping Sophie lay completely unaware of the chaotic life she about to start. A life with a clueless uncle who, although he loved her more than his own life, had no idea how to raise a kid, let alone a little girl, and was ultimately going to screw her up for life and send her to therapy for years to come.

A car door on the side of the road slammed, and Aaron's pulse quickened.

Was that the new nanny?

Liam had arranged everything. All Aaron had done was call her and have a brief five-minute conversation with her yesterday, letting her know she could start today. Hell, it was probably closer to three minutes. He was putting all his faith in Liam to not hire his niece some wingnut off the streets to take care of her. Lord knew Aaron had no clue how to pick a good nanny, the questions to ask, the credentials to look into.

Even if he did, he was in no frame of mind to be calling references and vetting potential hires. He'd hardly slept a wink in the last week. He couldn't.

How could he sleep when Dina was gone?

When Sophie needed him.

He'd spent every minute he could with Sophie in the hospital until she was released. More than he was probably allowed, but the nurses took pity on him because they knew the situation. Thank God for Liam. Aaron wouldn't have known how to start, explaining that his sister was dead and that she wouldn't be back to bring Sophie any more milk. She wouldn't be back to hold and bond with her baby. She wouldn't be back to take her home when she was well enough to be discharged.

He fumbled for his keys in his pocket as the grief crashed hard in his chest at the thought of welcoming Sophie to her new home and not having Dina there. He found his keys, but they fell as he struggled to hold the car seat, diaper bag and a grocery bag full of formula.

"Shit!"

His eyes flashed down to Sophie.

Please don't wake up. Please don't wake up.

A hand landed on his shoulder. "I got 'em," Liam said, releasing Aaron's shoulder and bending down to retrieve his keys. He didn't hand them back but instead walked toward the front door, put the right key in the lock and turned the latch, holding the door open for Aaron and Sophie.

Aaron stepped forward, but he stopped on the threshold.

Liam's hand landed back on his shoulder. "I know, man. This wasn't the home Sophie was supposed to be moving into. I know."

His brow furrowed as his mouth turned grim. "I don't have a nursery for her. I don't have a damn thing."

"But you have love," came a soft, feminine voice behind them.

Aaron spun around, making sure not to swing Sophie and wake her up in the process, only to come face to face with a woman with long dark hair and bright blue eyes.

"Ah, Isobel, you made it." Liam stuck one foot on the bottom of the door to keep it open while extending his hand toward the woman, in a plain white T-shirt and denim capris. "It's nice to see you again."

She took Liam's hand with a small, demure smile. "Nice to see you again too." Her eyes flicked up to Aaron's, and she extended her hand toward him. He took it, and they shook briefly. "I'm Isobel, or Iz. Nice to meet you." Her long throat jogged on a swallow as she glanced down. "I am ..." She blew out a breath. Her eyes lifted back up to Aaron's, and he could see she was tearing up. "I am *so* sorry for your loss." She shook her head, looked away and wiped beneath her eyes. "I know that you're probably really tired of hearing people say that, and I'm sorry. I wish ..." Her jaw ticked as she clenched it hard. "I wish I could say something more comforting."

Who was this woman? She was saying exactly the things he was feeling. He was tired of hearing that shit. He was tired of the pity eyes and the whispers behind his back. He was tired of it all. But at the same time, he wished there was something someone could say to him that would make everything right, that could help him make sense of it all, click it all into place.

But there wasn't.

Dina's death had been senseless and wrong. There was no reason for his sister to have died when and the way she did. It could have been prevented.

"I can't imagine ..." She trailed off and wiped beneath her eyes again. "I'm sorry." Tears slipped down her cheeks as she crouched down and stared into the car seat at a sleeping Sophie. "You didn't deserve this, sweetheart," she whispered, reaching out and stroking a finger over the top of Sophie's delicate little hand. "You didn't deserve this at all."

Liam and Aaron exchanged looks over top of Isobel's head.

Liam's own eyes were welling up, and his jaw was tight.

Ah, fuck. Aaron was on the verge too.

Shit.

He'd stayed strong while at the hospital each day. Sophie needed him to stay strong. But once he arrived home, shut the door behind him and stared into the cold emptiness of his house, he'd lose it. Consumed by that nauseating, emotional mixture of sick sadness and boiling rage. He tossed and turned in his bed, crying until he couldn't cry anymore, only to then go and kick the shit out of his punching bag hanging in the garage in the wee hours of the morning. Then, when he couldn't swing another punch, he'd crumple to the ground in a new heap of tears until his eyes drifted shut and he managed to catch maybe thirty minutes of sleep on the cold concrete floor.

The endless back and forth between crippling sadness and sheer madness was exhausting.

But the anger felt good. It felt better than the pain that threatened to tear his heart clean from his chest.

He imagined the punching bag was the face of Dina's shooter. The faces of those who don't believe that guns need to be regulated and controlled. The faces of all those who could have prevented his sister's death, Sophie becoming an orphan, if they'd just opened their motherfucking eyes and seen the reality of the world they now lived in.

His fists flexed, and he cracked his knuckles. His body was struggling now between rage and misery. Tears threatened, but fury bubbled.

They needed to get the baby inside. They needed to change the subject before he blew a fucking gasket.

He made a noise in his throat and lifted the car seat back up off the ground. "I'm going to get Sophie inside and unpack a bit." He cleared his throat again before turning around and heading into his three-bedroom rancher, making sure to show the other two his back as a lone, hot tear sprinted down his cheek.

He set Sophie's car seat on his brown leather couch, wiped his eyes, sniffed, stared at the wall for twenty seconds to get his shit together, then finally faced the other two.

Isobel and Liam simply stood in his living room, both their eyes focused on Sophie.

"I just bought some formula, so you can feed her that when she wakes up," he said, opening up the plastic grocery bag and pulling out a bunch of premixed bottles of infant formula. "Nurses recommended this one. Should be gentle on her belly."

Isobel's head bobbed. "Okay."

"Master bedroom is down the hall. I'll put Sophie in the one closest to the bathroom, and you can have the one next to the living room." He hooked a finger over his shoulder to let her know where the bedrooms were before putting his head down and opening up the diaper bag.

"You want me to live here?" Her voice was like a soft lullaby. She probably had a lovely singing voice.

He lifted his head. "You don't want to?"

They both glanced at Liam, who immediately held up his hands in surrender. "I am merely the agent. It's up to you two to negotiate the terms. I simply facilitate."

"I can't do this alone," Aaron whispered. "I can't. I don't know how."

Her eyes closed for a moment, and he held his breath. Was she going to leave? Say she couldn't do this either?

"Let's just take it week by week, how about that? I can stay for the first few nights to help you get settled, and then we can take it from there."

Tension fled from his shoulders, and he nodded. "Week by week."

She smiled. "One step at a time. We'll make it work. We'll figure it out."

Aaron swallowed, then put his head back down and began pulling things out of the diaper bag. Sophie would wake soon, and he'd have to change her diaper and possibly even her outfit. He wasn't sure the diaper bag had enough to last them. Eventually she would grow, and he'd have to get bigger clothes for her.

Eventually he'd have to go to Dina's.

He should have gone to his sister's condo over the past week while Sophie was still in the NICU, but he just couldn't. He'd pulled into the parking lot for her condo building three times, only to sit there for fifteen minutes, curse, yell, bang his hands on the steering wheel a bunch more and then toss the truck in reverse and peel out of there.

He couldn't go into that building when he knew she wasn't in there. He couldn't go in and see her half-finished cup of tea sitting on the counter like he knew it would be. See her plants that probably desperately needed watering or the pile of mail in her mailbox.

He couldn't.

"Would you like me to go out and buy a few more things for Sophie?" Isobel asked, her voice calm and reassuring. "Newborns really don't need much in the beginning besides love, a full belly and plenty of diapers."

"She's right," Liam piped up. "A few sleepers in case she spits up or shoots shit up her back, but other than that, they're pretty low-maintenance."

"We can go and grab things from the nursery when you're ready," Isobel continued. "When she needs them. But right now, all she needs is you."

He lifted his head to Isobel's face. "I'm not enough. She needs her mother."

She took a step toward him, her blue eyes fiercely focused. "You're going to have to be enough. That little baby needs you more than ever now. You can do this."

A squeak that sounded like a baby guinea pig drew their attention to the couch. Sophie stretched and made a silly face, scrunching up her features before she slowly opened her dark eyes. She stared up at both of them, blinking several times before yawning wide.

"Oh, that's a good sign. I'm already boring her," he said dryly.

Isobel leaned down and gently unbuckled Sophie from her car seat before reaching in and pulling the baby free, cradling her against her chest. "Hi, Super Sophie," she cooed, kissing Sophie's forehead a couple of times. "Did you have a good sleep?" She pressed her nose against the baby's head and inhaled deeply. "Mmmm, nothing quite like that new baby smell." She let her eyes flutter shut and rocked them both gently back and forth. "They need to figure out a way to bottle it."

Sophie yawned again, showing off her gummy mouth and tiny pink tongue.

Isobel opened her eyes when Sophie began to squawk and bop her head against Isobel's shoulder. "Oh, she's rooting. Must be hungry. Go see your uncle, baby. I'll go and fix you a bottle." She passed Sophie to Aaron, her movements careful but sure. She seemed far more confident holding such a small creature than Aaron was. He felt like he was going to drop her at any moment.

Immediately, once she was in his arms, he sat down on the couch and laid her on his lap.

Isobel grabbed the bag of formula and bottles he'd bought at the grocery store and took it to the kitchen.

"Babies are more resilient than you think," Liam said. "I mean they don't bounce when you drop them, particularly on their heads, but you also don't need to hold her like she's a Ming vase either."

Aaron shot him an irritated look. "She is a fucking Ming vase. She's *more* priceless than a Ming vase. She's all I have." He choked out that last part and fixed his eyes back on a curious and alert Sophie. Her little arms jerked, and her fingers wrapped tightly around his index finger, holding on for dear life. "You're all I have."

Liam coughed, shifting back and forth on his feet. "Right. Sorry."

Aaron let out a slow breath and lifted his head back up, pinning his gaze on Liam. The guy looked like shit. Which was probably exactly how Aaron looked. Bags beneath his eyes, untidy short beard, worry lines, bedhead.

"I'm sorry," he finally said. "You've really stepped up for Soph and I. We couldn't have done it without you. You're a true friend to Dina." He swallowed as the emotions threatened to ransack his composure. "You're a true friend to all of us."

Liam's jaw wobbled, and he sat down on the other end of the couch, running his hand through his dark blond hair, then dragging it down to scrub over his face. He tugged on his chin. "Ah, man. Ain't nothing right or true about any of this. It's fucked up, is what it is. Not Dina. Anybody but Dina."

Aaron clenched his jaw so tight, he thought his eyes were going to bulge clean out of his head.

Anybody but Dina was fucking right.

Liam grunted, drawing Aaron's attention away from his dark thoughts. "So listen, no pressure or anything, join if you want, come when you're ready, but ... I'm a single dad too, and over the last few years, I've gotten to know other single dads. Through work and other ways too. I started a club. The Single Dads of Seattle. We meet every Saturday night at my place for poker. You're probably not ready to come tomorrow night, but the offer is always there.

"Some dads hang out with their kids other days during the week, playdates, whatever. But what it mostly is is a group of men who all fucking get it. We get how hard it is to be a single father. Some of us are full-time single dads, some of us part-time. We have each other's backs. Babysit for each other if needed. We're a brotherhood. Or a *fatherhood*. A family."

A family.

Aaron was about to say he wasn't ready to socialize when Isobel's voice interrupted his thoughts.

"Who's ready for a bottle?" she asked.

He lifted his head up from Liam's face to the gorgeous young woman coming toward them.

Fuck, she was young. What was she, twenty-five? Twenty-six? There was no way this woman was a day over thirty. Unlike Aaron, who was not only a day over thirty but a good eight years over.

He lifted Sophie off his lap and stood up, grabbing—well, more like snatching the warm formula bottle from Isobel's hand. "I'll do it." He grunted, moving over to the window, cradling his niece in his arm and offering her the bottle.

"Oookay," Isobel said, not seeming to be affected by his gruffness. "So, are you wanting me to stay over tonight? Because I didn't bring anything. I'd have to run home and grab a bag of clothes."

He didn't bother turning around to face her but grunted an answer. "Yeah. Go get your stuff, then come back."

24

There was a pause, then footsteps heading toward the front door. "Okay, I'll be back shortly." Another pause. "Text me if you need anything." Then the front door shut, leaving Aaron and Liam alone once more.

Aaron felt his new friend's presence before Liam entered his peripheral vision. "Dude, don't fuck the nanny," Liam said. "I know she's hot. Fuck, she's crazy hot, but you can't fuck your nanny."

Aaron adjusted Sophie in his arms, tilted the bottle up a little more and then glared at Liam. "Don't you think I know that?"

"Knowing and doing are two different things. Tread lightly, my friend." He slapped Aaron on the shoulder. "And get some sleep. You look like shit."

Aaron focused back on a guzzling Sophie. "I look how I feel."

Liam hung his head and squeezed Aaron's shoulder in a comforting and brotherly way. "You and me both, man. You and me both."

Chapter 4

Isobel slid in behind the steering wheel of her white Toyota Corolla and put the keys in the ignition. She didn't put the car into reverse. She didn't move. She just sat there and stared at the garage door to Aaron's house, wondering what the hell she'd just gotten herself into.

He was hot.

Boy, oh boy, was he hot.

Big, muscly, a force of nature like she'd never seen before.

And that hair. Dark red, thick and lush with just the smallest hint of a wave.

She'd always had a weakness for redheaded men. *Outlander* had ruined her. Now all she lusted after, fantasized about was a big, tall Scotsman lifting his kilt and taking her hard and fast on a bed of heather.

She squeezed her eyes shut.

That didn't help a bit.

Those arms. Holy Batman. Those weren't even arms. Those were tattooed tree trunks busting out of a thin black cotton prison. He needed to release those glorious beasts for all the world to admire.

And lick.

Oh crap.

She slammed her palms on the steering wheel and rested her forehead on top of the back of her hands. "No, no, no."

She should be marching back into that house and declining the job. Say something came up and she would find him a replacement nanny. That she couldn't work for him. Couldn't live with him.

Holy mother.

Aaron wanted her to live there.

She was going to be under the same roof, day and night, with the sexiest thing she'd ever laid eyes on.

And were those dog tags beneath his shirt?

Was he some kind of soldier? A fighter pilot? A sniper? Oh dear heaven and earth, a SEAL? Was he a SEAL?

She whimpered as she lifted her head up, jumping when she came face to face with the man who had her whimpering. His head cocked to the side in confusion, her purse in his hand.

Oh crap!

He wandered around to the driver's side door and waited for her to roll down her window.

"Everything okay?"

Swallowing, she nodded. "Yeah, just, uh ... I have a bit of a headache." He didn't have a baby in his arms anymore. Why not? Her eyes searched his big frame for signs of a tiny baby hiding somewhere. Oh, now she really was losing her mind.

Lack of sex will do that to a person.

"Where's Sophie?" she finally asked, having not let the oxygen reach her brain before asking the stupid question. Obviously, Sophie was folding the laundry in the house while lip-syncing to Green Day.

She's probably in the house sleeping, you moron.

"She fell asleep after her bottle. Liam's holding her. I came out here to grab the bassinet I bought. Noticed you forgot your purse." His blue eyes seared her skin until a tingle, not at all unpleasant, ran through her, ending firmly between her legs.

He held out her purse.

"Right." She took her purse from him. "Thanks. Can't forget this." She smiled at him, but every bit of it was forced and awkward. She wanted to put the car into drive and plow headfirst into his garage door hard enough to knock herself out so she didn't have to think about how his eyes twinkled in the sunlight or his tattooed biceps rippled when he crossed his arms over his chest. What did the tattoos mean?

She couldn't quite tell from the angle and the fact that they crept up beneath the sleeve of his shirt. What she could tell was that they were hot.

She didn't want to stare too long at his arms, or his chest, or his shoulders, stomach, thick thighs, the V of his legs ... fuck. Where *could* she look?

His face.

Damn, that was hot too. But safer territory than anywhere else on his body.

She smiled another awkward smile, hoping he hadn't caught her ogling his arms.

He didn't smile back but instead pinched his brows together and looked down the bridge of his nose at her.

Isobel squirmed beneath his intense gaze.

"You're coming right back?" he asked.

She nodded for the umpteenth time. "Yep."

He nodded once. "Okay."

"Bed!"

She groaned inwardly, then groaned again and even harder when his eyes grew wide.

She shook her head, her face on fire. "I mean, bedding. Do you have a bed for me? Or should I bring some of my own bedding and a blow-up mattress or something?"

Understanding slowly crossed his face. "Guest room has everything you'll need. Just bring your clothes."

She was staring up at him but let her eyes travel down the length of his frame, and of course they stopped on what was right smack dab in front of her, the V of his thick, powerful thighs in his well-worn jeans.

Aaron cleared his throat, forcing Isobel's neck to nearly snap in two, she flung her head back up so fast. "Get going," he ordered, his tone gruff and almost mean. "Get back soon." Then he headed past her toward his truck, which was parked beside her car in the double driveway, and retrieved the bassinet from the pickup bed. He walked toward the house right in front of her car but didn't bother looking at her.

She couldn't decide if that was better or worse.

She waited until she heard the front door of the house close before she tossed her car into reverse and pulled out of the driveway.

Only then did she realize how soaked her panties were and how much her nipples ached. She glanced down her body at her breasts. Her bra had no padding, and it showed. Oh boy, did it show. Hard peaks poked out beneath the thin white cotton of her T-shirt.

She paused at the end of his driveway and bonked her head on his steering wheel again. This was such a bad idea. Such a bad, bad, bad idea.

She glanced once more at the house, only to see Aaron standing in front of the living room window, staring at her.

Fuck.

Averting her eyes, she checked her blind spot, her rearview mirror, and then backed out into traffic as fast as she could.

She needed to get away from the pheromones and testosterone and whatever that incredible manly smell was. It was driving her loony. She wasn't able to think straight.

"Bad idea," she repeated. "Bad, bad, bad."

She needed to turn the job down. She had to.

But then her mind wandered to sweet baby Sophie and how badly she needed a village around her. A team of people devoted to taking care of her, making sure she had all the love she'd ever need.

She couldn't abandon that baby.

Her heart wouldn't let her.

While in Aaron's kitchen, she'd checked his fridge and pantry, and the guy had no food. Some beer, two onions, half a bag of carrots, some weird-shaped pasta and six packages of ramen noodles were all she could find besides eight different kinds of barbecue sauce and a bottle of Frank's Red Hot. Had he been eating takeout all week since his sister passed? Had he been eating at all?

She decided that she'd take a detour on her way home and stop off at the grocery store to refill his fridge and pantry. Maybe she could cook him a nice dinner as well. Steak and baked potato with roasted veggies and maybe an apple pie for dessert?

The clock on her dash said it was only one o'clock. Plenty of time to grocery shop, pop home and then head back to Aaron's house to whip up a pie.

Aaron's house.

Her new home?

Her home away from home?

Her work home?

She shook her head, then turned on the radio to drown out her thoughts. She was turning into Tori, overthinking everything. She needed to just take this job day by day, hour by hour, minute by minute.

Aaron and Sophie needed her.

The fates had put them into her life for a reason.

They needed her help, and she had help to give.

Aaron's massive chest flashed into her mind as she came to a red light. "Yeah, keep telling yourself that," she murmured. "You're doing this to help them, *riiiight*. Not because you want what your sister has. Tori mixed business with pleasure and got the relationship of a lifetime. She's doing her boss, and life is just peachy." She caught her reflection in the side mirror. Her cheeks were flushed pink and her pupils wide. She exhaled as she hit the accelerator when the light turned green. "Just peachy."

Anger coursed through him as he paced the living room in front of the big picture window, a screaming baby on his shoulder, inconsolable and nearly purple in the face.

Where the fuck was she?

She said she was going to be right back. How far away did she live? Canada?

He held Sophie away from him and gently turned her around in his arms to smell her butt for the millionth time. He'd changed her like four times since Isobel left. Then another two times after Liam left half an hour ago. Surely the baby didn't still have more shit in her.

He grabbed the bottle off the coffee table and placed Sophie into the crook of his arm. "You hungry, Super Sophie?" he asked, unable to make heads or tails of his own thoughts from the incessant screaming and the thundering pulse inside his brain.

She refused the bottle and instead increased the volume and intensity of her wail.

He'd never liked loud noises, never been able to handle the sound of people screaming ... not since Colombia anyway. Not since the fire.

He propped Sophie back up on his shoulder and bounced her, walking back and forth in front of the living room window.

"What's wrong, baby?" he asked in the calmest voice he could muster. He pulled her away from his shoulder again and held her along his forearm.

Her entire face was scrunched up as if she were in agony, her eyes shut, tears streaming down her chubby cheeks, mouth open exposing her pink gums.

What the hell was wrong?

31

Why couldn't he fix her?

He was used to fixing things.

A broken table? A cracked foundation? He could fix that.

Fuck, even a corrupt government he could fix ... well, he and his team. His brothers. A couple of well-placed explosives, snipers on the roof and a sharp knife for those that managed to escape, and all was right with the world once more. The bad guys were gone.

Yeah, he was a fixer.

Yet he couldn't fix Sophie.

Had he broken her?

Could you break a baby?

The sound of a car door slamming in the driveway had him racing to the front door. He flung it open just as Isobel was making her way up the path with her arms loaded.

"Where the fuck have you been?"

She lifted her head up, panic in her eyes as she took in the screaming Sophie and his obviously frazzled, near insane demeanor.

"I stopped to get groceries," she said calmly. "You have no food." She placed all her bags at their feet and took Sophie from him, cradling the shrieking infant against her chest, making cooing and shushing noises as she rocked and swayed her body away from Aaron and into the living room. "It's okay, baby. It's okay. Does your tummy hurt?" She laid Sophie down on the couch, unsnapped the three snaps between her legs and pulled her shirt up over her belly. "Is it gas, sweet pea?" Gently, she pressed the tips of her fingers over Sophie's stomach, prodding and moving around. She turned to face Aaron, who was standing like an idiot in the foyer. "In that green fabric shopping bag is a jar of coconut oil. Please bring it to me."

What the fuck was she going to do with the coconut oil?

But he didn't question her. Like a good soldier, he snapped into action. He grabbed all the bags that had groceries in them and lugged them into the kitchen, finding the oil and bringing to it her.

She had Sophie's tiny feet in her hands and was doing a bicycle motion, pushing her knees up toward her stomach. "Can you open the jar for me, please?"

He knelt down next to them and opened the jar, watching as she scooped out a small amount onto her fingers and then proceeded to rub it into the baby's stomach.

She smiled. "Ah, there's the bubble."

Bubble?

She turned to face Aaron. "She's gassy. Probably the formula. It might take a bit for her tummy to adjust to it if she was getting donor milk at the hospital. I'm massaging out the gas bubbles." She did another slow sweep of her hands over Sophie's stomach, and the baby farted. Isobel smiled again. Sophie stopped screaming. "Pushed that one right out."

"That's all it was?" he asked, mesmerized by her magic hands and the sudden silence in the house.

She shrugged, continuing to massage the baby. "Yeah, maybe. I mean, she is a month old, and the whole *witching* hour or *purple crying* thing can start at this age too. Might have been that. But my money is on it being gas."

"Purple crying? Her face did go purple. I thought I was going to have to give her CPR."

Isobel's giggle made everything inside him loosen and relax. "That's not quite it. I'll send you the link. Some babies just scream bloody murder at a certain time every day for a few weeks after they're born. Nobody knows why. Apparently, my sister was one of those babies." Her grin warmed him. "I wasn't. You?"

He shook his head stiffly. "No clue."

And he had no way of ever finding out either. He had no idea who his parents were, let alone what kind of a baby he'd been.

"Get a bit of oil on your fingers," she ordered. "I'll teach you how to do it."

He did as he was told, watching as she swept her fingers gently over the baby's stomach. Sophie had calmed now and was just watching the both of them with curiosity.

"I love you," Isobel said softly.

What? His head snapped up from where he'd been watching Sophie, only to see the side of Isobel's face. She wasn't fazed a bit by her slip-up.

Had he heard her correctly? Was he losing his mind?

Wouldn't surprise him if he was.

"It's called the *I love U* baby massage. Now watch my fingers. Down on the left side, like the letter *I*. Do this a few times. Then across the top of the tummy and down, just like an upside down and backward *L*." She did the *L* a few times. Sophie stopped kicking, and she splayed her legs out, locking her knees, watching Isobel with the same fascination as Aaron. "Then lastly, the upside-down *U* for the *U* part of *I Love U*. Up one side on the right, through the ascending colon, over the top of the tummy or the transverse colon, and then down through the descending colon on the left. Up, over, down." She reached for his fingers and placed them on Sophie's soft stomach. Her fingers landed on top of his. "Not too hard. Just enough pressure. Up, over, down."

His hands were huge beneath Isobel's small, dainty ones and even bigger over top of Sophie's belly. But he did as she instructed as she guided him, and using the pads of his fingers, he massaged Sophie's stomach. He swept down the side of her stomach, and she farted.

Aaron chuckled, lifting his eyes to Isobel's. She was smiling too. She had a beautiful smile.

"Good job, Uncle Aaron. Farts are good."

"Farts are good," he murmured, continuing to work Sophie's belly.

Isobel pulled her hands away from his and sat back so he had more room. "You're doing a great job."

He let out a rattled breath. He didn't feel like he was doing a great job. He felt like he was fucking up this whole parenting thing right out of the gate. Sophie hadn't even been out of the hospital twelve hours, and already he was probably traumatizing her for life.

"She likes it. See how her limbs have stopped flailing and she's just lying there still, watching you? It's because she trusts you."

Aaron snorted and reached for more coconut oil. "It's because I'm relieving her gas. I'd stare in awe at someone too if they cured my indigestion."

"No, it's not just that. Look at the way she's looking at you. There's love in those eyes. Trust."

He didn't realize it until that moment, but he'd been resting his elbow on Isobel's knee. He sure as hell realized it now and hastily removed it, clearing his throat as he scooted away from her and that floral and feminine scent that she'd filled his home with the moment she stepped inside.

"How do you know all this shit?" he asked, starting back at the beginning and doing the letter *I* on Sophie's belly. The baby's eyelids were becoming quite heavy. Was he actually massaging her to sleep?

Isobel shifted on the couch but thankfully not closer to him. "I've been a nanny for a while now. You pick up on this stuff. I also signed up for this infant care program after I completed my CPR training. Figured it would come in handy, and it has. I've always loved kids, always wanted to be a mom someday, so why not learn the basics before you're sleep-deprived and in the trenches of parenthood?"

"Why not indeed," he grunted.

"A little gentler," she instructed, placing her fingers back on top of his and guiding him along Sophie's belly again, helping him ease up on his pressure. "They're durable but not indestructible."

He grunted again, the slippery feel of her fingers intertwined with his slippery fingers making a dull ache form in his chest.

35

BOOK 4

The woman was sweetness incarnate. Long dark hair, piercing, bright blue eyes, rosy cheeks, heart-shaped face, soft, full lips. She was what wet dreams were made of.

She pulled her hands away and stood up. "You got this. I'm going to go put the groceries away." Then before he could mutter something along the lines of *you don't know where anything goes,* she abandoned him to his now sleeping niece and sauntered her fine ass into the kitchen. Leaving him to wonder how he was going to do this with such a gorgeous and intriguing woman living under his roof but also knowing, more than anything, that he couldn't do it without her.

Chapter 5

After the feel of his fingers beneath hers, and the warmth of his big body so close, his elbow on her thigh, Isobel needed some space, and she needed it pronto. Extricating herself from her tight spot on the couch, between a sleeping Sophie and a nervous, kneeling Aaron, she made her way into the kitchen to begin putting away all the groceries she'd bought.

She made a point of not really paying attention to what was going on in the living room. The man was too distracting, and she had work to do. Out of the corner of her eye, she caught him heading down the hall with a sleeping Sophie on his shoulder, but then he didn't return.

Probably for the better.

It gave her a chance to collect her thoughts as well as figure out where everything was in his kitchen. She also had dinner to prepare.

It'd taken her longer than she anticipated to get all her stuff from home and then go grocery shopping, so by the time she arrived back at the house, it was nearly four thirty.

Aaron's face when he'd flung the front door open and demanded to know where she'd been had been both laughable and pitiable. The poor guy was in over his head, and he knew it.

Her heart went out to him. Which is why she hadn't taken his snarky tone personally. He was just frazzled and scared. She'd known that the moment she walked into the house. Not only was he grieving the loss of his sister—something Isobel wouldn't wish on her worst enemy—but he was also coming to terms with the fact that he was now a parent.

A *single* parent.

To a little girl.

A little girl who would need the world from him.

That had to weigh on a person. No matter who they were. She couldn't imagine what Aaron was dealing with at the moment, and although she didn't know the man, she had this visceral pull, this deep desire to help him. To help Sophie.

The moment Liam had told her their story, she knew she needed to help. She knew she needed to be there for them. Her heart had ached all week from when Liam had called her, until Aaron had called her asking her to meet him at his house when he brought Sophie home. She'd cried several times over the week at the thought of Sophie not having her mom in her life.

Isobel loved her mother. She loved both her parents equally, but she had a special bond with her mother and sister. She couldn't imagine growing up without either of them.

When Isobel got her first period, Tori and her mother had celebrated as though Isobel had won the lottery. Isobel and her sister were allowed to skip school, their mother called in sick to her job at the mayor's office, and all three of them went and got mani-pedis, facials, and massages. Then they grabbed lunch at the Elliott Bay Social Club, went to the Emerald Bay Mall and bought new underwear, bras and a *period positive* outfit, which was an outfit you felt good about yourself in while you were at your most bloated and gross-feeling during your period. So for most women—day two.

And poor little Sophie would never have that in her life. She would never have her mother taking her to celebrate such a momentous occasion. Her mother would never help her get ready for her wedding or hold her grandchild if Sophie decided to have children of her own. These were all things Isobel couldn't wait to experience herself with her own mother, and Sophie would never have that.

She stood over the counter peeling carrots, hot tears streaming down her face at the thought of Sophie growing up without a mother. And poor Aaron, losing his sister, and in such a horrific way.

It would destroy her if something ever happened to Tori. She was her best friend.

Once she had the baked potato wrapped in foil, made up an herb medley for the vegetables and a dry rub for their steaks, and put her apple pie in the oven, she wandered down the hallway to go and find Aaron. She needed to know how he liked his steak cooked.

She was a medium kind of girl, but if he was anything like her father, he'd be a medium-rare or even rare man.

Earlier, he had kindly taken her bags to the room that was designated for her, but she hadn't had a chance to check it out or put anything away. She had time though, and the soft sound of a rumbling snore drew her farther down the hall toward the bedroom next to the bathroom, the one he was going to turn into a nursery for Sophie.

The door was slightly cracked open, so she just gave it a gentle nudge, and what she saw made her ovaries damn near explode and her heart quadruple in size.

Aaron, splayed out on a queen-size bed, asleep, snoring, with a sleeping baby on his chest.

Be still my heart.

She swallowed, her mouth suddenly full of saliva and her panties equally damp.

Had she ever seen anything sexier?

No. She could confidently say she hadn't.

Sophie's cheek pressed over his heart, and her eyes were glued shut. Her little mouth formed the perfect rosebud pout. Aaron looked more relaxed than she'd seen him all day. A sense of peace surrounded him, a sense of calm. But at the same time, she could see that he hadn't allowed himself to completely let his guard down. Whatever those dog tags represented, the man was used to sleeping lightly and always remaining aware of his surroundings and potential threats.

He probably knew she was standing there, probably felt the air in the room shift or heard her heart racing.

Because it was certainly racing.

She allowed herself to watch them for a moment more, studying the one bicep she could see and the tattoos that peaked out beneath his sleeve. It looked like initials or cursive words in a beautiful black script, but she couldn't make out what it said. She wanted to get closer, lift the hem at the sleeve and see how far up the ink went. Trace her tongue over it ...

She shook her head as if that would bring her clarity and then retreated before her thoughts turned into actions and she was kicked out on her ass for sexually harassing her boss. She closed the door behind her and headed to the room that would be hers.

She began emptying her duffle bag into the dresser drawers and setting her toiletries and makeup on the nightstand. Might as well get comfortable. There was no sense living out of a suitcase if she didn't have to.

Her new bedroom was nice. Sparse, but nice. There was no art on the walls or superfluous furniture, but the bed seemed comfortable when she sat on it and bounced a few times, and there was a nightstand and dresser. What you would expect for a guest room in the home of a bachelor. The sheets were white, the quilt on top dark blue. There were no throw pillows and no extra blankets or throws stashed in the closet. And why would there be? This was the home of a man who probably knew how to survive on the bare minimum. He could probably stretch an Oreo cookie for a week, sleep in mud and blood, in the extreme cold or sweltering heat, and all for the mission. The last thing on Aaron's mind was comfort.

She blew a strand of hair off her forehead. She'd have to grab some comfort items from home the next time she was there.

Home.

It was so weird that she wasn't going to be sleeping in her own bed tonight. Wasn't going to be leaving work, only to return when the sun was up.

She'd never been a live-in nanny before. How did it work?

They hadn't even discussed hours or pay. Days off or vacation time. She still had design commissions she had to finish. Would he let her do that when she was off the clock? Would she ever be off the clock?

What did Aaron do for work? Did he still serve with whatever military organization he'd been a part of? Would he be gone for months on end on another mission, or was he taking time off to get acquainted with Sophie and figure out this parenting thing? Could he take paternity leave?

She had so many questions.

Why hadn't she asked them when Liam had called her and offered her the job?

Why hadn't she asked them when Aaron called?

She'd never been so impulsive accepting a job before, never been so irresponsible.

Why?

The clearing of a throat behind her made her jump and drop the bra she had in her hand. She spun around to find Aaron, cradling a groggy Sophie, staring at her.

Oh yeah, that's why she'd thrown responsibility and protocol out the window. Because the story of the man and infant in front of her pulled at her heartstrings so hard, she thought they might snap.

"You fell asleep." She put the bra she'd dropped in one of the dresser drawers and stepped toward them. His tired blue eyes followed her movements. "I can change and feed her if you'd like to try to get some more shut-eye." Without asking for his permission, she took Sophie from him and brushed past his broad chest in the doorframe, taking great care not to inhale his sexy manly smell, and made her way into the living room.

Sophie started bopping her face against Isobel's shoulder, which meant she was looking for food again. She headed into the kitchen, where she'd put the bottles. "Guess we'll have to wait on that diaper change until after we feed you."

She didn't bother to look behind her, but she knew Aaron had followed them through the house.

"You cooked?" His voice was hoarse from lack of use, but it was also deep and gravelly and made her nipples instantly tighten.

"Figured you could use a good meal. How do you like your steak?"

"Steak?"

"Yeah, I picked up a couple. Plus baked potatoes, roasted veggies and apple pie for dessert." She grabbed the prepared bottle of formula from where she'd had it warming in a cup of water on the counter and took it and Sophie back into the living room, once again not making eye contact or waiting for Aaron. He followed them anyway.

She sat down in his La-Z-Boy recliner and propped Sophie up in the crook of her arm, the infant's hunger warbles getting stronger by the second.

"Ah, here we go." She placed the bottle nipple into Sophie's mouth, and immediately the baby started to guzzle. "That's better," she cooed, beginning to rock them in the chair. She was staring down at Sophie's angelic little face, but she knew Aaron had stopped in front of them. He blocked out enough light from the living room window, and his red hair was like a flashing light on the top of a cop car. It was hard to miss. She lifted her head and her eyes. "Over dinner we should hammer out the details of my contract," she said. "Go over my hours and days off and stuff."

He was staring at her in a most unsettling way, and not *serial killer going to murder you in your sleep* unsettling, but more of a *panther stalking his prey* unsettling. But when she mentioned days off, his nose wrinkled up in confusion and the intense look was gone. "Days off?" He scratched the back of his neck. "What do you mean, days off? What do you mean, hours?"

Oh boy.

She flashed him a giant smile. "Well, this is a job. So I'm entitled to days off and scheduled hours. Do you have a job? Are you wanting me to be with Sophie while you're at work, and then you can take over once you're home? Would you like me to cook meals? Clean? What is my job description, besides keeping your niece alive?"

His eyes went wide. "I, uh, I have no idea. I kind of just thought you'd always be here for us. For Sophie, I mean." The man was so lost.

Her heart went out to him.

It was so odd to see a big man, with such an intimidating presence, enormous muscles, chiseled jaw and eyes that you just knew saw absolutely everything, seem so small. So helpless and lost. So broken.

She shook her head and smiled again. "We can talk once we have some food in our systems. I figured out your barbecue, but if you're particular about how your meat is cooked, you're more than welcome to man the grill."

He nodded. "Okay. Now?"

The timer for her pie in the oven started to beep.

"Sounds good. Potatoes and veggies are already on."

He nodded, turned around and then headed toward the kitchen, appearing lost in his own home. In his own skin.

Isobel watched as he opened the door to the patio, the tongs and plate of meat in his hand. She only caught his profile, but what she could see broke her heart even more.

He was crying.

Chapter 6

Once he'd collected himself and tossed the meat onto the flames, Aaron opened the patio door and stepped back into the kitchen. Isobel had her back to him and was humming a soft tune as she gently swayed in front of the counter.

It gave him another moment to compose himself and wipe his eyes before she turned around.

"What the hell is that?" He instantly berated himself until it hurt for his harsh tone. He really had to work on that. Hunger and lack of sleep had never been his friends, but right now they were his mortal enemies, and they were making his mood take a serious nosedive.

Thankfully, Isobel was unfazed by his tone. Instead she simply smiled and kissed the top of Sophie's head. "It's one of those stretchy baby wrap things. There's a baby boutique next to the grocery store, so I swung in there and grabbed it. The lady who ran the place showed me how to put it on. Sophie loves it. I put her in after her diaper change, and she passed right out again. And don't you just love the color? I love periwinkle."

What the fuck was periwinkle?

She balanced a plate on either hand and did a little hip swivel. "And see—hands free."

"I'll, uh … I'll pay you back for it," he said, putting the plate that held the raw meat into the sink. He cleared his throat. "We can talk scheduling at dinner too."

"No need to pay me back for the wrap. I'll get lots of use out of it, and when she grows out of it, I'll just sell it." She paused. "Or hang on to it for when I have my own babies." Her cheeks flushed a brilliant, sexy pink, and she cast her eyes down to the top of Sophie's head. "This little one is making my biological clock kick into overdrive." She kissed Sophie as she moved about the kitchen with ease and familiarity.

Aaron stood there stunned.

He also wasn't sure how he felt about her confidence in his home. Even though he knew she wasn't over thirty, she was sure as hell mature. And knowledgeable. Particularly when it came to babies.

"I like my steak medium," she said, wiping her hands on a hand towel. "If that's what you came in here to ask?"

He grunted and nodded. "Yeah. It was. Okay." Then he spun on his heel and opened the patio door again, wishing he had a beer in his hand ... or an entire bottle of rye.

A few minutes later, with the steak steaming on the plate, along with the veggies and potatoes in the foil, he brought their dinner into the house.

Isobel had set his small two-seater kitchen table, and she'd been kind enough to pop him a bottle of beer. It looked like she was having water though.

"The meat will need to rest a bit," she said, not turning to face him. "So you might as well leave the veggie and potatoes in the foil so they don't get cold."

She turned around from where she'd been hunkered over the sink. Sophie was no longer in the baby wrap thingy, and Isobel was holding a piece of blood-soaked paper towel to her finger.

Aaron plunked the plate of food down on the dark granite counter top with a *thunk* and was around and grabbing her wrist instantly. "What happened?" He held up her hand and removed the paper towel. Blood poured down her hand and wrist from the pad of her left index finger.

She shook her head and made to pull away, but he tightened his grip on her wrist. "It was nothing. I couldn't find your bottle opener for your beer, so I tried

to use a knife like I've seen my dad do a million times, and I got myself good."
She tugged away again, but he fixed her with a look he hoped she took as a firm
no. "Looks worse than it is, I swear. I'll live," she protested.

"Where's Soph?" He dabbed the paper towel to the cut, but it immediately
filled with blood again. It was a deep cut and long, too, spanning across the entire
pad of her finger.

"We were both getting hot in the wrap, and I didn't really want to eat over
her head in case I dropped food on her, so I put her in her bassinet. She's over
in the living room."

He glanced to where she pointed with her other finger but then turned back
to her face. "You might need stitches."

Her gasp made his whole body stiffen.

"No," she whispered. "I don't do needles."

"Well, it's pretty damn deep, and I don't have the proper stuff in my first
aid kit to freeze the area." He held the paper towel against the cut and applied
pressure. She winced. He loosened his grip a bit. "Sorry," he murmured. "But
you really should get it looked at. They might not stitch it, but they could
cauterize it."

Her eyes went wide, and her lip wobbled. "No. No needles. No cauterizing.
That means they'd burn it."

"I know what cauterizing means," he said blandly. The fear in her eyes tugged
at something deep inside him, and he softened his tone. "If they freeze it, you
won't feel the stitches."

Her bottom lip trembled, and her eyes grew wide with fear. "But I'll feel the
needle for the freezing."

"Well, yeah, but ..."

She shook her head. "But no. I'll just wrap it with some gauze and Band-Aids
and stuff. Keep it clean." Her chuckle was forced, an obvious front for her fear.
"I'll have a cool scar to share at parties, along with an embarrassing story about

how I sliced my finger open because I'm too lazy to ask you where your bottle opener is."

"I don't have one."

"How do you open your beer then?"

He hated to be the bearer of bad news, but she had to know. "They're twist-off. Otherwise I use my teeth."

She hung her head, and he heard a muttered "Fuck."

He couldn't stop his lips from turning up into a half smile. She was something else. "Sorry."

She shook her head before lifting it back up to look at him. "You'll damage your teeth if you keep doing that, and you have such a nice smile." Long lashes blinked over sapphire-blue eyes. Eyes he could easily get lost in. Eyes he could easily picture staring up at him as he hammered her body into a mattress until she was forced to squeeze them shut as she opened her plump lips and screamed out his name.

Fuck, where did that thought come from?

He dropped her wrist and turned away. "I'll go to the garage and grab my first aid kit if you're going to be a stubborn ass and not go to the ER." Then he vacated the kitchen as fast as he could, stopping only half a second to stare at a snoozing Sophie on the floor in her bassinet, but it was enough time to hear Isobel murmur from the kitchen, "*I'm not the stubborn ass. You're the stubborn ass.*"

He returned from the garage with his first aid kit moments later, only to find Isobel bouncing a crying baby in one arm while holding yet another blood-soaked paper towel over her bleeding finger.

Growling at the impossible woman who had just entered his life, he set the first aid bag down on the kitchen counter and opened it up. Isobel wandered past him, grabbed another bottle for Sophie off the counter and attempted to juggle the newborn into the crook of her arm without releasing the paper towel.

"Whoa!" he said, abandoning the kit on the counter and rushing to save Sophie from the fate of the floor. "What the hell?" Aaron wasn't sure, but had he not swept in, the baby probably would have been face-first on the tile before either of them could blink.

"I had it," Isobel grumbled.

"No, you didn't. Learn to ask for help. Learn to recognize when you need to go to the hospital. Don't be a baby. Only babies are afraid of needles." He positioned Sophie into the crook of his arm and snatched the warm bottle from Isobel's hands before she could protest. He turned around, showing her his back, and proceeded to feed his niece. "Seeing as you're such a know-it-all, you can bandage yourself up." Then he wandered into the living room to continue feeding Sophie in peace.

Isobel glared at Aaron's back as he stalked his sexy frame into the living room with Sophie.

What a complete ass.

A complete ass with a very *fine* ass.

Shut up. Shut up. Shut up.

Continuing to glare at him, with a small bit of hope that lasers might eventually shoot out of her eyes and singe him a little, she opened up the first aid kit.

And holy shit! What a first aid kit.

It was like something you'd see in an ambulance car or something.

More than just the little pocket kit of Band-Aids and iodine the Boy Scouts used. No, this was a proper medical kit with defibrillator pads and a big round squeezy thing for when a person is intubated and everything.

Keeping the pressure on her cut, she rummaged through the kit for the gauze and bandages. It would be interesting to do it all one-handed. She glanced at the man next to the window rocking gently, but like hell was she going to ask for help after his little outburst.

She got it. He was grieving.

But did he have to be such an ass?

Everyone grieves differently. There is no right *way to grieve. No timeline. No cure. It's an entity all on its own.* Her mother's words came back to her. She'd said the exact thing to Tori and Isobel after their grandmother died and they were struggling to make sense of it all. Tori had lashed out in anger, Isobel had grown quiet, and their father, who had lost his mother, had retreated to their family cabin for a week, where he didn't speak to a soul.

She blew out a breath. "Everyone grieves differently," she muttered, the frustration in her shoulders leaving with her exhale.

She grabbed a roll of soft, white gauze and began to unravel it.

"That's not how you do it."

Jeez, the man was like a ninja. How did he sneak up on her like that?

With a grunt, he placed a once-again sleeping baby into Isobel's arms, grabbed her finger and went to task cleaning the cut.

"Thank you," she whispered, resting her nose against the top of Sophie's head.

He grunted again, his eyes barely flicking up to her, but when they did, his gaze quickly moved from her eyes to Sophie's. "Are babies supposed to sleep this much?" He put his head back down and began wrapping the gauze around her finger.

"Wake cycle of about forty-five minutes or so," she said. "But that might also mean she's up a lot tonight. Her days and nights could still be switched. She's also not *technically* a month old. She's brand new, as she was a preemie. Their sleep patterns are all over the place, and they get hungry a lot because their tummies are about the size of an egg."

"How do you know all this shit?" With medical tape, he secured the gauze in place, the force of breaking the tape from the roll making his arm muscles bunch in an incredibly sexy way.

"After Liam called and asked me to take the job, I bought a few books on infant care. The youngest child I've looked after was three months and hadn't been preemie or in the NICU, so Sophie is foreign territory for me. I wanted to be prepared."

He released her finger, then went about cleaning up the first aid kit. "I guess I should have read some books too." She could tell he was deliberately avoiding making eye contact with her. He was looking anywhere and everywhere but her face.

"You've had a lot on your mind," she said quietly, gently burping a snoozing baby now that she had her other hand back. "It's okay. You'll figure her out. Just like she'll figure you out and have you wrapped around her little finger in no time." She attempted a smile, but his scowl and unwillingness to look at her made the corners of her lips dip.

Not saying a word, Aaron zipped up the first aid kit and left the room.

Was he always a man of such few words?

She walked over to the bassinet in the living room and put Sophie back down. The baby squeaked a bit, but when Isobel found a soother in the diaper bag and offered it to her, Sophie settled right back down.

Wandering back into the kitchen, she went about plating their dinner. Hopefully, the meat wasn't overdone now, or even worse—cold.

This time she heard his footsteps behind her.

How could he sometimes be in stealth mode and other times elephant mode? Was it a conscious thing?

She set Aaron's meal in front of his beer and then took a seat in front of her own plate across from him.

He sat down, picked up his knife and fork and dove in like a man who hadn't eaten in days—possibly weeks.

The sound of cutlery on the plate as he sawed away at his steak was intense and echoed around the quiet kitchen like a chainsaw on an old-growth fir.

With far less vigor, she started on her own meal.

The silence between them was deafening. Awkward. Strained.

At least that's how it felt to her.

Was it all in her head, or did he feel the tension too?

She took a sip of her water and cleared her throat. She could have had one of his bottles of beer, but she didn't want to assume she could, and plus, she was on the job and didn't really want to be drinking on her first day of work.

"So, um ..." She exhaled, clenched her jaw, unclenched and then stared straight at him until he lifted his head to look at her. It was a damn long moment before he did. But once he did, she struggled to get a read on his mood. Hopefully it was a touch happier now that he had some food in his belly.

He lifted one eyebrow. Obviously, he was waiting for her to continue.

Right!

She swallowed. "Should we take this opportunity of us at the same table, while Sophie's sleeping, to discuss my contract? Hours. Wage. Expectations." Damn, the man had nice eyes. Bright blue with yellow around the center. The colors worked with his dark red hair and tanned complexion.

Aaron finished chewing his steak, took a sip of his beer, then leveled his gaze back on hers. "What do you want?"

Well, that wasn't the response she'd been anticipating.

"What do you mean *what do I want?*"

"What kind of hours do you want? What kind of pay?"

She shook her head, still confused. "I'm not the one who has a baby she needs help with. What do you even do for work?" She pointed at his chest. "Are you in the military? Are you going to be going off on missions for months on end? What do you need from me? Let's start with that. What do you want from me?"

Something animalistic flashed in his eyes, but he quickly caught it, chained it and tossed it in a cage. But that didn't stop her heart rate from skyrocketing from that brief look.

He took another drink of his beer. She should have been irritated with his stalling, but she wasn't. It simply gave her an opportunity to check out the long, muscular line of his neck and the heavy drop and lift of his large Adam's apple as he swallowed.

Mother Mary, that was hot.

"I need you to be here for Sophie," he finally said. "Whenever she needs you."

Isobel fought the urge to grumble and instead bit down hard on her tongue for a moment. "So you want me here more than a typical forty-hour work week? Is that what you're saying? Are you paying me salary or hourly? Are you deducting my living costs from my wages? Because I *have* a home, and if you're going to charge me room and board, I'll just go live at my apartment with my sister and show up in the morning and leave when you return home from work." She wrinkled her nose. "Which, by the way, you still haven't told me what you do."

A muscle in his jaw ticked. "I'm in construction. Carpentry."

She pointed at his muscular chest again. "But you used to serve?"

"Used to. Retired now."

"Army? Air Force? Marines?"

"Navy."

Did her vagina just spasm?

Did she dare ask the next question? Did she dare ask if he was a SEAL?

"I work eight to six Monday through Friday and some weekends. Depends on the job. I need you here with Sophie when I'm at work and when I'm here because I do paperwork at home at night."

Okay, now they were getting somewhere.

"Do you own your own company?"

He nodded.

Did this guy have a word limit each day and if he went over, he lost a limb?

"I can do eight to six Monday through Friday. But I will need days off as well. I do have a life and another job."

His eyes went wide, then his brows narrowed. "What other job?" The tone of his voice wasn't angry, but it wasn't innocently curious either.

"I'm a graphic designer. My business is small, but I do have a few clients and commissions. I also have a dog walking business, but I've already found another person willing to take on all my clients if your need for me extended beyond full time."

More grunts and this time a couple of grumbles as well. He scooped sour cream and bacon bits onto his baked potato. "You can have Saturday and Sunday off, but I'll need you here for Saturday nights. I'll pay you more. You can do your design stuff while Sophie naps."

"So I'm off the clock when you walk in the door after work then? If that's the case, I may as well just go home and come back in the morning."

"Fuck," he muttered. "I didn't think about that." He lifted his head up. "I need you during the night."

Whoa.

Realization how that must have sounded dawned on him, and his cheeks flushed an adorable pink. "I mean I need you here at night for Sophie. I need you to get up with her. I can't be up all night with her and then at work all day. I'll fucking cut my hand off with the circular saw."

"Hence, why we're having this discussion."

His eyes hardened. "I don't like your attitude right now."

Isobel blinked and sat back in her chair, dropping her fork to her plate with a loud clatter.

What attitude? She had an attitude?

"*My* attitude?"

He nodded. "Don't think I didn't pick up on that sarcasm."

"I'm sorry," she said softly. She set down her steak knife, planted her palms on the table and looked him square in the eye. "Look, I get that you're grieving. I get that you're in over your head here. But I *want* to help you. When Liam told me your story and about Sophie's mother"—she swallowed and a sob caught in her throat—"it gutted me. Nobody should have to go through what you and Sophie are going through. I want to help."

A protective shield slammed down around Aaron. His eyes shuttered. His jaw tightened. His posture stiffened. "You think I *like* this?" he gritted out.

Her head shook. "What on Earth gave you the impression I thought you were enjoying this? I would think there was something seriously wrong with you if you did. Your sister just died. You are now raising her baby. Your life is a mess. But I am also *not* the enemy here. All I've done since I got here is help. All I've wanted to do since I got here is help, but you're making it very difficult. I know nothing about you, nothing about what you want from me, and yet I'm still trying to make this work. You, however, have given me the cold shoulder since I arrived, which is not something I deserve at all." She shook her head and glanced at her knitted fingers in her lap. "I know you're grieving but—"

"Don't fucking say that again." His words were soft but clear, and they cut like a freshly sharpened blade.

She inhaled and slowly lifted her gaze to his.

"You'll work Tuesday through Saturday," he said. "I'll take Sunday and Monday off. You'll work seven in the morning until seven at night with the understanding that if Sophie wakes up after midnight and before six o'clock in the morning, you are to get up with her. I will pay you overtime for everything beyond forty hours. You get two weeks' vacation, which will become effective after a three-month probation period. Research what a competitive live-in nanny wage is and come to me with a number. I will not charge you room and board. I'll pay for groceries. You'll eat here. I will get you a car seat for your car, and you can bill me for gas." He stood, shoved his unfinished plate of dinner

54

away, grabbed his beer and stalked off toward the garage, leaving her sitting there staring at their plates wondering what the hell she'd just gotten herself into.

Chapter 7

Aaron finished his bottle of beer and then windmill-hurled it across the garage and into the retracting door, causing it to smash and fall to the concrete floor. It was moderately satisfying but not enough.

He wanted to smash. He wanted to hurt. He wanted to maim and demolish. He wanted to shatter. Just like his heart had shattered a little over a week ago. And just like it repeatedly did over and over and over again every time he looked down at his niece and saw his sister staring back at him. And it would continue to shatter until nothing but dust remained. Because the pain would never end. It might subside over time, but it would never disappear. And it would resurrect itself countless times over the days, weeks, months and years to come. The wound might scab over, but then, when Sophie grew old enough—inevitably looking just like her mother—and curiosity began to consume her, he'd have to explain to her what happened to her mother, and the scab would be picked and the wound would be open and exposed once again.

He needed to learn how to live in pain. Day-to-day pain was his life now. His present and his future.

He glanced down at the demolished beer bottle, and fury rippled inside him.

Who the fuck did Isobel Jones think she was anyway?

She waltzed her tight little ass into his house and made herself at home. What the fuck?

She bought groceries.

She cooked.

She stood up to him.

She ... was willing to help and go above and beyond for a total stranger. A stranger who was grieving. A stranger who was angry. A stranger who was neck-deep in a life he didn't think he ever wanted and was most certainly sure he had no idea how to live.

It was the pity in her eyes that made him see red. The sadness and desperation to fix his situation. Next thing he knew, she'd be trying to fix him, to fix his heart.

He was the fixer. Not her. But he was unfixable.

His heart, at least the biggest part of it, was gone. All that remained of it, he gave to Sophie, but he knew very well that it wasn't enough. That he'd never be enough for her.

He scrubbed his hands over his face and up into his hair, pulling on the ends until there was pain. He screamed and pulled harder. He screamed louder and pulled even harder.

Nothing he did could distract him from the hollow ache inside his chest. No amount of pain anywhere else in his body could mask the agony of losing Dina.

He went to the beer fridge he kept in the garage and opened the door, pulling out another bottle of San Camanez Lager and twisting off the cap. It wasn't quite a smile, but a flurry of something light, something not heavy or angry, fluttered through him when he stared at the cap, and his lips twitched slightly out of the deep frown.

That woman was fucking stubborn.

Who didn't want to get an injury treated properly?

He'd never been able to understand people's fears of modern medicine or needles. That shit was necessary for survival. You suck it up, buttercup, bite down on a strip of leather and let whoever has the sewing needle close the gaping wound before your intestines spilled out.

Fuck, she would have gotten a local anesthetic and not felt a goddamn thing. Unlike his time in Medellin when the henchman for a Colombian drug lord had stabbed him in the gut with a rusty machete.

Thank God he was with Colton, their team medic. Since it was more than just a superficial cut, Colton had his work cut out for him. Aaron had grabbed their emergency first aid kit, bit down on a strap of leather and let Colton, one of his brothers, darn his abdomen like it was just a hole at the bottom of his sock.

They'd poured enough brandy into the wound first to get a sumo wrestler drunk, then burned the needle and cauterized his flesh with a lighter to stop the bleeding. All without any pain meds or freezing. All he had was the dregs at the bottom of the brandy bottle to numb his pain. Even then, he'd still gone into septic shock a few days later, needing to be airlifted to Bogota for surgery.

Yeah, getting a finger stitched up at the hospital was a walk in the fucking park.

He wasn't ready to go back into the house yet. Wasn't ready to face Isobel and the pity in her eyes.

He exhaled as he slowly slid down against the beer fridge, his back to the cool metal. With his free hand, he ran his fingers over the tattoo on his left arm.

Vos potest conteram ferro.

You can't break steel.

Or the most equivalent translation they could find.

Since she was ten, Dina had hounded Aaron for the two of them to get matching tattoos, something that would solidify their bond as siblings and all the other person would ever need. He didn't think they needed tattoos to symbolize that, but whatever. When he turned eighteen, he got his first one. A black and white rose—which was Dina's birth flower—on his right shoulder. She'd been both elated and also jealous as all get-out. He got the larkspur—the July birth flower—on his other shoulder a week after Sophie was born.

He got a couple of other tattoos when he turned twenty-one, this time to celebrate getting his journeyman ticket for construction and Dina turning eighteen. A hammer and saw creating an X on his right bicep with the date he passed his test beneath, and then the Latin saying *Vos potest conteram ferro* on his other bicep.

Dina had gone with him to get the latter of the two tattoos, and he surprised her for her birthday by paying for her to get her own as well.

She got the same saying across her ribcage.

It was a silly saying, but it was the mantra they lived by their entire lives. They were the Steeles. They were tough. They were resilient. They could bend, but it would take a lot to break them.

After they'd been moved to their third foster home in a year and a half, Dina, who had only been six at the time, was developing anxieties and fears that could only be explained by the lack of security and roots. So Aaron started telling her every night before they went to bed that you can't hurt steel.

He explained to her the properties of steel and how they were similar to Dina and Aaron.

Just like Dina was a tough cookie with a hard shell and a no-nonsense personality, steel has a high tensile strength. It's difficult to fracture. It takes a lot of pressure, a lot of strength to break steel. And Dina was the same way. Her years in the system, not knowing who she could trust—besides Aaron—had forced her to grow up far quicker than she should have, and as a result she was slow to trust, slow to warm up to people and even slower to accept help. She rarely broke down and cried, rarely showed her vulnerability to anyone but Aaron. Her outer shell was six inches thick and almost impenetrable.

So while Dina slowly grew cynical of the world, Aaron was forced to bend and change shape to keep the peace. Like steel, he was ductile. When the need called for it, he put on his big brother hat, or his father hat, or his friend hat. On occasion, he even had to put on his mother hat and explain things like menstruation and training bras to Dina.

He kept the peace between Dina and their foster families. When Dina would shut down or refuse help, lash out in frustration or pain, he had to ramp up his willingness to *join the family*—as much as he would have rather not.

Dina's favorite comparison between her and steel was that they were both lustrous and shiny. That always made her giggle when Aaron compared her to the sparkle of a chrome bumper freshly washed and drying in the sun.

She'd shake her head, tossing her red curls over her pillow, and roll her eyes, calling him a goofball.

"And you're durable," she would say. "Long-lasting and resistant to wear and tear."

He'd tuck her in. "I try to be." Then he'd show her the scar on his elbow from when he fell off the jungle gym at school. "Wear and tear right here, but I'm still going strong."

She'd take his hand, pull him in so their noses touched, and they'd whisper the mantra that kept them going: "Strong as steel. You can't break steel."

They'd say it three times before he'd kiss her on each cheek, then the forehead, and tell her he loved her.

She'd say it back, close her eyes and fall asleep holding his hand. Every night, he held her hand until she fell asleep. Until he knew she was off in dreamland, dreaming of their future and life outside the foster home, life outside the system.

Aaron wasn't sure what time it was when he finally stood back up. He'd fallen asleep on the concrete floor of the garage, and his ass, back and hips were paying for it.

He hadn't even finished his beer.

It was warm as monkey piss now, so he dumped it on the back lawn, threw the cover over the barbecue and went into the house through the door from the patio.

The house was dark and quiet. The kitchen clean.

Had she left?

Panic at the thought of Isobel gone swam through him, and he raced to the front window in the living room.

Her car was still in the driveway.

Thank fuck.

His stomach rumbled in protest at his stupid decision to abandon his dinner, so he made his way back into the kitchen and opened up the fridge.

Stubborn and thoughtful.

She'd placed his dinner plate in the fridge with a piece of plastic wrap over it.

He pulled it out, pulled off the plastic and tossed it into the microwave, then he grabbed another beer out of the fridge, twisted off the cap and took a long swig, waiting for his steak to heat up. It would probably overcook in the microwave, be tough and rubbery, but it served him right after he'd left dinner the way he had. He'd only taken one bite of the meat, but the rub Isobel had made had been amazing. From what he could tell, the woman knew how to cook.

The beep of the microwave drew his attention away from thoughts of his new employee slash roommate, and he grabbed his dinner, choosing to sit at the counter and eat, rather than at the table.

He was two bites into his steak and practically moaning from how good it tasted when the sound of an infant wailing down the hallway made him pause mid-chew.

Crap.

He dropped his fork to his plate and took off at a steady lope down the hall toward Sophie's room.

He was almost there when the sound of Brahms's "Lullaby" made him stop in his tracks.

"Lullaby and good night, with pink roses bedight, with lilies o'er spread ..."

He knew her singing voice was going to be soothing and beautiful.

She alternated between gentle hums and soft, quiet lyrics.

With an ache in his heart, he stepped forward and peered into the dark room. Isobel stood with her back to him, swaying softly.

He entered the bedroom, the floor creaking on the threshold of the door from his big frame and causing Isobel's body to stiffen and the singing to stop. She turned around to face him, Sophie in her arms.

Aaron's cock immediately jerked in his jeans.

Fuck.

Isobel's pajamas, although not a see-through teddy, were hot as fuck—a tight black tank top with a low cut and blue and black plaid pajama pants that hung disastrously low on her hips, showing off a very tight, very tanned midriff. And fuck almighty, was that a navel piercing?

He held back the groan deep in his throat as best he could and averted his eyes to the floor, then to the top of Sophie's head, and finally to the dark, blank wall behind Isobel's head.

"I tried feeding her, but she wasn't interested," she whispered. "Just wants to be held." She began to rock again, humming the same lullaby as before.

Sophie's eyes were open, but they were hooded. Her limbs were limp too, and she kept yawning.

"Dina used to sing that song to Sophie when she was pregnant with her. She'd rub her belly and sing Brahms's 'Lullaby' before bed."

Her eyes flicked up to his, unease on her face. "Do you want me to sing something else?"

He shook his head, taking a step forward until he could smell her hair and whatever luscious body wash she'd used in her shower. "Soph seems to like it."

"Do you want her?"

He shook his head again. "No, she seems too content." Trying his damnedest not to focus on Isobel's cleavage, he pinned his gaze on her bandaged hand. How had she managed to shower with it on? He picked up her hand. "How's your finger?"

She made a face but didn't pull away. "It hurts. Throbs actually, and I can't tell if the bleeding has stopped or not. Showering was interesting. Used plastic wrap, a Ziploc bag and an elastic band."

The corner of his mouth twitched. A real MacGyver.

Then the image of her naked and soapy in the shower flashed into his mind, and he dropped her hand and took a couple of steps back.

He hadn't been with a woman in a while, let alone one as young and fit as Isobel.

This was not a good idea. He needed a nanny he wasn't going to have dirty dreams about. He needed a Mrs. Doubtfire, not a Mary Poppins.

He gnawed on the inside of his cheek until he tasted blood. The pain was his punishment for his thoughts. For fuck's sake, his sister had just died, leaving him to raise his niece all on his own, and yet the thoughts that entered Aaron's mind as Isobel's cleavage stared him down were anything but pure.

He cleared his throat, determined to focus on the wall behind her. "Listen, I'm sorry for earlier."

She adjusted Sophie in her arms slightly, but that only pushed her breasts farther out of her tank top.

Fuck me.

"It's okay. I'm sorry if I said something to upset you. We can hammer out the work details tomorrow. Liam said that he would take care of my wages if you couldn't. I'm not worried about not getting paid, I just need to know what you want."

What he wanted ...

What he wanted was to put Sophie back in her bassinet, turn Isobel around, pull down her pants, bend her over the bed and get lost in the sweet heat of her body. He wanted to forget the last week and just feel good, even if temporarily. He wanted to hear her scream out his name as she came around his cock, her orgasm rippling through her so fiercely her knees threatened to buckle and he had to wrap an arm around her waist to keep her standing.

"I can afford to pay you," he said, shoving the dirty thoughts to the back of his mind for later. "Liam doesn't have to."

Her smile was dismissive. They needed to move on to another topic.

Her expressive blue eyes looked tired, and the yawn that followed her smile confirmed it. Aaron was tired too. His impromptu nap in the garage hadn't done anything for his energy or fatigue. If anything, it just made him feel more exhausted than before, and now his back ached.

Isobel picked up one of Sophie's arms, then gently let it drop like a wet noodle. She lifted her eyes to his and smiled again. "Out like a light." With slow, careful movements, she moved over to the bassinet on the bed and leaned in to put Sophie down. Only that move just showcased her luscious ass and caused her pants to pull down enough to reveal a small, discreet—fresh-looking—tattoo on her left hip.

Aaron's jeans were suddenly very uncomfortable.

But he couldn't look away. He stared at her ass. He stared at the three-inch-long tattoo of a stick figure girl with an *I* in the center of her triangle dress. It appeared as though she was meant to hold hands with someone, but it was just her on Isobel's hip.

Who had the matching tattoo?

Just as slow as her movements had been before, Isobel stood up and backed away, pulling up her pants and covering the tattoo in the process.

"I put your dinner in the fridge," she whispered as they made their way out into the hallway. She didn't shut the door because he hadn't brought the baby monitor over from Dina's yet and wasn't sure how well they could hear Sophie cry if her door was closed.

"I saw that and heated it up, thank you. You're afraid of needles, and yet you have a tattoo and belly button ring?" It was out of his mouth before he could stop it. Now she'd know he'd been staring at her ass and her body.

She pivoted and lifted her tank top, tugging her pajama pants down enough to show the whole tattoo. Now his jeans were really uncomfortable. "Yeah, well, I was hammered when I got them."

His brows pinched. "They're not supposed to tattoo or pierce drunk people."

She shrugged and released her clothing. "I consented first. Tori and I have always wanted to get matching sister tattoos, so we did it for my birthday last month. A friend of ours is training to be a tattoo artist and did it for us in her studio. I signed the waiver, then pounded tequila like it was water until she was able to get close enough without me spazzing out. The belly button was pretty easy. I just shut my eyes and it was over in a second. The tattoo was a bit more of a challenge."

He nodded. "I see."

"Childhood injury during a blood draw," she said, a memory of a past trauma flitting behind her eyes and causing a muscle in her jaw to clench. "We went on a family vacation down to Central America, and I caught a bug while we were in Guatemala. The nurse or whoever was doing the blood draw couldn't find a vein and kept sticking it in and pulling it out, then her hand slipped when she was about to stick the needle in again, and she got me good. My whole arm bruised. I was barely four at the time, and the whole thing was pretty traumatic. I've had a real fear of needles ever since. They usually have to sedate me before I consent to getting any kind of blood drawn or a vaccine."

Aaron scratched the back of his neck. Well, now he felt like a real ass for condemning her earlier. Some fears, some trauma were unexplainable, with no real discernible cause, while others were deep-seated, rooted years in our past from one lonely incident. And then they haunted us forever.

Aaron had a trauma like that—and it haunted him on the regular.

"I'm really sorry that happened to you," he finally said. "Sounds like it was really scary."

She nodded. "It was. And I know that it's silly that I'm a twenty-six-year-old woman who is still afraid of needles, but those memories still come crashing back the moment I see somebody snapping on the latex gloves and coming at me with a syringe."

He nodded. "Understandable."

She cleared her throat. He could tell she wasn't a fan of the conversation topic. "You've quite a bit of ink yourself." It wasn't a question. Only a few of his tattoos were visible at the sleeves of his shirt. The rest were on his back and shoulders. Was she going to ask what they all meant? He really hated when people did that. Tattoos were personal, and sometimes their significance wasn't meant for the whole world.

He grunted, waiting for the onslaught of inquiries.

He got none.

She yawned again and stretched, lifting her arms above her head and pushing up to her tiptoes. A sliver of skin at her midriff peeked out at him, tempting him. Her belly ring sparkled and winked at him. Taunted him.

Oh fuck me.

"I'm going to bed," she said, rubbing her eyes.

Bed.

Why did that word cause every muscle in his body to wake up?

He was exhausted. He needed sleep. His muscles shouldn't be rousing; they should be getting ready to rest.

It's because you want to take her *to bed. And do wickedly dirty things to her until the sun comes up and you feel even remotely human.*

He glanced down at her feet. Fuck, even those were cute. Painted a bright pink and two of her toes had rings on them.

He cleared his throat and stared at the wall behind her.

Fuck, he was a coward.

"Okay, well, good night." Then he turned on his heel and headed back toward the kitchen, hoping his beer was still cold and his meat was still warm.

He was seconds into his steak when the cry of an infant yet again interrupted his meal.

He waited until he heard Isobel rouse in her bedroom and saw her shadow walk down the hall before he took another bite of his steak.

Would any of them ever sleep again?

How did parents do it?

How did anyone have more than one child?

These questions plagued him until he finished his dinner, jumped in the shower and saw Isobel's almond- and honey-scented body wash sitting on the counter. Then different thoughts entered his mind, and with the shower running extra hot, his eyes closed and his hard cock in his hand, he relieved the pressure.

Hoping to God the nanny wouldn't be hot in the morning but knowing full well he was royally fucked.

Chapter 8

With Sophie back in the stretchy wrap carrier, Isobel was free to get things done around the house. Not that she had much to do, as it wasn't her house and Aaron hadn't provided her with a list of things he'd like done, but she wanted to feel productive. She decided to get dinner for that night prepped, and while perusing his chest freezer in the garage for inspiration, she noticed a pile of Aaron's dirty laundry just sitting on top of the washing machine in the garage, so she put in a load.

He probably hadn't done laundry in well over a week.

She guessed that he'd spent nearly every minute at the hospital over the past week, probably like Sophie's mother had until …

Dear God, her heart hurt and tears welled up in her eyes every time she thought about Aaron's sister.

A gentle knock on the front door had her abandoning her station at the counter washing lettuce and padding her bare feet across the house.

Tori had texted that morning and asked if she could come by for baby snuggles.

Isobel jumped at the chance to see her sister. She had so many questions for her. Mainly concerning how Isobel was supposed to work for a such a hot guy and not melt into a puddle of goo every time he looked at her.

"Hey!" Tori beamed, stepping over the threshold and into the house. It was only nine o'clock in the morning on Saturday, but already the sun was out, and it was hot. That's what you got the last few days of August in beautiful Seattle.

"Hey." Isobel stifled a yawn and leaned in to peck her sister on the cheek. Tori pecked her back.

Tori's eyes softened as she took in a snoozing Sophie in the carrier. "Oh my God, she's perfect." She ran her hand over the top of Sophie's downy-haired head before leaning in and giving her a big sniff. "My ovaries ..." she whined. "Gah. Mark wants to wait a couple of years before we have kids, but I keep telling him that he's not getting any younger."

"At least he's on board now. He wasn't before."

"True."

"And besides, you're focused on grad school right now. And that business management course. How on earth could you handle a pregnancy, let alone a baby? You're not even living together yet."

"Touché. We will be soon though. I just want to finish my business class first before we shack up."

They wandered back into the kitchen, and Tori took a seat at the kitchen table, where she could watch Isobel prep dinner.

"So I'm here for baby snuggles. Gimme, gimme." She held out her hands and wiggled her fingers. "I can feed her a bottle if she wakes up. I just need to cuddle."

Grinning, Isobel gently pulled Sophie from the wrap, her little body all scrunched up and warm. She didn't even bother to wake up when Tori took her. Instead she simply stretched, made a pouty face and then turned her cheek into Tori's chest.

"She's beautiful," Isobel's sister cooed, standing up with the baby in her arms and grabbing a light blanket that was draped over one of the chairs. "That perfect little nose." She draped the blanket over Sophie's body before settling back down in the chair. "So dish. How's the new job?"

was about to open her mouth when the door from the patio opened walked a sweat-drenched, hot-as-fuck Aaron. His gray tank top was ʃ, his face a mottled red and covered in sweat and his hair damp. He had ʃds in his ears and running shoes on.

ʃhe thought he was still sleeping.

She could not have been more wrong.

Tori's mouth dropped open.

Aaron's eyes narrowed on her before flashing up to Isobel. He wanted to know who the hell was in his house and holding his baby.

Donning the biggest, most reassuring smile she could, Isobel wiped her hands on a tea towel and stepped out behind the counter. "Aaron, this is my sister, Tori. Tori, this is my boss, Aaron." She was having a hard time not looking at him. The way his tank top clung to his stomach and chest left very little to the imagination, and his biceps and tattoos were in full view. "She texted me and asked if she could come meet Sophie, get her baby fix. I hope you don't mind."

Tori stood up from the chair and offered Aaron her hand. "You have a lovely home."

He grunted and took her hand, though the reluctance in his body language was palpable.

"Going to take a shower," he said. "Need to go get more of Sophie's shit from Dina's today." Then he headed past them and down the hall.

Tori and her sister remained quiet until they heard the shower start.

"Uncle John with no shirt on, sitting in a kiddie pool eating sauce-covered chicken wings," Tori finally said.

Was her sister having a stroke?

Isobel looked at Tori as if she was suddenly speaking in tongues. "Huh?"

"That's what I would picture in my head when I was having dirty thoughts about Mark ... before we ... you know."

70

Isobel snorted and rolled her eyes, wandering back to her lettuce at the counter. "And look how well that turned out. You're now madly in love with your boss and planning a future together."

Tori lifted a shoulder. "I'm just saying, you're going to need some kind of a distraction if that sex on a fucking shish kebab is your boss. Especially if he's wandering around the house looking like *that*. Was he all broody like that yesterday? I see a darkness around him."

"He just lost his sister. Of course, he's in a dark place. He's grieving." Memories of Aaron snapping at her last night and telling her not to say that word again interrupted her thoughts. "I'd be in a dark place—hell, I'd be destroyed if something ever happened to you. I get where he's coming from, so I'm trying to give him some space. Give him a bye."

Tori's eyes said she understood. "I'd be a fucking wreck if something happened to you too."

Isobel blew her a kiss.

Tori caught it.

"But you need something to mentally distract you from that gorgeous hunk, otherwise you're going to wind up in a world of trouble."

"And you think thoughts of our barrel-chested, hairy-as-fuck disgusting uncle will help?"

Tori bent her head and nuzzled Sophie's head. "It can't hurt. At least he's finally being useful."

Isobel cracked a half smile. "True."

Her family thanked the universe after every big Jones family gathering that *Gross Uncle John* wasn't a blood relative. Tori and Isobel's dad's sister had just chosen unwisely, thus inflicting the plague onto the rest of them.

They heard the shower stop, and Tori's back straightened. "So what are your hours? What days do you work? Mark's heading to poker tonight. Is Aaron heading there too? Are you supposed to watch Sophie? Gabe's with the respite worker tonight, so I'm free if you're free and want to grab dinner or catch a movie."

Isobel nibbled on her lip in thought before speaking. "We started talking about my schedule last night, and he got all upset and stormed off. From what he said, he wants to me to work Tuesday through Saturday, including Saturday night so he can eventually start going to poker night, I'm assuming. But I get Sunday and Monday off. However, he also said he wants me to get up with Sophie between midnight and seven in the morning, so I don't know if that includes Sunday and Monday." She shook her head. "It's all so messy. I'm working twelve-hour days, seven to seven, and he said to come to him with a wage in mind." Her eyes bugged out. "I've never had to do that before. How awkward."

Tori flattened her lips into a thin line. "Yeah, sounds messy. Maybe today he'll be in a better frame of mind. Yesterday had to be a bit overwhelming for him."

She nodded. "Yeah. I'm going to offer to go to his sister's place on my own. If the roles were reversed, I don't know if I'd ever be ready to go to your home and through all your stuff."

"You want help?"

The bathroom door opened, and Isobel couldn't stop herself if she tried. Her eyes flew up from her sister's face, and she watched a towel-only-clad Aaron saunter his big, wet frame down the hall toward his bedroom.

He had more tattoos on his back—oh God!

His door shut, and she finally released her breath.

Tori let out a low whistle. "You are fucked, you know that, right?"

Isobel's gaze dropped down to her lettuce. "Yep."

Isobel tied the stretchy wrap at Aaron's back, careful not to let his fresh manly smell or the heat from his body make her sway too much. "You just go for a walk with Soph. Tor and I will take care of the rest, okay?" she said, stowing her gasp when Aaron spun around and the intense pain in his blue eyes made her want to do everything she could to take away the hurt.

He'd trimmed his beard, tidying it up a fair bit so it was now just a short scruff hugging his chiseled jaw. Oh boy, did he ever look good.

She shoved down the desire to swoon. They were standing outside of Dina's condo building, and ever since they arrived, Aaron had been twitchy and extra grunty.

"I'll text you when we're done and you can wander back," Isobel said, taking a step away from Aaron.

He nodded before kissing the top of Sophie's head. "She's going to be okay? Not overheat?"

"She's in a diaper and a onesie. She should be okay. If she gets too hot, you can always pull the wrap off her legs like this." She showed him how. "Oh, I almost forgot. I found this in the back of my car from one of my previous kids." She plopped a big, floppy yellow sun hat on top of Sophie's head. "Probably a bit big, but it'll do the trick until we find her her own."

His smile was small and tight. "Thanks."

Her head bobbed. "No problem."

A car door on the street slammed, drawing their attention away from each other. Seconds later, Tori walked up the pathway, followed by her super-good-looking doctor boyfriend, Mark.

"Brought reinforcements," she said. "Gabe is with Mark's mom for a few hours. So, Mark can either be some muscle, or he can ..." Her eyes darted between the two men.

Or he can babysit Aaron.

"I don't need a babysitter," Aaron growled.

Mark slapped him gently on the back. "Never said you did. But how about a friend? How about a guy who's done the newborn thing, done the single

73

dad thing? I'm an overflowing fountain of knowledge." His grin was wide and boyish.

Tori rolled her eyes. "And not the least bit modest about it."

"There's a sports bar not too far from here, and although they don't advertise it, there is a small section that allows kids. The owner is a fellow single dad, but by choice." Mark shook his head in disbelief. "Just had a baby via surrogate. Cute little thing, Willow. We can go grab a beer, stare out at the traffic and not say a fucking word to each other. How's that sound?"

Aaron's hard gaze softened just a touch, then he turned and started to walk. "Fine, but you're buying."

Mark's smile grew even wider, his green eyes twinkling with mischief in the warm summer sun. "I like him." Then he took off at a steady lope to catch up to Aaron.

Isobel turned to Tori and rested her hand on her sister's shoulder. "Thank you."

Tori shrugged, and the two headed toward the front door of Dina's condo building. "I figured as much as Aaron thinks he wants to be alone, he really doesn't. And Mark's done all that shit. As much as I'd never agree with him to his face, he really is a fountain of knowledge."

Isobel unlocked the front door to the condo, and they made their way toward the elevator. "Yeah, your boyfriend's ego is already big enough. You don't need to inflate his head any more than it already is."

They stepped on to the elevator.

Isobel felt her sister's hand brush hers, and they laced their fingers together. Tori squeezed, then Isobel squeezed back.

"Thank you for coming with me. I couldn't imagine Aaron having to do this, but I also wasn't looking forward to doing it on my own either. I never knew the woman, but I know two very important members of her family, and the hole her death has caused in their life is enormous."

Tori squeezed her hand again. "You're an amazing person, Iz. A big heart and a tremendous friend. I just hope that when some of the grief-fog clears, Aaron can see that. I don't want to see you get hurt or taken advantage of."

Me too.

The elevator door opened, and they both stepped out, still holding hands. Dina's unit was a few doors down the hall. They stopped when they came to unit 409.

"Ready?"

Isobel put the key in the lock, turned it and then pushed the door open. "No."

"Me either."

Then they stepped inside.

Chapter 9

"That seems to be the last of it," Mark said, dusting off his hands on his khaki shorts and leaning against Aaron's black truck. "You guys need a hand unloading everything back at the house?"

Aaron shook his head, lifting his hand to block out the glaring sun. "Should be okay, thanks." For the first time in what felt like ages, but was really just over a week, his heart didn't ache nearly as much as it had. Sitting with Mark on the patio at the Prime Sports Bar and Grill had been therapeutic.

And it was a bonus that the owner, Mason, was a fellow new dad as well, because when Sophie started to lose her shit and root around like an anteater in the soil, Mason ran to his back office and brought out a bottle of formula.

"Can never be too prepared," he said with a grin. "Us dads need to stick together."

Mark had offered to feed Sophie so Aaron could finish his steak sandwich.

"You coming to poker tonight?" Mason asked, snuggling his own newborn daughter, Willow, against his chest. "My mom has been staying with Willow for a few hours so I can duck out." He yawned. "I have to say, as much as I know they say *breast is best* and all that jazz, formula has its pros too. Anybody can feed my baby, and I get a bit more freedom."

"Formula saves lives," Mark said, tilting the bottle up a little farther for Sophie.

"That it does," Mason agreed, adjusting Willow. His new tattoo that said *Willow* on his left forearm was bright and shiny in comparison with the other faded and older tattoo sleeves. He turned to face Aaron. "So, poker?"

Aaron wiped his mouth with his napkin before responding. "Not tonight, but I will soon. I'm not really into socializing at the moment, but I know I also can't become a recluse. I need to make Sophie some friends."

Both the other men snorted.

"That'll come. Just take it one day at a time," Mark replied. "The invitation is always open."

Aaron nodded. "Thanks. I'll keep that in mind."

"She's fed, changed and buckled in," Isobel said, bringing Aaron's thoughts back to the now and the fact that the four of them were standing out on the sidewalk in front of Dina's building. All of Sophie's things, including her crib, dresser, clothes and toys, were all packed up in the box of his truck.

Tori rubbed Mark's back, and the way she looked up at him was so full of love, anybody who drove by would know they were mad about each other. "Ready to go?"

His eyebrows waggled. "Sure, but I think I'm going to take my girl for some ice cream before we go back and pick up Gabe."

Tori's blue eyes glimmered. "How about gelato instead?"

Aaron didn't need to see it to know that Mark had reached down and pinched Tori's butt.

"Anything for you, babe," Mark practically purred.

Aaron fought the urge to make a gagging face and instead just looked away. But looking away meant looking at Isobel, and she too seemed uncomfortable in the romantic exchange between her sister and Mark.

Interesting.

"Call me if you need anything," Tori said, leaning forward and hugging her sister, pecking her on the cheek before they broke their embrace. She turned to Aaron. "The same goes for you. Anything you need, just give a shout."

It was a struggle, but he forced a smile and thanked her.

Mark and Tori looped their arms around each other and took off down the sidewalk toward his car, his hand boldly making its way into the back pocket of Tori's jeans.

Isobel blew out a breath. "Those two are like teenagers." She opened the passenger side door of Aaron's truck and climbed in.

He walked around to the driver's side and climbed in behind the steering wheel. "How long have they been together?"

Why the fuck did he care? Why was he asking this?

"She's been working for him since January, but I don't think they started sleeping together until maybe February or March. Made it *exclusive* and *legit* around March, I think. There was some serious drama there."

Aaron hated that he was curious how Mark and Tori managed to make the employer fucking the employee thing work, but he knew better than to ask.

"Hungry?" he asked, throwing the truck into gear and figuring food was a better topic of conversation than sex and relationships.

Hell, *anything* was a better topic than sex and relationships.

"Starved. Didn't you just eat though?"

"Can always eat." He shrugged.

Especially since he had hardly eaten anything at all last week. He was making up the calories now.

She craned her neck around to look in the back seat. "Soph's asleep."

He glanced in the rearview mirror at the mirror set up and poised on the car seat. Sure enough, his little niece was back in dreamland, her lips big and pouty as she sawed logs. "Feel like a burger?" he asked, stopping at a red light and getting his bearings. There was a pretty decent burger joint a few blocks away, and thankfully, they had a drive-thru.

She made a noncommittal face. "I could eat a burger."

The light turned green, and he made a hard right. Moments later, they pulled into Ralph's Burger Barn and got in line for the drive-through.

"What do you want?" he asked, regretting his gruff tone the moment he barked it out.

She leaned over the center console to check out the menu board. The fact that her body and that incredible almond vanilla scent was so much closer was not lost at all on him ... or his cock.

Fuck.

"I'll get the sesame ahi burger with yam fries," she said, sitting back in her own seat.

"Tuna?" he said, looking at her with disgust.

"What? I had red meat last night. I try not to eat it more than once a week. Haven't had fish in a while." She glanced out her window, ignoring his blatant disapproval.

Shaking his head, Aaron pulled ahead to the speaker and gave their order.

They were on the road in no time, driving in silence, which was normally how Aaron liked it, but for the first time since Isobel walked into his life, he didn't welcome the quiet. She'd gone above and beyond her job description today—and yesterday for that matter—and continuously took his foul mood in stride. She deserved more than grunts for answers and his cold shoulder.

He just wasn't sure how to open the door of conversation. Had he glued it shut with his earlier behavior? Was there a common ground they could travel that was simply platonic and friendly?

Somehow it just felt easier being curt and closed-off with her, because deep down, he wanted to grab her dark ponytail in his fist, tilt her blue eyes to the sky and crush his mouth against hers. Could he find a happy medium between being angry at her and wanting to fuck her?

He'd never been good at happy mediums.

"How would you like to divide and conquer?" she asked, breaking the silence as he maneuvered his truck through traffic. "I prepped dinner, so it just needs to be thrown on the barbecue. Salad is made. Chicken breasts are marinating. I figure since it's like four o'clock now, we can have a late dinner." She twisted her face up. "I mean, really all that can be saved until tomorrow and we can just call these burgers dinner too. Have a snack later in the evening if we're hungry."

Aaron grunted and nodded once. That sounded fine to him. He ate when he was hungry, not when the clock told him to.

"Would you like to assemble the crib and I can take care of Sophie, or would you like to spend some more time with her and I can put together the nursery?" Isobel asked, craning her neck around to peer into the back seat of the truck. Aaron could see in his mirror and the mirror he had facing Sophie that she was still out like a light.

"I can put the crib together," he murmured, happy that she'd broken the silence but not sure how much gusto he should give the conversation. "That's a man's job."

She made a disgruntled noise in her throat, then spun in her seat to face him. "You better get over that misogynistic viewpoint and fast, my friend. You're raising a little girl, and she needs to be taught there is no such fucking thing as a *man's job* or a *woman's job*." She shook her head. "Fuck, even if Sophie was a boy, you should still be teaching him that there is nothing a girl can't do." They came to another red light. He glanced at her. She was pissed. Anger burned in those bright eyes, and heat flushed her cheeks. She looked like she was ready to tear out his jugular.

Jesus Christ, that fire started quickly.

He quickly held up his hands in surrender. The last thing he needed was a pissed-off feminist. "Sorry. Sorry. That's not what I meant. Fuck." He raked his fingers through his hair. "I didn't mean to anger the feminist."

Was that a growl?

Yep, he was pretty sure she growled.

"Anger the feminist? Are you fucking kidding me right now? Every goddamn person on this planet should be a feminist. Feminism isn't about female superiority. It's about gender equality. That there isn't anything you can do that I can't. That we should be paid the same if we do the same job and given equal

opportunities." She crossed her arms over her chest and huffed. "What fucking century are you living in, buddy?" She glanced out the window. "*Anger the feminist*. Well, you've sure as shit angered her now."

Holy fuck. An uncomfortable heat raced through him, not only from embarrassment but also at the thought of pissing her off so much he could lose her.

He couldn't lose her. He just couldn't.

"I just meant that I wouldn't know where to put all her clothes and stuff. I made the crib, so I can put it back together."

She scoffed, her arms tightening across her chest, pushing up her cleavage. "Bullshit. You're backpedaling. You put clothes in a goddamn dresser. I took the crib apart, so I'm pretty sure I could put it back together. You better become a feminist right quick, otherwise you will be enlightened, and you won't like how it's done."

He swallowed. "Sorry."

She shook her head again in frustration and pointed at the road. "The light is green. Go."

He cleared his throat and nodded, feeling like he hadn't just received a slap on the wrist. He'd received his entire ass handed to him.

"And another thing ..."

Oh fuck. He struggled not to roll his eyes and kept them positioned on the road ahead.

"There are but *three* things a man can teach a boy that he cannot teach a girl." He saw her hold up her hand and three fingers out of the corner of his eye. "Three."

She paused. Was she waiting for him to ask what they were? Did he want to know?

Thankfully, she didn't wait for him to ask and began counting them out on one hand. "And they are: how to pee standing up, how to clean a foreskin, and how to grow up and not become a rapey bastard. *Everything* else, and I mean *everything* else can be taught to a girl."

Rapey bastard?

He nodded, keeping his eyes glued to the road. "Okay. I'm sorry, I, uh, I was wrong. There is no such thing as a man's job. I will do better by you and by Sophie."

"Is that a promise?" she asked, her tone having softened a touch but not completely. They came to another red light. He turned his head and stared at the side of her face until she pivoted to look him. "Well?" she asked, cocking an eyebrow.

He nodded again. "It's not just a promise, it's an absolutely. I will do better."

Triumph flared behind her eyes. "Good." She glanced forward. "The light is green."

He shifted his eyes forward again but then slid her the side-eye as he waited for the car in front of him to turn left. "Do you forgive me?"

Her narrowed gaze told him she was weighing her options. "I do, but I don't want to hear any more chauvinistic bullshit come out of your piehole ever again." She glanced into the back seat. "Particularly around Sophie."

He blew out a breath just as they turned into his driveway. "Never again."

She opened her door before he'd even turned off the truck. "Good. Now spend some time with your niece, because *I'm* going to put the nursery together." Then she walked to the back of the truck box, popped down the tailgate and began heaving things out. He was still in the driver's seat, staring at the garage door and processing the last five minutes, when he saw her head toward the front door with her arms loaded.

She turned back to face him, a glare back on her beautiful face. "Chop, chop."

Aaron's eyebrows nearly flew off his face.

Chop, chop.

No woman had ever spoken to him like that before. No woman besides Dina, that is. And even Dina hadn't ripped out his throat like Isobel had.

The woman had fire. And not just a single flickering flame like that of a birthday candle. No. She was a raging wildfire, unstoppable, relentless and fierce.

She wasn't feisty. No, that word was condescending to a woman like her.

She was a force to be reckoned with. She put up with his bullshit but also put him in his place. Women who could do both were a rare breed. He could just imagine Dina doing a big fist pump and then high-fiving Isobel.

Isobel, a kind heart, a gentle soul and a warrior all rolled into one very attractive package.

He opened up his truck door and climbed out, only to see her standing on his front stoop.

"You have the keys," she called out, irritation rolling off her in waves. "Chop, chop."

Chop, chop.

He dropped his head as he approached her, struggling to hide his smile.

Then it dawned on him. For the first time in over a week, he didn't have to force a smile. Instead he was trying to hide it, and it was all because of a woman he hardly knew who had taught him more about kindness, compassion and feminism in twenty-four hours than he'd learned in thirty-eight years.

"Licking your wounds?" she asked, the edge to her tone almost gone.

He lifted his head, loving the challenge in her eyes. "Something like that."

Her brow furrowed and she angled her head to the side, studying him, concern filling her eyes where the rage and irritation had once been. "You seem different. Everything okay?"

You mean besides the verbal ass-whooping you just gave me?

He reached past her and unlocked the door but kept his eyes on hers. His smile was big and genuine. "Yeah. I think it actually will be."

Chapter 10

They were five weeks into the new arrangement, and thankfully, Aaron, Isobel and Sophie had finally fallen into a bit of a routine.

Sophie was proving to be a very easy and agreeable baby, as Mason and Mark could attest to, as apparently their children were not. Or at least that's what Aaron had come back from poker night saying, a big, cocky grin on his face.

Isobel was tired, but she knew that was to be expected, and it was giving her a good idea what motherhood would be like when she finally had children of her own.

It was Wednesday afternoon, and they were in the final day of September. The first half of September had been blistering hot, but when Isobel threw open the blinds that morning, the day was overcast, and her phone said the temperature was a pleasant sixty-four degrees.

The door chimed to The Lilac and Lavender Bistro as Isobel propped it open with her foot and wheeled the big, fancy jogging stroller inside.

It was after the lunch rush, so there were only a handful of patrons in the small seating area.

"Be right with you," called a familiar voice from the back.

"Take your time," Isobel replied, her eyes going wide as she took in all the decadent confections and desserts in the glass case next to the cash register.

"Iz, is that you?" A dark, curly head popped out from behind the corner. Paige smiled, her golden-brown eyes sparkling. "About time you showed up." She made her way around the counter and hugged Isobel. "I can't thank you enough for the beautiful logo. We're getting so many compliments on it." She pointed to the logo that had recently been painted onto the front door.

Isobel also noticed that the logo—two sprigs of lavender and a droopy lilac bunch over *The L & L Bistro*—was stitched onto the top left corner of Paige's chef's coat. "I'm so glad you like it."

Paige was all smiles. "I love it." She clapped her hands together. "Now let's fill your belly. On the house, as promised."

Isobel smiled at the same time her stomach rumbled.

The door behind them chimed.

Paige smiled again but also rolled her eyes. "The usual?"

Isobel turned to see a beautiful sandy-blonde haired woman in ballet attire. She looked a touch ill. "You know me well. And some of that ginger iced tea too, please." Paige nodded, then retreated back to the kitchen.

The newcomer made a face and then sat down in the nearest chair. "Morning sickness should be gone after lunch, no?"

Isobel smiled sympathetically. "Oh crap. I'm sorry. But congratulations."

The woman's green eyes flicked up from Isobel's face to the stroller. She stood up to take a peek at the sleeping Sophie. "How old?"

"Three months, I think."

The woman's eyes narrowed. "You don't know how old your baby is?"

Paige returned. "It's not her baby. It's Aaron's. Or Aaron's niece, I should say." She handed the woman a tall glass of the ginger iced tea. "This is Tori's sister, Isobel."

Understanding immediately dawned on her face as she sat back down in the seat closest to the front door and took a long sip of the iced tea.

"I'm the nanny," Isobel confirmed. "She was born July twenty-first but was four weeks early, so her corrected age is around eight weeks." She counted on her fingers. "Yeah, eight and half weeks. Sorry."

Paige turned to face Isobel. "Iz, this is Violet, Adam's girlfriend and Mitch's sister."

Ah, okay, it was all starting to make sense now. She'd heard about all these people, but only met a handful of them.

The door chimed again, and all three women turned to see Tori stroll in with Gabe in tow. "Hey! Is this a meeting of the minds? A meeting of the better halves?"

Gabe ran off to the back corner where a small table full of toys was set up, and he went to work stacking red blocks. Tori took a seat across from Violet. "Baby still giving you grief?"

Violet nodded, wiping the back of her wrist across her mouth. "There's no reprieve. Every minute of every day, I feel like I'm seasick."

Paige made a face that said she understood all too well. "Yep, that's what my pregnancy with Mira was like. Freakin' awful. Bet you're having a girl." She bent down and retrieved something sinfully delicious from the glass case, plopped it onto a plate and brought it over to Violet. "One caramel apple fritter."

Violet smiled at her. "Thank you."

"Is it wrong that I'm excited to see you get fat?" Tori asked, standing back up, playfully hip-checking Isobel on her way to check out the glass case.

Violet dove into the fritter, but her eyes said all the words she couldn't.

Paige burst out laughing. "I have to admit, I'm kind of looking forward to that perfect dancer's body getting all bloated and round too."

Violet swallowed. "You two are bitches."

Tori pointed at something interesting in the glass case. "You still have lilac churros left?" Her eyes grew big and hungry. "You never have any left by the time I get here."

Paige moved her eyebrows up and down. "I may have tucked a few aside with the assumption that you and Gabe would be stopping by." She bent down again and retrieved the churros, placing them on a plate and sliding them across the counter.

Tori giggled with glee, grabbed the plate and, like a chipmunk with nuts, ran to the table with Violet and took a giant bite. She shut her eyes and moaned. "This is almost better than sex." Her eyes opened. "Notice I said almost? Because there really isn't anything better than sex with Mark."

Violet licked caramel off her thumb. "I can't even think about sex right now. I feel disgusting." Her eyes flared and focused on Paige. "I don't even want to hear how the sex with my brother is dynamite. I see the smile on his face when he gets home. I don't need the details."

Paige bit her lip. "Well, you're sleeping with my ex-husband, so ..."

Violet burped, her face going an unsettling shade of puce. "Not currently I'm not."

Isobel's eyes had just continuously bounced back and forth among the three women. Tori had filled her in a bit about the tangled web of Paige, Violet, Adam and Mitch, but hearing it firsthand just made her brain hurt.

"What can I get you?" Paige asked, drawing Isobel's attention away from the family tree in her head. "Your sister got the last of the candied lilac churros, but I still have a couple of lavender ones, as well as lavender scones, some sfogliatelles and white chocolate pound cake cupcakes."

Isobel's mouth watered. "I can't decide. Everything sounds so good."

"Or I can make you something savory. The menu board is behind me up there. Anything you like."

Her stomach rumbled as she read the words *lemongrass and ginger prawn taco with homemade apple and cabbage slaw*. "I'll get the prawn taco," she said before she could change her mind or risk a stroke from her inability to decide. Normally she was better at choosing things. She'd close her eyes and let her finger do the work.

Paige's eyes lit up. "Excellent choice. I'll be right back."

"Pull up a seat," Tori said, shoving the last bite of the churro into her mouth. She pushed out a chair, and Isobel wheeled the stroller closer and sat down.

"You're not going to share any of that with Gabe?" Isobel asked, checking behind her to make sure Gabe was okay in the play corner. His block tower had reached an impressive height.

Tori grabbed her water bottle from her purse and took a sip. "He doesn't like them. Paige will give him a 'cookie' with red sprinkles before we leave, and he'll be over the moon." She made air quotes when she said *cookie*. "They're actually really healthy, with like a quarter cup of coconut sugar or something in the entire recipe. She tosses in chia and flax and a bunch of other healthy stuff. But then she rolls them in sprinkles so the kids can't see all the extra stuff."

"They're a kid favorite with all my dance students," Violet chimed in. "Not sweet enough for me, but then I've always liked my sugar. And now that's all this baby will let me keep down. Sugar and pickles." She shook her head. "How am I supposed to grow a healthy human eating that?"

"So." Tori placed her elbows on the table, linked her fingers together and rested her chin on her fingers. "How's life with the hot, broody boss? It feels like forever since I've seen you or talked to you. Feels weird."

It definitely felt weird. Normally, Isobel and Tori never went more than a day or two without seeing each other. Now they were coming up on a couple of weeks.

Isobel groaned and averted her eyes. "They're fine."

Violet sat forward. "Hot, broody boss? Oh, do tell."

Isobel shot her sister a look that said she was not happy with Tori's little outburst. "My boss—Sophie's uncle—is incredibly good-looking. Like tattooed, muscly, dog tags, scruff, bright blue eyes, grunty, that sexy penis-line thingy on his hips—hot."

Violet's eyes widened. "Go on."

Isobel rolled her eyes. "The first few days were tough. He was really distant and angry. But I get it. He just lost his sister, and now he has to not only grieve but raise her baby. That's a lot to take in. But now ..." She watched Paige walk across the restaurant with her meal.

"What'd I miss?" Paige asked, plunking a beautifully put-together plate down in front of Isobel.

"We're hearing all about Isobel's sexy boss and how they're having a hard time keeping their hands off each other," Violet said, thanking Paige for her second iced tea.

Paige grabbed another chair and brought it to the table. "Okay, dish."

Ah, damn it.

Isobel groaned, then glared at Tori, who was all smiles. "We've done a fine job keeping our hands off each other, thank you. I don't think he's attracted to me that way, anyway. Problem is, I don't even know if he likes me. And not in a romantic like-like way, but even in just a friendly way."

All three women's brows pinched.

"What do you mean?" Tori asked.

Isobel took a bite of her wrap and shut her eyes just like Violet had. It was incredible. She chewed her food slowly, savoring every flavor.

"I'm about ready to take that away," Violet said. "I have another dance class soon, and I'm not leaving here until I hear everything."

Isobel swallowed, took a sip of her sister's water bottle and then continued, albeit reluctantly. "He's just so weird. Not mean or anything, but not super chatty or friendly either. But *crazy* polite. Like ridiculously polite and proper. It's kind of freaking me out."

The three women exchanged curious but also knowing looks.

"Seems to me he likes you," Violet said, sipping her ginger iced tea.

Isobel shook her head. "Nope. I've been around the block enough to know when a guy is attracted to me. I thought he might too, at first. You know, the old ponytail-pulling thing."

All the women groaned.

That was not something any of them would teach their daughters. Violence of any kind was not a way of showing attraction. Society was so fucked up.

"But then he went from being rude and angry to overly polite and distant. Aaron Steele is not attracted to me. Like once Sophie's in bed, we don't sit up and chat or anything, get to know each other—as friends. He retires to bed, goes out for a run or goes to the garage to work on God only knows what. Maybe paperwork or something."

"And what do you do?" Paige asked.

"I work on my graphic design commissions. It's win-win, I suppose. But it just feels weird, you know. I live in this man's house, cook his meals, clean, take care of his niece like she's my own child, and he treats me like the help."

"But you *are* the help," Violet said slowly.

Isobel blew out a frustrated breath. "I know. I don't know what I want, but I know it's not what's going on right now. We have a routine, but it's so businesslike. He knows nothing about me and hasn't really given me any openings to ask about him. I have no idea who I'm working for."

"What do you want from him?" Tori asked. "The man *is* grieving. He's also trying to run a business and figure out how to transition from uncle to father. He's going through a lot."

Isobel pouted and took another bite of her wrap. "I know. It's just with all the other families I've nannied for in the past, the parents made a point of getting to know me. We bonded, just like I bonded with their children. I eventually became another member of the family."

"Eventually," all three women said at the same time.

"It's only been a few weeks. Give him time." Paige reached across the table and rested her hand on Isobel's.

"But I also think he wants to bang you," Tori said. "You may think he's not interested in you, but I saw a look in his eye that first day I met him. There was something there. A twinkle or whatever you want to call it when he looked at you."

Violet and Paige both snorted laughs.

"And you *definitely* want to bang him," Isobel's sister added. "And who wouldn't? That man is *fine*."

Paige licked her lips. "We need to plan an ambush or something on poker night so that we can meet this mysterious new dad. See just how hot he really is."

Violet cleared her throat. "Ahem." Playfully, she planted her hands on her hips. "And what about Mitch?"

Paige's grin was saucy and mischievous. "Hey, it doesn't matter how you get your appetite as long as you go home to eat." She wiggled her eyebrows up and down playfully.

Tori tossed her head back and laughed. "I love it. I'm going to remember that one. Repeat it to Mark after a barbecue with Mason and baby Willow makes me all hot and bothered. That man is *damn* fine."

Paige and Violet nodded.

Isobel's lips twisted in thought. "I thought at first he was still upset with me for snapping at him a few weeks ago, and that's why he was all closed off, but his actions would prove otherwise."

Tori slammed both her hands down on the table. "You snapped at him?"

"He said assembling a crib was a man's job."

Eyes rolled around the table, and lips made shocked little *O*'s.

"Oh no he didn't," Violet said with a headshake.

"I put him in his place and then some. Don't worry."

Paige's nod was curt, her brows pinched. "Good."

"He even came home a few days later with a baby tool belt for Sophie and a onesie that said *Future Handyman*, but with a Sharpie he'd added one of those little upward arrows and a *W* and *O* in front so it read *Future HandyWoman*."

They all laughed.

"Well, at least he's learning. Turns out you can teach an old dog new tricks." Tori chuckled. Her eyes followed Gabe as he carefully made his way down past the tables toward them. He stopped a mere six inches in front of her. "Hey, buddy. Ready to go?"

"Toooori," he said, his face rosy and his smile wide.

"You want your cookie for the road?" Paige asked, standing up and moving back behind the dessert case.

Gabe nodded and followed her.

"Okay, you tell me which one you want. Just point, and I'll grab it."

Tori turned back to Isobel. "How often has Uncle John come in handy over these past few weeks?" Her smile was all too telling.

Isobel glanced at the still sleeping Sophie. "More often than I'd care to admit."

Tori laughed. "Been there, sister. You are screwed, and not in the good way."

Isobel blew out a breath. "Don't I know it."

Chapter 11

As Isobel was walking back to her car with Sophie snoozing once again in the stroller, she stopped in front of what looked to be a new business. It was bright inside but fairly open concept and sparse with the decor. There were several rooms, all sectioned off by walls of acrylic glass, and inside were tables and stacks of dishes, glassware, china—all things breakable. She glanced up at the sign—*The Rage Room: You break it because you paid to.*

Without hesitating, she opened the door and awkwardly maneuvered the big stroller inside, hoping to God that the *bing* of the door didn't wake Soph.

A gorgeous woman with tattoo sleeves, a bright shock of hot pink hair, two hoops in one nostril and impeccably done smoky eye makeup stepped out from the back. Her smile took her from gorgeous to stunning. "Hi, I'm Luna. Welcome to The Rage Room. You here to let out some fury?"

Isobel's eyes went wide and her smile even wider. "I'd like to book a room, please."

Aaron was just getting into his truck to head home for the night when a text message popped up on his phone. It was Isobel.

I have a surprise for you. Please meet me and Sophie here.

Her message was followed with a map and address attachment. But there was no venue name.

He texted back, frustrated at her cryptic message.

I'm tired. Just wanna shower, eat and go to bed.

She sent him a picture of her and a kind of smiling Sophie. Isobel had a fake pouty face, and Sophie looked like she was getting ready to shit herself.

She texted back.

Pleeeeeaaaase! It'll be worth it, I promise.

He grumbled, punched the coordinates into his GPS and started his truck. It was only a ten-minute drive from his jobsite and on the way home. She really was the least demanding, least inconveniencing person alive.

He tossed the truck into first gear and pulled out onto the road, hitting voice to text. "Be there in five."

His phone pinged a minute later to reveal her face yet again, but this time she was smiling.

He was tempted to make that picture the wallpaper on his phone.

Over the last month, he had remained as professional as humanly possible when it came to his drop-dead fucking gorgeous nanny. He was polite, courteous and above all *professional as fuck*. Sure, he tugged one off nearly every night in the shower, but if it meant keeping Isobel as his nanny and not having a lawsuit on his hands, he'd suffer through. Besides, she didn't seem to be interested in him that way anyway. She was so busy with Sophie, going to baby groups and the story time at the library. It seemed like they were out and about every day, all day. The woman was exhausted by the time 8 p.m. rolled around, retiring to her room and not coming out unless Sophie squawked.

Exactly ten minutes later, he pulled up to the strip mall. There were a bunch of different businesses all in a row: a dance studio at the end, a photography studio, a bistro, a liquor store and now a new business—*The Rage Room*.

What the fuck was a rage room?

He shut off his truck and climbed out, double-checking on his phone he had the right place, but when Isobel and Sophie stepped out of The Rage Room, he put his phone away.

"There's Uncle Aaron," Isobel cooed, walking toward him, holding Sophie in her arms.

She passed Sophie to him, and he pecked her on her baby-soft cheek. "What are we doing here?"

Isobel's smile dissolved over half of the anger that burned like a tire fire inside him. "Come on in and I'll show you." It looked like she was tempted to reach for his hand, but instead she simply clapped hers in delight and then skipped, yes, *skipped* toward the front door.

The bell chimed, and a woman with pink hair and tattoos stepped out from the back. "Your room is all ready for you," she said with a smile. "Big one at the back. Your wife paid for extra stuff, too, so go crazy. Nothing is off limits." Her pierced nose wrinkled. "Well, besides the acrylic glass walls." She shrugged and placed a clipboard with a waiver on the counter in front of him. "I mean you can try to smash the acrylic glass, but I doubt it'll break." Aaron's biceps bunched as he hoisted Sophie up onto his shoulder and signed the waiver. "Well, you might, actually, so please don't try."

What the fuck was this woman talking about? What had Isobel gotten him into?

He really just wanted to get home, shower, eat and go to bed. It'd been a long day on the jobsite, and his back was fucking killing him.

Isobel chuckled beside him. "Here, hand me Soph."

He passed off the baby and followed the pink-haired lady and Isobel down the short corridor toward the back, where a room made out of four acrylic glass walls housed tables and shelves loaded with various dishes, vases, lamps, glass and wood.

The pink-haired woman pointed to a rack that held various things, such as baseball bats, crowbars, tire irons, even a sledgehammer. "Your weapons." She grinned as she handed him a pair of leather work gloves, safety goggles and a hardhat. "And your protective gear." She stepped out, and Isobel and Sophie followed her.

Aaron paused in the doorway, confused. "Iz, what is all this?"

She patted Sophie's back and bounced her. "It's a rage room. A place to let the anger out. Figured you might need it." Her blue eyes glimmered. "I'm going to take Soph for a walk. You've got thirty minutes to do as much damage as you can. If you need more time, that's not a problem. She has my credit card and will just charge me for the extra time." She made to walk away but then turned back, hope shining in her eyes. Eyes that saw straight through him, eyes that terrified him, eyes that he continually got lost in, drowned in nearly every night as she sat across from him at the dinner table. Her smile was small but true. "I hope this helps." Then she took Sophie, and the two of them left the building, leaving Aaron in a room alone with his demons.

Isobel wasn't sure what she was going to return to. Aaron had seemed confused and irritated with her before she left. Left him in a room with Old Country Roses china and a baseball bat.

Would he find the ability to let his anger out therapeutically, or would he just be angrier than before?

Isobel smiled at Luna, who was behind the desk, as she wheeled the stroller back into the front lobby of The Rage Room. "How's he doing?" she asked, tuning in to the sounds around her. She didn't hear any smashing or crashing or bashing. Was he done?

Luna shrugged. "He's been done for about ten minutes. He left."

Isobel's eyes narrowed, and she studied Luna's face like the woman was suddenly speaking another language. "He what?"

She shrugged again. "I asked him if he wanted to wait for you, and he said no. That you guys had your own vehicles and he'd meet you at home."

Isobel's mouth opened and closed repeatedly. "Did he at least smash stuff?"

Luna nodded. "Yep. Go see for yourself." She jerked her head down the corridor toward Aaron's rage room. "Not too many people destroy the table too. That man had a lot of power behind his rage."

Isobel left Sophie and the stroller next to the front desk and jogged down the hallway toward the end. She braced herself for what she was about to see.

Even then, she hadn't been prepared.

Every single thing was demolished.

Battered and shattered, shredded and annihilated. You couldn't tell what anything was, even if you tried. Not even the table looked like a table anymore. It was just a series of toothpick-size splinters and screws scattered around the thrashed room space.

She swallowed down the lump in her throat.

Maybe this rage room hadn't been such a good idea.

Was he even more enraged now? Was she going home to a man on the warpath?

She didn't jog, but her walk was brisk as she made her way back to the front. "How did he seem when he left?"

Luna's lips turned down into a dismissive pout. "He seemed fine."

"Not fuming mad, like he was going to go home and smash more stuff?"

She shook her head. "No. I even asked him if he needed more stuff to smash, and he said he was good. Seemed eager to get going."

Isobel was crazy confused.

"You want to book another day?" Luna asked. "We host parties too. Birthdays, bachelorette parties, networking, team-building, that kind of thing. Nothing quite brings people together like destroying shit." She laughed, revealing a shiny green tongue stud. She handed Isobel a card. "We even have a rewards program. Nine rage days and the tenth one is free."

Isobel took her card and stowed it in the back pocket of her jeans. "Thanks. I'll keep this in mind."

Luna was all smiles. "I already stamped the first one for you. Only eight more to go."

Isobel smiled as she pushed open the door. A chilly wind off the water was blowing through the city, and it was starting to rain. "Thanks, Luna. Nice meeting you."

Luna waved. "You too. Take care."

Isobel pulled the rain cover over Sophie's car seat and set off on a quick jog toward her car.

By the time she got Sophie loaded and the stroller stowed, the sky had opened up and it was a downpour. Only with the wind, it was more of a *sidepour* and pelting Isobel in the face with big droplets as she opened her car door and slid behind the steering wheel.

It was rush hour, and the streets were slammed.

She rested her forehead on the steering wheel for a moment and took a couple of deep breaths.

Maybe it was a good thing they weren't going to be getting home any time soon. Perhaps it would give Aaron a chance to cool off.

One could only hope.

By the time she got home, Sophie was officially losing her mind in the back of the car, and Isobel was on the verge of tears herself.

It was still coming down in buckets as she pulled up to the garage door, tossed the car into park and opened the door. She'd forgotten her rain jacket in the house, and her car umbrella was busted and she hadn't bought a new one yet, so even though she was already wet, she was about to get soaked.

As she prepared herself for the second round of drenching, a dark shadow in a black raincoat ran past her. He opened the back passenger door, ducked inside and then, as quick as he came, retreated back to the house with a still-wailing Sophie.

Isobel scrambled after him, covering her head with her purse—not that it would do much good.

She burst inside and slammed the door against the assaulting wind, wiping her wet hair out of her eyes and shaking off the drops that clung to her sweater.

The sound of Sophie crying had disappeared down the hallway, along with Isobel's sexy, surly boss.

The clock in the living room said it was six thirty. She was still technically on the clock for another thirty minutes. Should she go relieve Aaron?

Did she want to see him?

First, she needed to get out of her wet clothes, then she could tackle the repercussions of her actions with Aaron.

She opened her bedroom door, and what sat on her bed nearly knocked her flat on her ass—a big, beautiful bouquet of flowers. Peonies and lilies, ranunculus and daisies. All her favorites. All dazzling.

There was a card tucked into the top, and she pulled it out.

Just like the man who had undoubtedly given her the flowers, the card was to the point, with zero frills and zero emotions.

THANK YOU!

That was it.

But it was enough.

She let out the breath she'd been holding, and her shoulders abandoned her ears. She'd been tense on the drive home. And not just because Sophie was freaking out in the back. Isobel was nervous that Aaron was going to be mad with her for booking him the rage room, for trying to help him find an outlet for his pain.

And even though he still might be furious with her, he also seemed grateful.

She peeled out of her damp clothes and pulled on a pair of blue and white plaid pajama pants and a dark blue hoodie. She tossed her damp ponytail up into a messy bun on the top of her head and took her now dry body and her exquisite flowers out to the kitchen.

Thankfully, she'd had the forethought that morning to put together a hearty turkey and quinoa soup in the slow cooker. She'd also made cheese and jalapeno biscuits during Sophie's morning nap.

She really hoped Aaron hadn't waited for her and had already fed himself. She would feel terrible if he was starving because she'd been trapped in rush-hour traffic.

"There we go, baby," she heard his deep, soothing voice coo as she padded barefoot down the hall and into the living room. Aaron was sitting in his La-Z-Boy chair with Sophie in his arms and a bottle in her mouth. "Fresh diaper and something in your belly, you're an easy gal to please."

His tone seemed chipper. Okay, maybe *chipper* was the wrong word. But he didn't sound angry or irritated. That didn't mean much, though, because he was always pleasant and sweet with his niece.

Isobel slowly approached him from the side, gauging his body language and whether he threw up his walls as she got closer. He didn't look at her, but he also didn't appear to brace himself for her presence. She took a deep breath. "How'd it go?"

He glanced up at her, the smile he'd been giving Sophie falling just a touch when his gaze reached Isobel's face. "It was good." He tilted his head toward the flowers. "Thank you."

She clutched the bouquet to her chest. "They're amazing. Thank you."

He nodded, then turned back to Sophie. "Go dish yourself up some dinner. You must be starving."

She sucked in a deep breath, pushing a strange ache out of her chest. She assumed he'd already eaten, but knowing that he had hurt her heart.

She nodded without saying a word and took off toward the kitchen.

"I'll just finish feeding Sophie here and then join you," he called after. "That soup smells great."

She nearly tripped over her own bare feet and bashed her hip into the table. She spun around. "You haven't eaten yet?"

He was looking at her now, the blue of his eyes practically glowing, the smile on his face directed at her. "No, I waited for you."

Chapter 12

It was Saturday afternoon, and Isobel was in the middle of folding laundry. The television was on in the background with the news yammering away.

She'd become slightly obsessed with the recent crime spree happening in Seattle. Jewelry stores were being robbed almost weekly, and the police still hadn't been able to catch the guy or guys involved.

Though the authorities weren't sure whether it was one guy or an organized group. Either way, it was very interesting to follow. She had always been intrigued by crime shows, particularly the unsolved ones. She loved any kind of a mystery. Maybe that's why she was so into Aaron, despite how moody and angry he was. The man was a huge mystery, and she found herself wondering when he'd reveal the next clue, allowing her to get just one step closer to cracking the case—or in this instance, his hard, armored shell.

She went to turn up the volume on the television when her phone started to vibrate on the coffee table.

The call display said it was her friend Mercedes.

She hit *answer* and hadn't even put her ear to the receiver when Mercedes's demanding voice blasted over the other end. "Why aren't you returning my text messages?"

Isobel scrunched up her nose. "What text messages?"

Mercedes's scoff could probably be heard in Australia. "Check your phone, my *dear*. I've been messaging you for nearly two hours."

Sure enough, there were like twenty missed text messages from Miss Mercedes Porter.

"Crap, sorry. Sophie was fussy and wouldn't take a bottle, even though I knew she was hungry. Then she had a poop explosion, so I had to change her—and me—and then do laundry, feed her, put her down—"

"I get it, you're in pseudo-mommy mode. Can you talk now?"

"I can. What's up?"

"Get your dancing shoes on, pretty lady. We're hitting the town tonight. I just got a promotion. You are now friends with the head buyer for the entire women's line for Orchid Apparel."

Isobel dropped the towel she was about to fold. "Shut up."

"No, you shut up."

"Like corner office, brass nameplate promotion?"

"Mhmm. And a company credit card." She whistled. "I get to go to fashion shows, rub shoulders with potential distributors and designers."

Mercedes and Isobel had met in art school. Mercedes was studying fashion, while also doing a fashion merchandising degree online, and Isobel was getting her degree in graphic design. They'd instantly become friends, and although Mercedes had a big mouth, her heart was even bigger. She was *the* friend to have when the chips were down. She was the first person to show up to lend her support, a bottle of wine and a tub of ice cream in the crook of her arm. And if it was a breakup, she even brought a small metal garbage can, and a lighter. Then she'd encourage Isobel, or whoever had been dumped, to light the guy's stuff on fire.

Only once did they set off the sprinklers in Isobel's apartment.

"I've got us on the list for Emerald, Social Club, Touch and The Ballroom. We don't have to go to all of them—or we can—but we're on the VIP list at them all, just in case. I can come grab you early. We can grab a drink at Prime Bar first before we head out. The bartender there is fucking gorgeous."

Isobel snorted. She was pretty sure Mercedes was talking about Mason.

She was about to say she couldn't wait when the coos and warbles of Sophie on the baby monitor reminded her that she was on baby duty Saturday nights. And Aaron went to play poker with his single dad friends.

Ah, crap.

"I can't," she said glumly, stowing the baby monitor in the back pocket of her jeans and heading off down the hall to go grab Sophie. "I have to work. Aaron goes to poker night."

"Fuck. I hate how much you work. Seriously, it's not right."

Yep. Big heart. Big mouth.

Isobel bent at the waist and picked Sophie up out of the bassinet. "Hey baby." She propped her up on her shoulder and wandered back out to the living room. "I'm sorry, Mercedes. Could we go out Sunday?"

Mercedes whined. "I made the plans for tonight. Everyone else can go tonight."

"I'm really sorry. I would love to go celebrate your new promotion, but ..." she kissed the top of Sophie's head. "Work comes first."

"You can go."

The deep voice behind her made her squeak and nearly drop her phone and the baby in her arms. She spun around to find not only Aaron, the owner of the voice, but another man, a very attractive, very broad, very tall man standing next to him.

"What was that?" Mercedes yelled into the phone. "What just happened?"

"I'll call you back. Just gimme a minute." Then before Mercedes could protest—because oh, she would—Isobel hung up.

"This is my friend Colton," Aaron said. "We worked together."

Colton stepped forward, his smile wide and perfect. He thrust out his enormous hand. "Pleased to meet you. Heard nothing but good things."

Isobel's core tightened. Good things from Aaron? What had he said about her?

"You guys worked in construction together?" she asked, passing Sophie off to Aaron when he asked for her.

Colton shook his head. "No."

He left it at that, and the glint in his eyes said she shouldn't press further.

"Liam's making me host poker tonight," Aaron said, returning with Sophie in his arms and a bottle. "He's getting renovations done to his place. New floors. I told him I had a friend in town. He said the only way Colton—who doesn't have kids—could come to poker is if he tripled his buy-in and I hosted."

Isobel shook her head and resumed folding laundry. "Oh, that Liam. He doubles the buy-in for those who are no longer single and triples it for those who are childless. A true mastermind, that one."

"Where are you going?" Aaron sat down in his La-Z-Boy chair and began to feed Sophie. Since the night in the rage room, Aaron had been a fair bit calmer around her, still not super-friendly, but certainly calmer—and definitely still very polite.

"My friend Mercedes just got a promotion at work and wants to go out to celebrate. She's put our names on the VIP list at a bunch of different hot spots. The woman has crazy connections. I don't know how she knows so many people."

Aaron didn't look up at her, but a strong, sexy muscle along his jaw ticked. "You can go." He finally lifted his gaze to hers. "Not that you need my permission."

Now it was Isobel's turn to hide her eyes. She brushed her hand in front of her mouth to mask her smile. He was cute when he was trying to be a feminist.

There was hope for this one yet.

"Thanks. I'm not leaving until later tonight. I can put Sophie down if you like?"

He nodded. "Do what you can until the guys arrive, then take the rest of the night off." He booped Sophie on the nose and smiled down at her. Isobel's insides liquefied and her heart constricted.

"You're really figuring this dad gig out, huh?" Colton said, wandering over to the couch. "Looks good on you." He tossed his head back and whooped out a laugh. "Never thought I'd say those words. That fatherhood looked good on you." He shook his head. "And now Cahill is married with one on the way. Who's next?"

Aaron lifted an eyebrow at his friend.

Isobel watched the exchange.

Colton shook his dark, close-cropped head. "Don't look at me. No way, man. Never. I'm a lone wolf. A bachelor. Ain't no dirty diapers or wedding bells in my future—not ever."

Aaron rolled his eyes. "Never say never, dude. Rob says he's never been happier."

"Yeah, well, it helps that he married a fucking billionaire heiress," Colton scoffed, rolling his eyes.

Aaron pursed his lips together. "I don't think he cares about any of that shit. I wouldn't."

Isobel wondered if they even knew she was still in the room. The way they were talking about their friend Rob and his wealthy wife but also the candid and optimistic way Aaron was speaking showed a new side of him she'd never seen before. And she liked it.

Isobel cleared her throat. "Does six work for dinner?" Thankfully, she'd taken out more than enough meat with the intention of leftovers for tomorrow. Aaron could eat a lot, and she assumed his handsome friend with the dark amber eyes could also put it away when he wanted to.

Aaron grunted, not bothering to look up at her. "Six works."

She turned away, her heart hurting a little at how cold he still was toward her. Would it ever change? Did he even like her?

"Iz?"

She turned back around to find him looking straight at her. "Thank you. For everything." His smile was small but genuine, and it made all the butterflies in her belly take flight at the exact same time.

She teetered back and forth on her feet, smiled back and tucked a strand of hair behind her ear. "You're welcome." Then she headed down the hallway with an added spring in her step, only to stop on the threshold of her bedroom door. She shouldn't eavesdrop, but she had a hard time stopping herself.

"She's cute," Colton said, dropping his voice down several octaves. "Crazy cute. Must be hard remaining professional around that."

She strained her ears until her whole brain hurt trying to listen for Aaron's answer, but she couldn't hear a thing. Did he know her door wasn't closed?

Probably.

The man was a retired something or other. He probably had specially trained ears. Could hear a worm beneath the soil like a robin.

"So why are you here?" It was Aaron's voice, and although low, it was clear. So either he hadn't responded to Colton's earlier question, or he'd mouthed his response, figuring she was eavesdropping. Damn, he was smart.

"Rob's old lady is sick as a dog with morning sickness. Wark's on a mission, same with Blaze and Ash."

"They sent you to check up on me? Make sure I don't go off the deep end?" She heard the gentle patting sound of Aaron now burping Sophie. "I don't need a babysitter. I'm not going to off myself like Brandon. I'm fine."

"Says who?"

"Says me."

"Dude, your sister fucking died. In a mass shooting no less. And she left you her newborn baby to raise. That would fuck with anybody's mind, let alone someone who's been through the shit you've been through. Have you found anybody to talk to? A therapist? Gone to the veterans' center for help?"

"When the fuck would I have time for that? I work all goddamn day, then I'm home in the evenings with Sophie. I need her to know I'm here for her. That she has at least one person who won't abandon her."

Isobel clutched her chest and leaned back against the doorjamb as a tear slipped down her cheek. He was hurting so badly, and there wasn't anything she could do to help him.

"You're not your parents, man. You're not, and you never will be. Sophie didn't end up in the system like you and Dina because she has you. You know what being an orphan is like, and I know you're not going to take your own life and abandon her, but that doesn't mean you don't need help."

Aaron and his sister had been in foster care? What happened to their parents? How long had they been without a family who loved them? And now that Dina was gone, did Aaron have anyone?

A growl she'd come to know well rumbled down the hallway. "I'm doing the best I fucking can right now. Now back off. If you've come to get me to spill my guts and cry on your shoulder, then you can get back in your fucking rental car and get lost. I don't need a babysitter. I told you that."

"Okay, okay. I'll back off ... for now. But the best way to get through this shit is to talk about it."

"Yeah? Who the fuck told you that? You watching Dr. Phil or something?"

"Rob. Actually. And Admiral Cahill. Been out to see the fam on the farm a fair bit. Admiral's been taking me to the veterans' center there in Texas. It's helped a lot. Particularly to process the shit that went down in Colombia."

The squeak of Aaron's La-Z-Boy recliner followed by a gruff grunt and booted footsteps had her retreating into her room, but she didn't shut the door.

"You can sleep on the couch," Aaron said. "I'm going to go change Soph." His heavy steps grew louder the closer he got. Hastily, she closed her door, leaving it open just a crack.

"You can't run from your past," Colton called back. "Otherwise it'll haunt your future forever."

Aaron walked past Isobel's door grumbling, "Stupid chatty motherfucker. On his goddamn period wanting to talk about feelings and shit." Isobel held her breath until she knew he was in Sophie's room. Then she heard, "All right, Super Sophie, let's change your little bum. I felt all kinds of thunder rumbling. Did you give me any lightning? Oh, whoa! Gross, baby. Gross."

Isobel smiled and held in a laugh as another tear slipped down her cheek. He was hurting, he was haunted, and yet when that baby needed him most, he rallied, plastered on a smile and gave her what she needed. He gave her everything.

Even if it took everything out of him to do it.

Chapter 13

By seven thirty the house was full.

Aaron hated it.

Crowds had never been his thing, even before the Navy, even before his tours in the Middle East and South America.

And although The Single Dads of Seattle weren't necessarily a crowd, his house wasn't anywhere near as big as Liam's, and it felt tight.

Colton was busy playing bartender, mixing drinks and whetting whistles while Liam bounced Sophie in his arms and Isobel was off in her bedroom getting ready. Once the doorbell had started to ring—didn't these men know better than to ring a doorbell in a house with a baby?—she'd made herself scarce, taking off down the hall to get ready.

He'd been wondering for a while how much of his and Colton's conversation earlier she'd heard. Particularly that part about whether or not he was able to keep things professional. Colton's grin had been huge when Aaron gave him the stink eye and mouthed the words "So fucking hard." God forbid Isobel hear him say that. He'd probably be scouring the want ads for a new nanny before sunrise.

Things between them had been good. Or at least he thought they were good. Painfully platonic was how he best described it.

Professional, polite and perfectly *plain*.

Which was the absolute opposite of what he really wanted.

But if he wanted to keep her, he had to hide his urges, hide his attraction and keep his distance. And over the weeks, an arm's length was beginning to seem like not enough. He could still smell her at an arm's length, and she smelled fucking fantastic.

He'd been pissed off with her at first for booking him a room at that Rage Room place. How dare she? But then he thought about it, and wasn't that the whole point? Wasn't he meant to be angry? The angrier you were, the more crap you demolished.

More bang for your buck.

And once he got going, he *really* got going.

He'd smashed shit in that room up good. Channeled all his fury, all his hate and pain about Dina, about Colombia and the Velasquez family into the aluminum baseball bat and went ape-shit on the room. It hadn't taken him long to destroy the place. Maybe ten minutes—if that. Then the next ten minutes were spent working on his tactical breathing. *Hold air in the lungs for four seconds. Exhale for four seconds, emptying all the air from the lungs. Keep the lungs empty for four seconds and repeat.*

It was how they reduced stress and re-centered themselves in the field. How he and his brothers coped with the never-ending shit storm that rained down on them.

He hadn't realized how much anger and pain he had bottled up inside of him until he started to let it out, until he picked up the bat and swung it into the ugly yellow lamp on the bookcase.

That first swing, the sound of the lamp smashing and the bookshelf cracking, had reawakened something inside him. A beast. *The* beast. The same beast that had come forth in Colombia. He'd morphed into a killing machine then, avenging those he loved, and he morphed into that same killing machine again in the rage room. Seeing that ugly lamp disintegrate into nothing more than shards of jagged ceramic in front of his very eyes had given him joy.

Bloodlust.

And he needed more.

He'd roared, yes, actually roared after that and began to swing and smash and hammer the bat down on everything and anything breakable—which was all of it. And he didn't stop until there were tears in his eyes, sweat on his brow and nothing but chips and splinters at his feet.

A shattered world because of a shattered heart.

When there was nothing left to destroy, he dropped the bat in a deafening clatter, fell to his knees, head in his hands, and wept. Wept for Dina. Wept for Valentina and Miguel. José and Rosita. For Sophie, who would never know her mother. For his buddy Brandon, who'd taken his own life because he couldn't cope with the real world after he left the battlefield. He didn't stop until his chest heaved and his knees ached.

But even then, he didn't stand up.

He kept his head down and began to breathe.

Inhale. Hold. Exhale. Hold. Inhale. Hold. Exhale. Hold.

Only once he could count the beats of his pulse with the ticking of his watch did he stand up, wipe his eyes and step out of the room.

Then he drove to the grocery store, bought the biggest bouquet of flowers they had and headed home. He knew Isobel would probably be disappointed that he hadn't waited for her—and it gutted him to think he'd hurt her—but he needed a bit more time to compose himself and regroup before he saw her. He didn't want her to see his red eyes or blotchy skin. She had the uncanny ability to see right through him, and he knew that if she walked into The Rage Room and saw him as he left his session, she'd know he'd done more than just smash shit to smithereens.

He didn't want her to see the beast.

To see his bloodlust or the aftermath of his ire.

Because the rage room had done more than just provide him with an outlet to channel his fury, it had allowed him to revisit all the recent pain in his life.

His losses—and there were many—opening up old wounds that hadn't quite scarred over but were at least no longer fresh. Now they were fresh again, at the forefront of his mind, and he needed time to let them scab over before he saw her. Before she looked at him with those eyes, that smile that made the whole world a better, brighter place.

They'd shared dinner that night, and although they didn't talk much, he enjoyed sitting with her. Watching her mouth move and her long throat swallow.

He'd never considered himself a throat guy. But for some reason, he really loved Isobel's throat. It was long and sexy as hell. He loved to watch her swallow food as he secretly envisioned her swallowing *other* things.

Was there such thing as a throat fetish?

Thankfully, she didn't press him for conversation, which he appreciated. She seemed to know that he wasn't much of a talker and that after his session in the rage room, he *really* wasn't interested in talking.

The rest of the week had been nice. Once his scabs healed over and he was able to go minutes and then eventually hours without thinking about Brandon or the Velasquez family, he felt better. He slept better. He'd even cracked a joke at work, which had all the guys on the jobsite pausing to look at him like he was from outer space.

He had to wonder, though, was it really the rage room that helped him? Or was it Isobel? Just her presence alone calmed him, grounded him, reassured him that he didn't have to go this alone.

He'd always have triggers that brought back the horrific memories of Brandon, Dina and the Velasquezes. The rage room had just been a *big* trigger. But being with Isobel each morning and each night was its own kind of therapy. Watching her with his niece, seeing her dote on Sophie as if she were her own daughter, brought him a sense of peace he hadn't felt since the day he got Dina away from her last foster home and became her legal guardian.

And now Isobel was heading out on the town to go flirt and drink and dance. He hated the idea of her being ogled and petted by gropey frat guys as they slurred their words and spilled their drinks all over her. She deserved so much more than that.

You mean you?

Fuck no. Aaron was unworthy of her. It was *him* who didn't deserve *her.*

But, as she had so passionately educated him on the ways of the modern feminist, she did not need his permission to go out. He was her boss, not her keeper. So even though he didn't like the idea of her going out, he had no say in the matter.

And that just pissed him the fuck off.

"Nice place," a low, calm voice said, drawing him from his thoughts. Aaron turned around to see Atlas, a big, tall blond man with gray eyes, looking around the dining room. "You do this yourself?"

Aaron nodded. "Bought the place but then gutted it and renovated it."

Atlas nodded. "Cool."

He was a man of very few words, but then again, so was Aaron. The two got along well. Atlas didn't bother making any more small talk and instead just nodded and wandered over to the bar.

Liam had brought over his poker chips and card table, as Aaron's small two-seater kitchen table hadn't even worked for him, Colton and Isobel to eat at. They'd dined in the living room.

Aaron was busy opening bags of potato chips and pretzels when a high-pitched whistle had all the conversations in the house pausing. He lifted his head to see Isobel, looking hotter than he'd ever seen her before, *clickety-clacking* her heels down the hallway.

She was in some weird bright red jumpsuit thing with a low-cut neck. Did chicks call them *rompers?* Whatever the fuck it was called, it hugged all her curves, showing off those sexy hips and luscious ass, but it was also modest and feminine in the way the fabric billowed and flowed. Aaron knew nothing about fashion, but he knew what he liked, and he liked that look on Isobel. He liked it a lot.

And apparently, so did the other men in the house.

Heat raced through his veins from the look Zak was giving her. Like she was a ripe red raspberry on the bush and he couldn't wait to pluck her and taste her.

Fuck Zak.

"Looking good, Miss Jones," Zak said, sidling up next to her as Isobel accepted a vodka soda from Colton. "Heading out on the town tonight?"

Isobel was all smiles. "Sure am. A friend just got a promotion, so she wants to go celebrate. And I need to dance. Haven't danced in far too long."

Zak's eyes raked her from tip to toe, his smile growing just a touch wider when they landed on her chest. "Well, you shouldn't have any problems finding a dance partner. You look lovely."

"Thank you. But I usually prefer to just dance with my friends. The club scene can be such a meat market. Not really the kind of guys I'm interested in meeting, you know?"

Zak nodded. "I couldn't agree more. Not looking to date, myself, so I stay away from those places altogether. But if you asked me to dance, I would probably make an exception."

Aaron wanted to snap his neck.

"We miss you at the gym. Was it something we did?" Zak took a step closer to Isobel when Mark tucked in next to the counter and grabbed a drink from Colton. Zak did not step away again when Mark left.

Zak was a dick.

"Nothing you did." She chuckled. "I just don't have time for the gym right now. I've been tossing Sophie in the jogging stroller and going for a run most mornings after Aaron's headed to work. I'm getting my workouts that way while the weather is still decent." She took a long sip of her vodka soda, the line of her throat bobbing as she swallowed. She finished her drink and put the glass down on the counter, nodding at Colton when he asked if she'd like another.

"Well, when you're ready to come back, let us know. I'll hook you up with a discount in the childcare center too if you need it."

She batted her long lashes at him and flicked her ponytail over her shoulder, laughing. "Thanks, Zak. Always a plus to have friends in high places."

Was she flirting with him?

Did Isobel have a thing for Zak?

The motherfucking space station could probably see that Zak had a thing for Isobel, but was it mutual?

Had they ever acted on it?

Had they slept together?

Were they sleeping together?

Aaron bet Zak got a lot of tail. He probably rarely ever failed at picking up a woman. The guy was jacked. Even more than Aaron. Taller too. With tattoos down both arms, dark red hair, blue eyes and a megawatt smile. Plus, the dude owned a fucking gym franchise. He probably had little gym bunnies hopping all around him morning, noon and night.

Aaron wanted to punch a hole through the fucking wall. He wanted to punch a hole through Zak's fucking flirty-ass face.

He'd stopped listening to Isobel and Zak's conversation. He was too deep in his own head. But when Isobel's laugh, a laugh he'd never heard before—warm and carefree—swam around the kitchen, and all because of something Zak had said, Aaron's blood began to boil. He was close to losing it.

"Need ice," he muttered to nobody, taking off in the direction of the garage at a breakneck speed. It would not bode well for him—for anybody—if he put his fist into Zak's face. It might make him feel better for half a second, but after that he'd feel worse than he did now. Also, Zak could probably hold his own in a fistfight, and Aaron might find himself flat on his ass with a broken nose and a black eye faster than he could say, "The only easy day was yesterday," the official motto of the United States Navy SEALs.

Blowing out a long exhale, he shut the garage door behind him and paced back and forth in front of his truck. Where was The Rage Room when he needed it the most? He could punch the punching bag, but the whole house would hear that and know something was up. The same if he threw something or hollered. He needed a pillow to scream into. He needed to soundproof the garage and reinforce the beam so that it didn't shake half the house when he beat the living shit out of the bag.

Why did he join The Single Dads of Seattle so soon? He wasn't ready to socialize. He wasn't ready to talk preschools and shitty diapers, sleepless nights and dance recitals. He wasn't ready for any of it.

And fuck if he ever thought he would be.

He wasn't a dad. He was an uncle hanging on by a thread the width of a fucking pubic hair.

Every morning he woke up hoping that the day would be easier than the last. That yesterday wouldn't be easier than today, that he'd finally feel like he was Sophie's dad and not just the consolation prize who was inevitably going to send her into years of therapy because he himself needed therapy, he was so fucked up.

And then there was Isobel.

Perfect, sweet, smart, kind, beautiful, patient Isobel.

How she hadn't run for the hills already was beyond him.

She was a fucking saint.

It drove him damn near mental to see her flirting with Zak in the kitchen. Drove him over the edge most nights when he went to take a shower after her, only to smell her body wash in the bathroom, feel the steam from her shower where her naked wet body had just been. He knew it was wrong that he jerked off in the shower every night to thoughts of her, but he couldn't stop himself. It was the only way he could temper the urge to knock on her door—no, knock *down* her door and claim her as his.

His back was to the door, but his training kicked in immediately, and his entire body stiffened. He knew it was her. The momentary volume increase from the men in the house followed by the soft *click* of the door closing made his breathing turn rapid.

Suddenly, her hand was on his back, slowly moving up to his shoulder.

He swallowed and squeezed his eyes shut.

She's the nanny.

Don't fuck the nanny.

Don't fuck the nanny.

Do. Not. Fuck. The. Nanny.

"Aaron," she whispered. Fuck, her voice was like warm honey. So sweet, so smooth. "Is everything okay?" She squeezed the top of his shoulder. "Can you turn around and look at me ... please?"

That last word did it. That faint, almost timid *please.*

He turned around, wrapped his fist around her ponytail and took her mouth like she held all the answers, all the oxygen, all the hope in the world.

Her hands fell to his chest, and she pushed him away.

Careful not to frighten her with his need, he let go of her hair and took a step back. He ran his hands through his hair and looked away. "Fuck, I'm so sorry, I don't know what I was—"

"No, you were just standing on my foot." Then she leapt up into his arms, wrapped her legs around his waist and took his mouth with the same intensity as he'd taken hers—possibly more.

Aaron groaned as she tugged on his hair, deepening their kiss, forcing her tongue deeper into his mouth. She whimpered but didn't pull away. Instead she opened wider for him and sucked on his tongue like it was his cock—or at least how he hoped she sucked cock. Holy fuck. She nipped his bottom lip, smiling as a groan made its way up from the depths of his throat, and he palmed her breast. Her giggle was light and girly. He wanted to make her do it again.

He moved them over to his workbench and plunked her butt down. Her ankles locked around his back, and she pressed the apex of her thighs against his hips.

He moaned. Fuck, she felt good. And she smelled goddamn amazing.

He knew that the moment they stopped kissing, the moment they pulled away from each other, he'd have to find a new nanny for Sophie, but for the moment, for just one brief moment in what was one of the worst times of his life, he didn't feel pain. In Isobel's arms, with her legs wrapped around his waist, the heat of her nestled up tight against his erection, her lips sucking on his tongue, all he felt was good. Fuck, he'd even go so far as to say he felt great.

The attraction wasn't one-sided. He'd have never guessed it. But now he was fucking thrilled he'd been wrong.

All the tension and stress, the feelings of inadequacy, the grief and anger lifted off his shoulders, replaced by the silky softness of Isobel's arms as they wrapped around him tightly and her fingers toyed with the hair at the nape of his neck.

The moment they stopped kissing and she removed her arms, the weight would drop back on his shoulders. The tension and stress. The responsibility of being Sophie's dad. The anger he felt over Dina's death. Over the Velasquez family. There was just so much death.

The doorbell chimed.

Only in this case, it wasn't *saved by the bell*. The spell was broken by the bell.

Isobel was the first to break their connection, pulling away from his mouth and lifting her arms from his shoulders.

And just like he expected, all the stress dropped right back on them. Only a new weight was added, too—the weight of what he'd just done.

He'd kissed his nanny.

"Isobel, where are you?" a woman's voice called throughout the house.

Isobel's eyes went wide. Her flushed face and puffy lips were sexy as hell and made Aaron want to lock the garage door and forget about everyone on the other side of it for the rest of the night.

"That's Mercedes," she whispered. He backed away and helped her off the workbench. "She's here to pick me up."

119

He nodded and scratched the back of his neck, not sure what to say after what they'd just done. He cleared his throat. "Listen, I'm really sorry. I—" His words were as strained as his zipper.

She pressed her finger against his lips, her smile wide and seductive. "Don't apologize. Don't. Please. I have to go. We can talk more about ... *this* tomorrow." She walked toward the door. "Have fun tonight. Or at least try to. Try to win, too." Then she opened the door and headed out into the house, leaving Aaron standing in the garage, confused as fuck and with a raging boner.

Chapter 14

Isobel touched her mouth and smiled as the memories of Aaron's lips, his tongue, his hands, his ... all came flooding back.

That hadn't been at all what she'd gone into the garage for, but damn if she wasn't pleased with the surprise.

Always one to pick up on people's emotions almost before they did, she could tell Aaron had not been happy that she and Zak had been as chatty as they were. Or that Zak was as close to Isobel as he had been. Aaron's body grew tighter by the second, his cheeks flushed a ruddy color, his nostrils flared, and if the man had hackles she could see, they'd be standing straight up.

The kiss had surprised her. But it was the best kind of surprise.

Here she thought he disliked her. Tolerated her for the sake of Sophie and that the attraction was entirely one-sided.

How happy was she that she'd been wrong?

"What's with the smile?" Mercedes asked, having to yell over the loud music as they sat at their VIP booth in one of the nightclubs. Isobel had lost track of which club they were at. They'd been to at least three. And it was just her and Mercedes left. All the other celebrators had headed home for the night, claiming exhaustion, CrossFit the next day or some other *millennial excuse,* as Mercedes put it. Isobel felt bad, but she would have just as soon gone home too. She was tired, and truth be told, she wanted to get home and explore that kiss more with Aaron.

A nudge had her blinking a few times.

"Hmm?" Mercedes hummed. "What's with the smile? You look like you're in a trance."

Isobel shook her head. "Oh, nothing. Just thinking about something."

"Is it that houseful of super-sexy men you just left? Because I've been thinking about them too. Especially that one with the military haircut and amber eyes. What was his name again?"

Isobel took a sip of her martini. "Colton. That's Aaron's friend."

"He was hot."

"Excuse us, ladies." Two men, probably a good five years younger than Isobel and Mercedes, approached their table. "But we couldn't help noticing that the two of you are all alone this evening," the taller of the two said.

They were both well dressed, with name-brand polos and pants, expensive watches and equally pricey haircuts. The cologne that drifted over with them reeked of money and privilege.

Isobel was immediately turned off.

"Might we buy you a drink?" the other one asked. His eyes were a deep dark brown, so dark Isobel wasn't sure if it was the club lighting or the man actually had no discernible pupil.

She hoped that Mercedes would bust out her inner bitch and dismiss them. Isobel was in no mood to be entertaining puppies. It didn't matter how cute, put together and friendly they were. She had a real man waiting for her at home.

Oh dear lord. One kiss and he's already your man? Get over yourself.

Yeah, but it was the best kiss she'd ever had, so …

"Sure," Mercedes piped up. "We're just celebrating my promotion."

One guy went on one side of Mercedes. The other scooted in next to Isobel. They were trapped.

Her body temperature went up. She squirmed away from the guy next to her and practically sat on Mercedes's lap. How could she get it through to her friend that these guys were con artists?

"What's your promotion?" tall guy asked, flashing a big, white smile. His teeth were freakishly straight. Those had to be veneers. Or possibly even all new teeth entirely.

"Purchaser for the entire women's division. I'm in fashion." Mercedes tossed her long, blonde hair over her shoulder and grinned. "What do you guys do?"

"We're on the college swim team," they said in unison, puffing up their chests and flashing more dazzling fake smiles.

Mercedes, always a heavy drinker when partying, was several drinks further along than Isobel and a shameless flirt when she was into her cups. She stroked the arm of the guy beside her. "Ooh, swimmers. I bet you have swimmer's bodies underneath those shirts."

Isobel rolled her eyes.

"Wouldn't be getting ready for the Olympic qualifiers if we didn't," the one beside Isobel said, scooting in closer to her.

"I'm Vance. This is Troy," tall guy said, wrapping his arm around the back of the booth behind Isobel.

She didn't want to be rude or harsh on Mercedes's night, but she was getting a really bad vibe from these guys. They were players. They were cads. Garbage wrapped up in a very expensive package with a pretty velvet bow.

Drinks arrived at the table seconds later, and the guys passed them out. They were all smiles. All creepy, way too big, way too fake smiles.

"To promotions," Vance said, lifting his martini glass in the air. Troy followed suit. Mercedes was next.

They all sat there waiting for Isobel to lift her glass too.

Mercedes cleared her throat and elbowed Isobel. "Drink," she murmured. "Don't be rude."

With another eye roll, hesitantly, she clinked their glasses.

Mercedes tossed back her martini in two sips.

Isobel nursed hers for a while, sipping it slowly. It was a good drink. Better than the ones they'd been drinking all night. Better gin. But she also knew her limit and when she'd had enough. She didn't want to feel like shit in the morning, so she had no intention of finishing her drink, no matter how good it was.

Good drinks aside, she barely heard a word Vance spoke to her. Her mind was elsewhere. She was wondering how and when they could ditch the Speedo twins and she could get back to Aaron. Get home. She was tired of the club scene. And not just tonight. She was tired of it altogether. Getting too old for the meat market, the loud music, the overpriced drinks, the skeezy guys on the prowl. She wanted to find a good man who she could cuddle up on the couch with, with a bottle of wine, a plate of nachos and a good movie.

Was that too much to ask?

Did guys like that exist anymore?

They had to.

Her sister had found one.

Mark was the real deal. A real, honest-to-goodness doctor with a kind heart, a full head of hair, a great sense of humor and an awesome kid. And more importantly, he loved her sister implicitly.

Isobel wanted that.

She needed to find her own Mark.

"Another round," Vance called, signaling the waitress.

Isobel went to shake her head, but Mercedes elbowed her again and said, "Totally."

And that was the last thing Isobel remembered hearing before the night got crazy and the world went dark.

Her mouth was full of cotton, or at least it felt like it was. She'd been drinking gin martinis but couldn't remember her mouth ever feeling like this after a night out with Mercedes. She didn't recognize the smell or the sounds around her either. This wasn't her apartment or Mercedes's place. This wasn't Aaron's house.

Male laughter made her eyes flash open.

Where was she?

Pushing herself up to sitting, she realized she was on a couch in a strange living room. Alone. More laughter from down the hall had her standing up and creeping toward the noise. She was still a little wobbly on her feet. Had she really had that much to drink? She didn't think she did. She hadn't felt pass-out drunk.

"Who first?" She recognized that voice. It was one of the guys from the club earlier.

"We'll do blondie upstairs. She clearly wanted it. Was all over me. Besides, I don't know how the fuck we're going to get into that jumpsuit thing without cutting it off her. Fuck, those things are ugly."

More laughter, as well as the sound of eating.

"She might wake up if we leave her though," the other one said.

"Yeah, but her struggling is part of the fun."

More laughter.

"I do like it when they put up a fight. When they pretend that they don't want it, when we really know they do. They always want the *D*." That sounded like Troy, he had the deeper voice.

Goosebumps raced down Isobel's arms, and her gut churned violently.

Her struggling is part of the fun.

Oh God, she was going to be sick.

"Sounds good." Chewing. "We should get going though. Finish up."

Crap!

She scanned the living room for a weapon. Nothing. Not even a decent lamp.

Her father had made sure both Isobel and Tori knew the basics of self-defense. Had it just been one guy, Isobel could probably take him out. But there were two of them, and she was still feeling the effects of whatever drug they'd given her—because clearly, she'd been drugged. She knew what it felt like to be drunk, and this was beyond that. Her wits were not all there. Neither was her spatial awareness, and the way her limbs felt as if she was constantly moving through Jell-O, the two guys together could easily overpower her.

"Should we *rock, paper, scissors* to decide who goes first?" one of the guys asked.

Disgusting.

The hallway offered nowhere to hide. Neither did the living room. The stairs were at the end of the corridor though. Mercedes was upstairs. Would they go to the living room to check on Isobel? Could she go find Mercedes and get them out of there?

"One more slice." The sound of a crunching beer can had Isobel, with her high heels in her hand, booking it down the hall on tiptoe toward the stairs.

She still had her purse, thank God. And her phone. Once she was at the top of the stairs and out of earshot of the kitchen, she called Aaron. She needed help. She needed to find Mercedes. She needed to get them out of there.

"Hello?" Aaron's deep rumble grounded her, calmed her racing heart. "Iz, what's wrong? Where are you?"

Her voice shook. "Aaron ... I think we were drugged. I woke up in a strange house on a couch. I don't remember drinking enough to black out. I have to find Mercedes."

"Where are you?" Panic filled his voice.

She glanced out a window at the end of the hall. "I—I don't know. I have no idea. I don't even remember how we got here. I don't remember anything. W-we met a couple of guys at the club. I got a weird vibe from them right away, wanted to leave, but Mercedes wanted to stay. They kept buying us drinks ..." A boisterous guffaw from the kitchen made her stomach lurch up her throat. She dropped her voice to an even lower hush. "I'm scared, Aaron."

"Is the friend finder app turned on on your phone?"

Her head pounded, and her vision was a touch blurry. She pulled the phone away from her ear.

"Never mind. Yes, it is. I know where you are. You're four miles away. Hold tight."

She shook her head, tears of fear welling up in her eyes. "Aaron, there are men downstairs. I—I think they plan to—" Voices at the foot of the stairs had her pausing. "They're coming," she whispered, opening the closest door, which appeared to be a bedroom. She turned on the light.

"Isobel!" Aaron screamed into the phone. "Isobel!"

Isobel was frozen in place as she took in her friend lying unconscious on a bed. Her black miniskirt was still in place but pushed up to reveal Mercedes's pink lace underwear. Her emerald off-the-shoulder shirt still covered her body. But it was her face that was what made tears drip down Isobel's face. A big cut across Mercedes's cheek was fresh with dried blood. Had she put up a fight and they hit her to get her here?

Had Isobel fought them? She ran over to the mirror. There were no cuts or scrapes on her face. Did she go with them willingly? She couldn't remember.

"IS-O-BEL!" Aaron yelled through the phone.

Noise in the hallway had her ducking into the clothes closet. She was just inside, door closed, breath held, when voices and laughter filled the room.

"IS-O-BEL!" he screamed again.

She put her ear to the phone and whispered. "I can't talk. Text only." She texted the rest of her message to him, her fingers trembling with each letter.

In the same room as Mercedes now. She's passed out. Big cut on her face. I'm hiding in the closet. Both men are in here. I think they plan to assault her.

He texted back.

Stay quiet. We're almost there. It's going to be okay. Don't hang up. Put the phone to your ear.

Swallowing, she put the phone back to her ear.

"Just listen." His deep voice soothed her. "I'm here for you, Isobel. I'm not going anywhere. We'll get you out of there. Both of you. Don't be the hero. We'll save Mercedes. We'll save you both. You can do this. You've got this. Don't be the hero, baby. Got it?"

Tears dripped down her cheeks as she struggled to swallow down her sob and not make a bunch of noise.

Her eyesight had adjusted to the small, dark closet. She spied a metal baseball bat leaned up against the corner.

Bend with your knees. Eyes on the ball. Don't forget to follow through with your swing.

Her dad's words came back to her. He'd coached her softball team for years, all the way through junior high and senior high. Her team had gone to nationals four times in six years, and they won nationals twice.

Isobel had played shortstop. But she wasn't nicknamed *the homerun kid* for no reason. She could knock a ball clear out of the park almost without even trying.

"Isobel!"

She put her ear back to the phone.

"We're two minutes away. Stay safe, baby. Stay down. Stay with me. I need to know you can hear me. Text me something. Anything."

Her entire body shook as she struggled to text out the words.

Sophie.

"Good, baby, good. You're still there. That's good. We're almost there. Just a couple more blocks. Stay with me. Stay quiet. I won't let them hurt you. We can't let anything happen to you. Sophie loves you. You're the best thing that's ever happened to us."

Us?

But she didn't have time to think any harder on Aaron's obvious blunder when the sound of belt buckles being released drew her attention to the room on the other side of the door.

"Aaron," she whispered, turning her head into a bunch of hanging dress shirts. "They're getting undressed. I can't stand by and do nothing. I can't let them hurt my friend."

Her fingers wrapped around the neck of the baseball bat. She tucked her cellphone into the pocket of the jumpsuit, and her other hand fell to the doorknob.

"ISOBEL!" Aaron screamed at her in her pocket.

She was about to open the closet door when the sound of a door being kicked in downstairs had her pausing.

"What the fuck?" Vance hollered.

"Fuck!" Troy murmured.

The bedroom door opened at the same time feet thundered up the stairs.

She opened the closet door just a crack.

The sound of men fighting filled the air, but none of that mattered. She had to wake up her friend. Racing around to the other side of the bed, she propped Mercedes up in the crook of her arm and sat one butt cheek on the bed. "Come on, sweetie. Wake up. You need to wake up."

Colton appeared in the doorway, his fists bloody. "Is she conscious?"

Isobel shook her head, a tear dripping down her cheek. "No."

He was around the side of the bed and scooping Mercedes into his arms faster than Isobel could blink. "Cops are on their way. Ambulance too. But we've got to get her out of here."

Isobel followed them down the stairs. "Where's Aaron?"

"Here." She spun around at the sound of his voice next to the kitchen and heaved herself into his arms, the tears now falling with abandon.

"Oh thank God."

His hand fell to her back, and he began to rub, shushing and cooing words she didn't bother to understand but felt reassured by nonetheless. "It's okay. It's all right. I'm here. You're safe."

She pushed away from him. "Who's with Sophie?"

If he and Colton were here, who was with Sophie? Was she in his truck?

His eyes softened, and he pulled her head back to his chest, chuckling softly. "Liam was still over when you called. He's with her. It's okay."

Her body relaxed. The sound of Aaron's racing heartbeat next to her ear was one of the most beautiful things she'd ever heard.

"Isobel?" Mercedes's voice on the couch had her leaving Aaron's embrace and rushing over to her friend. Colton had a small first aid kit open and was treating Mercedes's cut. He also had a bottle of what looked to be smelling salts.

Isobel fell to her knees in front of her friend. "I'm here."

"Wh-what happened?"

A knock at the door had Aaron leaving the living room. The space instantly felt colder, bigger, more foreboding. It amazed her how much of an impact his presence had. How much safer she felt when he was near.

Voices filled the strange house. Four heavily armed police officers, two male, two female, entered the living room.

The tall redheaded female cop appeared to be in charge. "Where are they?" she asked, directing her questions to Aaron.

With a glare in his eyes, he jerked his chiseled chin the direction of the kitchen. "In there." The other female cop and the bald male cop took off to the kitchen.

The redheaded cop's badge said Rose. Her eyes softened when she approached Isobel and Mercedes. "Hello, I'm Officer Rose." Her gaze zeroed in on the cut on Mercedes cheek. "Fuck," she muttered under her breath before sinking down onto her knees next to them.

Mercedes's breathing increased, and she reached frantically for Isobel.

"It's okay. It's okay," Isobel cooed, taking her friend's hand. "We're safe now."

"I'd like to ask you ladies some questions," the officer said. "But we can do it wherever you feel most comfortable."

"They should probably get bloodwork to determine what was put in their drinks," Colton said, standing up and closing his first aid kit. "Those motherfuckers need to burn."

Officer Rose cleared her throat and the look in her eyes hardened. She didn't appreciate Colton telling her how to do her job, that was clear. But she remained professional and simply nodded. "Agreed. Now let's get you two out of here."

"Agreed," Aaron said, wrapping an arm around Isobel's waist and steering her toward the front door.

He never let go of her after that. Never let her out of his sight, even when they went to the police station and the hospital. He was always there. Always with her, making her feel safe and cared for.

And when they finally got home and he released her hand, it felt weird.

She knew they'd only had one kiss, but now she knew the pull toward him she had wasn't one-sided, and she desperately wanted to find a way to hold his hand again, kiss him again, be in his arms again.

She just needed to figure out how to get there—and stay there.

Chapter 15

Holy fuck!

Aaron needed a drink.

Thankfully, Liam was still at the house, even though Sophie was asleep, and he had a drink waiting for Aaron.

Aaron nodded and swallowed down half his scotch, letting the liquor slide down his throat into his stomach. It had a mild burn to it that he enjoyed, that he needed.

When Isobel called, Aaron's heart leapt up into his throat. Then the tone of her voice caused his heart to shatter. The terror, the grogginess, every word she spoke sent white-hot shards of rage and fear coursing through him. He knew something was wrong with her before she said she was drugged. She didn't sound like herself, didn't sound like the smart, confident woman he'd come to know, come to …

It'd taken everything he had and Colton physically restraining him for Aaron to not choke the life out of the two scumbags with their zippers down.

"The district attorney will be in touch with Isobel and Mercedes within a few days," Liam said, tipping back his scotch. "She's a fair attorney. I like her, and she'll do right by the women. She'll file the charges, and Isobel and Mercedes will just have to take the stand and testify. We need to nail those motherfuckers to the wall."

"Fuckers shouldn't be breathing," Aaron muttered. "Had to restrain myself. If Colt hadn't been there, I probably wouldn't have."

"And I'd be representing you for homicide, so it's a good thing he was. Where is he now?"

Aaron leaned against the kitchen counter. "He took Mercedes home. She was really shaken up, so he offered to stay on her couch until she felt better." He glanced at the knuckles on his right hand. They were cut up, bloody, swollen and red.

"Should probably put some ice on that," Liam said blandly.

"Probably," he grunted.

"You still need me?"

Aaron shook his head. "No, man. We're good. Thanks for sticking around and staying with Soph."

Liam grabbed his half-empty bottle of scotch off the counter and punched a couple of things into his phone before shoving it into his pocket. "No worries, man. Anytime. Sophie loves her Uncle Liam." He tucked the steel poker chip case under his arm and headed toward the front door. "Bring the card table with you next weekend, okay? The Uber is two minutes away. I'll wait outside. Let you get to bed."

Aaron finished his scotch and put the glass in the sink, following Liam to the door. "Don't know if I'll be able to sleep after all that shit."

"Adrenaline?"

"Yeah."

"I get that. I'm the same way after a big win in court. I feel fucking invincible. Want to leap from tall buildings and run up walls or something equally stupid."

Aaron grunted and held the door open for Liam. The nights were getting cooler. Fall was closing in on all of them. "Not sure I'm invincible, but I'm definitely not tired."

Liam slapped Aaron on the shoulder. "You'll figure out something. Let me know if you need anything. Let Iz and Mercedes know this isn't going to get swept under the rug. Those privileged little twats are going to get theirs and then some."

Aaron hung his head and nodded. "Thanks, man. Appreciate it."

Headlights illuminated the driveway. "Anytime, man. See you next weekend." Then Liam headed off toward his Uber, leaving Aaron alone in the house, save for his infant niece and the traumatized nanny who was asleep in her bedroom.

They'd gone straight to the hospital, where a poor and rattled Isobel needed to be held in a vice grip between Aaron's arms and legs in order to sit for the bloodwork.

She hated needles.

Tears streamed down her face and her body tensed like an iron rod as the gray-haired nurse approached with the kit to collect blood.

"I can't," she sobbed, shaking her head and burying her face in his chest. "I can't. I hate needles. I can't. I don't care what drug they gave us. I can't."

As if she were one of the skittish horses on the Cahill farm back in Texas, he brought his voice down to a soothing coo and rubbed her back. "You need to, Iz. It'll be quick. I'm right here. Not going anywhere, babe. I got you. Shh. It's okay, baby. I got you. I'm here."

She shook her head. His T-shirt was damp from her tears. "Can't they just determine what drug it was from Mercedes's blood test?"

"They might have given you something different. We don't know. You woke up sooner than she did. She's still pretty loopy." He tucked a stray wisp of hair behind her ear and ran his finger down her jaw, tilting her head up so she was forced to look at him.

Eyes the same shade as the wide-open sky in the heart of Texas blinked back at him, red-rimmed and full of fear. "I'm scared, Aaron."

"I know, baby, I know. But I'm here. I'm not going anywhere, okay?"

Swallowing, she nodded. "Promise?"

"I promise, baby. I'm right here. Squeeze my hand as tight as you have to. Bite it if need to. I'm here for you. Not going anywhere. Never."

He made eye contact with the nurse, who'd been standing behind Isobel waiting for her to calm down. She approached gingerly. Isobel tensed even more in his arms as the nurse appeared on her left side.

"Here, Iz." She'd been sitting sideways on his lap, but he moved her so she straddled him. He wrapped his arms tight around her, keeping her in place.

With gloved hands, a kind smile and calm movements, the nurse lifted Isobel's arm.

Isobel jerked it out of her grasp. "I can't."

"Eyes on me," Aaron ordered, adopting the tone he used to use when he was training new recruits.

Her eyes widened, her back straightened and her head snapped up from where she'd been staring at the nurse.

"Good girl. Now stay focused on me. Don't look anywhere else but me, my eyes, okay?"

She nodded.

"I need to hear you say it, Iz."

"Okay. Your eyes. Look at your eyes."

"That's right."

The nurse lifted her arm one more time. Isobel went to pull away, but Aaron swung his arm out and secured her arm to the armrest. He pushed down hard on her wrist so she couldn't move it, his other arm pulling her tighter against his chest.

They were nose to nose, breathing the other in. He couldn't see anything but her.

It was all he wanted to see.

Isobel winced when the needle went in. Her pulse quickened beneath his arm, and her breathing hitched. Hot little puffs of air hit his lips quickly, and pain raced behind her eyes.

"You're doing great, baby. So great."

"Almost done," the nurse said.

"Almost done," he repeated. "You're so brave, Iz. So brave. You got this, baby. Just a couple more seconds, then it'll be all over, then we'll go home."

Her lips trembled. They were so close now, he felt them quiver against his own and ached to quell her nerves with a kiss. Take her mind away from the now, from the last several hours, and go back to the garage, go back to when it had just been the two of them, her hands in his hair, her body soft and pliant against his.

"And we're all done." The nurse tapped him on the shoulder. "You both did great. Don't leave the cotton ball on for more than about twenty minutes, otherwise it'll bruise."

They still hadn't broken eye contact, still hadn't pulled away.

Aaron waited until he knew they were alone in the small bloodwork vestibule before he pulled his gaze away and helped her down off his lap.

He went to sit down in the other chair, but her arms around his neck, drawing him in for a hug, stopped him.

She pressed her face into his neck, hot tears dripping onto his skin. "Thank you." The sound of soft sniffs muffled her words.

He wrapped his arms back around her waist, his body relaxing in her embrace. His nose brushed her hair, and he inhaled, shutting his eyes when the scent of her bodywash stirred something dangerous inside him.

"Ready to go?" Colton's voice from around the corner had them both finally separating.

Isobel linked her hand with Aaron's.

She didn't want to let him go. He understood that. It was common after a trauma. He'd seen a lot of that during recovery missions. The hostage or victim became attached to whoever had rescued them, only feeling safe around that one person.

So why did he feel the same way about her, then? He didn't want to let her go. Not now. Not ever.

136

Isobel felt disgusting.

Her clothes needed to be burned.

She also needed to go and buy a jumpsuit in every fucking color of the rainbow.

Had that been the only thing that had saved her from being raped? The fact that it was the Fort Knox of clothing? She needed to add more of those to her wardrobe. Maybe that's all she should wear from now on.

A pain in the ass to take off when in a public bathroom but hard to get off in the event of a sexual assault.

Fuck, what a mess.

She peeled off her clothes, bra and underwear too and tossed them into a pile in the corner of her room. Maybe Aaron would let her have a trashcan fire in the backyard tomorrow. Purge her world of the memories of tonight. She'd have to see if Mercedes wanted to burn her clothes too.

She needed a long, hot shower. She needed to wash away the traces of the night. The smell of Vance's grotesque cologne, the gin, the scent of their house of toxic masculinity. Shivering despite the warmth of the house, she grabbed her towel off the back of her door and wrapped it around herself.

Aaron was probably in bed by now, so she figured she could just duck across the hall to the bathroom wearing only a towel. He did it all the time. Why couldn't she?

She opened her door and stepped out into the dark hallway.

Hand on the bathroom doorknob, she paused when she heard Aaron's bedroom door open. Then there he stood, wearing nothing but a towel.

Her jaw dropped.

She'd only ever seen his naked back. He was always leaving the shower in a towel. She'd never seen his front before. And what a front.

How many abs did the man have? Did his abs have abs? Was that normal?

137

Could she count them without him noticing?

And that puffy pink scar that ran up from his hip bone to just below his left nipple—how on earth did he get that? It looked like it'd been deep. Had Colton been the one to stitch him up? He'd mentioned on the ride to the police station that he'd been their team medic. She still didn't know what *team* he was referring to.

"I can wait if you're going to have a shower," he said, his eyes struggling not to travel the length of her body. "I can't sleep though. Adrenaline and all that. Been a while since I punched somebody unconscious."

She nodded, her eyes focused on his scar. "I need to clean the night off. I won't be able to sleep either."

Uncle John in a kiddie pool eating saucy chicken wings.

She needed to thank Aaron for coming to her rescue. If he hadn't picked up his phone, hadn't been there, shown up when he had, she didn't want to think of the alternative.

She rubbed her lips together. "Thank you," she whispered, still fixated on the thick, long scar. "For rescuing Mercedes and me." Emotion choked her, and she struggled to get the next words out. "If you and Colton hadn't shown up ..." Slowly, she lifted her gaze to his.

Fire burned back at her in his dark blue irises. But he didn't say anything.

Why wasn't he saying anything?

She felt like she needed to keep talking, otherwise she'd surely do something she would regret, something he was clearly not sending her signals for, even though she wanted him to send those signals off like a bright orange flare in a dark starless sky.

She dropped her eyes to the floor and nudged a fluff on the wood with her big toe. "And thank you for helping that nurse at the hospital. I know I'm a big baby when it comes to needles ..."

"You're not a baby," he whispered. "You're one of the bravest"—he swallowed—"kindest, sweetest people I've ever met. I don't know what Sophie or I did to deserve you, but we can't do this without you."

Holy crap.

"Which is why ..." His hand adjusting the corner of his towel drew her attention back to his torso. He scratched at his facial scruff with the other. "Look, Iz, about earlier tonight ... the kiss. I'm really sorry. I was unprofessional and inappropriate. It will never happen again, I swear. Please don't quit. We can't lose you."

She shook her head. "Don't."

Please don't apologize. It's the only good memory I have of tonight. Don't take that away from me.

"But I shouldn't have taken advantage—"

"You didn't." She needed him to know that she was a willing participant in their kiss. Hell, she'd jumped up on his hips and demanded more from him. She'd been more than willing. She was still more than willing.

His head shook, and he blew out a breath. "But I did. You're my nanny."

Despite how utterly violated she felt after the night from hell, standing there in the dark hallway with Aaron, she felt nothing but safe. "But I could be more," she whispered, lifting her head.

His eyes grew wide. His mouth parted. "Iz, I really don't want to take advantage. I don't want you to think I'm using you. You've had a rough night—"

"Aaron, I want this," she blurted out. "I want you."

He shook his head. "I need to hear more than that. After tonight ..." He rubbed the back of his neck. "Fuck, I need like a consent form or something."

He was so cute when he was trying to be a gentleman. But at the moment, she didn't want a gentleman. She didn't *need* a gentleman. She wanted Aaron. Her hero, her muscly roommate and the man who was holding her heart captive.

"Please?" she whispered, wondering if that was what he wanted to hear.

"Is that a yes?" he asked, his voice hoarse and gritty.

139

With her heart pounding, she nodded. "It's more than a yes. It's an absolutely." Then, just like earlier that night, she leapt up onto his hips, but not before they both dropped their towels. His mouth was on hers and she wrapped her arms around his neck as he propelled them forward into the bathroom. She reached out and flicked on the light, never pulling her lips from his. He pushed the shower door open and blindly turned on the water at the same time she slid down from his hips.

Somehow, they stepped inside, never breaking the kiss. Warm water poured down on them from the enormous rainfall showerhead, making their bodies slippery and their mouths damp.

He cupped her breast with one hand, kneading and caressing, pinching her already hardened nipple. She gasped into his mouth from the slight snap of pain when he tugged. But her gasp quickly morphed into a smile and a whimper for more.

His erection was hard against her hip, demanding attention. She wedged her hand between them and took him in her palm. He groaned the instant she wrapped her fingers around his length, thrusting up, encouraging her to stroke him.

The shower soon filled with steam, the water no longer warm, but hot—or was that simply the blood running through her veins?

His free hand wrapped around her long, dark, damp hair, which hung down her back, and he tugged, forcing her to break their kiss and tilt her head skyward. His teeth raked up her throat, nipping at the side of her jaw and down toward her ear.

Isobel's lips parted, and water droplets fell on her tongue and in her eyes, forcing her to squeeze them shut again. His mouth continued on its journey, down her neck, her shoulders, her chest, until he found a nipple and latched on, sucking hard and scissoring his teeth back and forth.

She arched her chest up, pushing her breast against the rough scruff of his face, eager for the wet heat of his mouth and the teasing torture of his teeth.

She continued to pump him root to crown in her hand, reveling in how soft his skin was, yet how hard—and he still appeared to be growing. She ached to drop to her knees and take him in her mouth. Taste him, feel his hand on her head, see the passion and fire in his eyes as she gazed up at him and took him all the way to the back of her throat.

His hand released her breast, and he brought it down her torso, dipping two fingers between her plump folds. She knew she was wet—and not just from the water.

When he found her heat, he groaned against her breast, causing a shiver to sprint through her and settle deep in her belly.

He rubbed her clit, gentle circles with just the pads of his rough, calloused fingers. But it made her knees buckle and her nipples grow even harder. On instinct, she thrust her hips against his fingers, desperate for more.

"That's right, baby," he murmured, kissing his way across her chest to her other breast and latching on to the other nipple. "So fucking sweet."

Isobel grew frustrated. As much as she was loving the foreplay, loving his mouth on her breasts, his fingers between her legs, they weren't moving fast enough. The water would be cold by the time either of them came, and they still had to wash up too.

Aaron certainly knew his way around a woman's body. She'd been close several times, but just when she thought he was going to help her leap off the cliff, he'd pull back. The man was a master at edging, pushing her nearly to the brink only to scale back and leave her damn near insane from the buildup of it all.

In frustration, she pulled her breast from his mouth and stepped away, causing his fingers to slip off her clit. He blinked at her in confusion; water droplets clung to his eyelashes and ruddy scruff like tiny crystal beads. His intense dark blue eyes were full of pupil, and his nostrils flared like those of a wild animal who'd just caught the scent of his mate.

Licking her lips, she sank to her knees, pushing him back against the wall in the process. She gripped his length again and angled him into her mouth, taking him to the back of her throat almost immediately.

"Jesus fuck," he ground out, his hand slamming against the shower wall. The other fell to the top of her head. His hips bucked just slightly, but she liked it. Liked that he was helping to set a pace that worked for him. It worked for her too.

With her free hand, she cupped his soft, hairless ball sac and tugged, just until she heard him grunt, inhale and then moan out an exhale.

Using her hand to pump, she dipped her head and took a ball into her mouth, sucking and licking, rolling the delicate piece around in her mouth. She released him with a soft *pop*, then gave the same attention to the other one.

He gathered her hair in his fist again and held on tight, working himself in her palm.

"Mouth again." He grunted. "Deep."

Smiling, she took his cock back in her mouth, taking him deep just like he'd ordered.

"Fucking God," he gritted, tugging harder on her hair, pushing himself farther down her throat. "So fucking good, babe." He tapped her head. "Gonna come soon."

She started to hum, stroking him faster, twisting her wrist as she brought her hand up.

"Fucking humming." He groaned. "Fuck, babe. Gonna come." He tapped her head again. "Can't hold it."

She tightened her grip around his cock, pushed him to the back of her throat, tugged down gently on his ball sac, and he let go.

Warm, salty semen shot down her throat in thick spurts. She swallowed it down as quick as she could, making sure to contract her throat muscles around the head of his cock to heighten his pleasure. His knees wobbled, and his thighs began to shake.

She dared to take a peek up at him. She always loved watching a man come when she had him in her mouth. It was so raw, so primal, so male.

And Aaron was no different. His head was back against the shower wall, his mouth opened just slightly, his eyes shut, and every muscle in his body and face was clenched tight. Every abdominal muscle stuck out. His biceps bulged. His pecs twitched.

He was the most masculine thing she'd ever seen in her life. He was absolutely gorgeous.

When the final spurt of cum fell across her tongue, Aaron released a long, slow breath. His damp lashes fluttered, so Isobel quickly closed her own eyes before pulling him free.

Hands came up beneath her arms, and she found herself on her feet. His mouth was on her once again as well, stealing her breath and capturing her heart.

"Fucking amazing." He pushed his fingers back between her folds and flicked her clit. "Best head I've ever had."

She grinned against his mouth.

A compliment like that shouldn't make her feel as good as it did. Hell, he could probably say "Good girl" and she'd purr like a fluffy kitten, rub up against his shin and ask for another.

Yet his praise meant the world to her. His affection, his attention, his desire for her meant the world.

"Wanna fuck you, baby," he murmured against her mouth. "Condoms are in the bedroom though."

Right. Condoms.

"Gonna wash you first. Take care of you." Pulling his mouth from hers, he gruffly spun her around, her back to his chest. The sound of bodywash being squeezed out echoed around the small space. Seconds later, he began to run her bath pouf over her skin. Her arms, her back, her butt. He made sure to spend extra time between her legs, flicking her clit from time to time with his fingers just to keep her on her toes and make her knees turn to jelly.

Down her thighs, her calves and finally her feet. It felt incredible. His hands, the attention, it was exactly what she needed.

"Hair now."

A man of very few words, he sure knew how to take care of a woman, make her feel like the most important person on the planet.

His fingers on her scalp were magic. If given the chance, she could probably orgasm from that alone, the way each scrunch, each scratch, each tickle at the nape of her neck sent tingles spiraling through her. Warmth pooled deep down in her belly, and her pussy pulsed.

"Head back."

She did as she was told, and he ran his fingers through her tresses to help rinse away the suds, combing through until she was clean.

"Love your hair, babe," he grunted, biting her shoulder. "So long."

She turned around again and looped her arms over his shoulders. "Long enough to wrap around your hand when I'm ..." She lifted an eyebrow.

His eyelids dropped to half-mast. "Yes." He reached behind her and fisted her hair into a ponytail once more, tugging her head back so she was forced to look up. His teeth found her neck again and scraped along the front of her throat.

She blinked a few times, the spray from the shower blurring her vision. "Take me to bed, Aaron. Make me forget tonight."

The look he gave her pushed her just one step closer to orgasm. Keeping his eyes on her, his nostrils flaring, he reached over and turned off the shower.

She couldn't stop the smile that erupted on her face as he opened the shower door, wrapped her back up in her towel, scooped her up and carried her down the hall to his bedroom.

The only thing that would have made it better was if he'd kicked open the door and tossed her onto the bed.

Oh well. Maybe next time.

Chapter 16

He knew it was wrong.

A big fucking mistake, that's what it was.

But how could something that felt so good, so right, be wrong? How could something as amazing as sinking between Isobel's luscious thighs, getting buried in her heat, be a mistake?

Because she's your nanny.

His cock pulsed like it had a heartbeat of its own. It certainly had its own *brain*, as it wasn't paying attention to any of the logic Aaron was spewing.

Her nails dug into his back, banishing any negative thoughts and bringing him back to the moment. She was beneath him, he was inside her, and that was all that fucking mattered. All that fucking mattered was Isobel and the way she responded to his touch, the way she mewled and whimpered and arched her back when he took a sweet, cherry-red nipple into his mouth and sucked it hard. The way she wrapped her legs around his waist and thrust her hips up to meet his. The way she sank her teeth into his shoulder when he pinched her clit.

That's all that fucking mattered.

That and the fact that he hadn't felt this good in a long time. Too long.

And it wasn't just the fact that it was the touch of a woman he'd been so long without; it was that it was Isobel. Not just any woman would have cut it, would have been the balm to soothe the pain in his heart. But Isobel had the touch. She held the magic.

And it was a magic he didn't ever want to let go of.

"Aaron," she breathed, digging her nails harder into his back. "Fuck."

He pumped harder into her, feeling her walls quiver around his cock as she climbed the mountain. He could tell she was close. He'd gone down on her when they'd first come to his bedroom, and she'd come twice on his tongue. He'd never tasted anything so goddamn sweet in his life.

She was an easy little nut to crack too, which was a bonus. Responsive and eager.

And the way she gave head—holy fuck!

He'd had a fair few women on their knees in front of him in his thirty-eight years, but none of them could hold a candle to Isobel. His Isobel.

Eager to please and so fucking generous. He could still remember the feeling of her throat swallowing as he blew his load across her talented little tongue. She'd taken him so fucking deep. So, so fucking deep.

"Harder," she panted, tracing her tongue around the shell of his ear. "Please."

Her plea tore at his heartstrings. She was still hurting, still reeling from the night. Who the fuck could blame her? Aaron was still reeling too, but in a different way. He was filled with rage. She was filled with fear.

She lifted her fingers from his back and placed them on either side of his face. "Kiss me. I want to be kissing you when I come. Connected in every way."

Connected in every way.

She tugged on his ears, bringing his lips down to hers. He shoved his tongue into her mouth and she began to suck it, mimicking the way she had sucked his cock earlier, the way he'd hoped she'd sucked cock when they'd kissed earlier in the garage.

Oh boy, she did not disappoint.

She squeezed her muscles around him, drawing him deeper inside her perfect body, her wet heat surrounding him just the way her mouth had in the shower.

146

He swiveled his hips, slammed down into her, and she came.

She came so fucking hard.

Her body stiffened beneath him, her muscles clenched up tight, and her whimpers poured into his mouth as she rippled around him. She increased her grip on his ears, pulling his face harder against hers. A pain throbbed in his skull from the tension, but he welcomed it. The same as when she tugged on his hair or clawed up his back.

She was a woman who knew what she wanted, who took as much as she gave, demanded as much as she acquiesced, and he loved that. Loved that she wasn't afraid to ask for what she wanted from him. No head games, no drama. Just Isobel. Perfect, sweet, smart, sexy, kind Isobel.

She released his ears and pulled her mouth away from his, turning her head, allowing him to dip his face to her shoulder, into her damp, sweet smelling hair.

"Bite my shoulder when you come," she whispered. "Mark me."

Aaron groaned.

Mark me.

"Mark me as yours."

Fuck yes.

Reaching behind him, he grabbed her leg behind her thigh and pushed her knee into her belly so he could hit her deeper.

She moaned when his belly slapped her clit, her head thrashing side to side on the bed, hair flying everywhere.

Could she come again?

He'd love to try to get her there.

Her hands came up and she cupped her breasts, pulling on her nipples and biting her lip as she brought herself more pleasure.

Aaron had never seen anything more fucking beautiful.

"So fucking sexy." He growled, his head falling back to her shoulder as his balls tightened up and his cadence began to wane. He was close.

"Aaron ..."

"Iz ..."

He pushed her leg up more. Her hips leapt up to meet his, and he was done.

Tossed over the cliff, from the plane, off the skyscraper into the abyss. You name it, he did it. No parachute needed because he fucking flew. When he was with Isobel, he fucking flew.

With each hard pump into her body, he came harder. His teeth sank into her shoulder, and her quick inhale and then low moan told him she liked it. He was giving her what she wanted, what she'd asked for.

"Oh God."

Fuck, yeah. Another one.

She grappled at his back, her nails once again raking down from his scapula to his glutes and back. She was marking him too—fuck yeah.

Her tight little pussy with just the perfectly trimmed triangle of hair pulsed around his shaft as he drove into her, the last of his cum spurting out into the condom until he collapsed against her, spent and finally exhausted.

Thank fuck.

Maybe now he could sleep.

Maybe now they could both sleep.

Once he knew she was done, he rolled off her, removed the condom, tied it and stood up. Not bothering with clothes, he went to the bathroom to dispose of the condom and wash up. He thought when he got back to his room she'd be gone, off in her own room, but she wasn't. She was still in his bed.

Hmmm.

"All done in the bathroom?" she asked, slipping her lithe frame from the bed and padding barefoot down the hall. He heard her brushing her teeth and the toilet flush. She was probably going to head to her own room now. Like him, she seemed exhausted. He climbed into bed, shut off the light and pulled the covers up to his waist.

Tucking his hands behind his head, he stared up at the ceiling, willing sleep to come. Only every time he closed his eyes, he saw Isobel back on her knees in the shower. His cock in her hot little mouth, her eyes shut and a smile curving up at the corner of her lips.

"Big fucking mistake," he breathed out, shaking his head.

The bathroom door opened, and he heard the light flick off. Moments later, she returned, a slim shadow in the dark room. She didn't say a word but climbed back into his bed, snuggled up against him, put her head on his shoulder.

She exhaled, her breath across his chest making his nipples tighten.

Aaron grunted, and his body went stiff. And not in the good way.

What did she expect from him?

What did she want from him?

He wasn't a snuggler. He wasn't a boyfriend.

Fuck, had he ever been somebody's *boyfriend*?

He'd been somebody's fuck buddy. He'd been a devirginizer. (Her words, not his. Totally consensual. She was just tired of being a virgin, and they were friends in high school.) He'd been somebody's itch-scratcher. Somebody's hero. Hell, he'd even been somebody's revenge sex, but he'd never been anybody's boyfriend.

It wasn't in his makeup. He didn't know how to be a boyfriend.

The closest he'd come to dating somebody had been Heather Alvarez, but that was mostly just about sex when he was home in Seattle between deployments. They might have said the *L* word, but he couldn't remember. He knew she was still hung up on her ex from high school, but they were there for each other when they needed a release, when they needed company. Plus, she was a fucking amazing cook, and her family owned a Puerto Rican restaurant, so even when things between them ended, they ended platonically, because no way was he giving up Heather's mother's Mallorca. No fucking way.

Hell, when Heather's new husband (her ex from high school whom she'd gotten back together with) needed help finding his long-lost sister, Heather had called Aaron. Aaron had put the McAllister family in touch with Rob Cahill, his buddy in arms, and Rob had, of course, found Skyler. Now the two were married, with a baby on the way.

Aaron shook his head.

He never thought he'd see the day ol' Rob would settle down. Never thought he'd see the day ol' Rob would put his demons to bed and live a normal life.

Aaron hadn't witnessed the horror Rob had seen in that Peruvian brothel, but he knew what was in there. He knew why his buddy had fallen off the rails and took to the bottle like he did.

A lot of them did.

Some of them couldn't handle the memories and took their own lives.

Like their buddy Brandon.

And Brandon had left behind a wife and new baby.

He clenched his jaw tight at the thought of his fallen brothers, at the thought of Brandon struggling with what he'd seen, what he'd done, all the lives he hadn't been able to save.

Then he started thinking about his own failures. That last mission in Colombia that would haunt him until his dying day.

"Aaron?" Her whisper brought him out of his head, and he was grateful for it. When he started to think about Colombia, about the Velasquez family, he quickly began to spiral, and it was always a tough climb back out of that deep, dark hole.

He cleared his throat. "Yeah, babe?"

"I know I've already said it, but ... well ... thank you again for saving me tonight. For being there for me ... and Mercedes." Her fingers splayed out over his chest, but then she gripped his dog tags. "You're a real hero, you know that?"

No, he wasn't.

He'd failed Dina, he'd failed in Colombia, and if Isobel stuck around long enough, he'd probably fail her too.

150

"I'm just glad you're safe," he said with a grunt. Emotion began to claw at the back of his throat, and he struggled to get the next words out. "If anything had happened to—" He swallowed.

Isobel propped herself up on her elbow, but her fingers tightened even more around his dog tags. She gazed down at him, and even in the darkness of the room, he could tell her eyes held a conviction to them, a heat and seriousness. "But it didn't, because you were there."

He shifted his body, untucked his hands from behind his head and drew his index finger down over her cheek. She shut her eyes and leaned into his touch.

"I like this side of you," she said, her voice soft and almost angelic. She batted her lashes and pinned her gaze on him once again, her lips tilting up on one side. "I mean, don't get me wrong. I like the powerful, alpha side too, but this gentle side is a nice change. I usually only see you like this with Sophie." She snuggled in tighter to him, her fingers still wrapped around his dog tags. "Will you tell me about your time"—she shook her fist with the dog tags—"when you needed these?"

He cupped her jaw, then bent his head low and brushed his lips over hers. "Not tonight."

Not ever.

But she didn't need to know that right now.

He didn't want to scare her away. As much as her presence in his bed confused the hell out of him, he also didn't want her to leave, and he worried that if he started talking, he might not stop—and then she'd run scared.

"But one day?" she asked, with hope in her tone.

His other hand wrapped around her back, and he began tracing the length of her spine with his fingers. Gooseflesh on her satin-soft skin rippled beneath his fingertips. He pressed another kiss to her lips. "Sleep now, babe."

She smiled against his mouth and released his dog tags, burying herself even deeper into his arms. "Okay." Her head rested on his chest, and her fingers spread out over his heart. "I like being here with you," she whispered, a yawn following her words.

His heart beneath her hand tightened, and he swallowed. "Me too."

She blinked up at him. Her smile was placid and tired. "Goodnight, Aaron."

Unable to look at her for fear she might see more than he wanted her to, he closed his eyes and dropped his mouth to her head. "Goodnight, Isobel." Then he tucked his nose against her hair so her scent and softness surrounded him, and he willed his heart rate to slow down and sleep to take him.

It didn't.

Within moments, he could hear Isobel's deep, even breaths. She was out.

Of course she was. It'd been a crazy, terrifying night, and she was probably exhausted.

Thank God she hadn't had more of her drink—a full dose of the date-rape drug and she'd still be out of it, probably for a day or two. He wondered how Mercedes was fairing. Thankfully, he trusted no one more than Colton to take care of someone when they were ill or injured. The man was a top medic and a stand-up guy. Mercedes was in good hands.

Isobel shifted next to him, her fingers wrapped around his dog tags again, and she tucked her knees up until she was in the fetal position. Her head now sat in the crook of his arm. She made a face of discontent, like she was reliving some trauma.

Was she dreaming about tonight?

His hand fell to her hip, and he pulled her tighter against him, his other hand wrapping around her fingers until she released his dog tags. He went to pull away, but she grappled for his free hand and linked their fingers together. Only once they were holding hands did her face relax.

Her pouty lips turned up into a smile, and she let out a contented sigh.

Aaron pecked her on the top of the head, then shut his eyes.

He hated how good this felt. Hated how right she felt in his arms because now, he had something to lose. Just like Colombia, he let his heart take the lead, and now when shit hit the fan—because it would—he had a whole hell of a lot of something to lose.

Chapter 17

The sound of a warbling baby and the beep of the microwave roused Isobel from her slumber. She stretched, pointing her toes and reaching her arms above her head. Parts of her body tingled, and a dull but pleasant throb between her legs reminded her of last night.

She rubbed her shoulder, remembering Aaron's teeth. He'd marked her, just like she'd asked.

Smiling, she rolled over in bed and pushed her face into his pillow, inhaling deep.

Ahhh.

It smelled just like him.

Manly, musky, fresh and oh so delicious.

She was about to get up and go see to Sophie when she remembered that it was Sunday and she technically had Sundays off. So far, Aaron seemed to be doing all right when left on his own with his niece. Sophie was also an easy baby, so that helped. She seemed to get that Aaron was simply doing his best. She didn't demand too much from him, didn't prefer Isobel over him and seemed to settle quite quickly when Aaron picked her up and put her against his chest.

Last Sunday, Aaron had let Isobel sleep in, albeit not in his bed this time, and when she woke up, she found him wearing Sophie in the stretchy wrap and making pancakes on the griddle. The man didn't cook very often (well, besides grilling on the barbecue), but he managed to make a mean breakfast.

She could smell freshly brewed coffee—another thing (besides all things in the bedroom and breakfast) that Aaron was very talented at, as well as something that smelled an awful lot like waffles.

Her stomach rumbled at the thought of homemade waffles with maple syrup or fresh fruit and whipped cream.

Then her nipples pebbled and her core clenched at the thought of Aaron covered in whipped cream. Mmmm. Yes, please.

Taking one final whiff of his pillow, she swung her legs out over the bed, grabbed the nearest shirt she could find—his big, black T-shirt—and tossed it over her head. She fixed her hair up into a big, ol' messy bun on the top of her head with the hair elastic she kept around her wrist and headed out to the kitchen to see what was cooking.

She stopped in her tracks when she entered the kitchen. He was singing. And dancing. Well, swaying ... or something, but whatever it was, his ass in those gray sweatpants wiggled and taunted her the way a proud male bird flapped and flittered his plumage for a potential mate.

She released a slow breath.

Down, girl.

"Making waffles with my baby. She can't eat them yet, but when she can, she's going to love them. Love them so. Just like she loves her Uncle ... whoa, oh, ohhhh," Aaron sang, shaking his hips and pulling a waffle out of the iron and flipping it onto a plate. *"Sophie Boo Boo, what can I do? What can I do, ooh, ooh, oooooh."*

Isobel snickered. He didn't have the greatest voice, but it wasn't terrible either. Her father certainly had worse. Aaron's voice, although not pitch perfect, was deep and manly—soothing. "Morning," she piped up when there was a break in his song. "Nice singing."

His hips stopped swaying, and his back went stiff.

She wandered around the counter and sidled up next to him, grabbed a coffee cup from the cabinet and poured herself a cup.

Aaron took his coffee black, but he had the creamer sitting out for her like he did every morning.

"Those smell amazing," she said, turning around and leaning against the counter, cradling the coffee mug in both hands and lifting it up to her nose. "Blueberry?"

He grunted and then nodded, not bothering to turn around and look at her.

"What time was Sophie up?"

"Three, five and eight."

She glanced at the clock on the stove. It said eight thirty. Sophie would be ready for a nap soon.

"Well, thank you very much for getting up with her at night and then this morning. I really appreciate you letting me sleep in." Isobel yawned, put her mug down on the counter and stretched up onto her tippy-toes. Her bare butt hit the edge of the counter. Perhaps his shirt wasn't as long as she thought.

Whoopsie daisy.

"Can I help with anything? Eggs? Bacon?"

He grunted again. "Bacon's done. No eggs. You can wash and de-stem the strawberries though."

She bobbed her head and opened the fridge, grabbing the strawberries. "Sounds good. Have you heard from Colton? I'm going to text Mercedes soon. She usually sleeps in on Sundays, so I'll wait another hour or so. I hope she's doing okay." She walked over to the sink, opened up the plastic container of strawberries and turned on the faucet.

Was Aaron not going to ask her how she was doing?

About not only her near-assault and drugging and the trauma from it all but also about all the sex and the fact that she'd slept all night in his bed, snuggled up tight against his warm, hard body.

She'd never slept so well, so soundly in all her life.

Was it the endorphins? The adrenaline? The exhaustion? Or was it Aaron? The pheromones, the attraction and the way his body made her sing from the mountaintops, over and over and over again.

She waited a moment longer to see if he'd ask her how she was, or at the very least turn around, but he didn't. Not even a glance over his shoulder.

She cleared her throat and turned off the faucet for the sink. "Um, what are you and Sophie going to do today?"

She had the next two days off, and although when she woke up, she thought maybe she'd stick around and spend the day with Aaron and Sophie, the cold shoulder she was getting from Aaron made her reconsider.

"Gonna toss her in the stroller and go for a run," he said, still not turning around.

"Oh, that's a good idea. Looks like it's a nice day. Soph loves when I do that. She passes right out."

Grunt.

Irritation and unease ran neck and neck inside her. Why was he behaving like this? Had last night meant nothing?

Even if he didn't want to spend the rest of his life with her, she deserved to see his goddamn face. Deserved some eye contact. Deserved some conversation.

Shoving down her snarl of irritation, she grabbed a paring knife out of the knife block on the counter and began removing the strawberry stems.

The silence between them was excruciating.

Well, he couldn't ignore her at breakfast. They'd be forced to sit across from each other. He'd have to look at her then. Have to talk to her.

Out of the corner of her eye, she watched him pull the plug for the waffle iron from the wall. He put the waffle batter bowl in the dishwasher, taking what seemed to be a lot of care *not* to turn in her direction.

"'K, catch you later," he mumbled, then without so much as a glance back or a "*Thanks for the fuck last night,*" he was gone.

Isobel stood there at the sink, knife in her hand, knuckles aching from her tight grip. She didn't move, didn't blink, barely breathed, until she heard the door from the garage close and she knew he was gone.

Only then did she pick up the plate of waffles and heave it against the wall.

She was wearing his T-shirt.

Fuck.

And it looked damn good on her, with her soft, sun-kissed legs poking out beneath, her hair up in a messy bun on the top of her head. Was she wearing anything under the shirt? Probably not. They hadn't exactly tumbled into bed wearing any clothes, and he hadn't heard her go to her room at all.

No, she was in his shirt, and only his shirt, wandering her tight little ass around his kitchen. It'd been all he could do to keep his boner at bay. Something about wearing a baby on his chest and sporting a stiffy just felt fucked up.

In addition to looking hot as fuck and making him want to put Sophie in her bassinet in her bedroom and then bend Isobel over the kitchen table and take her from behind, she'd been super-chatty and annoyingly perky.

She wanted more from him.

He knew the moment he kissed her, the first time, and then the second time and every time after that, that he was making a colossal mistake. Fucking the nanny was a big no-no. She'd either be a stage-four clinger and want to fix him, move in permanently and play house for the rest of their lives, or she'd take from his brush-off that last night had been a one-off and be scorned, furious and probably bring him up on sexual harassment charges.

He hadn't even been running for ten minutes, and already Sophie was asleep.

A hill was up ahead. He picked up speed. He needed the pounding of his pulse in his ears to drown out his thoughts. The screaming of his calf muscles to distract him from the pain he felt in his chest.

Nearly at the top, his body demanding he surrender and stop, he pushed himself those last few yards, sprinting until his breath tasted metallic and spots clouded his vision.

A horn *beep-beeped* behind him as he put the brakes on the stroller and wandered around the sidewalk to catch his breath.

He wasn't on the road, wasn't in anybody's way. What the fuck?

"Hey! Quite the climb."

Lifting his head and using the hem of his shirt to wipe the sweat from his eyes, Aaron blinked until he saw that it was Mark. He'd pulled over, rolled down his window and was smiling.

Aaron gave him a nod.

"You're not too far from my place. Run over for a beer."

Aaron wrinkled his nose. "Is it even noon?"

Mark shrugged. "It's Sunday. Who the fuck cares what time it is?"

Fair enough.

"Go through the next two sets of lights. Turn right on Meadowlark, then left on Quail. 1356 Oriole Drive, at the end of the road. Can't miss it. Big tire swing in the front hanging from the spruce." He glanced back into his car and smiled, then nodded. "Gabe asked if that's a baby in there. He loves babies."

The windows of Mark's car were tinted, so Aaron hadn't seen Gabe in the back. From what he knew, Mark's son Gabe was on the autism spectrum. That's how Mark and Tori had met. He'd hired her to run therapy programs with Gabe.

Hmm. Maybe Mark might be able to offer him some insight into his Isobel dilemma.

Or he'd kick the living shit out of Aaron for defiling his girlfriend's little sister.

Ah, fuck.

Up shit creek without a paddle in sight. And it appeared there was also a hole in his canoe and no bailing bucket.

He was sinking.

Mark nodded. "See you in a bit. I'll have a cold one waiting for you." Then before Aaron could turn down the invitation, Mark merged back into traffic and was gone.

Sophie's eyes popped open, and she made a face that said she was thinking about shitting her pants. Isobel kept diapers, wipes, extra clothes, formula, water and bottles in the bottom of the stroller—a better prepared SEAL he'd never met. So he wasn't worried about being ill-equipped to handle a morning out with his niece. That wasn't it at all. Sophie made another face, and the sound of a small rocket ship taking off filled the quiet street.

He debated undoing her straps and turning her around to survey the damage. Was it up her back? She didn't seem put out. Perhaps he'd finally managed to secure a diaper properly and keep the explosion contained.

"Shall we go?" he asked, glancing up the street in the direction Mark had gone.

Sophie blinked back at him.

He nodded. "Okay then. Let's get this over with."

He took off on a jog again, his feet heavy because, well—his canoe was at the bottom of the creek and his socks and shoes and pockets were now full, full of shit.

Mark was going to kick his ass.

Or Tori would.

Yeah, his money was on Tori.

Chapter 18

"This is a nice surprise," Tori said, opening the door for Isobel and welcoming her into Mark's home. "What brings you by?"

Isobel pursed her lips together and followed her sister into the kitchen of Mark's beautiful Seattle home. "Men fucking suck, that's what."

Tori had grabbed the kettle and was filling it up with water but stopped, turned off the tap and set the kettle back on the stove. Without saying a word, she wandered over to the far wall and slid a panel open to reveal Mark's impressive wine collection.

Humming, she tapped her chin for a moment before grabbing a bottle of red close to the top, closing the panel and wandering back toward Isobel. "I was going to put on a cup of tea, but I'm guessing we need something stronger."

Isobel simply lifted her eyebrows. "I'll be leaving my car here then and cabbing home because I might just need the whole bottle to myself."

Tori grabbed two glasses from the kitchen cabinet, popped the cork and poured them each a glass. She slid one across the quartz countertop to Isobel. "Let's go sit out on the patio in the backyard. It's sunny out, and with blankets on our laps, it's the perfect temperature."

Nodding, Isobel took her wine and immediately tossed a good portion of it back before following Tori out to Mark's gorgeous backyard.

"So," Tori started, curling her legs up under her and draping the plush cashmere throw over her lap, "dish. What did Aaron do? I'm assuming it was Aaron."

Isobel blew out a long breath and swirled her wine around her glass before starting. "Partially, yes. But it's just men in general, really. I swear you found the only good one left."

Tori snorted. "After weeding through a sea of duds. You *do* remember my soon-to-be ex-husband, right? King of the Douches. Captain of the Twat Squad. President of the Fucknuggets."

Isobel's lip twitched. One night while drinking, Tori, Isobel and Mercedes had come up with increasingly hilarious and offensive names for Ken. It'd been therapeutic and fun.

"Governor of the Cuntasauruses," Isobel added.

Tori clinked her wineglass with hers. "I like that one." Her face grew serious. "What happened?"

"I went out with Mercedes last night to celebrate her promotion."

Tori nodded and sipped her wine. "Yeah, she messaged me too, but I just can't do the club scene anymore. I'm done with that shit."

So was Isobel.

"Anyway, eventually it was just Mercedes and me. She wasn't ready to go home, and I didn't want to abandon her, so I stayed around."

Tori's eyes narrowed. "What happened, Iz?"

Isobel swallowed. "We met a couple of guys. I got a bad vibe from them right away, which is saying a lot considering that generally I try not to let those vibes cloud my judgment."

Scoffing, Tori rolled her eyes. "I keep telling you to go with your gut and stop giving people the benefit of the doubt. People suck. Chances are that man with the lost puppy doesn't really have a lost puppy."

Isobel sniffed and nodded. "I know. I know. And these guys definitely didn't have a lost puppy. They drugged us."

Tori's hand flew to her mouth, and she planted her feet on the ground, her wine sloshing around in her glass. "No."

"I woke up in a strange house on their couch."

Tears welled up in Tori's eyes, and at the same time, she grabbed Isobel's hand and pulled her over to the same couch as Tori, holding her baby sister. "Did they?"

Isobel snuggled into the warmth of her big sister. "No. Score one for jumpsuits and rompers." She forced out a laugh. "Tough to take off to pee, but also tough to take off to rape."

"Fuck," Tori breathed. "And Mercedes?"

Isobel shook her head. "No. Aaron and Colton showed up before they could. I was in the closet in the room where Mercedes was still unconscious. If the guys hadn't shown up … I had a baseball bat in my hand." Her entire body trembled at the memory of last night, the fear, the fury, the need to fight for her friend. She'd never been so terrified in her life.

"Oh fuck, honey." Tori wrapped her arms tighter around Isobel and began to rock them back and forth. "You called Aaron?"

"Yeah. I didn't know what else to do. I probably should have called 911 first, but …"

But she felt safe with Aaron. Cared for. She knew he'd never let anything bad happen to her. And he hadn't.

Well, at least not physically. Emotionally was another story. He'd shown him another side of himself last night, a softer, gentler side, and then this morning, she didn't even recognize him.

What happened between when she said goodnight to him, he kissed her and they fell asleep and when she walked into the kitchen to find him making breakfast with Sophie?

"Then what happened?" Tori asked.

Isobel shook her body, hoping some of the tension slipped off her shoulders. "Cops came. They got our statements, and then we had to go to the hospital to check to see what kind drug they'd given us, in case it was toxic or had some messed-up side effects or something and for evidence."

"And?"

She shook her head. "I got a call earlier this morning, and it was just your run-of-the-mill date-rape drug." She laughed again. *Just your run-of-the-mill date rape drug.* As if it were aspirin or something. No biggie. "I only sipped my drinks, so there wasn't as much in my system. Mercedes was downing the drinks like they were water, so she was pretty messed up."

"And Aaron?"

"We ..."

"He slept with you after you were nearly raped?" Tori pushed Isobel away for a moment, held on to her arms and shook her. "What the fuck? I'll fucking kill him."

"It wasn't like that. I initiated it. I needed it. I needed to forget. I needed a distraction."

Tori's eyebrow drifted toward her hairline. "I can feel a *but* coming on."

You'd think they were twins, the way Isobel and her sister were connected. "But I think it meant more to me than it did him. I really like him. And perhaps deep down I hoped that last night was the beginning of something." She shook her head, pulling at a stray thread on the seam of the blanket. "He couldn't even look at me this morning. Hardly even spoke to me. Never asked how I was doing. Nothing. I wasn't expecting a proposal or flowers, but some freaking eye contact would have been nice. Is that too much to ask?"

Tori's blue eyes, the same shade as Isobel's, turned dark and stormy. "No, it's not. That motherfucker."

"I don't know what to do. Do I just pretend like nothing happened? That it was just a one-off, go back to the way things were? Can we go back to the way things were? Do I want to?"

Tori grabbed the wine bottle off the glass and wicker patio coffee table and topped up both their glasses. "You drink until you find a solution," she said with a forced laugh. "And if you don't find a solution, you don't go back there until you do. It's your day off, right?"

Isobel took a sip of her wine. "Yeah, today and tomorrow."

Tori nodded. "All right then." She clinked her glass with Isobel's again. "How's Mercedes?"

Isobel shook her head. "I have no idea. I've been texting her all morning and haven't heard back. Tried calling her too but no answer. I swung by her place on the way over, and her car was gone."

"Is it safe that she's alone, after what she's been through? Should one of us go over and sit with her?"

Isobel shrugged. "I would if I could find her. Aaron's friend Colton is with her, I know that. Or at least he was. He's some kind of military or whatnot like Aaron. He was their medic. I'm sure she's safe with him."

Commotion at the gate from the front yard had them pausing their conversation and glancing behind them. Gabe came tearing through the gate, followed by Mark, and then finally a very sweaty Aaron and the stroller with Sophie.

Isobel's heart stopped, and her eyes grew wide.

Aaron's went even wider when he finally saw her sitting there with Tori, their wineglasses extra full.

Mark retreated into the basement, coming out moments later with two beer bottles. He handed one to Aaron before sitting back in the empty wicker patio chair. "Ah, nothing like a cold brew after a run, am I right?"

Aaron's eyes hadn't left Isobel since he arrived.

She took a deep and grounding breath before speaking. "Hello."

His already flushed face grew even more ruddy. "Hi."

"Do you need a change pad or something for Soph?" Mark asked, tipping back his beer.

Aaron shook his head, setting his beer down on the coffee table. "No, thanks. I've got everything." Without saying another word, he unclipped Sophie from her stroller, grabbed the go-bag from underneath and headed into the bottom floor of Mark's house.

Gabe, who had been busy playing in his sandbox, went to follow them, but Mark reached out and grabbed his son by the waist, hauling him into his lap and making Gabe erupt into giggles.

Mark was all smiles until he noticed that neither Isobel nor Tori was smiling. His face grew very serious, and he stopped tickling and bouncing Gabe. "What's wrong? You guys look like somebody just died."

Tori's eyes lasered in on her boyfriend. "Iz and Mercedes were drugged and abducted last night. Narrowly escaped an assault."

Mark's green eyes went wide. "Holy fuck!"

Tori grunted. "Aaron and Colton saved them."

"And where are the fuckers now?"

"In custody," Isobel replied, her eyes drifting to the open basement door. She had no idea how far in Aaron had wandered and whether he was still within earshot. Chances are he was.

Tori leaned forward and put her lips next to Mark's ear. Isobel didn't have to hear her sister to know what she was telling him. His wide eyes grew fierce, flew to Isobel, softened, flew to the open door and then filled with rage once again.

"Need me to kick the shit out of him?" Mark whispered, directing his question to Isobel.

Hmm. Interesting thought.

She still had no idea what kind of military organization Aaron belonged to, but based on his physique and size, he'd probably mutilate Mark with a couple of well-placed punches. And Mark was no slouch, so that was saying a lot.

Tori leaned forward again and whispered something else to Mark.

Isobel could stare into the man's green eyes all day long, they were so expressive and bright. He nodded, then turned and kissed Tori's cheek. "I love how big your heart is," he murmured.

Tori's smile was small, and the softness in her eyes as she looked at Mark spoke of just how deep their love was.

Isobel wanted a love like that.

Can't eat, can't sleep, can't think love.

Aaron appeared at the door a moment later, Sophie in the crux of his arm wearing a new outfit. His eyes fell back to hers. "Have you checked your phone?" he asked, passing Sophie off to a grabby-hands Tori before stowing the go-bag in the bottom of the stroller.

Isobel shook her head. "No, why?"

"Just do it."

Hating his tone and how distant he was being, she glared at him as she grabbed her phone.

There was a text message from Mercedes.

Oh thank God.

She opened it up, and her jaw nearly hit the floor.

"What?" Tori asked, grabbing the phone and turning the screen toward her. "What happ—holy fuck!"

"What?" Mark asked.

Tori grabbed the phone from Isobel and held it toward Mark. "Mercedes and Colton just flew to Vegas and got married."

Chapter 19

Aaron watched Isobel's reaction to Mercedes and Colton's message. She was hard to read. Normally she wasn't. Normally she was an open book, a glass house. She wore her emotions right out in the open on her face.

It was one of the things he liked most about her. No head games. No drama. No lies.

But at this moment, he had no idea what she was thinking or how she was feeling. He also had no idea how much of last night she'd told her sister.

He glanced at Tori.

Laser beams practically flew out of her eyes at him.

Shit. Isobel had told her everything.

"Well, that's a surprise and a half," Mark said, handing Isobel back her phone. "Colton didn't strike me as the settling down type, and Mercedes—" He whistled. "The man's got his work cut out for him, that's for sure."

"Understatement of the century," Tori said blandly.

Aaron shifted back and forth on his feet. It was only a matter of time until Tori told Mark everything she knew, then he'd have no allies left.

"Okay." Mark stood up. "You two need to get a move on." He fixed his green-eyed gaze on Isobel and then Aaron.

They both looked at him quizzically.

He rolled his eyes. "We're taking Soph for the afternoon while you two go figure some shit out. We'll bring her home in a bit."

The pit in Aaron's stomach dropped.

Fuck. Mark knew everything too.

Aaron scratched the back of his sweaty neck. "I don't know if that's such a good idea."

Tori propped Sophie up on her shoulder. "Nonsense. It's a great idea. You have formula in the go-bag, right? Diapers? Clothes?"

Slowly, Aaron nodded.

"Great. We both know what we're doing with children, babies too. She'll be in good hands. This will give you guys a chance to talk without distractions." She reached down and took the wineglass away from Isobel. "I suggest you do it sober, though."

Isobel glared at her.

Tori was all smiles.

"Best get a move on," Mark encouraged. "This is her car seat on the stroller, right?" He shook the handle of Sophie's bucket car seat. I can just secure it into my car, no problem?"

Aaron grunted. He didn't like being told what to do and when to do it. Not by anyone.

"All right then. We'll bring her back around four or so. Should give you two lots of time. After all, if you're going to *play* like adults, you need to act like adults and talk this shit out."

Tori snorted. "Pot, kettle."

He gave her the side-eye. "I'm better now, right?"

The look she gave him was all love. "You are, dear. Very much so."

Mark's grin was wily and triumphant before both he and Tori turned serious once again and pinned a very parental, very stern look on Aaron that said a million things, all of them threatening.

He needed to get out of there before one of them lost their cool and tore a strip off him for defiling their little Isobel.

If only they knew how dirty their little Isobel could be.

Mark cleared his throat. "Go."

Blowing out a breath and grumbling something at her sister, Isobel stood up and headed in the direction of the yard gate. "I'll drive," she muttered, not bothering to wait for him or even to hold open the gate.

Aaron could hear Mark's chuckle as he followed her up the stone path on the side of the house. "Good luck, buddy," Mark called. "You're going to need it."

Isobel pulled into Aaron's driveway and turned off the ignition. She huffed out a breath and didn't open the car door. Instead she simply sat there and stared ahead at the closed garage door. "You hurt me," she whispered.

Aaron's gut lurched at her words.

The last thing he wanted to do was hurt Isobel. He'd hack off a limb, gouge out his eyes, impale himself on a rusty spear before he intentionally hurt her.

"I'm sorry," he murmured.

She turned to face him. "What's going on with us? I don't get you. I've been your nanny for over a month now, and I hardly know a thing about you. This is unlike any nanny job I've ever had before. The parents usually want to know who the hell is with their kid all day."

He fought the urge to say that Sophie wasn't his kid, but instead he gnashed his molars together and didn't say anything.

"And then"—she forced out a laugh—"I thought we'd turned this corner last night when we kissed. I honestly thought you didn't even like me. I thought the attraction was one-sided."

So did he, but from his side.

"You were so caring, so reassuring when I called you in a panic, when I called you for help." She swallowed, the sexy line of her throat jogging as she pushed down the emotions. "You're the first person I called. I called you before I even thought about calling the cops." She stared straight ahead at the garage again, her fingers twisting in the fabric of her sweater. "I feel safe with you. I don't know why, because I have no idea if you *are* a safe person. For all I know, those dog tags could mean you were in the military but then went rogue and became a gun for hire or a mercenary or something."

"I was a SEAL." Damn, all he wanted to do was reach out, grab her hands and bring them to his lips, reassuring her that she was *safe* with him, that he'd never intentionally hurt her.

But he couldn't. He couldn't lie like that when he had no clue if she actually was safe with him. He'd let people down before. He could do it again.

Probably would do it again.

She spun back around to face him, her eyes wide, lips parted. Pink flooded her cheeks, and her nostrils flared. He was used to this reaction from women. They always got turned on when he or his buddies told them what they did. Sometimes it was fun to watch the way the women changed. Their visceral reactions to being around men who lived dangerously. "A SEAL as in a Navy SEAL?"

What was it about danger that turned women on?

She licked her lips.

"Yes. Colton too." He could give her that. She deserved the truth. "We were the good guys, I swear. Saved more people than we killed." He pressed his lips together and breathed deep through his nose. "Or at least that was the goal."

Good guys was a relative term, but she needed to know he wasn't some gun for hire who would sell his soul to the highest bidder.

Maybe that was because he didn't really have much of a soul to sell anymore anyway.

The way the blue darkened in her eyes told him she believed him but was still curious and probably skeptical.

"I failed in my last mission." He swallowed. "So after I tied up some loose ends, I retired and moved back here. Started up the construction company."

"Thank you for sharing," she whispered.

"You're welcome."

They both dropped their gazes to their laps.

"I'm sorry that you failed your mission. I hope it was fixable."

He resisted the urge to laugh. Oh, he'd fixed it all right. Fixed it good.

He'd gone rogue and went on a fucking killing spree.

Yeah, he'd fixed it.

Her pained sigh brought his eyes up to her face. "What are we doing, Aaron? Why were you so closed off this morning? You didn't even look at me. I'm not expecting a diamond ring after last night, but I do think I deserve eye contact." She lifted her head and fixed her eyes on the side of his face until he looked at her. He didn't want to, but he knew he had to. "I deserve respect," she said when he finally looked at her.

She deserved the universe.

Hearing the rawness in her words, he closed his eyes, unable to look at the hurt on her face any longer.

"I'm sorry. Last night took me by surprise. I never thought it would happen. It never *should* have happened." He ran his fingers through his damp hair, and like the coward that he was, opened his eyes and focused on her pink tennis shoes instead of her beautiful face. "Hell, Liam even warned me. He told me nothing good could come from sleeping with my nanny. But then seeing you last night flirting with Zak ..."

She made a dismissive noise in her throat and shook her head. "Zak flirts with everyone. And I mean everyone. He mostly does it because he's not interested in dating right now, but he finds it fun. He flirted with Tori when Mark was being a dink to her, pushed Mark to step up. Maybe he was trying to do the same to you?"

Had that been Zak's angle all along?

Good thing Aaron hadn't put his fist through the man's face.

He hung his head and stared at his black jogging shorts. "Well, Zak aside, I understand if you want to quit. I took advantage of you. I should have known better—"

She stomped her foot on the floor of the car and crossed her arms in front of her chest, pushing her breasts up. "How many times do I have to tell you that I wanted you too? I *want* you too."

His cock lurched in his shorts.

Down, boy.

She reached for his hand across the center console and placed her fingers on top of his, her touch soft but sure and steady.

Fuck, he needed steady in his life.

"We can start slow," she offered. "Take a few steps back, if you want."

The only steps he wanted to take were into the house and back to his bedroom. He wanted her naked on his bed with his face between her legs. That was where he'd been happiest. That was where he'd felt steady and sure. Buried in her softness, in her sweetness.

"I'm not sure what you expect from me," he asked.

"Did you enjoy last night?"

Did the sun rise in the east? Did beer taste good? Of course, he enjoyed last night.

"I'll take that facial expression and your silence as a yes," she said, a cute smile tilting her lips up on one side. "So did I. Why can't we do that? Why can't we just enjoy each other and continue doing what we were doing?"

"You'll want more eventually," he said, hoping she understood he wasn't trying to be an asshole and just simply stating a fact.

"Maybe you will too."

She didn't deny it. She would. She knew she would.

He shook his head. "I can't give you more. It's ... when people get close to me, they get hurt. It's just a fact."

Her little button nose wrinkled. "Who would want to hurt me? Or you?"

"Doesn't matter."

"Is this about Dina?"

His sister's name sent a red-hot poker directly into his heart. He snarled and flung the car door open, choosing not to answer her rather than bite her head off and say something he would ultimately regret. He heard the driver's side door open and then slam shut and her footsteps behind him as he approached the front door.

Not bothering to turn around, he slid the key into the lock and opened the front door.

She followed him but didn't say a word.

He needed a drink. He'd had three sips of his beer at Mark's before being sent on his way to *kiss and make up* or whatever the fuck Mark and Tori expected him and Isobel to do. It didn't matter that it was only noon. He needed a fucking drink.

Halfway into the kitchen, he stopped.

Waffles and plate carnage littered the floor.

What the fuck?

Isobel's footsteps stopped behind him. "I was angry," she said, her voice only a touch sheepish. "You treated me like a piece of meat. Good enough to sleep with but not good enough to sit and have breakfast with. Not good enough to look at after the fact. You didn't even bother to ask me how I was this morning. And after everything I went through last night, I think I deserved that."

Was that a sob?

No.

Fuck, no.

He spun around. Her eyes were red-rimmed and brimmed with tears.

"I'm trying really hard here, Aaron. Really fucking hard. I know you're struggling with all of this, and I'm trying to give you space, but it's getting tough. Your walls are near impenetrable. But last night, I thought ..." She wiped her wrist beneath her nose. "I was scared, and you helped me. You showed me compassion and care. You gave me strength when I had none. I wanted to replace the memories of last night with something better, with something good. I didn't think that what we did last night would make it difficult for you to look at me the next day. Would make it difficult for you to be around me, to talk to me. Had I known it would, I wouldn't have—" She turned her head and wiped beneath her eyes.

Oh, fuck.

An ache filled his chest.

In a couple of long strides, he ate up the distance between them, grabbing her by the shoulders and bending his knees until they were eye to eye. What stared back at him fucking killed him.

But he didn't know what to say. An apology would be hollow and lackluster. Or at least that's what he thought. An apology wasn't enough. What he had to give her, what he had in his heart just wasn't enough.

She blinked damp, spiked lashes at him, looking through him, seeing all of him.

As she went to speak, he crushed his mouth to hers, smothering her words. He released her shoulders, wrapping his arms around her waist and tugged her into his body. She groaned and gripped his T-shirt tight, his dog tags too. It was like she was holding on for dear life. But it was actually him who was holding on to her. Grappling for the last remaining threads of his sanity, of his humanity ... of his soul. Sweeping through her mouth, his tongue swirled around hers, massaging and sucking, tasting a delicacy he knew he didn't deserve.

He knew it was wrong. The whole thing between them was wrong. It'd been wrong the first time he'd kissed her, then the second and every time after that. But he couldn't stop.

He wanted her to demand they stop, to see the man that he really was and realize she was better off walking away. That he couldn't give her what she needed, what she deserved.

He also wanted her to beg him for more, to take what she could from him, what he could offer her, even if it wasn't much.

She pushed him away, her chest heaving with heavy pants, her eyes bright and lips puffy. "What are we doing, Aaron?" She stepped away from him and turned around. "What do you want from me?"

Fuck if he knew.

Could everything and nothing be the right answer?

He wanted everything she had to give him, but he also knew that it was better to ask her for nothing, because how could you ask someone to give you all they had when you had so little to give in return?

She spun to face him. "I like you. I'm attracted to you. I want you. I also love my job. I'm in love with your baby, and I don't want to lose Sophie." She swallowed. "Or you. But if this is going to be too much for you, I can step back. I can just be the nanny." Her blue eyes turned fierce. "But don't fuck with my heart. Don't fuck me and then not even look at me afterward. I'm a person, and I deserve respect. I'll take a lot of crap, but I won't take being disrespected, grieving or not. I don't deserve it."

Had he ever met a stronger, more confident woman in his life?

Fuck, no, he hadn't.

Isobel Jones did not play games. She wasn't dramatic. She wasn't wishy-washy. She was blunt, up-front and candid. And hell if it didn't make him want her even more.

He took a step forward. "I don't have a lot to give," he said softly. "I'm not whole, haven't been for a while."

She planted her hands on her hips. The hips he desperately wanted bare and in his palms as he watched her bounce up and down in his lap. "What does that mean?"

"It means I can try. I *want* to try. I *want* you, but I don't know if that'll be enough. If *I'm* enough."

Her eyes softened, and she took half a step forward. "Why don't you let me be the judge of that, hmm?" She closed the distance between them and looped her arms around his neck, resting them on his shoulders. "You're an amazing man, Aaron. Hurting, lost and confused, but you're still amazing. I wish you could see all the things that I see. How good you are with Sophie, how much love you have for her. You have so much love to give, I just wish you were able to see if for yourself. I wish I could help take away your pain."

"You can't fix me," he whispered. "I'm unfixable."

She tilted her head to the side, and a small, almost indiscernible smile lifted the corner of her mouth. She shook her head. "I'm not trying to fix you. I'm trying to show you that you're not broken."

You're not broken.

He rested his hands on her hips and pushed her T-shirt up and leggings down just enough so that his palms rested on bare skin. She was warm to the touch and soft all over.

He needed more softness in his life.

Isobel, Sophie, they'd been exactly what he'd needed to take away the jagged edge that had begun to consume him, cutting through the last remaining shreds of his soul.

Heat and need swirled in the intense cornflower blue of her eyes. "How can I take away your pain? How can I ease the hurt?"

"Sounds to me like you're trying to be a *fixer.*"

He could feel the warm puffs of her breath against his mouth now that they were so close. "I prefer the name Wonder Woman, but whatever." Her smile was wicked, but even with the sudden restless gleam in her eyes, there was no denying her sweetness. No denying the true nature of Isobel and how giving and genuinely compassionate she was.

"You're most definitely Wonder Woman," he breathed, flicking his tongue out and tracing it along her bottom lip. "I'm in awe of you."

Her fingers curled around his neck, and she took his mouth, propelling them forward until his calves hit the wooden kitchen chair and he was forced to sit down.

The woman knew what she wanted, and she wasn't afraid to ask for it. Wasn't afraid to take control.

He wasn't quite sure how he felt about that. At least not until she straddled him and pushed her breasts against his face and ground her hot cleft against his titanium-hard erection, which she could undoubtably feel, as his jogging shorts left very little to the imagination.

She bent her head and traced her tongue over the shell of his ear. "Condom," she whispered.

"Bedroom," he grunted, grabbing her ass cheeks and rocking her against him.

Without another word, she stood up, reached for his hand and led him down the hallway to his bedroom. The confidence in her gait and the smile on her face made his balls tighten up and his pulse thunder in his ears.

When they entered his bedroom, she released his hand and went to get undressed, but he stopped her.

Last night, they'd already been naked. Today he wanted to unwrap her himself.

"Let me." He gripped the hem of her T-shirt and slowly drew it over her head. She lifted her arms to help him. Her bra was nothing special. Simple, white cotton with a tiny satin bow in the center. But it was sexy as fuck on her.

She was wearing dark gray leggings or tights or whatever the chicks were calling them these days. The skin-tight stretchy pants that had taken over the bottom halves of nearly the entire global female population. Thankfully, Isobel rocked them. Her ass was perfect and tight, her thighs soft and luscious, and as he pulled the leggings down, sinking to his knees, he kissed a trail down her quads to her shins. He pulled off her cute little pink tennis shoes and socks, discarding everything but her bra and panties in a pile next to the bed.

It killed him not to stop and fold it all.

Everything in his room, in his home was neat and orderly.

Everything had a place.

Disorder bred chaos.

Order saved lives.

But he wasn't about to take time away from Isobel and her body and the way she was watching him to give in to his OCD. He'd fold it later.

Still on his knees, he guided her over to the bed, then lifted her foot, planting kisses up her instep toward her ankle, her calf and knee. He swirled his tongue around the back of her knee until she squirmed and inhaled.

"That tickles," she whispered.

He did it again, only this time, he nipped her skin, then reached up and pushed his fingers beneath the elastic of her panties. The damp patch made the white cotton near translucent, showcasing the small patch of dark hair she kept so neatly trimmed.

He fought the urge to lift his head and push his nose into it. Inhale her sweet, musky scent.

His fingers moved through her slick, pink folds until he found her clit. She pushed down on his hand, encouraging his quest.

He was going to take his time. Savor her. Do this right.

He'd already hurt her more than he could bear. He needed to make amends and apologize properly.

Lazily, he stroked her clit, felt it swell beneath his fingertips and more warm wetness trickle out onto his knuckles.

He dragged the tip of his tongue up her inner thigh, pushing his nose against her mound when he reached the juncture of her legs. Removing his fingers from her clit, he flicked it through the fabric with his tongue. She lurched on the bed, then fell to her back.

He smiled, repeating the whole process to her other leg before finally peeling her panties down and tossing them with the rest of her clothes. Still on his knees, he pulled her butt to the edge of the bed, spread her legs wide, tossed them over his shoulders and kissed her clit.

Her hips leapt off the bed.

He did it again.

They leapt again.

Grinning, he sucked one of her soft, pink folds into his mouth, loving her flavor and the way it slid like warm honey across his tongue. He could drink her down all day long.

His fingers found her cleft, and he pushed one, then two inside her, feeling her ridges pulse and contract around him.

His dick was raging now. Pulsing in time to the beat of his heart as he ate Isobel out with the intensity of a starved man. Because he was starved. He'd been starved for the touch and compassion of a good woman for far too long.

She seemed to see all that he was—or wasn't—and yet in many ways that was okay. She didn't ask for more.

At least not yet.

There would come a time she would ask him for more, and when she realized he had nothing left, nothing more to give, she'd walk away.

He couldn't focus on that now. That was pain for later. Pain he would endure alone. Right now, there was a woman who wanted to heal his heart, take away his pain and in return fill a hole he thought would be empty forever.

"Aaron," she whimpered. Her hand landed on his head. Propping herself up on her elbows, she gazed down at him, her eyes glassy, her lids hooded. "Everything okay?"

Ah, fuck.

He'd stopped.

He'd fucking stopped.

Stopped his tongue, stopped his lips, stopped his fingers.

He was so inside his own head, he'd forgotten about his body. He'd forgotten about Isobel's body.

Grunting, he flicked her clit. "Sorry, babe."

She put her head back down. "Whatever you did a second ago, do that again."

Son of a bitch. What had he done a second ago? He hadn't even been paying attention to what he was doing.

Shit.

Christ.

"You were sucking on my clit and swirling your finger just—oh, oh, yeah, just like that—" Her leg spasmed on his shoulder, knocking his ear.

Thank fuck.

He sucked on her clit, drawing the sensitive nub into his mouth.

"Ooooh," she crooned, filling his mouth with more sweetness.

He wanted to make her come. Then he wanted to flip her over onto her belly, push her legs together, cover her body and fuck her into the mattress until she was putty.

Using the flat of his tongue, he swept it up through her cleft, laving at the lips and twirling it around her clit, sucking on the hood, which she seemed to really like.

Her pussy quivered around his fingers. She was getting close.

An easy nut to crack and with more tells than the world's worst poker player.

"Another finger," she panted, pushing her body down onto his face, shamelessly taking what she wanted from him and telling him what she needed. He fucking loved it.

He added another finger.

She tensed around him, the rise and fall of her hips growing more and more erratic. "Oh, fuck, yes." She cupped her breasts, pulling her bra down to expose her nipples, her fingers tugging and tweaking until they grew strawberry-red and pointy.

Aaron knew he should probably just shut his eyes and get to work, but it was fascinating and sexy as fuck to watch her. She was so animated, so comfortable in her own skin and with her own body and pleasure, he was mesmerized.

He sucked hard once again on her clit, pressed up on her G-spot with his middle finger, and she detonated.

A warm gush filled his mouth as she convulsed and rippled around him, her body bowing on the bed, her hips pressing up to his face as she rode the waves of ecstasy.

He'd shut his eyes when she started to come but opened them again to watch her, enamored with the beauty before him and how unabashedly she allowed herself to experience pleasure. She pulled at her crimson nipples until they were so far away from her breasts, Aaron figured they must hurt, but she continued to do it, tugging and twiddling, pinching and fiddling. Her mouth opened and her chest heaved as she crested the climax and began to fall back down to Earth, her body slowly relaxing, the tension vacating her muscles. A soft sigh released from her parted lips, and her hands fell away from her breasts to the bed.

He licked up through her cleft, and her leg spasmed again.

He chuckled as he pulled away. She'd been like that last night too. Highly sensitive right after her orgasms. He loved it.

He stood up and removed his jogging shorts and boxers, followed by his shirt. She'd blinked her eyes open just in time to watch him toss all the clothes into the hamper.

She crooked a finger at him as a small, sultry smile coasted across her lips. Lips he didn't think he'd ever get tired of kissing. Lips he knew he'd never get bored of watching wrap around his cock and suck him like a pro, swallowing every drop like a champ, batting her lashes at him and asking for more. And most importantly, they were lips he loved to watch curl up into a smile. She had the best fucking smile.

He would never grow tired of Isobel. Never.

The same couldn't be said for her though. She'd probably grow tired of him by the year's end. Possibly sooner.

Stowing the niggling thoughts of self-doubt in the back of his mind, he grinned, making his way around the bed to his nightstand. He located a condom, tore open the package and slipped it on.

Placing one knee in the bed, he gripped her by the ankles and then, with a flick of his wrists, flipped her to her belly.

She let out a loud and surprised squeal and then an *oof*.

He hovered above her body and unhooked her bra, freeing it from her chest and arms and tossing it to the floor with the rest of her clothes. Kneeling her legs apart, he pushed two fingers back inside her and pumped. "I love it when you tell me how you want me to eat your pussy. Love a woman who knows what she wants, where she wants my tongue and how many fingers she wants inside her."

Isobel groaned as he slipped a third finger in. When she pushed her butt up into the air just a touch, he had to temper his desire. He'd like nothing more than to take her there, take her tight hole and watch her shatter into a million pieces as he pumped three fingers in her pussy and shoved his tongue down her throat. Fill her up with all of him and watch her come undone.

Another time though.

Soon.

"I want more than just your fingers inside me now," she whispered, maneuvering a hand beneath herself and beginning to rub her clit.

He shook his head and, using his free hand, pulled her arm out from under her. "Nope. It's my turn now. I'm in charge. You come when I tell you to come. You put your arms, your legs, your ass where I tell you to put them."

She craned her neck around to look at him, a cheeky little curl to her lips.

"Can I make one final request, please?" She batted her lashes at him with far too much sass. He'd have to consider spanking some of that attitude out of her.

He gripped his dick in his fist and gave it a couple of tugs. "Fine, one."

She licked her lips. "Kiss me."

Chapter 20

Aaron's kisses were the absolute best.

Fierce and passionate. Driven and hard.

The man kissed the way he did everything, full throttle, no holds barred, and to the max.

When she asked him to kiss her, she'd been expecting him to just lean over her body and kiss her quick. What she got—what she loved—was so much more.

He splayed himself over her completely, his weight pressing her into the bed, his arms on top of hers, fingers intertwined with hers, mouth devouring hers. His tongue swept into her mouth and demanded entry, wet, hot and powerful. He pried her lips open, swirled his tongue around hers and forced her to acquiesce to his control. She was pinned, unable to move—not that she wanted to—but either way, she couldn't even cup his face, so she just let him take over the kiss. He bit her lip hard, tugging and nibbling. She tried to nip him back playfully, but he pulled away, smiled and then dove back in, spreading her mouth open wide and plunging his tongue inside.

She tasted her release on his lips. It just spurred her on. His heavy weight on her pressed her hips into the bed, and if she wiggled just right, she could get her labia to open and her clit could get some lovin'.

But Aaron was wise to her games, and when he figured out what she was doing, he reared up off her body and a harsh, unexpected smack landed firm across her left buttock.

"Eek," she squealed, a rush of heat blooming from her struck bottom up through the rest of her body. She blinked open her eyes and glared at him over her shoulder. "What was that for?"

"I told you that I will tell you when you get to come. I'm in control. You were disobeying me." A slow grin crossed his handsome face and made her heart skip a beat. "Understood?"

Biting her lip to keep herself from smiling, she nodded. Then she ground down against the bed again, brought her hand beneath her and flicked her clit, all the while continuing to watch him.

Heat flooded the dark blue of his eyes. "You're a brat. "

Her lips twitched as she tried to flatten them, determined not to smile. "You love it." Ah shit, she was smiling.

His dark red brows furrowed, and he shook his head. "Miss Jones, you simply will not learn."

Did the air whistle? It sure as heck sounded like it. Down came his palm once again, this time on her right cheek. She jerked on the bed, inhaling from his strike. But like before, the pain lasted mere moments, and what replaced it was a warm, pleasant throb.

He spread his body back out on top of hers, running his hands over her arms, spreading them out on the mattress so her body made the letter *T*. "Follow my lead," he said, pushing back up to his knees.

She nodded, the excitement of the spanks and what he had planned next making her want to finally obey. She wasn't sure she could submit entirely—it'd never been in her nature—but she was curious about the position he had her in and what was to come of it.

She watched him out of the corner of her eye. He pushed her knees back together so she lay face down on the bed, arms out, legs touching. He scooted up over her, his knees on either side of her legs, arms on either side of her shoulders.

Levering up onto one hand, he grabbed his cock and slowly breached her body.

They both moaned at the same time.

In this position, with her legs closed, she was tight. She felt all of him. Every hard, solid inch of him. He slid into her channel with ease, her arousal making both of them slick. Once fully seated, he began to move.

Everything felt good.

She'd never had sex in this position before. Her legs had always been spread. This was new. This was exciting. This was incredible.

"So fucking tight, Iz. So fucking tight," he murmured next to her ear. "Love your tight little pussy and the way it hugs my dick just right. The perfect fit."

The perfect fit.

With each measured thrust, he pushed her body harder into the bed, her clit bounced against the mattress, and her pebble-hard nipples demanded to be pinched. She was going stir-crazy from how good it felt, but she was on the verge of insanity from not being able to make it all feel even better.

He kissed a hot, wet path across her shoulders, sinking his teeth into the nape of her neck and scraping them down to her right bicep.

She moaned, pushing up just a touch to welcome him in deeper.

His groan behind her said he approved the assist and very much enjoyed it.

A hand worked its way beneath her, and fingers found a nipple. They tugged until she gasped and squirmed.

"Just because I liked it doesn't mean it was allowed." His voice was a rough and strained tenor behind her. "I control your pleasure, remember?" He pinched her nipple harder. Heat coiled in her belly, and she ground her clit down against the bed again.

"Iz, you're really a terrible submissive."

"That was your first mistake there, stud. I'm nobody's submissive. Not in the bedroom, not ever."

Was that a growl behind her?

Before she could blink, let alone get her rocks off, he was off her and out of her, and she found herself being hauled up to her knees.

Was he mad? Was he honestly expecting her to submit to him or get out? Was he going to tell her to put her clothes on and go get Sophie?

Sure, she was a bit of *marshmallow,* as her mother called her, but she was no doormat. And contrary to what a lot of her exes believed, there was a difference. She was a strong, independent woman with a soft heart. She'd never let a man tell her what to do, and she had no intention of starting. Once in a while, she relinquished control in the bedroom—somewhat—but most of the time (perhaps it was because she'd never really found a partner who truly satisfied her), she took matters into her own hands and told the guy how to get the job done. Took the reins, climbed on top and made it happen.

It was a hard habit to break.

Maybe Aaron could help her?

She was about to suggest they try again. He could even tie her up if he wanted to, that way she really couldn't move, but the look in his eyes told her plans had changed and she needed to just wait.

So she waited.

Watching her with hooded eyes, he moved until he was propped up against the headboard. He took his heavy, latex-encased cock in his hand and stroked it. "What do you want, Isobel?"

Phew.

Grinning like a cat that had just had a whole bowl of warm cream placed in front of her, Isobel crawled across the bed, tossed one leg over his lap and hovered just above him.

"Little control freak," he whispered, taking his cock and angling the tip at her center.

"Nuh-uh." She lifted one eyebrow before shaking her head and tilting her hips forward so the tip of him hit a different part of her. She sank down just a touch so he got the idea.

He was no dummy.

Lust filled his eyes, his lips parted, and warm puffs of air escaped him, hitting her lips, which were just inches from his. "Iz, we don't—"

She put her finger to his lips. "I thought I was in charge."

His throat bobbed on a hard swallow, but the wicked and triumphant gleam in his eyes told her he wasn't at all unsure of it.

Using his fingers, he trailed a path of wetness up from her center and between her cheeks, lubricating her tight hole. A hole she hadn't given over to a man in quite some time, and even then, she really hadn't found one who knew what the hell he was doing back there.

She couldn't quite put her finger on why she wanted to go there with Aaron, particularly now. All she knew was that she did.

She really, really did.

He pushed a finger inside her, then another, scissoring them to stretch her out. She squirmed in his lap. It was a sensation she was familiar with, but it'd been a while.

"Don't have to, Iz, we really don't."

She pressed her lips to his, lifted up and waited for him to remove his fingers and replace them with something else. "Shh," she whispered against his lips. "I want this. I want you. I trust you."

The fire in his eyes seared her soul, opened her heart and made everything inside her tingle.

She felt the tip of his cock press against her anus.

"Push out, Iz," he whispered, his words strained, his breaths coming out in ragged pants. She had one hand on his chest and one on his shoulder. The pulse in his neck against her thumb beat wildly.

She did as she was told, pushing out with her muscles at the same time she sank down, breathing out with each luscious inch she took in.

"Jesus fuck, Iz," he groaned. "Not gonna last long like this."

Once he was fully inside her and she had acclimatized to his size, she lifted up just a touch. "Fingers," she whispered, moving a hand between them to find her clit.

His eyes flared.

"Two."

Awe filled his gaze as he pushed two fingers into her pussy and began to pump. Slowly, finding their rhythm, she began to move. Up and down, she moved in his lap, taking him out to the tip, then back down to the root, all the while rubbing her clit as Aaron's fingers plunged inside.

She was close in no time. Full. Full of Aaron, just the way she needed it to be.

"Baby," he ground out, bucking up into her, the cadence of his fingers inside her beginning to ebb as he approached the pinnacle. "So fucking good. So, so fucking good. Not gonna last."

She reached for his free hand with her free hand and laced their fingers together. They needed to come together.

Her face was just above his, their lips close but not touching, eyes focused on the other. He had the most incredible blue eyes. Dark and stormy, with bright bursts of yellow around the pupils. They were unique and beautiful. Unusual and tumultuous, just like Aaron.

"Fuck, Iz, so good."

She lifted up, swirled her hips, then captured his mouth at the same time she dropped back down.

They both shut their eyes and came. His tongue pushed into her mouth and swept inside as his cock pulsed and her whole body tightened. Every muscle inside her went rigid, even her toes curled, and her legs cramped as the orgasm ricocheted around her body like the ball in a pinball machine.

Aaron pulled free from the kiss and tucked his face into her shoulder, kissing along the bone as he descended down from the ether.

"You're incredible, Iz," he said, his voice muffled as he continued to pepper kisses over her flushed skin. "Never met a woman like you."

"I've never met a man like you either," she said, pulling her hand from between them.

He snatched her wrist and brought her fingers to his mouth, sucking each one off like it was butter pecan ice cream on the hottest day of the year. A new rush of need whirled through her, and she clenched around the fingers he still had inside her.

His eyes had been closed, but when he was done licking off her fingers, he opened them, and what looked back at her was a need, a lust, a desire so intense every molecule of oxygen fled her lungs at once and her eyes stopped blinking.

Isobel's bottom lip dropped open.

Something akin to terror flashed behind Aaron's eyes before it vanished just as quickly, and a big smile brightened up his whole face. He pulled his fingers from her pussy, licked those clean too and then gently helped her climb off his lap.

The condom hung—very full—off his semi-hard cock. He tugged it off, tied it and then, with his other hand, reached for hers and hauled her up to standing. "Come on, sexy, let's go have a shower." He propelled her ahead of him and then slapped her butt. "You might not submit to me, but I bet I could make that ass a very purty pink in the shower."

Grinning, she wiggled it and tossed him a wink over her shoulder. "Is that a challenge?" She released his hand and skipped toward the bathroom.

The animal noise behind her made her speed up, continuing on past the bathroom and out into the rest of the house. She heard him stop at the bathroom to probably toss the condom in the garbage, only to see his sexy frame emerge seconds later.

She sank her top teeth into her bottom lip as she bounced on the balls of her toes in the living room, looking down the hallway at his big, shadowed frame, the large, long, puffy pink scar on his abdomen appearing to almost glow.

His nostrils flared, and his gait morphed into more of a prowl. Goosebumps prickled along her skin as his smile grew wily. "Oh, Iz, you won't be able to sit down for a week if I catch you."

She took off toward the kitchen, knowing full well he would catch her, trap her and make good on his promise.

And she was totally, one hundred percent okay with that.

She just hoped that when he finally caught her, he'd also want to keep her.

Chapter 21

A shower, two orgasms, a meal and then another orgasm in the kitchen later and Aaron and Isobel found themselves sitting in the living room with Liam (who had shown up literally seconds after Isobel's kitchen orgasm) discussing Dina's celebration of life.

"As per your wishes," Liam started, his son Jordie playing quietly on his iPad next to him on the love seat, "I delayed the celebration of life until things with Sophie got settled. I booked the rental space for next Saturday. Everybody at work knows. They're appreciative you wanted it held on a weekend."

Aaron grunted.

"Not that that would have mattered, though. Dina was loved by all, and we would have shut down the firm on a Tuesday to honor her."

Aaron grunted again, his eyes focused on the television screen above the fireplace.

The television, although on mute, had the news playing in the background. Things with the jewelry store robberies were escalating. Store owners were getting gun permits and talking about fighting back.

Not what they needed at all—more people with guns. Good guys or not, they needed less guns in hands, not more.

Isobel rubbed his back affectionately and laced the fingers of her other hand through his, resting them on his thigh. "It's okay. I know it's tough to talk about."

Liam's eyes lasered in on Isobel's hands. She watched his gaze bounce back and forth between Aaron's face, then hers. Suddenly it all dawned on him. He pursed his lips and shook his head, causing the dark blond swath of hair over his forehead to bob. "Ah man, you caved."

Aaron grunted for the umpteenth time, removing his gaze from the television and focusing it on Liam.

"I mean obviously you caved. Look at her." Liam held his hand out toward Isobel. "And she's amazing. Smart, great with kids. But you guys ..." He ran his fingers through his hair. His dark brown eyes were a mix of amusement and concern. "Just be careful, okay. Mark and Tori wrote up a relationship and work contract. But they also don't live together. This could get mucky. And if they do, I'll represent the first person to come to me. I love you both, so it'll be hard to pick a side, but money eases my pain."

"You're an arrogant fuck," Aaron ground out.

Liam's grin was huge. "It's one of my best qualities."

Isobel rolled her eyes. Aaron grunted next to her.

After Liam finished laughing, his eyes found Isobel's, and his gaze turned avid and sincere. "Seriously, though, I don't want to see you get hurt." His eyes bounced to Aaron. "Either of you."

"And we appreciate that," she said, admiring the way Liam's nose wrinkled and the lines next to his eyes creased when he got serious. He was a handsome man, there was no doubt about that. Trouble was, he also knew it. "But we're taking it slow."

Skepticism crossed his charming features. "The orgasmic glow around both of you would say otherwise."

Isobel's face caught fire.

"What's an *orgasmic glow?*" Jordie asked, lifting his head from his iPad. His eyes, the same dark shade of brown as his father's, squinted in curiosity. "Is it like a glow stick?"

Liam chuckled awkwardly and ruffled his son's hair. "Something like that, kiddo. I'm just saying that Mr. Steele and Miss Jones look so happy they're practically glowing."

Jordie's mouth tilted down in a frown of understanding. "I got an *orgasmic glow* when we went to Legoland this summer."

Isobel dipped her head to hide her smile and bit the inside of her cheek to keep from laughing.

Out of the mouths of babes.

"You sure did," Liam said, clearing his throat. "Though, let's just say you were happy. An orgasmic glow doesn't really work for Legoland."

Having already lost interest in the subject, Jordie shrugged and returned his attention to his iPad.

Aaron made another noise in his throat, only this one sounded more like a Harley revving its engine. "Anyway, dude, thanks for getting all that shit for Dina's service sorted. I appreciate it."

Liam nodded. "You're welcome."

Isobel was about to see if Jordie wanted a snack when there was a knock at the door. She checked the ornate, handmade driftwood clock above the mantle. It said four o'clock.

Sophie was home.

Opening the door for her sister, she didn't expect to see Mark and Gabe follow in her wake.

"Saw Liam's car in the driveway," Mark said, wandering into the house.

Jordie's head popped up from where he'd been focused on his iPad, and when he saw Gabe, he abandoned the tablet entirely, and the two little boys began playing with the Ziploc bag of toy cars Gabe had arrived with.

"Full house," Aaron murmured, taking Sophie from Isobel after she'd removed the baby from her car seat.

"You okay?" Their eyes locked and fingers brushed as she passed him the baby.

He nodded. "Yeah.

"Should we order pizza, have them stay for dinner?" she asked.

He made a face that said that was the last thing in the world he wanted to do, but instead of saying as much, he nodded again. "Okay."

Her eyes went wide as she tried to gauge his true feelings on her suggestion. "You're sure?"

Unease stared back at her. "No. But I know it's the right thing to do. Order the pizza. I'll be okay."

"All right," she whispered, resting her hand on his thigh and giving it a reassuring squeeze. "I'll go order some pizza for five o'clock."

Mark had kicked back in the armchair like he owned the place, animatedly chatting with Liam. Tori was unpacking the dirty formula bottles in the kitchen, and the two little boys were playing cars down the hallway.

Isobel's heart swelled as she took it all in.

This was exactly what she'd always wanted. A home full of people. Friends and family, children and everyone in between. She wanted her house to be the go-to home for social gatherings, playdates and dinner parties. She wanted to be mom to her own children as well as *other* mom to her friends' children. A person everyone knew they could rely on and trust to set a plate for them at the dinner table if they needed it.

She wanted a village.

Was this the start of her village? Or was this just a mirage, a fake village blurred by the haze of orgasms still in the air and all the dopamine in her system?

Would it ever be her village? Or was she simply the hired help for a villager but not a villager herself?

"So," Tori started, having rinsed the bottles in the sink and set them to dry on the drying rack, "did you guys kiss and make up?"

Isobel averted her eyes, a smile tugging at her lips.

"Oh, well then. Good for you."

She felt his heat at her back before she heard a word. He certainly knew how to turn on stealth mode when he needed to.

Tori's eyes flew up from the diaper bag to behind Isobel. "I'm going to go see what Gabe and Jordie are up to." She left the kitchen but not before turning around to mouth something dirty at Isobel.

Isobel rolled her eyes.

"You sure you're the younger one?" Aaron said, propping Sophie up on his shoulder.

"Sometimes I wonder," she said blandly.

Holding Sophie against him with one of his big palms, he cupped the side of her face with the other, his thumb caressing across her cheek while his pinky finger lay directly over her pulse. She leaned into his embrace and stepped into his body. "I'm going to try my damnedest not to screw this up," he said, tilting his head down so their lips were no more than an inch apart. "I'm not good at the boyfriend thing. Never really done it. But I can tell you're worth it."

I can tell you're worth it.

Not wanting to read too much into his sentiment, she told the butterflies in her belly to settle down and instead simply smiled at him. Her hand fell on top of his over Sophie's back. "Let's not put a label on it for now. Let's just do what feels natural, what feels right and take it from there. I don't ask for much."

"Just eye contact after sex?" His lips twitched.

"Before, during, after. Whatever. Just don't shut me out."

His lips brushed against hers. "Hard to make eye contact during when I'm behind you."

"Is that a suggestion for later?"

He tightened his grip on her jaw. "It's a promise." Their tongues tangled, and she moved her hand from Sophie's back to press it flat over his strong, thumping heart.

A heart she already found herself growing to love. A heart she hoped she could help heal.

A heart she hoped would one day love her back.

Chapter 22

"Something smells good," Aaron said, walking up behind Isobel Tuesday night, cupping her butt and planting a kiss on the crown of her head. He'd been late getting home from work, but she'd held dinner for him, and his stomach grumbled at the smell of the Mexican spices that hit his nostrils when he walked through the door.

She stood over the stove, pushing ground beef around in the skillet. "Almost done with the taco meat. You have time to run and shower before dinner if you want."

He made a dismissive noise, pinched her butt cheek again until she squeaked and then stepped away. A plate of taco fixin's sat on the counter, and like a bad boy he grabbed a handful of shredded cheddar cheese and sprinkled it into his mouth. "Where's Soph?"

"Down ... for now. We had a rough day. She was really fussy."

He paused. "Why?"

"Well, for one, she's a baby. Two, I think she might be coming down with a cold. She was struggling to breathe when I fed her her bottle, and she's been spitting up a lot. I might sleep in her room tonight with her, just in case she spits up in her sleep."

"We could move her bassinet into our room."

Her body stilled. The spatula paused in her hand.

Then it hit him.

He'd said *our room*. Like his room was now his *and* Isobel's. They'd been sleeping together all of a few days, and suddenly he'd moved her in.

Fuck.

Granted, yes, last night she'd stayed in his room. But they hadn't done a heck of a lot of sleeping. He'd picked up another box of condoms on his lunch break today as they'd depleted his stash last night.

With the spatula in her hand, she slowly turned around to face him, her mouth open just slightly, hesitation in her eyes. "Um."

Ah, fuck. Was she going to go all female on him and make a big thing about it?

He'd slipped up. Big deal.

She must have noticed not only the horror on his face but also growing irritation. He chalked up most of that to hunger. He was fucking starving. Something passed behind her eyes before she shook it off, nodded and then turned back to the stove. "Whatever you want to do. I don't mind staying in the other room with Soph though. That way you get a decent night's sleep."

Yeah, but then Isobel wouldn't be in their bed.

Ah, fuck. He'd done it again.

Their bed.

It wasn't *their* bed. It was *his* bed.

He just preferred when she was in it too.

"I got a surprise for you," she said, changing the subject—thank God.

He lifted one eyebrow. "Yeah, is it you naked with your lips wrapped around my dick later?"

She rolled her eyes. He smiled. It felt weird to smile. He'd been doing it so rarely lately, and yet she pulled more from him than anybody—well, maybe not Soph. "No, it's not that. But play your cards right there, soldier, and maybe you can have two surprises." She pointed to the table where half a dozen papers were spread out.

He walked over and picked them up, thumbing through each one. They were logos for his construction company. All beautifully designed with his company name, easy to see and very eye-catching. He lifted his head.

She was standing there watching him, her cushiony-soft bottom lip between her teeth, eyes eager but also with a wary apprehension behind them. "I noticed you don't have a company logo. I Googled to make sure, but I couldn't find one. I did up a few mock logos that I thought you might like." She lifted one shoulder like it was no big deal that she spent a bunch of time designing something for him. "I got this new design program, so I was just playing around." She took a step toward him. "I won't be offended if you don't want to use any of them, but if you like one, you can have it."

How did he get so lucky? This incredible, generous, patient, smart, creative, beautiful woman had been handed to him on a silver platter, and each and every day she just kept surprising him. Giving him more.

He didn't deserve her.

He thumbed through the designs again. The one that caught his eye was the cobalt blue and silver design with bold block letters and sort of a pitched roof overtop. *Steele Construction, Inc.* was easy to read and very bold. He pulled it from the bunch and then cleared his throat. "I like this one."

Her smile made everything inside him turn molten hot and his balls tighten in his pants. "Awesome! It's yours." She turned back to the kitchen and began humming over the stove once again, her hips and that rocking ass swaying to the tune.

He bit down the groan that threatened to break free and instead cleared his throat. "I'm going to go shower," he grumbled, needing to wash his body and clear his head. The sexy woman in his kitchen muddled the fuck out his brain. He was halfway down the hall when the doorbell chimed.

"Shit!" Isobel gritted, practically flying out of the kitchen. "Shit, shit, shit, shit." She nearly beat him to the door. "Don't people know a baby is in the house? I need a damn sign on the door. *You wake the baby, you take the baby.*"

She glanced at him over her shoulder, seeing the worry in his eyes, and a nervous chuckle breaking past her lips. "Not that I'd give your baby away, but you know what I mean."

He was behind her as she flung the door open, curse words and threats of throat-punching spilling from her mouth.

"Hey!" Mercedes smiled, holding up her hand to show off a big fancy diamond. Colton was right behind her, grinning like a dumbass.

Aaron felt Isobel's frustration slip away instantly. She lunged for her friend and wrapped her arms around Mercedes's neck. "Hi! Oh my God, you two!"

Mercedes and Colton followed them inside.

"Gonna go shower," Aaron grunted, shooting a glare in Colton's direction before heading back down the hallway.

Stupid motherfucker getting married. What had he been thinking?

"So I need the whole story," Isobel said as all four of them sat around the living room eating tacos—Aaron really needed to make a decent-size kitchen table. Not that he liked the idea of entertaining, but it just made sense. Because of course, Isobel had invited them to stay for dinner. She wanted to hear all about her friend's elopement.

Aaron couldn't give two shits.

It was Colton's mistake.

The man had made his fair share over the years. Like that chick in Guadalajara who'd handcuffed him to the bed, then robbed him blind, but not before she'd generously given him crabs.

Aaron rolled his eyes at the memory before diving into one of his tacos.

Isobel had taken to making tacos every Tuesday, and it was something he'd grown to really look forward to.

Taco Tuesday followed by sex had been on the menu tonight.

Dinner, sex and more sex before Isobel passed out in his bed with her head on his chest and his hand cupping her butt.

Now he had to wait for all of it except the tacos.

He glared at a gabbing Mercedes. Guests and entertaining had not been part of the plan. They were cutting into sexy time.

Mercedes put her taco down and wiped her mouth with her napkin, her smile so big, Aaron was having a hard time believing it was real.

"It's hard to explain," she started. "When you know, you just know. After Saturday night, I realized I wanted nothing to do with the bar or dating scene anymore. I'd been convincing myself that that was what was fun, that was how to have a good time." She shook her head, her gaze falling on Colton next to her. He reached for her hand, and they rested their clasped fingers on the couch. "A good time is being with someone you love. Cuddled up on the couch watching movies, eating nachos, drinking wine. I don't want the superficial, fake good time anymore. I want the real deal. I want a life, a partner, a future." She squeezed Colton's hand. "And I found it all."

"Yeah, but why'd you have to get married?" Isobel asked. "Couldn't you just date?"

"Why delay the inevitable?" Colton asked with a shrug. "We want to start our future now. Start our family now."

Isobel choked on her water. "Family?"

Mercedes nibbled on her lip. "Well, not *right*, right away. But soon."

Colton's smile was wicked. "We're just practicing right now."

"Colton saved me." Mercedes's eyes welled up with tears, and she turned back to look at her husband. "He took care of me. He makes me feel safe and loved, cared for and cherished. I've never met a man like him before, and I don't want anybody else."

Colton leaned over and pecked his new wife on the cheek. "And I've never met a wild, beautiful, smart, funny woman like Mercedes before. It was just meant to be."

Barf.

The two of them turned to face each other, staring into each other's eyes like a couple of lovesick morons.

Aaron's stomach turned from their sappy and mushy display.

Who the fuck was the man in front of him? He sure as hell didn't recognize him. Sure, he *looked* like Colton Hastings, their team medic, special operative, man-whore, but he certainly wasn't acting like him. Colton Hastings, aka the man-whore from Massachusetts, had sworn up, down and sideways that he'd never let a piece of tail tie him down. That marriage was for suckers and kids just drained your bank account. He'd laughed hysterically when Rob announced he was marrying Skyler, then he'd hit on every woman at their wedding, finally taking the receptionist from the hotel's front desk back to his room for the night.

The guy was definitely who you wanted on your six when out on a mission, but he wasn't exactly who you let around your little sister. Colton had only met Dina once, and Dina had had a boyfriend at the time.

Yet now, here Colton was, married and talking about babies.

They were in the fucking Twilight Zone.

"What you gonna do for work?" Aaron asked, feeling the need to finally say something. He'd been quiet since the newlyweds showed up, not sure how to handle their news or their over-the-top public displays of affection.

Colton released Mercedes's hand and picked his taco back up off his plate. "Not sure yet. Mercedes's place is big enough for the two of us, so I'm moving in with her. Thought about maybe trying out for the fire department. The academy has a new enrollment soon." His mouth turned up at one corner, the white scar that ran through his lips on the left making his smile seem just a touch evil. "Or I have a friend here in town who runs a construction company. He mentioned the other night that he's short-staffed and looking for laborers. I feel like I'd be a real asset on the job site, what with my medical background."

Ah, fuck.

Aaron lifted an eyebrow, leveling his gaze on his friend. "Yeah? You think so?"

Colton chewed his meal, a dumbass grin on his face. "I do. I mean, you'd be my reference anyway, right? Who knows me better than you?"

Aaron clenched and flexed his jaw muscle in thought. "You know how to run a circular saw?"

Colton nodded. "Helped my daddy build his barn last summer. Thing's still standing, not getting any complaints from the pigs or chickens, so I couldn't have done that bad of a job."

Aaron grunted. "Tomorrow morning then."

Colton smiled, tipping up his beer. "Thanks, man. You won't regret it."

He better fucking hope not.

"So, what's going on with you two?" Mercedes asked, pointing at Aaron and Isobel with her bejeweled hand. "I'm picking up on some serious sexual tension." The woman's bright gray eyes twinkled with her own dopamine and heavily sexed-up glee. "Has Mr. Sheffield finally decided to tap that?"

Aaron looked at Isobel for clarification. Pop culture references had never been his forte.

Isobel rolled her eyes, reading his frustration and conveying a bit of her own with a glare across the room at a pleased-as-punch smiling Mercedes. "She's referring to the old television show *The Nanny*. Mr. Sheffield was the boss."

Aaron groaned.

He wasn't sure if he felt sorry for Colton for being lassoed by this woman or if his buddy deserved her.

"We're taking things slow," Isobel said, glancing at Aaron. "Right?"

Aaron picked up his beer and guzzled half of it before nodding. "Yeah, slow."

Though the way he'd hammered her body repeatedly into his mattress Sunday night had been anything but slow. He'd shocked the shit out of both of them with his intensity. He'd been fucking insatiable.

Once he, Iz and Soph were alone again Sunday night—Tori, Mark, Liam and the kids having headed home after pizza—and he could finally breathe, they cleaned up, bathed Soph, put her to bed, and then he'd taken Iz in every room of the house. They'd christened every countertop, every chair, every sofa, every flat surface in his rancher. Then when they ran out of flat surfaces, he bent her over the hood of his truck in the garage and fucked her there too.

No wonder they needed more condoms.

"Why go slow?" Mercedes asked. "If it's right, it's right."

He could practically feel the heat radiating off Isobel's cheeks. He could definitely see them changing color out of the corner of his eye.

But his woman was all class. She shrugged. "Everybody is different. We're content with the way it is."

Mercedes rolled her eyes. "You mean *he's* content with the way it is. Someone to watch his kid, make his meals, clean his house and warm his bed, with zero commitment or promise of a future."

Colton's mouth made an *O* that said *"Oh snap,"* and his eyebrows nearly cleared right off his forehead. Mercedes's eyes narrowed on Isobel, one blonde eyebrow ascending in challenge.

The two women seemed to have a stare-down.

Aaron held his breath. If one of them started to take off her bangles and hoops, they were going to have a catfight. His gaze bounced between the two women. Neither of them wore bangles or hoops. How the fuck would anybody know if they were going to fight?

"That's enough," Isobel finally said, her voice low but crystal clear.

Mercedes rolled her eyes, shook her head and picked her taco back up, taking a big bite. "All I'm saying," she started again, tucking her food into her cheek, "is that I don't want to see my friend get hurt. You have the biggest heart on the planet, Iz. I've seen it shatter once or twice, and it's the most gut-wrenching thing in the world. I don't want to see it happen again because you've given yourself over completely to somebody who isn't prepared to do the same."

What. The. Actual. Fuck.

Rage pumped hot through his veins, and he had to rein in his desire to grab the blonde woman across the table by the hair and heave her out into the backyard.

It was raining. Might cool her off a bit.

He needed to cool off too. Needed to calm the fuck down.

Mercedes wasn't exactly wrong, but where the hell did she get off spouting this shit?

Had Colton said something to her? That Aaron was a shell of a man, incapable of love, incapable of anything but putting his head down and getting the job done?

The only love he'd been able to give anybody had been Dina, and when she died, so did his heart. He was scraping the bottom of the barrel, so to speak, trying to gather up the remaining fragments he could to give to Sophie, but he knew it would never be enough. It certainly wouldn't be enough to give to an incredible woman like Isobel.

"Has he told you about Colombia?" Mercedes asked.

Motherfucker.

Isobel turned to face Aaron, shaking her head as hurt and confusion clouded her sky-blue eyes. "No. What happened in Colombia?"

"Babe." Colton's hand rested on Mercedes's arm. "That's Aaron's story. I told you my story because we agreed to start our marriage off with no secrets, no demons or monsters in the closet. But Colombia isn't *your* story to tell."

Mercedes pursed her lips together. "She has a right to—"

"It's his story," Colton said again, his tone laced with a harsh edge of warning.

Mercedes shut her piehole and cast her eyes down to her lap. "I'm sorry."

Well, holy fuck. Colton was able to get the little big mouth to shut her trap. Someone needed to.

"Sorry, bro," Colton said, clearing his throat. "Didn't mean to—"

"It's fine." Aaron sniffed, stood up and took his empty plate to the dishwasher. "I'm tired. Gonna head to bed." He turned back to face his friend, making sure to avoid the penetrating stare of curiosity from Isobel and the equally infuriating glare from Mercedes. What the fuck did she have to glare at him for? "See you at the office, nine sharp. Gonna need some steel-toed boots."

Colton stood up, smacked his heels together, tossed his chin in the air and saluted.

Oh brother.

"Sir, yes, sir," he hollered.

Aaron rolled his eyes. "If you wake Soph, you're fucking fired."

Colton's mouth snapped shut, and he nodded once before sitting down.

Aaron didn't look back toward the living room as he made his way to the bedroom, but he could feel her eyes on him. Feel her need to know more, her need for a connection. She wanted to know more about him, wanted more from him.

Meanwhile, he'd sooner forget it all. He'd sooner forget everything.

Chapter 23

He couldn't fucking sleep.

Not a goddamn wink.

Aaron lay awake and heard Colton and his loud-mouth wife leave, Isobel seeing them to the door and being the ultimate hostess. He heard her scurrying around the kitchen cleaning, then heading into the bathroom to shower.

His cock was like a steel rod, throbbing as he envisioned her killer body all soaped up, her nipples pebbled, her skin flushed from the warm water.

When the shower turned off, he fought the urge to spring up out of bed, throw open the bathroom door and fuck her hard against the sink. He'd make sure to rub his hands over the fogged-up mirror so they could both watch as he took her, her tits swaying with each pump of his hips, bringing her body to the brink and beyond.

But instead, he lay there, his fist wrapped tight around his shaft, a paltry substitution for the lush thighs and warm, tight pussy that waited just feet away from him.

The bathroom door opened, and he held his breath. Was she coming into his room?

That first night they'd spent together, he hadn't wanted her in his bed, knew how messy it could all get. But now he didn't want her anywhere else.

The slight creak of Sophie's door opening and shutting told him she wasn't joining him.

He released his dick and stared up at the ceiling.

Fuck, why'd they have to bring up Colombia?

He hadn't thought about that mission in days. He'd been sleeping well since Isobel joined his bed, curled her warm body next to his and chased away his dreams with her feminine scent and softness.

Fuck Mercedes. Fuck Colton.

He ground the heels of his palms into his eyes in an attempt to banish the memories, but they all came flooding back, whipping into a froth inside him until he could see the flames, ten feet high, and hear the screams—and they were deafening.

Much like Colt was their team medic, Rob their lead point man and rifleman as well as their top diver, Aaron specialized in unconventional warfare. A *charmer,* as he'd often been called, he was sent in first to win the loyalty and cooperation of the locals. Both he and Rob were fluent in Spanish, so they were the two usually dispatched first, particularly when they were down in Central and South America. But Aaron's red hair and blue eyes made him an anomaly that people seemed to flock to, whereas Rob, who was half-Mexican with dark hair and dark eyes, blended in and didn't draw much attention.

Aaron flirted, played dominoes and kissed babies while Rob snuck into the back rooms and pried open file cabinets.

And that's exactly what he'd done in Colombia.

Aaron's job had been to plant a mole inside the Muñoz Cartel. Only he got too close to the mole and his family, and they paid the price dearly for his mistake.

They became his weakness.

His heart was open and vulnerable.

And vulnerability can be fatal.

For everyone involved.

The sound of a baby crying in the room next door infiltrated his memories—his recurring nightmare—and had him bolting out of bed and throwing open his door. He was across the hall and in Sophie's room seconds later, flicking on the overhead light.

Isobel had Sophie in her arms and was bouncing her gently. She squinted at him in confusion, her eyes sleepy, her dark hair a wild mess all around her slender shoulders. "What are you doing in here?" she asked, making shushing noises to Soph.

"I heard her cry."

She raised her eyebrows. "Yeah, babies cry. Not the first time, won't be the last."

Ignoring her sass, he walked over to stand next to them where she sat up in the bed, the bassinet on its stand on the other side. He put the back of his hand on Sophie's flushed red cheek, then her forehead. "Does she have a fever?"

Isobel pressed her lips to Sophie's forehead. "Maybe a little. We should give her some Tylenol."

He shook his head. "No, I need to get her to the hospital."

I need to save her.

He turned and headed back to his room to throw on clothes.

Her voice followed him, and soon she was standing in the doorway of his bedroom, watching him slide into a pair of jeans and a gray Henley. "What are you talking about? Babies get fevers. Go grab the thermometer from the bathroom and check her out. I bet it's not as high as you think. We'll give her some Tylenol, and I'll stay with her. If it gets worse, I'll take her in the morning. It is cold and flu season, after all. And she's a preemie, so she's immuno-compromised. It's just a cold. In some cases, you're worse off taking babies to the hospital because of all the disease-ridden and infectious people there. She's more likely to catch something at the hospital than anywhere else."

He fastened his belt buckle, slid into his shoes and stepped toward her. He snatched Sophie from Isobel's arms with a force he immediately regretted but didn't have time to apologize for. "If you're not going to take her health seriously, then maybe this isn't the job for you."

Isobel's jaw dropped open.

"I'm taking her to emergency." He elbowed her out of the way and headed for the garage. Within moments, he had a screaming Sophie in the back seat of his truck and was racing down the highway toward the hospital, not that he needed to. The roads were practically empty.

By the time he arrived, Sophie had cried herself to sleep, and Aaron was verging on a heart attack.

He'd never heard her scream so much in her life.

Something had to be wrong.

He paid for motherfucking parking, grabbed the bucket car seat from the back and jogged toward the emergency room doors, praying to God that he'd gotten there in time.

"It's just a cold and a mild fever," the doctor explained, wrapping his stethoscope back around his neck. "Not much you can do for her besides Tylenol, a nasal aspirator and some infant menthol ointment on her chest for any congestion. Lots of fluids too. Kids get sick, and because she's formula-fed rather than breastfed, she's not getting the antibody buildup. Not a biggie though. It just means you need to be a bit more diligent about getting people to wash their hands before they handle her."

All the oxygen fled his lungs on a big sigh of relief.

She was okay.

The doctor clapped him on the back and chuckled. "First-time dad?"

Aaron grunted. "Something like that."

"I get it. Even though I'm a doctor, I still lost my shit the first time my oldest got sick." He tossed his head back and laughed. "Now, with my fourth, if there isn't blood or a broken limb, they walk it off."

Aaron's pulse thundered in his ears.

Walk it off.

He didn't think he'd ever be able to tell Sophie to *walk it off*.

Was he turning into what they referred to as a helicopter parent?

"You can get the mentholated ointment at any drugstore, the same with a nasal aspirator. I know it sounds gross, but the NoseFrida really is the best. Sucks all the gunk out." He scribbled something down on a piece of paper and handed it to Aaron, his eyes kind and patient as they took in Aaron's frazzled demeanor, exhausted eyes and bedhead. "All four of my kids scream like they're being waterboarded when we do the NoseFrida, but it works like a hot damn." He tapped his pen twice on the edge of Sophie's car seat, pulled the curtain open, gave Aaron one more smile of reassurance, then left.

Sophie had fallen back to sleep after her exam, a new diaper and a bottle of formula, all kindly provided by one of the nurses. He'd left the house without a goddamn thing. Not even his wallet.

Father of the year right there.

Fuck.

He grabbed Sophie's car seat, pulled the curtain open and came face-to-face with her.

She'd thrown on a pair of black yoga pants and a gray hoodie, her hair was up in a messy bun, and she was in those ugly-ass Ugg-style boots. Didn't stop her from looking drop-dead fucking gorgeous though.

Fear flashed in her eyes. Her gaze dropped down to Sophie, fast asleep, then bounced back up to Aaron. "Is she okay?"

He cleared his throat. "Just a cold. Mild fever."

You were right. I'm an idiot.

She blew out a breath and relaxed her shoulders. Relief filled her eyes. "Oh good. I'm late getting here because I swung into the twenty-four-hour pharmacy to grab some more Tylenol, a nasal aspirator called the NoseFrida, and some baby Vicks." She held up the bag. "Figured if they had to keep her in overnight or something, you might need this stuff." She lifted one shoulder, then teetered back and forth on her feet.

"Thanks."

God, he was an asshole.

Nibbling on her bottom lip, Isobel fixed him with a look that hit him square in the solar plexus. "I'm sorry I dismissed your concerns. I shouldn't have."

You should not be the one apologizing.

"I'm glad Sophie is okay. Are you heading home?"

He nodded, unable to look her in the eye, and began to walk toward the automatic doors. She fell in line with him but didn't say anything.

He wasn't sure if that was worse or not. The fact that she was being so sweet and understanding, not bombarding him with questions or *I told you so*. Or maybe she was quiet because she was upset and getting ready to quit. He'd been a complete ass before he left the house, and she had every right to up and leave with no notice. Nothing but a middle finger over her shoulder as she went on to change and enrich the life of another family.

They stepped outside into the pouring Seattle rain. The fog had settled in as well and lent the early morning an eerie and ominous feel. A rather poetic thought for his current mood, which was dreary, muddled and all around fucked up.

Where had she parked? He didn't want to drive home without her. He didn't want to *be* without her.

"I'm parked over here," she said, pointing in the opposite direction of where his truck was. "I'll see you at the house?"

The house.

Not home.

The house.

Fuck.

He nodded. "Yeah, see you." Then, like the dumb fuck that he was, he carried Sophie to the truck, clicked her seat in, then walked to the fence that separated the hospital property from that of a commercial building next door. He punched a wet panel as hard as he could, sending damp splinters flying and causing the board to snap in two.

He climbed into the truck behind the steering wheel and lifted his bloody hand in front of him. The pain was a welcome distraction from the agony in his chest. The storm inside him that just would not pass.

Would it ever get easier?

He turned on the ignition, tossed it into first gear and peeled out of the parking lot, only to see Isobel standing there on the sidewalk watching him.

She'd seen the whole damn thing.

Fuck him.

Chapter 24

"Here," Isobel said, handing Aaron a bag of ice cubes wrapped in a kitchen towel. "For your hand." She placed it over his knuckles as he sat in his La-Z-Boy recliner and stared at the empty hearth. "When you're ready, let me bandage it up for you, please." She didn't wait for his answer and instead took off back into the kitchen.

They'd arrived home at roughly the same time.

Isobel had taken charge once again with Sophie, getting her out of her car seat without managing to wake her up and putting her back to bed in her bassinet.

It was still dark out, and the clock in the living room said three in the morning. They should both really try to get some sleep.

Aaron wouldn't be able to fucking sleep if he tried.

He wasn't sure how long he sat there staring blankly ahead, but when a lowball of amber liquid over ice entered his line of vision, he jumped.

Had he been sleeping with his eyes open?

Wouldn't be the first time.

Normally he had better senses than that. Tuned into his surroundings and the people around him. He hadn't heard her in the kitchen getting ice, hadn't heard her sneak up on him.

What the fuck was wrong with him?

"Figured you could use one," she said, her voice gentle. "That hand of yours has really taken a beating over the last while. First beating up those creeps from the bar, and now that poor defenseless fence." She snickered. "Defenseless fence ... ha ha."

He took the glass and drained it, letting the liquor slide down his throat into his gut and numb his rage. The afterburn was a pleasant reminder that contrary to how he often felt most days, he was in fact still alive and kicking.

"Everything okay?" she asked, having sobered from her corny joke. When she sat down on the coffee table across from him, he felt a calmness surround them. She was open to hearing whatever he had to say. Unlike him, who constantly had his walls up, she had let all of hers down and was willing to listen. Her smile was small but warm, and her soft eyes encouraged him to confide in her.

He couldn't.

Some shit he couldn't talk about.

The rest he didn't want to talk about.

He didn't want to talk about Colombia or the Velasquez family.

He didn't want to talk about Dina and how he was fucking up everything with Sophie.

For fuck's sake, he should have known better than to take a preemie baby into an ER unless she was coding or had a temperature over one hundred and three. Now, if Sophie *did* contract something and got sick, he'd never forgive himself.

Child protective services should just come and take her now before he really fucked up.

Isobel's gaze bounced down to where their knees were touching, and she casually moved hers to the right so that they were no longer against his. She set a bowl down next to her, then took his hand from beneath the bag of ice and ran her fingers over the cuts and bruises.

Aaron winced. He refused to look at her. "It's fine."

"I can clean it up for you, bandage it if you'd like. Just like you did for my finger." She held up the finger she'd cut from trying to open the beer bottle with a knife a few weeks ago and wiggled it. "See, good as new."

Her hands were so soft, so delicate and feminine.

He fought the urge to thread his fingers through hers and instead grunted and pulled his hand away. "I'm fine."

Why was she being so nice to him when he'd done nothing but treat her badly?

He didn't deserve her kindness, didn't deserve her patience.

He didn't deserve her.

Nodding, pursing her lips and exhaling a clear huff of frustration, she stood up. Her hands fell to her sides and her shoulders slumped, fatigue noticeable in every move she made. "Okay then, if you don't need help with your hand, then I'm going to go to bed. Let me know if you need anything." She made to walk past him, but Aaron's arm shot out and his hand landed on her belly before she could retreat. He splayed his fingers out, his pinky wedging beneath the elastic of her pants.

He knew he shouldn't.

He wasn't in the right headspace. Wasn't thinking clearly, wasn't in a good mood. But fuck, he needed to be in a better mood. He needed to feel something besides the rage and grief that were threatening to consume him.

She must have understood, because she didn't step away. He could feel her pulse beneath her skin, her breath in her abdomen. Slowly, he trailed his hand down her stomach, pushed it beneath the waistband of her yoga pants and panties and past the small patch of hair.

Her whimper and slight parting of her legs had his cock surging in his jeans.

Two fingers explored her folds. She was slick in no time. He flicked her clit, and her knees wobbled.

"Aaron ..." she breathed, clenching around his fingers when he pushed two inside her channel.

"Sit on my face," he murmured, removing his hands from her and sliding down to the floor into a sitting position. He helped her out of her hoodie and pants until she was in nothing but a light pink tank top—no bra—and nothing else.

Her nipples were diamond-hard, and a slight shiver ran through her as he took her hand and guided her over him. He reclined down and waited for her to position her cleft over him. She did. Warm drips of honey fell on his lips as she seated herself on his waiting mouth. He lapped them up, grabbed her ass cheeks, brought her pussy down to his tongue and demanded more.

"Oh God." Her fingers threaded their way into his hair, and she tugged. "Yes."

Yes, this was what he needed in order to forget the rest of the world. This was what he needed to clear his head. He needed to get lost in a good woman, in an incredible woman. She would exorcise the demons from his mind, banish the fury, replace his bloodlust with a lust of a different kind.

Her hips bucked, and the globes of her killer ass rocked and flexed in his palms. Fuck, she had a great ass. And it wasn't just a great ass to fuck. The way it filled out jeans, yoga pants, shorts, it was like two halves of a fucking cantaloupe tucked into lacy panties just waiting for his fingers to squeeze. His hand to mark.

Once she filled his mouth with her sweet nectar, he was going to flip her over the couch, bend her nearly in half and fuck her until his balls were empty. Maybe then he could finally get some fucking sleep.

He twiddled his tongue relentlessly over her clit, back and forth, back and forth. She liked that. Made her gush even more, made her hips go all crazy-like and her fingers tighten in his hair, tugging until a snap of pain sprinted down his neck.

She was close.

His fingers crept along the round globe of her ass and one pushed her cheeks apart. He pressed against her anus. She didn't flinch or pull away. Dipping his digit down lower to gather some of her wetness, he trailed it back up between her crease before finally pushing in, breaching her rosette and feeling her tighten around him.

She moaned above him, the movement of her hips growing more and more erratic.

"Gonna come," she mewled, swirling her cleft over his mouth and causing his nose to knock her clit. "Gonna come so hard."

He pushed another finger into her ass, went ape-shit on her clit with his tongue, and she combusted. A gush like never before poured into his mouth from her pussy, drenching his face. He swallowed as much as he could, loving her flavor and how easily she came.

Once she released his hair and swung her body off his, he rolled over and stood up. Her eyes were out of focus and her cheeks flushed as she watched him unfasten his jeans just enough to get his dick out. He grabbed her by the arm, hauled her to her feet, bent her over the couch and drove home.

No pleasantries, no wasting time. He needed to fuck, and he needed to fuck now.

Aaron let out a grunt as he sank balls-deep into her slick heat, her body instantly contracting around his.

"Condom," she breathed, turning around to face him, her eyes no longer out of focus and instead filled with panic.

Fuck.

Fuck!

FUCK!

He pulled back out.

"Shit. Sorry."

"It's okay."

Was it okay to continue? Is that what she meant? Could they raw-dog it?

No, you fucker. You need to get tested. It's been a while. She needs to get tested, and you have no clue if she's even on any birth control.

Had they talked at all?

Nope, they hadn't. They'd just fucked. Not talking, just fucking.

Wow, he was a real class act.

She was still bent over the couch, ass in the air, glancing back at him, waiting patiently.

"Be right back." He took off down the hall to his bedroom, grabbed a condom from the dresser and was back in the living room in a flash.

She hadn't moved.

Well, she *had*, but it was only to move one hand between her legs.

Aaron groaned as he watched her touch herself. He ripped the condom packet open, slid it on, grabbed her hips and sank in balls-deep once again.

Fuck, it'd been so much better without the condom. Even that brief second where there was nothing between them had been pure fucking heaven.

He began to move, hard, really hard, slamming into her, taking all of her. The sound of flesh slapping flesh filled the dark, quiet living room. Her fingers still worked her clit, and every so often, she'd reach back and scrape her nails over his swinging nut sac, making his knees turn to jelly.

He palmed her ass cheeks, then slipped two fingers back into her tight hole.

Nothing was fucking hotter than the full visual of watching either fingers or a cock slide in and out of a gorgeous ass. Nothing.

"That's right, baby. Fucking take it," he ground out, baring his teeth. "So fucking hot. So fucking sexy, Iz."

She clenched her muscles around him, her pussy quivering on every plunge, squeezing on every draw. She was already fucking close.

Jesus Christ, how many times could this woman come a day?

He pumped his hips harder and faster into her, wanting to empty his nuts, needing to feel a release.

"Oh God, Aaron," she whispered, turning back around to face him, her eyes glassy and cheeks flushed.

With his free hand, he reached forward and pulled out her messy bun, snapping the hair elastic in the process. Her hair fell wild and free around her shoulders, hiding her face in a veil of dark silk.

He gathered up as much of her hair as he could into a tight ponytail, tugging hard until her neck arched back.

"That's right, baby. Just like that."

"Gonna come." Her voice broke with a sharp cry as her body went rigid and her pussy began to tremble around him. Wetness dripped down onto his balls as she continued to come, her body convulsing and spasming from the climax.

Aaron's sac tightened up, his belly did a flip-flop, and he let go. Leaning over, he sank his teeth into her shoulder at the same time he came. Warmth flooded his abdomen and bright stars shot behind his closed eyelids as wave after wave crashed through him until he was beaten and bruised and utterly spent.

He collapsed against her back, kissed the spot he'd bitten, then continued to kiss down her spine until he was forced to pull his fingers from her and tie off the condom. He kissed both cheeks of her ass a few times too, because he really couldn't get enough of them, before he helped her up.

He took off toward the bathroom to dispose of the condom and wash his face. He wasn't sure what to expect when he returned to the living room. He wasn't sure if Isobel was going to want to talk or what, but what he hadn't expected was to find the living room empty.

Had she gone to bed?

Was she in her room or Sophie's?

Could he open up Sophie's door to check?

Should he?

If she was in there, what would he say? *Hey, thanks for the fuck, but I'd rather not talk right now. I'm pretty fucked in the head.*

Oh yeah, that would go over *so* well.

He glanced at the bowl she'd brought over. It held a damp washcloth, dry cloth, antibiotic ointment, gauze and bandages. He grabbed it all and stalked to the bathroom to go and patch himself up.

It wouldn't be easy, as he was right-handed and it was his right hand that was all cut up. He really should have just let her do it for him. She offered, after all.

She offered a lot.

And she asked for so little in return.

All she asked for was respect, and he struggled to even show her that.

Even though he really did respect the hell out of her.

Why was it so hard to give her what she wanted?

He stared at himself in the bathroom mirror. What looked back was a scarred, angry man. A confused man. A fuck-up. A failure.

He had nothing to offer anybody. Least of all an incredible person like Isobel.

He did a half-assed job cleaning up his hand, and before frustration got the better of him, he flicked off the light and went out to the living room again.

He wouldn't be able to sleep in his bed knowing Isobel was just across the hall, all warm and soft, smelling of the sex they'd just had.

He needed space.

He needed help.

Chapter 25

It was Friday evening.

Dina's service was Saturday.

All day, Aaron had been a fucking wreck.

Thankfully, Colton understood, as did all the men at the job site, and they gave Aaron a wide berth. He was a shaken-up bottle of Coke, and his cap was half screwed off. It wouldn't take much to set him off.

So when he pulled into his driveway and saw an unknown car parked behind Isobel's car, anger and confusion raced through him.

Who the fuck was here?

He grabbed a beer from the mini-fridge in the garage, slammed it back in two sips, shut his eyes for sixty seconds and grounded himself.

He couldn't be this enraged when he walked in the door.

It wasn't fair to Sophie.

It wasn't fair to Isobel.

It wasn't fair to anybody.

He opened one more beer, finished it in one and a half guzzles, grabbed another, then headed into the house.

Laughter and baby noises filled the air, along with the smell of Italian spices and soft rock.

The house was warm, cozy almost.

Had she turned on the heat?

He never turned on the heat.

Put a fucking sweater on and an extra pair of socks if you're cold. Heat costs money.

At least that's how he'd been brought up in the foster care system, and then how he and Dina continued to live once they were on their own and with barely two pennies to rub together.

He made his way into the living room, where Isobel was sitting on the floor next to a woman probably in her late fifties, both of them staring lovingly at Sophie, who was doing some tummy time on her play mat.

A low, burning fire crackled in the fireplace with one of those fire logs.

He'd cleaned the chimney when he first moved in but hadn't had it in him to light a fire yet. He'd avoided fire altogether—besides the barbecue—since that night in Medellin. Since the house.

Where had she gotten the fire log? What gave her the right?

Isobel looked up, her blue eyes sparkling and full of joy. "Hey! You're home. How was work?"

Why did a question like that pull so hard at his heartstrings?

Because nobody since Dina has given two shits about your day, and it's nice to know somebody cares.

It also instantly dissolved a good chunk of his ire. He'd been ready to fight—who? He didn't know. But he'd entered the house with his hackles up, and then when he saw the fire, his anger had doubled, and he instantly needed to tear a strip off someone. But her words, her eyes, her smile and her kindness soothed the uncontrolled inferno inside him.

He was still angry, but he was no longer out for blood.

She stood up and wandered toward him. "My parents came to visit. They wanted to meet Sophie, as I can't stop talking about her."

Parents.

The sound of a toilet flushing, faucet running and door opening drew his attention down the hall. A big shadow appeared from the bathroom door. A *very* big shadow.

"These are my parents, Calvin and Harriet Jones."

The big shadow revealed himself to be a tall, broad man with dark hair and blue eyes. Hard blue eyes that immediately knew every one of Aaron's faults, secrets and *desires*.

Fuck.

Isobel's father stuck out his hand, his eyes still hard. "Calvin Jones. Nice to meet you."

Aaron swallowed, clenched his jaw and shook the man's hand. Jesus, his grip was tight.

"You have a lovely home." Isobel's mother's voice was soft and melodic like her daughter's. "And Sophie is just a little angel." She glanced down at Sophie, who was wriggling on her belly, flailing her limbs in every direction. She looked like she was in distress, but after the first time Isobel did tummy time with her and reassured him that babies needed this, he let her writhe—until she started to squawk in frustration. Then he scooped her up and did the rest of tummy time on his chest. She seemed to like it better there anyway.

"My parents popped into town for a visit," Isobel continued, chewing on the corner of her bottom lip, her eyes full of hope and joy as she looked up at him, "and well ... if you're okay with it, they offered to watch Soph tomorrow."

Aaron's brows furrowed. "Why?"

"So I can go to the service with you. Support you. It's really no place for a newborn."

"Dina's her mother." Heat rushed into his gut, and his back snapped straight. Of course Sophie was going to be there.

Isobel took a step toward him, her eyes gentle, her face wary. "I understand why you want her there, but she's still recovering from her cold. Her immune system is weak, compromised, and getting her around all those people who will undoubtably want to touch and hold her, it's not a good idea."

"I'll wear her. Put her in that wrap thing. There, problem solved."

A big, meaty palm landed on Aaron's shoulder, and he fought the urge to flinch it off. "Son, listen to Izzy. She knows what she's talking about. There are going to be lots of people there. You don't want to get little Soph any sicker." Calvin's voice was low and clear. The man was obviously used to giving orders and having them followed, no questions asked.

Well, so was Aaron.

"We've done the baby thing before. Not our first rodeo," Calvin went on.

Aaron gnashed his molars together so hard, he thought he might chip a tooth. His grip on his beer bottle made his knuckles ache.

His body stiffened; shoulders cinched up nearly to his ears. Calvin released his hold on Aaron's shoulder.

"I invited them to stay for dinner," Isobel went on. "That way they can get to know Sophie a bit before tomorrow."

The beep of the timer in the kitchen drew her attention, and she dashed away, slipping on oven mitts and pulling out what looked like chicken parmesan from the oven.

His stomach rumbled in anticipation of being full. He hadn't eaten anything all day.

Calvin had made his way into the living room and was down on the floor with Harriet and Sophie, the two of them with big smiles on their faces and making cooing noises at the now face-up Sophie, whose limbs still jerked and wiggled spastically.

Aaron took off toward the kitchen.

"I would have appreciated a heads-up instead of being ambushed," he whispered, his tone harsh. He was so close to her, he could smell her shampoo. He took a much-needed step back.

They hadn't had sex since that night after he'd taken Sophie to the hospital. They'd barely spoken since. His doing, not hers.

He didn't know what to say to her. Didn't know how to go about this whole thing. The dad thing. The boyfriend thing. The living together thing. The grieving thing. He was fucking it all up left and right.

Because he fucked everything up.

Always did.

People who got close to him got hurt, so it was only a matter of time before he failed Soph. Before he failed Isobel.

He needed to keep her away so that she couldn't get hurt.

What a load of shit.

By doing so, he was effectively hurting her.

It was all so fucked up.

Needless to say, things had been awkward during the day and lonely at night.

Very lonely. He missed her.

He missed the noises she made when she was close to coming. Missed the faint sigh of contentment that broke past her lips when she slept, the smell of her hair as it fell across his chest. Her softness. Fuck, she was just so soft. Like satin beneath his fingers—everywhere.

She set the casserole dish of chicken parm down on a hot pad, removed the oven mitts and turned to face him. "It wasn't an ambush. I live here too. Am I not allowed to have people over? To have my *parents* over? Besides, we need somebody to watch Sophie tomorrow. Who better than two heavily qualified people who have raised two daughters of their own?"

He gritted his teeth. "I don't like walking in not knowing who is in my house."

She shook her head and turned back to the stove, where she pulled a pot of steamed broccoli off the element. "I've been pretty cool about all the shit you've thrown at me these last few weeks. Particularly the last few days. Pretty damn cool, but I'm getting tired of it. I'm a good person, a kind person, but everybody has their limit of how much shit and abuse they're willing to put up with before they start throwing it all back over the fence.

"I never said a damn word about the other night after you took Sophie to the hospital, not a one. I let you use me, because it was what you needed. And because I ..." She paused, her back going stiff. "Because it was what I needed too. But I'm done." She turned back to face him. Pain flashed behind the blue in her eyes before they hardened. Now they were exactly like her father's. "I told you I was okay with our *arrangement* as it was, but that didn't even seem to be good enough for you. I give more, you take more, demand more and give less and less in return. I don't know a damn thing about you. Except that you've got the whole *asshole* routine down pat."

Worry tickled the back of his neck. He wanted to reach out to her, slam her body up against the counter, capture her mouth and give her back everything he'd taken from her.

But he had to stop using sex as his only real form of communication.

Problem was, he didn't really know any other way to express himself, to express how he felt about her, how much he wanted her, needed her. The woman was like oxygen, water, food and shelter—all of life's necessities rolled into one perfect little package.

So why couldn't he tell her that?

She pushed her shoulders back. "I'm going to start looking for my replacement."

No.

Dread dropped like a steamship anchor in his gut. He was going to be sick.

"I'll stay as long as I can, until someone else suitable is found, but I don't think this is working anymore. I thought I could help you. Thought I could glue some of the pieces back together in your life. Not fix you but help show you that you aren't broken to begin with. Just a little bit banged up, chipped away at. But you're making it damn near impossible. I love Sophie, and I love—" Her lip wobbled, but she caught it between her teeth, exhaled deeply through her nose before continuing. "And I love being in her life, but I can't work for you anymore. How you've treated my parents just now and their generous offer to help is the final straw. I've waffled with this decision all week, and your rudeness in there helped me make my decision. I'm a good person, Aaron, but I'm not a doormat."

Her words grew legs, kicked him hard in the belly and drove all the breathable air from his lungs.

Her glare faded, her eyes turned glassy, and her throat bobbed on a hard swallow. "Consider this my notice."

Isobel fought the urge to wince as Aaron's fingers gripped her shoulders and he shook her, fear burning in his dark blue eyes.

"You can't quit," he gritted, trying to whisper so as to not draw attention to them in the kitchen but clearly struggling. "You can't."

She dropped her gaze to his feet. It was easier than looking into his pained eyes. "I can't go on like this, Aaron. I can't."

A dark and surly noise rumbled deep in his throat. "Please."

"Tell me about Colombia. What happened? Why does Mercedes think it's something I need to know?"

If he expected her to give him her heart, to give him chance after chance to prove he was more than just the angry, grieving bugger he claimed to be, he needed to give her something in return. She didn't necessarily expect his heart—yet, but she expected him to trust her. She expected the truth. She expected him to confide in her and not just treat her like a nanny, a housekeeper and a concubine.

His mouth tightened, and fear flashed behind the deep blue in his eyes. "I can't," he ground out.

She glanced down between them at the floor. "Then I can't."

"Have you guys seen the news?" Isobel's father's voice entered the kitchen.

Isobel's head snapped up from Aaron's feet to find her father behind them at the edge of the kitchen, his own gaze intense and curious.

Aaron released her arms and fixed her with a pleading stare. "Please, Iz. Don't. Can we talk after dinner? Colombia was ..." He sucked in a sharp breath. "Colombia is not something I can talk about. But we need to *talk*."

She clenched her teeth and nodded, though there wasn't much he could say at this point to change her mind. She hadn't discussed everything with her parents, but she'd hashed it all out with Tori and the women at Paige's bistro over the past week, and they were all of the same mindset. Aaron was too damaged, and he needed to want to heal before she could even attempt to help him.

"Apparently there's been a slew of jewelry store robberies and carjackings taking place in the area over the past few weeks. Cops can't tell if it's an organized thing or not," her father continued. "You know to lock all your doors the moment you get in your car, right?"

"Yes, Dad," she sighed, distracted by Aaron and his visceral reaction to her giving him her notice. "I've been following the case."

It'd been several weeks now, and still they hadn't come any closer to catching the criminals. And now, the criminals weren't just robbing stores, they were jacking cars too. In the last ten days, two more jewelry stores had been hit, and the last time one of the clerks had been shot—not fatally, thankfully. So far, the news hadn't reported anything about any store owners whipping out guns. Though, unless they caught the guy or guys, it was only a matter of time.

"Right, my little mystery buff," her father continued. "You know to take your keys with you when you pump gas, lock your doors then too?"

She rolled her eyes. "Every time, Dad."

He stared at his phone. "Something fishy is going on with all these carjackings. Gonna talk to my buddy down at the precinct, see what he knows."

Isobel shook her head. Just like her, her father was addicted to the news. She got her love of crime and mystery from him. They often shared novels and would discuss them in depth over the phone after they'd both had a chance to read them.

A former Army Ranger and now security specialist, her dad always wanted to know how criminals got past high-tech security features, how they managed to thwart the experts.

"Dinner's almost ready, Dad," she said, stepping away from Aaron and the intense heat that radiated off his muscular frame. He smelled like sawdust, sweat and manliness. It was an intoxicating combination she needed to get as far away from as quick as possible. "Just need to toss the Caesar salad." She grabbed the bottle she'd prepared for Sophie off the counter and walked over to hand it to her dad. "Here's Soph's bottle if you or Mom would like to feed her."

Her father was a very astute man, always watching, always observing. No way was he ignorant to the vibe he'd just walked in on. "You okay, Izzy?" he asked under his breath. He was the only person she allowed to call her that. She typically hated the nickname, preferred her full name or *Iz*, but when her dad called her Izzy, she didn't mind one bit. "Need me to have a talk with him?"

She rolled her eyes. "It's okay, Dad, I've got this."

His lips flattened into a thin line, but his eyes, the same shade as hers and Tori's, softened. "He's hurting, sweetheart."

Wait, what?"

Her pinched brows must have given away her shock at her father defending Aaron.

"Remember when Nana died?"

Yeah, her father had been an absolute wreck. He'd escaped to their family cabin for a week, going completely off the grid.

"Multiply that by a million, then add a baby on top, and that doesn't even begin to describe the pain he's feeling. Cut him some slack."

Well, holy crap. She never in a million years would have expected to hear those words out of her father.

According to her mother, Calvin Jones had been a hard-headed, stubborn SOB with a real chip on his shoulder and an ego the size of Jupiter when the two of them had met. Her mother had actually tried to shake her father, break up with him and find somebody less—*dark,* as her mother put it. But her dad had been persistent. He wooed her mother, changed his ways, softened a bit and showed her a humbler side of himself.

It obviously worked, because the two had been married for what felt like forever, and they still seemed madly in love with each other to boot.

Though it took having children, particularly two very girly little girls, to really brought out her father's soft side. Calvin Jones was not afraid to play tea party, get his toes painted or dress up as a princess for Halloween when Tori wanted to go as the evil queen and Isobel decided she wanted to be a carrot (last minute) instead of the matching princess to her father.

"Maybe we should take little Sophie for a walk in her stroller so the two of you can talk," he offered, glancing out the window into the backyard. "It's not raining—for once. Might be nice to get the wee one some fresh air."

Isobel shook her head. "I can't ask you guys to postpone your dinner. Aaron and I can talk later."

Her father shook his head. "Naw, we'll be okay. We had a late lunch. Went to that Lilac and Lavender Bistro you and Tori have been raving about." His eyes went saucer-size. "We'll definitely be going back before we leave this weekend. I want like five of those sfogliatelle things."

Isobel lifted up onto her tiptoes and pecked her father on the cheek. "Thanks, Dad, but we'll be all right. Dinner in five, okay?"

He lifted one bushy eyebrow and cupped her cheek, then turned and took the bottle into the living room. Isobel and Aaron were once again in the kitchen alone—save for the tension hanging over them as well as her tendered resignation. Yeah, dinner was going to be a blast.

Chapter 26

Aaron filled up the kitchen sink with hot soapy water, put the chicken parm pan in to soak, then went to work putting the remainder of the dinner dishes in the dishwasher. Isobel and her mother had taken Sophie for a bath while Isobel's father said he had a few emails he needed to catch up on and went to go sit in the living room with his phone.

Aaron was a mess.

Although Isobel had been completely pleasant all through dinner, chatting with her parents, holding a fussy Sophie while eating with one hand and smiling across the living room at Aaron, things had been anything but relaxing. At least for him.

All through their meal, he kept trying to imagine her not sitting with him every night eating dinner, and he couldn't. He couldn't imagine her not there. Didn't want to imagine her not there.

He couldn't lose her. He just couldn't.

And not just as Sophie's nanny. He couldn't lose her from his bed, his house, his life.

A throat cleared behind him.

"Need somebody to dry?"

There weren't any dishes to dry, save for the chicken parm pan, and that was soaking. From the short amount of time Aaron had spent with Calvin, he knew the man wasn't an idiot. He just needed something to break the ice.

Aaron grunted, opened up the fridge and pulled out a beer, twisting off the cap and giving it to Calvin.

He grunted his own thanks and tipped it up for a long sip, eyeing Aaron over the bottle as he did. Finally, he pulled the bottle down, wiped the back of his wrist over his mouth and leaned back against the counter with a loud "Ah."

Aaron had spied the rest of the chicken parm in a Tupperware container on the counter and was tempted to cut himself another piece—Isobel made an amazing chicken parmigiana—but instead, he grabbed himself a beer from the fridge as well and opened it.

"You into all these microbrew beers that seem to be popping up everywhere?" Calvin asked, scrutinizing the San Camanez Island wheat ale label.

Aaron swallowed his beer. "Some of them."

Calvin made a face that said he wasn't of the same opinion. "I'm a Bud man, myself. Not sold on these fancy beers. Raspberry Sour. Apricot Saison. Chocolate Orange Ale." He wrinkled his nose. "Fruit doesn't belong in beer unless it's a lime down the neck of a Corona. And a Corona only belongs in my hand if I'm in Mexico. That shit tastes like horse piss. Same color too."

Aaron nodded and frowned in agreement. "Never could stomach the stuff myself." His head tilted down toward the floor, and he bent down to pick up a piece of fallen romaine lettuce from the salad.

"You like her, don't you?"

He nearly threw his back out with how fast he popped back up.

Calvin raised on eyebrow. "Love her?"

Aaron thought he was going to be sick. "Excuse me, sir?"

His other eyebrow joined the first. "Sir? Now there's a good start. You know, I see a lot of myself in you. Angry, hard, lost. I served too. Still haunted by a lot of the shit I saw and even more by the shit I did. Shit I can't talk about with anybody."

"Mr. Jones, I—" Aaron started.

But Calvin cut him off, continuing on with his speech, his level gaze telling Aaron he wasn't a man who appreciated being interrupted. "I hated the world for a long time. Had a big ego too. Figured I jumped out of airplanes, shot machine guns, drove tanks, I'm fucking invincible."

Aaron swallowed. Had he blinked?

He blinked.

His eyes burned.

"You know what though? You know what brought me to my knees, made me a real man, made me show more than just one emotion—the emotion that society says is the only one okay for men to truly express—having a good woman at my back. She showed me that real men are more than just angry. And then having two baby girls made me a fucking marshmallow. I've never cried more in my life than the days those two girls were born." He took another sip of his beer. "Okay, well, maybe when they graduated college. I was a fucking mess then too."

Why was he telling Aaron all of this? What was his point?

He must have read his mind. "I'm telling you all of this, son, because I was like you once. I nearly lost the best thing that had ever happened to me because I let my anger consume me. I know it's not the same, but right before I met Harriet, I lost my best friend. He killed himself shortly after we were discharged and returned home. He'd lost both his legs and couldn't cope with the change, couldn't cope with any of it. I blamed myself for not being there for him. I had my legs, had a good job and I was busy chasing skirts. Perhaps if I'd gone over more than once a week for a couple hours, I would have known how much pain he was in, how bad it really was. I let the grief and pain morph into anger and hate—because somehow it felt more acceptable to be angry at the world than sad. To hate the world rather than feel pain and loss because someone I loved was no longer a part of my world. I let the rage consume me. I nearly lost Harriet because of it."

"You had a family though, right?" Aaron gritted his teeth. How dare he compare their stories? Yes, losing a brother in arms was hard, but Aaron lost his sister. His blood. His only family.

It was not the same.

Calvin guzzled his beer, then put the empty bottle down on the counter. "Yep. Had a supportive mom, dad, sister, brother. So?"

"I had no family. I *have* no family."

"You have Sophie."

He could feel the rage beginning to bubble up inside him. He finished his beer and set his bottle down on the counter, bunching his fists at his sides and squeezing his jaw tight.

Calvin's head cocked to the side, and his eyes flicked down to Aaron's hands.

"That a bag in the garage?" he asked.

Aaron grunted.

He jerked his head. "Let's go."

His feet moved before he knew what he was doing.

"You got a lot of anger in there, son. Need to let it out somehow. Last place it should be directed at is a woman as kind, sweet and patient as Izzy. That girl has a heart made of gold with a marshmallow center." He opened the door to the garage and allowed Aaron to walk ahead of him. He grabbed Aaron's gloves off the hook, tossed them to him and then walked around to stand behind the bag.

Aaron pulled his T-shirt over his head so he was just in his black tank top and cargo shorts. He slipped on the gloves.

"Show me what you got, son." Calvin grinned, holding the bag steady.

Aaron bounced back and forth on his toes a few times before delivering a hard right cross to the bag. It didn't even jiggle. His cut-up, now scabbed-over hand from earlier in the week hurt like a bitch though. Why he decided to pick a fight with a fence panel ... fuck, he was a dumb fuck.

He shook it off and cracked his neck side to side, bouncing back on his toes.

Calvin pursed his lips together. "That all you got, son? Come on, a man like you, you've got more in there. I can see it. Let it all out."

Jab.

Jab.

Jab, jab.

"That's right. That's better. More. Let me see the rage. Let me see you seethe. Let it out."

Aaron hopped back on his toes, then stepped forward and drove his right fist into the bag in another right cross. Pain exploded across the top of in his hand.

Calvin lost his footing and stumbled back. "Good. Good." He caught the swinging bag and regained his position behind it. "Show me some kicks. Pretend the bag is my face. Really knock out my teeth."

Ignoring the pain shooting up his arm from his probably now bleeding knuckles, Aaron stepped back, bounced, turned to the side and then delivered an intense left side kick, once again knocking Calvin off his feet.

"Nice. Again."

Aaron did it again, this time with the right.

"Family is what you make it. It doesn't have to be the blood coursing through your veins that makes you a family. A family is made up of people who love you and who you love. People who have your back, who are there for you when the chips are down. Yes, Sophie is your blood—your niece, your daughter—but I know that there are a lot of people out there who would consider you family if you'd let them. If you let them in."

Aaron stopped, wiped his wrist over his sweaty forehead. "You talking about Isobel?"

"Izzy, Mark, Tori. All those single dads."

Shit, how much had Isobel told her parents?

"I can see the way she looks at you."

Aaron averted his eyes. He'd never really gotten close enough to a woman to have to deal with her father giving him the *hurt my baby, I'll hurt you* talk.

"I'm not one of those dads who blocks the threshold, crosses his arms over his chest, tells you about my gun locker, my knife collection and says that if you hurt my baby, I'll break your neck," Calvin said. Aaron met his gaze once again. The man appeared almost bored. "I raised my girls to be strong, independent women who can take care of themselves. They don't need their father threatening boys on their behalf. They can do that all on their own. I taught them self-defense, encouraged them to learn how to fight properly, take down a man twice their size if need be. Raised warrior princesses so they can rescue themselves from the tower, slay the dragon and claim the throne. We're merely their sidekicks, not their heroes."

Aaron's lip twitched. "Isobel has already read me the riot act about the fact that there are no such things as a *man's job* or a *woman's job*. She's tough as nails. She could definitely hold her own in a fight."

Calvin tossed his head back and laughed, slapping his thigh. The corners of his eyes crinkled, and his blue eyes glowed with love in the fluorescent lighting of the garage. "That's my baby girl. I raised her right."

"You certainly did."

Calvin sobered. "She's tough, but he's also soft-hearted. Been burned before because she let that empathy of hers cloud her judgement. Was nearly abducted as a kid when some man at the park convinced her his puppy was lost and he needed her to help him. Always tries to see the good in people, even when there isn't any."

Aaron stumbled where he stood, and a fear like he'd never felt before dropped like a lead weight in his gut. God, what if that was Sophie? He would lose his damn mind.

Calvin saw the fear cross his face and simply nodded. "Yep. Tori scared the guy off, thankfully. But Izzy's always been the bleeding heart. She gave her lunch away every day for a year to the homeless woman and her dog living on the edge of the school field. Never told a soul. Never complained about being hungry, never asked for more food in her lunch. She just gave it away. Sacrificed for another. Because that's who she is, that's who she'll always be. She puts everyone else ahead of herself. Even when her brain is telling her not to, her heart is telling her it's what she needs to do. She's always listened to her heart over her head."

Heat, not from his rounds with the punching bag, wormed its way up Aaron's chest. Why was Calvin telling him all of this?

"Izzy will risk hurting her own heart to save someone else's," Calvin continued, a slight edge to his tone. "She'll put her own happiness aside, always has. It's just who she is." His blue eyes turned dark, and he stared directly at Aaron, allowing everything to sink in.

It was a warning.

Aaron nodded and swallowed. "Understood, sir."

Calvin's smile was small but genuine. "Good."

He exhaled, then gripped the bag in front of him again, encouraging Aaron to start punching. Aaron began to hop back and forth on his feet, jabbing at the bag once again.

"Raising girls is hard," Calvin went on. He ran his hand through his short dark hair, his eyes going wide. "Especially during puberty. Holy shit. The hormones. The drama." He shook his head. "The mood swings. Oh brother, the mood swings. I'm going to tell you right now, always, *always* have tampons, Midol and chocolate in the glove compartment of your truck." Then his eyes softened, and he seemed to be seeing something buried in his memories as a serene smile slid across his mouth. "But it's so worth it. My girls are daddy's girls through and through. We text every day, send pictures and jokes. Talk on the phone weekly. I'd do anything for my babies—anything." He released the bag and stepped around it. "And you'd do the same for Sophie. You might not be her father, but you're all she's got." His head tilted to the side. "Unless you let other people in. Unless you build her a family, build her a village full of people who you can lean on, who *she* can lean on. People who love her. You don't have to do this alone. You don't have to be all she has, and she doesn't have to be all you have."

Aaron used his teeth to untie one of his gloves, slipped it off, opened the mini-fridge and grabbed a bottle of water. "Why are you telling me all of this?"

"Like I said, I see the way Izzy looks at you. She loves you, and I don't want to see my baby get hurt. I don't like your energy right now. You've got a lot of anger and hate in your heart, but I can see a lot of good in you as well. There's a lot of good buried beneath all the pain."

Aaron's hand paused midair, the water bottle poised inches from his mouth. "She doesn't love me."

Calvin's eyes narrowed. "I know my daughter. I see how she is with you. How she is with that baby."

Aaron shook his head, turned away and took a sip of the water. "She's in love with the *idea* of what this is. She's a domestic at heart. Wants the white picket fence, the house, the family, the dog, the weekend dinner parties. That's what she's in love with. She's not in love with me."

Calvin rolled his eyes and shook his head. "Then you're a bigger fool than I thought if you can't see it." He tossed Aaron his other glove again. "You got another pair around here? Do we need to go a couple rounds so I can knock some sense into you?"

He liked Calvin. Liked him a lot, actually. He reminded Aaron of Rob's dad Malcolm: to the point, rough around the edges, but with a real, genuine heart at the center of it all. He was the kind of man Aaron wished he'd had growing up. A real father figure to look up to.

Aaron opened up a small cabinet and pulled out another set of gloves. "You think you can take me, old man?"

Calvin's mouth split into a big grin. "Old man? Oh, son, I'll have you flat on your ass before you can blink, just you wait and see."

A short while later, covered in sweat, Aaron and Calvin left the garage, both of them smiling and tipping up beer.

"Ah, you were already warmed up," Calvin said with a laugh, slapping Aaron on the back and resting his hand on his shoulder for a moment. "I demand a rematch after I've stretched and gone for a light jog."

Aaron grinned as he took another sip of his beer. "You're on."

A quick glance in the kitchen and living room told him that Isobel and her mother were most likely down the hall in Sophie's room.

Aaron and Calvin walked into the living room and took a seat, Aaron offering his preferred La-Z-Boy to Calvin, which the man was grateful for.

"I don't know what the mission was that you're holding on to, but you've got to let it go." Calvin leveled his steely blue eyes on Aaron. "I know you've got one. We've all got one. That mission that was our last mission. Or the one that we can't let go of because we either failed or could have done more. We all have that mission. We all have that cross to bear, that load to carry on our shoulders for the rest of our lives. It came with the territory."

Why did he get the feeling Calvin Jones knew more about Aaron's past than he was letting on? The man certainly had a way about him that spoke of cunning, intelligence and stealth. Maybe he'd figured out a way to look into Aaron's time with the Navy.

He wouldn't know about Colombia, hell no. That shit was classified. But maybe he knew other things, other missions that Aaron had been a part of.

"You need to let that shit go," Calvin continued, his eyes softening. "Don't let it eat you up until there's nothing left of you but a husk of a man. Sophie deserves more than that. She deserves a daddy who is present and accounted for, not off living in the past, focusing on his failures." He hinged forward in his seat and looked Aaron square in the eyes. "Because, son, we all have 'em. We all have failures. We all have fuck-ups. But it's those of us who choose not to let those fuck-ups run our lives that still manage to find joy in the world, still manage to go on and live full lives with wives and children, friends and family. Choose joy, son. Choose to live a full life. Look to the future, not the past. Don't let the demons win."

Aaron's mouth dropped open, but his throat seized, and he was unable to speak. Hot tears burned at the back of his eyes, and he shut his mouth and gnashed his molars together until he could hear them squeak.

Calvin watched him. Didn't say anything for a moment but simply sat there, still hinged forward, elbows on his knees, and watched Aaron. Watched him battle with everything going on in his head, in his heart.

The man kept calling him *son*.

Normally, he hated when somebody called him that. He'd never been anybody's son, hated the façade that the term of endearment painted. And yet, when Calvin called him *son*, Aaron didn't hate it. It didn't sound like rocks in a blender the way it usually did. It sounded ... right.

Calvin cleared his throat, drawing Aaron from his thoughts. "You know, son, I have to thank you. Izzy told us what you did to save her and Mercedes that night." Calvin cradled his beer bottle between both hands and looked up at Aaron. Genuine fear clouded his eyes. "You saved those girls. Truly. Sure, Izzy knows some self-defense, and it might be able to help her in a mugging or in a one-on-one type situation, but you and I both know she couldn't have taken down both those guys. Not on her own, not after being drugged. I got connections at the precinct. Those fuckers are going to get theirs. Charges of assault, kidnapping, attempted rape, possession of illegal substance. We'll hang 'em up by their sacs and watch 'em swing."

That punishment was too good for men who hurt women. Those two motherfuckers didn't deserve to breathe the same air as Isobel—as any woman.

Aaron bared his teeth and sniffed. "The thought of their hands on her, sir ... Colton had to pull me off them or I would have ..." He picked at the beer label with his dirty, work-worn fingernails, unable to look the older gentleman in the eye. "I hate that I wasn't able to get there sooner."

Calvin's gaze turned gentle. "You got there in time. What matters is that you got there."

He swallowed, then finally lifted his head. "I wouldn't be able to live with myself if something had happened to her. I—" Aaron wiped a hand over his mouth and scratched at his close-shaved beard, stopping himself from saying anything more. Anything he might regret.

Calvin sat back in the chair and took another sip of his beer. "You know, even if you don't come to your senses about Izzy and how much you love her, realize how much she loves you, let go of some of that anger and embrace all the good life has to offer, I could never hate you. Probably could never even really be mad at you. I hope you don't break her heart, though, I really do." He let out a sigh. His head fell against the headrest, and he shut his eyes for a moment. "You saved my baby girl. I am forever in your debt. Anytime, any place, anything, you need it, just ask." He opened his eyes and pinned them on Aaron. "And I mean that."

Aaron looked away and clenched his jaw until he thought his molars might chip, and all to keep that goddamn tear from dropping down his cheek.

Chapter 27

Isobel and her mother returned from putting Sophie to bed only to find Aaron and Calvin sitting in the living room with beer in their hands and laughter between them.

It felt good to laugh. He was smiling.

The look Isobel gave him was one of utter confusion, but like the class act that she was, she stowed the puzzlement and instead smiled, pecked her father on the cheek and asked if he knocked Aaron down a couple of pegs.

Calvin chuckled warmly, wrapped his arm around his daughter and said he was demanding a rematch, needed to redeem himself.

Aaron found himself watching Isobel and her parents in quiet awe and total envy. He'd never had that. Never knew the love of a parent or parents. Never knew what it was like to know that even when you were at your absolute worst, at rock bottom and ready for the Earth to open up and swallow you whole, that there were people who loved you without quarter and would do anything to help make things better.

A few years back, Dina had hired a private investigator to look into their parents. Find out if they were still alive, if they had anymore siblings or family out there. His sister was on the baby train express and curious about their background and family medical history.

Unfortunately, what the PI found was not something neither Dina nor Aaron were ready to hear. Their father had been an alcoholic, and their mother a recovering addict with mental health issues. Apparently, shortly after Dina was born, in a drunken rage one night, their father killed their mother—and all over a twenty-dollar-bill that he wanted for booze, and she was holding on to for diapers.

Their father went to prison, obviously, where he was murdered by his cell-mate a few years later.

After finding all of out that, Dina told the PI to quit his investigation. She didn't want to know anything else, and frankly, neither did Aaron. If no family had come forward to claim Aaron or Dina, then they weren't worth trying to find in the first place.

Aaron was Dina's family, and Dina was Aaron's—they were all the other needed.

Calvin finished his beer, stood up from the recliner and stretched. "I'm gonna feel that round tomorrow, son. Might need to delay the rematch until I'm recovered."

Aaron finished his own beer and set it down on the coffee table next to Calvin's. "Name the time and place, and I'll be there."

Calvin's grin was wide but his eyes tired. He yawned. "Well, dear. Should we hit the road? These whippersnappers want us back here at fourteen hundred hours." He opened on eye and focused it on Aaron. "Right?"

Aaron smiled. "Yes, please, sir. I would really appreciate it if you would watch Sophie for us. Would certainly ease my mind to know she was being well looked after."

Calvin opened both his eyes and nodded. "Gonna spoil that little girlie rotten. No bedtime. Ice cream for supper and cupcakes for dessert."

Isobel rolled her eyes but made sure not to settle her gaze on Aaron. She was looking everywhere but him.

Damn. They really needed to talk.

"Not yet, honey," Harriet said, her hand falling to her husband's back and urging him to head toward the front door. "Maybe in a year or so."

Calvin's blue eyes twinkled. "I'm going to be her favorite." He shot a grin at both Aaron and Isobel, who followed them to the door. "Or at least that's the plan."

"Bye, Dad," Isobel sang, exhaustion in her tone. "And thanks for agreeing to watch Sophie, guys."

Harriet leaned forward and hugged her daughter, then Calvin got in on the hug, all three of them laughing.

Aaron stood back, hands in his pockets, eyes cast down.

But he wasn't like that for long. A big arm swooped out and drew him into the group hug.

"Can't forget you, son," Calvin said, wrapping his arms around Aaron's neck and pulling him in against Isobel's back. "We Joneses are huggers."

Aaron released his hands from his pockets and gently let one fall to Isobel's shoulder and then the other to her father's. He chuckled, but it was awkward, and he knew she wasn't laughing.

"All right, all right," Isobel said, prying herself out of the pile. "You two get some rest. You've got a wild baby to take care of tomorrow. Gonna need your beauty sleep."

"Nonsense," Calvin said, pretending to bat a lock of hair off his shoulder. "I'm as beautiful as they come."

Isobel groaned, grabbed the doorknob and opened it. "Go, before I die from all the corny dad jokes bouncing around the room. They're deadly."

They bid the Joneses goodnight and then Isobel shut the door, letting out a long exhale and slumping her back against the hard grain of the oak. "Love that man to the moon and back, but he's exhausting."

Aaron laughed. "He's not so bad."

He grabbed her hand and pulled her away from the door. Her eyes held the same confusion as earlier, only this time she didn't bother to hide it.

246

He made to tug her into the living room so they could talk, but she broke free from his grasp, her head shaking. "I'm tired, Aaron. I'm going to go to bed."

His face fell, as did his heart. They couldn't end like this. She couldn't quit. She couldn't quit him. "But you said we could talk."

She lifted her eyes to his. Her shoulders sagged. "I don't really think there's anything to talk about. This just isn't working. We're too different. You want a nanny with perks, and I want more."

He made to reach for her again, but she stepped away.

"I'm going to bed. I have to run to the cobbler in the morning to get my black heel that was being fixed. I'll take Sophie with me to give you some time to yourself before the service." Then before Aaron could protest, reach for her again or take her mouth with his, devouring her excuses and pouring out his heart, she was gone. Down the hallway and into her bedroom, where she promptly shut the door.

Shut him out.

He heard a roaring in his ears as the magnitude of his actions, his behavior finally came to an unbearably ugly head. He'd just driven away possibly the best thing that had ever happened to him and all because he was afraid of opening up. Afraid of letting someone love him out of fear of losing them.

Calvin's words came back on him like a song on repeat.

I let the grief and pain morph into anger and hate—because somehow it felt more acceptable to be angry at the world than sad. To hate the world rather than feel pain and loss because someone I loved was no longer a part of my world. I let the rage consume me. I nearly lost Harriet because of it.

And that's exactly what Aaron had done.

He'd allowed his grief to turn into rage until it was all-encompassing, and it drove away the woman he loved. Drove away his world. His sunshine. His summer. Because even though the days were getting shorter and darker, and the wind was cold, and the rain icy, when he was with Isobel, every damn day was summer.

247

Aaron stood in front of her bedroom door for a long time, his fist poised and ready to knock. Only he didn't. He just stared at the dark wood, willing it to open on its own, willing her to give him a chance to explain.

It never opened.

Eventually, his fist fell to his side, and he got ready for bed. He needed a shower after that impromptu boxing match with Calvin. Impromptu but needed. Impromptu but welcome.

He opened the bathroom door, towel around his waist, hair wet. Her bedroom door was still closed. He'd stared at her bodywash in the shower for a long time, hating the thought of never seeing it there again, never smelling the sweetness of it when he showered after her, never burying his nose in her hair as she rested her head on his chest or he spooned her from behind.

His fist pounded on her door.

Seconds later, it opened. A groggy-eyed beauty glanced up at him, yawning as she knuckled the sleep from her eyes. "Is Sophie okay—"

His mouth was on her. His hands in her hair.

The towel at his waist dropped, but he didn't care. He rushed into her room, taking her down onto the bed with him, spreading his body over hers.

The sheets and pillowcase smelled like her, were still warm from her body.

She didn't push him away. Didn't demand he leave. Instead, her arms wrapped around his shoulders, and her nails ran deep, painful tracks down his back. Yes. Any mark from Isobel was a mark he'd gladly take.

She arched into him, pressing her breasts against his chest. He released her mouth and dipped his head, taking a nipple into his mouth and sucking it through the thin fabric of her tank top. She moaned, cupping the other breast and tugging on the other nipple until it peaked hard beneath the cotton.

He pushed one hand beneath her shorts, cupping her mound and pressing his thumb against her clit. The sharp inhale of her breath told him he'd hit that sweet spot that caused her legs to flop open and a gush of warmth to drench his fingers.

He needed to prove to her that he didn't just want a nanny with *perks* anymore. He wanted what she wanted. A future, a partner. Someone to help him raise Sophie, to grow old with. Someone to be there every morning and every night and not as an employee, but as a co-parent, a teammate, a lover.

His lips made a trail down her abdomen, peppering kisses on every freckle, every soft, silky inch of her, committing the lush curves of her body to memory. His tongue swirled around her navel, flicking the little sparkly barbell piercing.

He was about to shuck her shorts off and show her exactly what she meant to him when the sound of a baby over the monitor on the nightstand filled the dark room.

Isobel sat bolt upright and pushed away from him, swinging her legs over the side. "She needs me."

He didn't bother hiding his erection and instead simply stood up. "Come back to bed when you're done."

She shook her head, regret and pain in her tired eyes. "I know I said I was okay with this just being what it is. But I'm not. I lied. I want more. I'm tired of always feeling like I've done something to upset you. I know you're angry, I get it, but I'm tired of it. I can't live like this. I'm a happy person, Aaron. A really happy person. And it's okay that you're not, but I can't live or work for someone who treats me like I'm a burden during the day and his private plaything at night."

"You're not," he protested.

She shook her head. "It's time I start listening to my head and not just my heart. And even though my heart is begging me to stay, to take the little you're willing to give me and be okay with it, my head is telling me I deserve more." Her bottom lip quivered and she averted her eyes, though he could tell they were beginning to well up with tears. "It's not fair, Aaron, the way you've treated me. And at this point, I'm really not sure if there's anything you can say to change my mind. You need to get some help, and I'm obviously not the one to do it." She swallowed, then turned her body away from him. "I have to go tend to Sophie. I would appreciate it if you were not in my room when I return."

She padded out of the room, not looking back. He heard her humming and shushing Sophie on the baby monitor. They had a formula dispenser in the nursery so they didn't have to walk all the way to the kitchen in the middle of the night for feedings. The *brrrr* and gurgle of the machine making a bottle mixed with her gentle singing. Once again, the words to Brahms's "Lullaby" made his heart ache for his sister.

"That's it, Super Sophie," she whispered, "that's a girl."

He could just picture her sitting on the edge of the bed, baby in her arms as she stared down lovingly at Sophie as she drank her bottle.

She was a one-of-a-kind woman. Kind and generous, patient and smart. But she was also strong—hella strong. She'd have to be to put up with all the mood swings and garbage Aaron had put her through over the last couple of months.

He raked his hands over his hair and picked up his towel. He'd fucked up so bad with her. So freaking bad.

Calvin was right. She loved him. Him, not the idea of him, not their little arrangement, but him. And he was too damn angry, too hurting to see it or let her in.

He went to his own room and pulled on his boxers then a pair of plaid pajama pants and a dark gray Henley. He couldn't let it end like this. Couldn't let her walk out of his and Sophie's life for good without letting her know what she meant to them.

What she meant to him.

The door to Sophie's room was open just a crack. He pushed it open more.

Isobel was curled up on the edge of the queen-size bed. Sophie was in the middle and a big pillow was on the other edge—not that Sophie was rolling yet but just in case.

Sophie was sleeping again, and so was Isobel, her hand on the baby's belly, Sophie's head in the crook of Isobel's arm.

She looked perfect there. A natural-born mother. Even to a child that wasn't her own.

He stood there for a moment, letting the image imprint on his brain. This selfless woman had taken on a newborn baby and a dark and damaged soul—no questions asked, no demands of her own. And in just a few short months, she had not only shown Sophie the kind of love usually reserved for that of a mother and child, but she'd shown him love as well. A love and connection he'd been searching for his whole life but didn't know it.

He pulled the pillow off the edge and lay down, careful not to disturb either of them. He wanted to rest his hand on top of hers where it lay on Sophie's stomach, but he didn't want to run the risk of waking her, so instead, he remained still, watching the woman he loved care for the child he loved and hoping to God she'd hear him out in the morning. Otherwise, tomorrow was shaping up to be one terrible day.

Chapter 28

Isobel propped open the door of the cobbler and pushed the stroller through, the bag with her fixed shoe swinging from her wrist. It was a drizzly day and a touch chilly, but unlike the last few days, when they'd been bombarded with a wicked wind, the breeze was mild and kept the raindrops from blowing sideways.

She made her way down the sidewalk past the various businesses in the strip mall. Most of them hadn't opened yet, as it was only nine thirty on a Saturday, but a few had staff milling around inside. She stopped in front of a jewelry store window, admiring a blue topaz pendant in white gold with small diamonds around it. She'd always loved blue topaz, loved the way it made her eyes pop.

She wasn't ready to head back to the house yet either.

Waking up in the bed next to Aaron and Sophie had thrown her for a loop.

When had he come in?

Why had he come in?

She'd nearly given in when he pounded on her bedroom door and kissed her. He just tasted so good—too good. And he smelled incredible. Fresh from the shower, all warm and wet and smelling like a forest with fresh fallen snow. She was weak to his advances and the way she felt when she was in his arms, when she was beneath him, when his lips were on hers.

His kisses made her forget all the heartache and confusion he caused her. Because he caused a lot. He was rude and angry, moody and dark.

She chalked a lot of it up to grief, but he couldn't use that excuse forever. It wasn't fair to her—it wasn't fair to any of them.

When she'd opened her eyes and saw him lying there, Sophie had only just started to rouse. Like a typical baby, she could grunt and squirm for a solid five minutes before bothering to open her eyes. It was her way of alerting the food provider that she was hungry and that they needed to get her bottle ready, otherwise, once the five-minute mark passed, shit was going to hit the fan.

But Isobel hadn't let her get past the five-minute mark. She hadn't even let her get past the one-minute mark before she scooped Sophie up, grabbed a fresh diaper and then headed to the living room, taking great care to close the door behind her.

She made Sophie a bottle, changed her diaper, fed her and then, once the baby was content and quiet, Isobel got dressed, and the two were out the door.

She didn't want to run the risk of bumping into Aaron and having to rehash the awkwardness of last night.

A cowardly move, she knew that, but today was going to be rough enough on him as it was. She didn't want to add to it.

So instead, she and Sophie headed out. Two girls on the town. They went to Paige's bistro and grabbed breakfast and a coffee, chatting up Paige and her hilarious employee Jane. Violet popped in, itching to have her sweet tooth satisfied, and then Tori showed up—probably because Isobel texted her.

The women rehashed the previous night and were divided. Tori was on team Aaron, as was Paige, but both Isobel and Violet were hesitant.

"He's broken," Violet said, shoving a danish into her mouth. "And far beyond your repair skills."

"Broken doesn't mean incapable though," Tori shot back. "He just lost his sister. I think fractured is a better word. And fractures can be fixed, they can heal with the right kind of tenderness and care." She fixed her eyes on Isobel. "And we all know that tenderness and care are your forte."

Violet wiped her mouth. "I know, but he's treating Isobel like a call girl. That can't go on."

"No, you're right," Paige added. "But maybe after today he'll be able to find some closure and begin to move on. If you love him—which I think you do—then maybe give him a second chance. If he doesn't start to make some real positive changes following her service and putting his sister to rest, then you can revisit your resignation."

Isobel liked Paige's plan.

She wasn't ready to give up on Aaron, but things did need to change. She couldn't continue to live her life on eggshells in his house, and she also couldn't continue to be expected to warm his bed at night but be okay being ignored by him all day.

A man in a black jacket and baseball cap bumped into her, shaking her from her thoughts. He didn't bother to apologize—even though she did, though she wasn't in the way. He wrenched open the door to the jewelry store and stepped inside, causing the door to chime.

Some people could be so rude.

Isobel glanced down at Sophie, who was busy gnawing on her fist. "What do you say, Super Sophie? Should we go back and see Uncle Aaron? Do you think he'll appreciate the pastry we bought him?"

Sophie simply blinked, then proceeded to try to shove her entire slobber-covered fist into her mouth.

Isobel's car was only about four stalls up, so she pushed Sophie down the beveled edge of the sidewalk and around to the trunk, where she stowed the stroller. She was just putting Sophie's bucket car seat into the back seat when the other back door opened and the man with a black jacket and a baseball cap slid inside.

He pulled a gun from inside his coat and held it on Sophie. "Get in the front and drive," he ordered.

Her eyes dropped down to Sophie, and her heart began to beat wildly in her chest at the same time her belly went tight with knots strong enough to hold back even the wildest of horses.

"NOW!" he bellowed, startling Sophie. The baby started to cry.

Swallowing, Isobel nodded, her hands shaking as she rested her fingers on Sophie's cheek. "I-it's okay, sweetie. I-it's okay."

He shook the gun and nudged her hand away from Sophie. "Fucking drive!"

She nodded again, then backed out of the car, shut the door, grabbed her phone from her back pocket and texted the only person she could think of the only words she could manage.

Carjacked. Help.

All the blood drained from Aaron's face and tendrils of terror curled into his stomach as he stared at the message from Isobel.

And she had Sophie.

Sophie and Isobel. The two people he loved most in the entire world were carjacked.

He brought up her GPS coordinates as fast as he could. She was on the move. Or at least her phone was. He assumed she was still in the car, otherwise if her car had just been stolen with her phone in it, she wouldn't have been able to text him.

Her phone had her on the highway heading northbound on the 405. It would take a miracle for him to catch up to her.

A fucking miracle.

But he had to try.

He had to do something.

Fuck, he didn't even know her license plate number. And she had a white Toyota Corolla, which were a dime a dozen. No way would the cops be of any help.

Besides, where were the cops when Dina was gunned down and bleeding out in that mall? They were fucking useless. The only reason the cops had been called that night when Isobel and Mercedes were drugged and abducted was because Colton called them. Aaron figured he and his buddy would just go in and take care of things themselves—like he had in Colombia. But Colton didn't think that the vigilante thing was a good idea. They needed to do things legally and call the police, especially since Aaron had Sophie to think about now. It wouldn't be good if he ended up in prison for killing a couple of frat boys. Colton was right, of course, but Aaron still didn't trust cops, still didn't think they were quick enough on the job.

He ran out to the garage and jumped in his truck, peeling out of his driveway like a bat out of hell. He set his phone into the holder on the dash and hit *call*.

Maybe, just maybe she would answer.

It started to ring.

And ring.

And ring.

He was sure her voice mail message was going to pop up next, but to his relief, she answered it.

"Hi, honey, how's it going?" Her voice was a sing-song chipper squeak.

Honey?

He stopped at a red light. "Not too bad, baby. Where are you?"

"Had to run to the cobbler to get my fixed shoe. Can't wait for our date tonight." The sound of heavy rain and heavy traffic competed with her trembling voice. She was fighting to stay strong, because she was strong. But she was also terrified.

"Me either, baby. Me either." He needed to keep her talking, needed to hear her voice. "What are you going to wear tonight, baby?"

"Oh you know, that little black dress you bought me with the *shell* lace pattern on it. You know the one ... I wore it when we stayed at the *Gas*light Inn in *Woodinville*."

Shell.

Gas.

Woodinville.

She was a fucking genius.

She was running out of gas, and was planning to stop at the Shell gas station in Woodinville.

Fuck, he needed to get there, and he needed to get there yesterday.

"Oh I remember, that was the night we ..."

"Mhmm."

"How's the little one?"

"She finally cried herself to sleep, poor lamb. Took her from Bellevue to Kirkland to fall asleep. Must be teething."

Bellevue to Kirkland.

Okay, so she was past Kirkland.

He didn't have much time.

Murmuring in the car had him straining his ears to listen.

"I-I'm going to have to let you go, honey," she said, the fear in her voice coming through the line with every shaky syllable. "I can't wait to see you tonight. Can't wait to—"

"Isobel? Isobel!" He slammed his hands on the steering wheel. "Motherfuck-er!"

The sonofabitch in the car must have caught on to them.

FUCK!

He brought up the friend finder app again and zeroed in on her coordinates. He was gaining ground on them. He'd just crossed Lake Washington and was now heading north toward Kirkland. He was maybe ten minutes behind them, give or take.

He increased the speed of his windshield wipers, as the rain was now coming down like a tropical monsoon.

She mustn't be doing the speed limit, or she was getting herself deliberately stuck behind slow cars. The woman was no dummy, and she'd been raised and trained by an Army Ranger. So although she was probably scared out of her skin at the moment, particularly with Sophie in the car, Isobel was capable of making rational, practical decisions that would ensure her and Aaron's niece's survival.

At least that's what he was choosing to believe at the moment. That's what he had to believe.

Oh please, Lord, don't let me be wrong.

"What the fuck was that?" the man in the back seat of the car screamed, leaning forward between the seats and grabbing Isobel's phone from where she had it tucked into one of the cupholders.

She glanced back into the car. Thank God Sophie was still asleep. "It was my husband. What did you want me to do? Tell him I've been carjacked and I'm currently on my way to the Canadian border?"

The man with the gun glared at her in the mirror. "Sounded like you were telling him where the fuck we're going."

She rolled her eyes. "I was making conversation. He'd suspect more from me if I didn't answer. We have a relationship like that, you know? Open lines of communication and all."

He was not a bad-looking guy. Short dark hair, hazel eyes, five o'clock shadow. But it was the dark bags under his eyes and the pock marks on his face that aged him. Without them, she would probably place him between twenty-eight and thirty-five. With them, he looked over forty.

She swallowed. "I'm running out of gas. I'm going to have to stop soon."

"No. No stopping."

She caught his eyes in the mirror. "Well, if we don't stop for gas soon, we're going to stop in the middle of the freeway. Which would you prefer?"

She felt like she was in the freaking Twilight Zone. Who sat and had arguments with their kidnapper slash carjacker while a baby slept peacefully between them? Nobody! What she should have done was run the car right into the nearest lamppost, then opened her door and run in a zigzag pattern as fast as her legs could carry her. But she had Sophie in the back seat, so nothing about that scenario was doable.

So instead, she was forced to drive out of town with her carjacker and hope to God he didn't tell her to pull off the highway, take her money, her phone and car and then leave her and Sophie dead on a back road.

No witnesses, right?

She tried to practice the tactical breathing her father had taught her all those years ago when she started having panic attacks at school. It had helped then, but it wasn't helping much now.

"Look," she started, "I'm going to have to stop for gas. You have a gun on my child. There isn't much I can do but do as you say. So if you tell me not to talk to anybody, I won't. If you want to get out and pump the gas while holding on to a screaming baby as insurance, go for it. But one way or another, I need to stop for gas."

A flash of unease drifted behind his eyes.

Yeah, the movies were a load of BS. All those highway chase scenes and everybody involved just happened to have started the drive with a full tank of gas?

Bullshit.

He knew she was right.

"I don't know where you intend for me to drive you, but if you want to get there, we need fuel."

His eyes darted back and forth. He glanced down at her phone, which by now had locked itself. She had a fingerprint reader to open it and a four-digit code.

He wouldn't be able to open it and see that she'd texted the words *carjacked* and *help* to Aaron.

At least she hoped he wouldn't.

He waved the gun in the air. "Okay, okay. Turn off and get gas."

The Shell station in Woodinville was coming up on the right. She knew it was there because she'd stopped at it once or twice on the way to her family's lake cabin.

Nodding, she shifted over to the far-right lane. "There's one up ahead."

His eyes turned fierce in the mirror, and he clutched the bag he was holding tighter against his chest. "If you pull any fucking funny business, I swear to fucking God I'll put a bullet in this baby faster than you can blink. You get the gas. You get back in the car. Got it?"

Her eyes met his in the mirror. "Got it. No funny business, I promise." Her lips trembled as she focused on the still-sleeping Sophie. Her little bottom lip stuck out all pouty and wobbled as if she were trying to suck. A tear slid down Isobel's cheek. "Please don't hurt her. Please."

Zero empathy glared back at her in the mirror. "Shut up and fucking drive."

Chapter 29

Aaron pulled his pickup truck into the Shell station just off the 405 on the outside of Woodinville. Her phone had her there.

She had to be there.

Unless the motherfucker tossed it out the window when they stopped for gas.

Dread coursed through him at the thought of her not being there. At the thought of Isobel and Sophie being on the road again with no phone, no way of tracking them, with some lunatic with a gun calling all the shots.

He wheeled around the gas station, searching for her white Corolla, but it wasn't at any of the pumps. Not parked out front of the convenience store either. It wasn't anywhere.

He was too late.

Her phone was here, but she wasn't.

Fear thundered inside him.

Where. Was. She?

He stopped and scanned the area. Looking for anything out of the ordinary, anything that might give him an idea that she'd been there. A sign, a baby blanket in a puddle, anything.

All he saw was a highway patrol car parked at one of the pumps, but he doubted those cops knew jack shit.

He was about to pull into a parking stall and go in to question the convenience store clerk when the sound of a horn honking at the intersection and the crunch of metal on metal drew his attention—as well as the cop's.

A car was heading in the wrong direction on an off ramp and had just been hit.

A white car.

A white Corolla.

Traffic had come to a stop as car horns filled the air and people hung out their windows, shouting at the driver.

The driver of the car that hit the Corolla was about to get out of their vehicle.

Nobody had stepped out of the Corolla yet.

The impact didn't look severe. Neither vehicle could have been going very fast. A couple of crunched bumpers was all it looked like from where he sat. It was a risky move for sure, particularly with Sophie in the car, but Aaron could just imagine that Isobel was desperate.

He gunned it and peeled out into the street—of course, alerting the cops. The police car's lights flashed and its siren *whooped* as it pulled out from the pump and followed him.

He ignored the police, instead getting as close to the intersection as he could before traffic got too tight and he was forced to park the truck and bail out.

He couldn't even remember if he bothered to turn it off or not.

It didn't fucking matter.

His feet hit the wet pavement and rain pelted him in the face as he ran full-tilt toward the stopped Corolla. It was hard to see inside the back window from all the rain, but he could tell that Isobel was behind the driver's seat and the carjacker was in the back.

He was in the back seat with Sophie.

He was in the back seat with Aaron's daughter.

The motherfucker was going to pay.

Slowly, cars and trucks began to back up, giving Isobel's Corolla space to back up to right herself, for the two vehicles involved in the collision to pull off to the side so traffic could resume.

He reached Isobel's slow-moving car and slammed his hand hard down on the top of the trunk, causing her to hit the brakes.

Perfect.

Then, with a rage so hot, so red, so intense, he acted in a fever and flung open the back passenger seat door, grabbed the man inside by the collar and tossed him out into the wet street.

It didn't matter that he had a gun, didn't matter at all.

He wouldn't for long.

Guns were the coward's choice of weapon. A real man fought with his fists. He fought with his wits. He fought with his own life on the line.

That's not to say that if Aaron had a gun on him at the moment, he wouldn't have put a bullet through the fucker's head. Because he would have. He'd put many a bullet through many a fucker's head, because it was just easier—and quicker.

But not today. Today he was out for blood.

He wanted to feel the man's nose break beneath his fists as knuckles collided with cartilage and bone. See the blood seep from his eyes as he made them black and blue.

It was hard to see through the rain, but he didn't have to have perfect vision. He just needed to see his target. And his target was currently scrambling on the ground, trying to grab his black bag. His gun was ten feet away in a puddle.

Good.

Aaron was on him in three strides, tackling him to the ground and sitting on top of the man's chest, his fists swinging, making contact each and every time with his face. The sound of bones crunching and strident wails from the man beneath him only spurred him on, made him hit harder, hit faster.

Nothing but the need to beat and punish filled his mind as his pulse pumped furiously through him, heating him from the inside out.

It wasn't until a horn honking directly behind him and the shrill call of a police siren filled the air that he slowed down, the kill-fog slowly dissipating inside his brain.

He was soaked through. Not that he'd worn anything besides a T-shirt and jeans, but all that was saturated.

Rain and blood mixed together and ran down his forearms. His knuckles ached from each punch. Once again, they were cut up and bloody—but it wasn't just his blood.

He looked down at the man beneath him. He was unconscious. He was unrecognizable.

A hand landed on his back. A hand he would know anywhere.

"Aaron?"

Without so much as a second thought or glance back at the fucker to see if he was still breathing, Aaron sprang up from his knees and whipped around, grabbing Isobel and wrapping his arms around her tight.

Her hands grappled at his damp shirt as she clung to him for dear life. Her wet hair stuck to her face.

More sirens filled the air, followed by the slamming of car doors and people's voices.

Aaron didn't care about any of it.

All he cared about was that his daughter and the woman in his arms, the women he loved, were safe.

Finally, he pushed her away, bent his knees so they could see eye to eye and ran his hands down her sides, making sure she was still in one piece.

Tears dripped down her cheeks, and her bottom lip wobbled as she struggled to rein in her fear.

He tugged her against him once more and ran his hand down her head, shushing her. "It's okay, baby. You're safe now. You're safe."

He felt her shudder against him, and her breathing slowly returned to normal. Only when he knew she was no longer crying, no longer trembling, did he separate them once more.

The sound of guns cocking made them both pause.

"Hands in the air," one cop bellowed. "Where we can see them."

Immediately, Aaron and Isobel tossed their hands into the air and faced the police officers. At least four of them were now hiding behind their open car doors, guns cocked and pointed on Aaron.

"Officer," Isobel yelled, "the man on the ground is the carjacker. He held me and my baby at gunpoint and made me drive him away from the jewelry store that was just robbed on Carnaby and Stanley. I have a baby in the car." She tilted her head toward Aaron. "This is Aaron Steele, the baby's uncle. He is *not* the bad guy."

Damn, his woman was strong. After everything she'd just been through, her voice was still steady as she pleaded her case with the police, the freezing rain pelting her in the face, her hair sticking to her neck, clothes soaked through.

"He is NOT the bad guy," she repeated.

Understanding and acceptance slowly dawned across each officer's face until finally whoever was in charge told them to stand down, and they dropped their guns from the "ready" position.

Aaron exhaled and dropped his arms back down to his sides. Isobel did too. She spun to face him, and he once again closed the distance between them, cupping both her cheeks in his hands. That's when he noticed that despite her tough exterior and the brave front she put on for the cops, she was terrified. Panic filled her eyes, and tears dripped down her cheeks. He wiped them away with his thumb, even though it was a futile gesture given how hard it was raining.

"How's Soph?" he asked.

She snorted, a small smile curving on her lips. "Still sleeping."

A throat cleared next to them, forcing him to release her face. He immediately wrapped a protective arm around her waist. No way in hell was he letting her go. Not ever again.

"Sir, ma'am," a police officer interrupted, "this the carjacker on the ground?"

Isobel nodded. "It is. He robbed the jewelry store in the Pier City strip mall on Carnaby and Stanley, then he took me and my—me and this man's niece hostage at gunpoint."

The cop's eyes flicked up to Aaron. "And how did you know where to find them?"

"I called her. She answered and gave me enough clues to figure out where to meet them."

His eyebrows rose beneath the brim of his dripping hat. "Wow. How clever."

An angry crow from inside the car caused all of them to turn their heads.

"She's up," Isobel said, slipping out of Aaron's grasp. "She's probably hungry."

"We're going to need to bring you both down to the station for questioning," the officer said, following Isobel to the car. She now sat inside, holding a bottle up for a guzzling Sophie.

Aaron was right there too. He stared down his nose at the police officer, who was a convenient five or six inches shorter than him. "Fine. Whatever. Let's just get everyone out of this rain."

"But we need to be home by two," Isobel shot back. "Questioning, statements, gun-wielding robber, carjacking or not, we have somewhere very important to be this afternoon. So unless you plan on arresting us for something, we will be leaving by one thirty."

The police officer stepped away, gesturing for Aaron to follow him. "She always this big of a tyrant?"

Aaron's smile went wide, his heart constricting and his shoulders finally free of the stress. "God, I hope so."

They left the police station at exactly one thirty and were home shortly before two. Sophie had been a trooper through the whole thing, hardly squawking at all once her diaper was changed and her belly was full.

And Isobel had been un-fucking-believable.

That woman had titanium balls hidden somewhere, because the entire time they were at the police station, she didn't break down once. She was steady and coherent, giving a rock-solid account of everything that transpired from the moment she stopped in front of the jewelry store to the moment the police arrived.

Obviously, because Aaron was rescuing Isobel and Sophie and the man he'd beaten to a bloody pulp was a felon, there were no assault charges—thank God.

But that didn't stop the cop who took their statements from reading Aaron the riot act about going all vigilante rather than calling the authorities.

Aaron had clamped down hard on the inside of his cheek with his molars and simply nodded rather than ask him where he and his buddies had been in August when a psychopath with an AK-47 ran into the Emerald City Mall. He'd never trust cops. Never. But he did have to tolerate them.

No sense adding punching a police officer to the report. Besides, his knuckles were killing him.

Isobel's car was being towed to a body shop, and they would hear later in the week whether the damage was fixable or not.

Aaron held the door open for her, and she stepped inside the house, both of them still damp, and now she was shivering.

"Go jump into the shower," he said, shutting the door behind them. "I'll tend to Sophie. You need to warm up."

She nodded. "My parents will be here shortly."

"Okay."

He was chilly but not freezing like she seemed to be, so he changed into some dry clothes, then tossed Sophie into the wrap on his chest and went about making a quick pot of soup.

Earlier that summer, he and Dina had gone to a farmer's market and bought a bunch of funky-shaped pasta. It wasn't until he'd cooked some up for them later that he realized what he thought were rocket ships were actually penises. It was an erotic pasta shop.

Oh, well. It was all he had.

Pasta was pasta.

He pulled the "rocket ship" noodles out of the cupboard and set the pot to boil.

He needed to get his wet and bloody clothes in the laundry before he forgot about them and they started to stink. Walking down the hall, he paused next to Isobel's room. A weird muffled sound echoed through the door.

She was crying.

She was so strong when she had to be, but everyone had a breaking point. Not even steel was completely indestructible.

He didn't bother knocking and instead slowly turned the knob. "Iz?"

She was sitting on her bed in her bra and panties, her wet hair hanging down all around her face. Fresh droplets of tears puddled on the tops of her thighs.

Adjusting Sophie in the carrier, he sat down next to her, resting his hand on her back. "Iz?"

They'd kissed when he'd found them, hugged and never stopped touching until they arrived home. But had that all just been the adrenaline? The fear toying with her emotions?

She lifted her head. Her sapphire eyes were red-rimmed, and tear tracks marred her face. She stared at him, her bottom lip jutting out and trembling ever so slightly.

"It's okay," he whispered. She needed to know that she didn't always have to be strong. He was here to be her strength, to be her rock.

Her nostrils flared, and she flung herself into his arms. It was awkward given Sophie between them, but they shifted and adjusted, and her head fell to his shoulder. And there she sobbed as he stroked her hair and gently hummed.

He wasn't sure why he hummed, but for some reason it felt right.

No song, no identifiable melody, just a soft, gentle hum of a tune that had simply popped into his head.

Big, hot tears dripped down onto his back, and her whole body shook as the entirety of the day finally came to a head. She'd been held at gunpoint, carjacked and then in a car accident. That was enough to make even the fiercest of warriors take pause and lose their composure.

And Isobel Jones was one of the strongest warriors he knew.

It wasn't long before her sniffles began to wane and she no longer shook as intensely. Sophie made a noise of protest between them, so Isobel pulled away.

Voices in the hallway had Aaron bolting upright.

"It's my parents," she said, wiping her nose with the back of her wrist. "I gave them a key last night in case they wanted to take Sophie for a walk. Sorry that they let themselves in. They're just like that."

He didn't care.

"Hello?" her father called out. "Anybody home?"

Isobel blew out a breath. "Suppose we need to tell them." She stood up and wiped beneath her eyes, grabbing her robe from a hook on the back of the door.

Once she tied the tails of the housecoat, he reached for her hand. "We'll tell them together. And then we'll go have some penis pasta."

Her nose wrinkled, and her lip curled up in confusion. "Penis pasta?"

Chapter 30

Hand in hand, they raced up the steps of the rented hall. The rain had stopped, and patches of blue sky fought their way through the bulbous gray clouds.

"I can't believe I'm going to be late to my own sister's service," he said, not so much mad as anxious. He'd been a nervous wreck on the drive over, tugging at his tie and cracking his neck back and forth. He felt like he was being strangled.

"It's fine," Isobel said, stepping ahead of him after he'd opened the door for them. "I blame the fact that there was absolutely no parking. What the heck?"

He shook his head. There must be some sports event or a recital or something going on nearby. They'd been forced to park in a parking garage nearly three blocks away, but only after he'd circled the block four times.

The sound of mingling voices and low music hit them before the wall of people did.

And it was literally a wall.

People filled the enormous room shoulder to shoulder. A sea of suits and black.

"There you are," Liam said, walking up, a program in his hand. "Was getting worried. Everything okay?"

"I was carjacked, held at gunpoint, kidnapped and then got in a car accident," Isobel said.

Liam's dark brown eyes narrowed. He paused. Then he tossed his head back and laughed. "Good one. You were home bangin', weren't you?"

Aaron ignored him. "Who are all these people?" Did Dina know *this* many people?

Liam looked at him like he'd just declared the Earth was flat and the moon was made of cheese. "They're here for you. For Dina."

"For me?"

He nodded. "Duh." His eyes scanned the room. "I see the pastor. I'm going to go let him know that you're here now so we can start the service." Then he took off across the room, waving and smiling at people as he went.

What the fuck would Aaron have done without Liam?

He wouldn't have Isobel, that was for sure.

He wouldn't have much.

Liam was a fucking lifesaver.

A large-bellied man with a short white beard and glasses made his way up to a small riser behind a podium and microphone. "If everyone could be seated, please."

The shuffle of chairs and bodies filled the room.

Isobel pulled him toward the front of the room. "Family sits at the front," she whispered.

He had no clue on the protocol. None.

They made their way up the center aisle toward the chairs at the front, and that's when he started to recognize all the faces.

And there were a lot of them.

His old boss from the construction site.

Rob and his wife, Skyler.

Rob's parents, Malcolm and Pilar.

Colton and Mercedes.

His ex-girlfriend, Heather, and her husband (Skyler's brother), Gavin.

Heather's mother.

All his brothers in arms: Blaze, Ash, Wark, Callaghan, Deck and Ryke.

And all of The Single Dads of Seattle with their partners: Mark and Tori, Adam and Violet, Mitch and Paige, Zak, Emmett, Mason, Scott, Atlas and, of course, Liam.

They were all here for him?

For him.

His feet became as heavy as a thousand sandbags, and his muscles refused to cooperate. He was frozen in place. Stunned. His pulse thundered in his ears, and his gut churned with unease. Why were they here for him? It made no sense.

Isobel tugged on his hand. "You okay?"

He shook his head. "I ... I can't."

Worry clouded her eyes. She squeezed his hand tighter. "Come with me for a second." She pulled him past the front row and over to where there was a small alcove and then a hallway. They ducked behind the wall, away from the crowd.

Finally, he could breathe again. Finally, his muscles worked in time with his mind, and he was able to relieve the tension in his neck and shoulders by cracking his neck side to side.

"What's wrong?" she asked, releasing his hand and placing both her palms on his waist. "Talk to me. Is it the crowd? Too many people? Do you not want to sit at the front? Do you not want to get up to speak?"

Oh fuck, he hadn't even thought about that. Now he wasn't just stunned, he was downright terrified.

She pushed past his coat and gripped the fabric of his dark blue dress shirt, pulling just a little to get his attention. "Please, Aaron. Talk to me."

He shut his eyes and started doing his tactical breathing.

Inhale, hold. Exhale, hold. Inhale, hold. Exhale, hold.

"All those people," he finally said, not yet ready to open his eyes. The darkness was comforting. The darkness was empty.

"They're here for you," she said softly. "Because they love you. Because they love Sophie and they love Dina."

He felt her body press against his, and finally, he opened his eyes.

"Are you overwhelmed by how much you're loved?"

He glanced down at her, his vision growing blurry.

She smiled sweetly and lifted her hand to cup his cheek. He leaned into her touch. "You are so loved, Aaron. They're here for you just as much as they are for Dina. Don't shut them out."

He quickly wiped his eyes with his thumb. "I don't want to shut anybody out anymore. Especially not you. Tonight, I'll tell you about Colombia. You deserve to know what happened."

She closed and opened her eyes slowly. "It's okay. If it's not something you want to share, it's okay."

He shook his head. "No, you need to know. I want to tell you. I want to share my life with you. My past, my present and my future."

"I like the sound of that."

"I hate that it took almost losing you to realize I can't live without you," he whispered, moving his hand to cover hers where it rested on his cheek. "Your dad was right. I love you, Isobel. Everything in this world means absolutely nothing if I can't have you in my life. Tell me I'm not too late, that you'll give me another chance. I want it all ... if you'll have me."

She blinked up at him again but didn't smile. Her eyes held promise though.

"I know I'm angry, and I'm going to really try to work on it. I'm going to get some help. Don't give up on me though, please. I need you. Sophie needs you. And not just as a nanny. She needs you as a *mom*." It felt weird saying that word but not wrong-weird. "And I need you as a partner, as my person."

Her eyes went wide, her cheeks rosy.

He smiled down at her, emotion catching in his throat.

Relief washed over her face, and he suppressed the urge to chuckle.

"You're everything I didn't know I ever wanted until I had it. Until I almost lost it. Say you'll give me another chance to prove to you I'm not the angry bugger you think I am. Say you'll stay." He chomped down hard on the inside of his cheek to keep himself in check.

She batted spiked lashes at him, and a lone tear slipped down her cheek. He cupped her face with his other hand and wiped it away with his thumb. The pulse in her neck raced beneath his finger. She swallowed. "I love you too. And I'll stay."

Chapter 31

"Come with me," Aaron murmured, his mouth next to Isobel's ear as she stood in front of the sink washing dishes.

She rinsed the soap from her hands, then dried them on a dish towel before giving him her hand and following him into the living room. It was the evening following Dina's service—and Isobel's carjacking—and both she and Aaron were exhausted.

"Can we wait and have sex tomorrow?" she asked, covering her mouth as a yawn took hold of her. "I'm really tired. Getting carjacked will do that to a person." She smiled a lopsided grin.

He rolled his eyes, leading her over to the couch and encouraging her to sit down. "We can. I'm pretty tired too. But I promised you something earlier, and I intend to keep that promise."

She cocked one eyebrow, unsure where he was going with this.

He cleared his throat and released her hand. His palm had grown quite sweaty, and she could tell he was growing more anxious by the second.

She shook her head. "You don't have to tell me if you're not ready yet," she whispered, leaning forward and cupping his jaw with one hand. "I appreciate your willingness, but if it's going to be physically taxing on you—don't. You've already been through so much today. We can wait."

His hand fell over top of hers on his face, and he leaned into her touch, shutting his eyes. "No. I need to do this."

Isobel nodded. "Okay. Take all the time you need. I'm not going anywhere."

He opened his eyes and a modicum of relief flitted behind them. He swallowed. "Okay, here goes."

"I loved Valentina," he started, shutting his eyes once again. The pain of reliving that day made his chest grow tight and his gut spin until he felt like he was going to puke.

"I've never been a boyfriend—per se, but I fell in love with her. I shouldn't have, but I did. She was the daughter of our mole, and my love for her, for her family became my weakness, my Achilles heel." He squeezed his eyes shut even tighter as the sound of Valentina's screams began to ring in his ears. "They were my mission. I was to protect them until they could be relocated to safety, and instead, I let my desperate need for a family take over, and that family paid the ultimate price."

He opened his eyes when he felt Isobel pull away, and a frisson of panic dripped down his spine, but she wasn't pulling away from him. Instead, she simply shifted where she sat on the couch and encouraged him to lie down and put his head in her lap. He did so, shut his eyes again and let her stroke his hair, his eyebrows, his face. Her touch calmed him, grounded him, and slowly, his heart rate began to even out.

He swallowed again. "After a few months of working with José—Valentina's father—and gaining pertinent information to take down the entire Muñoz Cartel, I ducked out one evening after dinner to meet with Wark—our new point man, since Rob had retired—to pass along the intel. Only we were ambushed, and I took a rusty machete to the gut."

Isobel gasped, her hand fleeing his face. He opened his eyes to find her covering her mouth, her own eyes wide in terror. "Is that where this scar is from?" she asked, lifting his shirt and gently running her fingers over the raised, pink flesh.

He nodded. "Yes. I was stabbed and Wark ended up losing a leg. Colton had been there too, and once we took out our enemies, Colt stitched me up as best he could. Blaze and Reeves showed up via helicopter to get Wark to a hospital."

"You didn't go too?"

He shook his head. "I had to get to Valentina. If the Muñoz Cartel knew about us, she and her family were in danger."

Colton followed him.

Only they were too late.

The entire house was engulfed in red-hot flames while José lay bound in the driveway, his guts drawn from his body as he died in agony listening to the screams of his family inside the house. Valentina, her mother, her son. They were all inside.

And there wasn't a damn thing Aaron could do.

Isobel sniffled above him, her eyes full of tears, her lips trembling. "Oh, Aaron. I'm so sorry."

Fuck, he knew he had to tell her everything, but he also knew what it would do to her. She was such a gentle soul. An empath who felt everyone's pain as if it were her own. No doubt she probably felt not only Aaron's pain, but the entire Velasquez family's pain as well.

He propped himself up from where he'd been lying in her lap and sat back up, drawing her into his lap and rubbing her back. It was his turn to comfort her, just like she'd comforted him.

"Is there more?" she mumbled, wiping the back of her wrist beneath her nose.

"You sure you want to hear it?"

She nodded. "Yes. I can take it."

He squeezed her tight against him. Of course, she could. She was a fucking warrior.

"Colton and I sat in the bush and watched the house disintegrate in the fire, watched José scream and cry in pain as they tortured him, dumped gasoline on him, until he finally succumbed to his injuries—or perhaps it was the grief first—and gave up fighting for his life."

"No!" She began to shake in his arms. He hugged her tighter.

"Then Carlos Muñoz himself stepped out of a blacked-out SUV. He lit a cigar, then set José on fire with the lighter."

The sharp inhale of her breath was followed by a rattled exhale.

It took everything inside Aaron not to leap out of the brush and go kamikaze on all their asses. Instead, seething, he clutched his abdomen, hands caked in his own blood, and watched them drive away.

It was a message to Aaron. A message to all of them.

And Aaron read it loud and clear.

It took eight weeks for him to be healed enough to move without considerable pain. Colton had done a half-decent job stitching him up, but Aaron had gone into septic shock and needed to be airlifted to Bogota for surgery.

Once he was discharged from the hospital, Aaron was granted a discharge on medical grounds, then he took off back to Medellin and finished the job.

They called him the Black Shadow because they never saw him coming until it was too late. Patiently, over the course of several months, he waited for hours in the dark, in the rain, in the blistering heat to take out his enemies.

To take them all out.

And he did.

One by one, he picked off every member of the Muñoz Cartel, until all that was left was Carlos himself. The smarmy, smug psychopath with more money than some countries and less morals than the Crips.

He'd found Carlos hiding alone in a bunker beneath one of his mansions, his family having fled to Ecuador.

"I hope you set him on fucking fire," Isobel gritted out, fury burning bright behind the pain in her wet eyes.

He shook his head. "No. But I finished him."

Quick and painless.

Merciful.

Though mercy was anything but what Carlos had shown the Velasquez family.

But torture had never been Aaron's forte. He preferred to get the job done swift and clean-like, then move on.

One shot in the back of the head. Just get it over with. End the nightmare. End Carlos Muñoz's reign of terror once and for all.

And he did.

Single-handedly, he took down one of the most powerful drug cartels, one of the most powerful men in South America, and then he was done.

The next day he flew home to Seattle, bought a house, started his business and found out his sister was pregnant. He hadn't looked back since.

Or at least he tried not to.

He tried very hard.

Booze helped. So did the punching bag in the garage.

And when things got extra hairy and he felt himself beginning to spiral, he headed to the local cage-fighting ring and went a few rounds with some of the guys. A lot of other veterans who understood his bloodlust, his fury, his need to hit and maim.

Only now he had Isobel and Sophie. They were his rocks, his home, his safety. Instead of wanting to hurt things when his past began to haunt him, he wanted to be around love and softness. Isobel and Sophie were where he could retreat to when the darkness started to close in around him and threatened to consume him. He had a good woman—a great woman who was nothing but light, and she and his daughter chased away the darkness, the anger, the pain.

"I'm so sorry, Aaron," Isobel said, her mouth against his neck, warm tears dripping down beneath his collar. "I'm so sorry for everything you've lost. It's been so much. More than anyone should ever have to go through."

"But I've gained so much too," he whispered, waiting for her to lift her head. He used the pads of his thumbs to wipe the tears from beneath her eyes. "You and Soph have given me so much. You've given me a sense of purpose again, a reason to keep going, to get up in the morning. You've given me love and hope." He pressed his forehead to hers.

Isobel hiccupped a sob, and fresh tears dripped down her cheeks. He wiped them away again with his thumbs.

"You saying you'll stay has given me more joy than I've ever had in my life. For the first time in a very long time, I have hope for the future. I *want* a future, and I want it with you."

Was it too soon to ask her to stay forever?

Ah, fuck it. He'd already put his heart on the line, told her about Colombia and what haunted him, and she hadn't run for the hills. Why not go all in? Why not lay it all on the line?

His forehead fell back to hers. "Forever, Iz? Will you stay forever?"

She lifted her head and gently pressed her lips against his. "I didn't think there was any other option."

Epilogue

2 years later ...

Aaron's head popped up from beneath the covers. "Was that a cry?"

Isobel rolled her eyes and huffed. "Nope. No cry."

"You sure?"

She grunted, then squeezed his head between her knees. "Yes, I'm sure. Your son is asleep in the corner of the room in his bassinet, and your daughter is asleep across the hall. I have the baby monitor for her room right here." She reached over to the nightstand and grabbed the monitor. "See, sound asleep. But for how long, we have no clue."

"I could have sworn ..."

"It was probably me making a happy noise, which I am no longer making, because you're paranoid. Now be a good soldier and get back to work." She glanced at the bassinet in the corner. Weston would be up any minute for a feeding—her boobs told her as much. They had a small window to get busy, and he was wasting it chit-chatting.

His grin was wicked and shiny with her arousal. "I love it when you're bossy." He pulled his fingers from inside her and gave her a quick salute. "Back in I go." Then he tossed the covers over his head and swept his tongue up between her folds.

"That's better," she purred, bucking into his face and biting her lips. Her breasts were engorged and ached, but no way in hell was she passing up the opportunity to have sex with Aaron. It'd been far too long, and sleep deprivation or not, leaking boobs or not, she was going to get an orgasm, whether Aaron got a tongue cramp or not.

"Mama!"

NOOOOOOOO!

Aaron tossed the covers back. "I definitely heard it this time. That Soph?"

Isobel scooted up the bed, then swung her legs over the side, pulling her pajama pants on. "Unless you think a three-month-old can say *Mama* already?" Man, lack of sleep and lack of sex turned her into a real sarcastic *biatch*.

He rolled his eyes. "I can go get her. Maybe you should just feed his nibs over there. That way when I get back, we won't be interrupted."

Good idea. Though she really hated the idea of waking a sleeping baby.

Her boobs were screaming louder than their two-year-old though, leaking like milky spigots too.

Nodding, she cursed their little cock-blockers, then walked over to the bassinet. Her chubby-cheeked son lay serenely on his back with his arms above his head and his mouth sucking at nothing.

Babies were so freaking cute—particularly when they slept and dream-nursed.

She scooped him up and wandered over to the glider rocking chair in the opposite corner, pulling her breast out as she sat down. Weston found her nipple, no problem, didn't even bother to open his eyes and reached up with both hands to hold her breast like it was a bottle.

Isobel closed her eyes and leaned her head back, setting them off to a gentle glide with her foot.

She could hear Aaron's deep voice across the hall as he dealt with Sophie and one of her nightly wake-ups. She wasn't quite potty-trained yet but hated sleeping in a diaper with pee in it, so whenever she peed in her diaper, she woke up and lost her mind, screaming until one of them changed her.

And then the whole big process was on repeat.

She needed her cup of water, her stuffed animal army all lined up in their proper order of rank along the foot of her bed. Her blanket needed to be retrieved from the depths of the abyss, also known as the tangled bedsheets. She needed her story, her night-night poem, her night-night song, and finally a kiss for each finger, one for her nose and one on each cheek.

Who on Earth had started this routine?

Isobel's father!

Right before Weston was born, Isobel and Aaron had gone away on a short weekend trip together without Sophie—a babymoon, as many called it. Isobel's parents had come to stay with Sophie, and in just four days and three nights, Isobel's father had created a new kind of monster at bedtime. A routine-demanding monster.

Sophie had that man so tightly wrapped around her pinky finger, her dad had a standing appointment every week with the chiropractor, his back was so twisted.

"But Papa did it for me," she would say, batting her long lashes at both Isobel and Aaron. "Why can't you?"

Then Aaron would cave, because he was the softy parent and Isobel was the hammer. The enforcer. The bad cop. She made the rules, and everyone else had to follow them. Otherwise, there would be consequences.

One of these days she'd shock the shit out of Aaron and be the good cop first, then he'd be forced to be the bad cop.

It would serve him right, always getting to play the hero while she doled out the discipline.

Raising tiny humans who didn't grow up to be colossal assholes was hard work.

Weston popped off but immediately began rooting again. Deftly, she switched him to the other side, feeling immediate release when he began to drain that breast.

Aaron loved her big milk-filled boobs. Kept buying her deep V-neck shirts to showcase the *girls,* as he called them. She just found her beach ball boobies uncomfortable and in the way.

Aaron's deep voice in song drifted across the hall and in through their open door. He was almost at the end of the routine. Hopefully, Sophie would be down until morning. She usually only woke up once.

Isobel began to hum the same tune, her eyes drifting shut once again as the song and the sound of Weston's guzzling blended into a pleasant background lullaby.

She wasn't sure how long she'd sat there, slowly humming, nursing and gliding back and forth, but when the weight of her son lifted off her lap, her eyes fluttered open.

"Little guy popped off," Aaron said, hoisting Weston up onto his shoulder and gently patting his back to work out a burp. He angled his nose to the baby's butt and gave a quick sniff, his mouth curling up into a smile. "First time in a while he hasn't shit himself post-feed. Think we're over that hurdle?"

Sleepily, Isobel pried herself out of the glider, stretching her arms above her head and yawning. "Maybe. Just means there's a new hurdle on the horizon. Remember the four-month sleep regression?"

He put Weston back down in his bassinet after the baby burped. "Don't remind me. Worst thing ever with Soph."

"Until the eight-month sleep regression," she said with a chuckle, sliding into bed, not bothering to take off her pajama pants.

Aaron climbed into bed beside her. "Hey, take your pants off."

She shook her head. "Naw, it's okay. I'm tired. You're tired. We can try again tomorrow night."

He made a growly noise in his throat, tossed back the covers and climbed over her. "No. Take your pants off and spread your legs, woman. I promised you an orgasm, and I intend to deliver."

Rolling her eyes, she smiled, though it took a lot of effort to lift the corners of her mouth. "You really don't have to."

Aaron's brows furrowed into a V, and he hooked his fingers into the waistband of her pants and tugged them off.

"Oh, all right, fine," she said, laughing. "You can go down on me. You can give me orgasms."

That smile. It was so mischievous, so wicked, it made her heart melt, her nipples tighten and her pussy clench every time.

He hunkered down onto his belly and shouldered her knees apart, dipping a finger into her still-wet folds. "Now, where was I?" he asked, twisting his lips in thought and staring into her pussy like it was a puzzle. He pushed a finger into her channel, and she gasped. "Ah, now I remember. I was riiiiight ... *here*." He swept the flat of his tongue up between her lips and laved at her clit.

Isobel's hips leapt off the bed. And her fingers gripped the ends of his hair.

She was seconds from coming, her fingers bunched in the sheets, head thrashing on the bed, when Aaron's free hand found her left hand. He pried her fingers free of the sheet, and something slowly slid onto her ring finger. His tongue never quit. His fingers inside her never ceased. The man was a true multitasker.

The orgasm was too close for her to think about anything else, so instead, she ignored the foreign thing on her hand and let the climax sweep through her. Her toes curled, her back arched, and her mouth opened in a silent cry as every muscle in her body clenched and she filled Aaron's mouth with her release.

His lips kept going. His tongue kept going. Around and around and around he swirled until another orgasm, fresh on the heels of the first, tore through her center. Eviscerating everything in its path, it left her boneless and pliant, bereft of coherent thoughts and panting on the bed with a sheen of sweat sprinkled across her limbs.

He lifted his head. "There we go."

She lazily lifted one eyelid. "You're a persuasive bugger, I'll give you that."

His smile could have given her another orgasm if she wasn't so damn exhausted. Then she remembered that he'd slid something onto her finger. She lifted her hand, and even in the dark bedroom, she could tell that it was one hell of a sparkler. Her eyes went wide, and she gasped.

"Figured we should probably make it official, no?" He shrugged, reaching for her hand and pushing the ring the rest of the way onto her finger. "I know we've talked about getting married. We should really do it. Not just talk about it but actually plan it and do it."

She licked along the seam of her lips, admiring the ring and the way it fit so perfectly on her finger. It was stunning.

His hand squeezed her. "You're it, Iz. My family, my heart, my future, my world. I want it all with you. You saved me from a well so deep, I wasn't sure I'd ever be able to climb back out. You made me happy again. Made me embrace the good in life and not just focus on the bad. You embraced Sophie like she was your own, and the way you are with our son makes me love you more each and every day."

A hot tear slipped down her cheek. She didn't think he'd ever said this much before in his life. At least not all at once.

He lifted his eyes from their intertwined hands. "Marry me."

More tears welled up in her eyes, and she hiccuped a sob as she nodded.

"Is that a yes?"

She nodded again, flung her arms around his neck and peppered kisses all over his face and neck. "It's more than a yes. It's an absolutely."

If you've enjoyed this book, please consider leaving a review wherever you purchased it. It really does make a difference and helps an independent author like me.

Thank you again.

Xoxo

Whitley Cox

Christmas with the Single Dad, Book 5

Chapter 1

"Can I touch your bicep?"

Careful to hide his eye roll, and instead plaster on a big fake grin, Zak Eastwood pulled his earbud out of one ear and sat up on the workout bench, coming face to face with a camel toe in hot pink spandex exercise pants. Slowly, he let his eyes climb the petite frame. Past the bare midriff with the spray tan, past the fake boobs stuffed into a tight white sports bra. Past the makeup (who the fuck worked out while wearing makeup?) to finally see long fake lashes batting at him shamelessly.

"Rockin' Around the Christmas Tree" played on the speakers overhead, competing with the rap in his one remaining earbud.

The woman in front of him took a half step forward, forcing the camel toe even closer to his head. He kept his eyes on her face. He just had to.

"I've just never seen such big muscles," she purred, tossing her shoulders back so her big fake tits pushed out toward him. "I see you here a lot. It shows."

He nodded. "Yeah, spend a fair bit of time here."

Because I own the place.

She thrust her hand forward, revealing pointy, sparkly gold fake nails with little green and red gems glued to them. "I'm Shadley."

He shook her hand. "Zak. Nice to meet you."

She nibbled on her bottom lip. "I know who you are. *Everybody* knows who you are."

He cocked a single eyebrow but didn't say anything.

"So can I touch it?"

"Touch what?" He was quickly losing patience with this woman. He knew what she wanted—that was being screamed from the tallest mountain—he just wasn't interested.

"Your arm." She lifted her shoulder.

The rap music in his one earbud switched to something heinously filthy. "Sure, have at 'er."

He had to keep the customers happy. Keep the members coming back for more. Even if that meant he pimped himself out a bit and let the gym bunnies hop around him constantly, wiggling their little cottontails. Not that he ever did what bunnies do best with them though. No freaking way.

She bounced on her toes, then stepped forward, reaching out timidly as if his arms had teeth and would suddenly lunge out and bite her.

Her hands were cold. Like fucking freezing. A chill ran through him, and his nipples tightened beneath his black tank top.

"Wow." She squeezed. "These are amazing. And your tattoos are so beautiful."

"Thanks."

She wrapped her hand around and beneath his arm, gripping his tricep. "I don't live too far from here. Just a couple of blocks. Was going to head home, have a bubble bath and some wine ..."

His mouth flattened into a thin line as he fought the urge to smirk. "Sounds like a great way to relax."

"I have a Jacuzzi tub, too. It's so big for little ol' me."

"You should get a Great Dane. They're huge."

He snorted in his head. He was fucking hilarious.

Her brows pinched, then relaxed, and she smiled a bleached-tooth smile. "I was thinking something a little less hairy and a little more muscly and inked up might be better company. What do you think?"

Commotion at the front desk drew his eyes away from the bunny in front of him. A regular patron whose name he couldn't remember—but really should—was just coming in and shaking off a ton of snow from her coat and stomping her boots.

The bunny cleared her throat. "What do you think? Feel like coming over for a bath and wine? I can massage out the aches from your workout."

He pinned his gaze back on the woman in front of him, careful not to let his distaste for her come out on his face or in his tone. "Thanks so much for the offer, but I need to get home. I have my kids tonight." No, he didn't, but she didn't need to know that. Finding out he had two kids usually scared the majority of the bunnies away.

She released his arm and stepped back a couple of steps. "Oh, you have kids." Ah, there it was.

That's right, little bunny, hop away now that you know I come with baggage.

He wiped his brow with his towel. "Two, a girl and a boy. Eight and ten."

Her smile was forced, almost grim. "How sweet."

Not into single dads there, little bunny?

She blinked her thick lashes, revealing what he knew to be *the smoky eye* effect with her shadow. Seemed a bit over the top for the gym but whatever.

His ex had been big into the *smoky eye*. Once she'd figured out how to do it, that is. For the first bit, Loni would come out of the bathroom looking like she'd just been punched in both eyes. Zak would laugh. Loni would pout and then head back in and try again. Eventually, she figured it out. Though he always preferred her—preferred most women with subtle eye makeup rather than dramatic.

He didn't begrudge a woman who wore makeup, got her nails done, took care of herself. Not in the least. He liked when a woman knew how to put herself together and dress up but also wasn't afraid to go out in public looking like a hot mess because she'd just killed it at the gym.

Life was all about balance.

Fake nails were fine as long as when the weeds needed to be pulled, she didn't mind getting a bit of dirt on her hands.

Or didn't mind breaking a nail as she raked them down his back when he was showing her how he liked to get his cardio workout.

He just wanted a woman who didn't prioritize that shit over the stuff in life that really mattered—like health and family. Besides, there wasn't anything hotter than seeing a ring of bright red lipstick around the base of his cock after a really good BJ.

However, he could tell in the mere two minutes she'd been standing there that Shadley or whatever the hell her name was, had probably never pulled a weed in her life, and definitely wouldn't be caught dead out in public looking like a hot mess.

She tilted her head in the direction of the women's changing room. "Oh, I think I hear my phone."

Fsst. Yeah, okay then.

You sure it wasn't the K-word that scared you off?

Kids! Nearly as terrifying as the word prenup.

And he would never *ever* get married again without one that was ironclad.

Shadley cleared her throat, then cupped her hand to her ear. "Yes, yes, that is definitely my phone. I left it in my locker. I better go check to make sure it isn't work calling me. I run a nail salon." She backed up a few more steps. "Nice to meet you."

He put his earbud back in and reclined down to the bench again. "Yeah, you too."

She was gone in a flash, leaving Zak chuckling to himself as he picked up the dumbbells again and resumed his pec fly reps.

Yeah, he could get any piece of tail he wanted. But he didn't want any. Not right now. Not for a long time. Loni had burned him bad. And she continued to make his life hell with the way she used their children as pawns in her manipulation and games.

She was a liar too.

Always with a new scheme up her sleeves. Always with a new ploy.

Her boyfriend was a liar too.

Zak fucking hated liars.

If he ever found a good woman again, he'd state right off the bat that if she lied to him, they'd be done.

No second chances, no do-overs.

Liars were the scum of the earth, and no way in hell would he have them in his or his kids' lives ever again.

Aurora Stratford nearly face-planted into the garland- and holly-adorned front desk as she shook her coat and stomped her boots. The temperature in her cheeks was that of a volcano, but her heart was on the verge of shattering.

Why?

Because he was talking to Shadley.

He. Zak.

He was talking to Shadley Taylor, the most beautiful woman at the gym.

Her squats were unbelievable, her makeup flawless. Like crazy flawless. Did she even break a sweat when she worked out at all? Did she even work out? Or did she simply come to the gym to be seen and cruise the weight section for fresh meat to sink her sharp fake claws into?

Over the past few months, Shadley had been talking with her girlfriends in the changing room—whenever Aurora happened to be in there at the same time as them—about trying to hook up with Zak. Looked like she was finally making her move.

Aurora tried not to let it distract her, but her eyes were glued to the two gorgeous people over in the weight room chatting.

And then Shadley touched his bicep, and Aurora nearly passed out.

Why did she torture herself?

Because he's gorgeous, and loving him from afar is better than never seeing him at all.

True.

Staring at him a few times a week was her guilty pleasure. Her dose of happiness at the end of the day, in a world filled with loss and stress and loneliness.

Once she swiped her key card, she took her snowy self to the women's changing room and got dressed for a workout.

It was exactly what she needed after a long day in the bullpen at her law firm. After a white-knuckle drive across town to the gym.

Why was it across town?

Because Aurora was attracted to Zak, and she let her heart run roughshod over her practicality.

Because Aurora was a thin-dime recent law graduate, first-year associate who exploited the *free two-week trial* membership at nearly every gym in Seattle, rather than pay a fee, because her ass was broke. Until she stumbled into Club Z, that is.

At a twenty-five-minute drive from her home and a twenty-minute drive from work, she knew it was stupid. There were over a dozen other fitness facilities and rec centers closer—and cheaper—to either work or home. But none of them had Zak.

The moment she walked in to claim her free two weeks and saw him doing chin-ups, she signed up for a lifetime membership. A LIFETIME MEMBERSHIP.

She was still paying it off.

But he was worth it.

The man was magnificent.

Stunning.

A tattooed god with a beautiful shock of dark red hair, rippling muscles, sparkling blue eyes and a smile that would make an entire nunnery fall to their knees and chant a thousand Hail Marys.

And he had absolutely no clue who she was.

The clock on the wall said it was eight o'clock. She'd been pulling twelve- and fourteen-hour days all week. Today was the first day she left the office before 10 p.m.

She climbed onto the elliptical machine once she'd filled up her water bottle at the fountain and grabbed a complimentary club towel.

She just needed to zone out and do cardio for an hour or so. Normally, she'd do thirty minutes of cardio and then weights, but she was just too damn tired for weights tonight. It was all she could do to keep her eyes open.

But she needed to keep her eyes open. She had the perfect view of her fantasy paramour. The perfect view of his ass, that is. He was doing squats in front of the mirror now, and the way his hamstrings and calves bunched and flexed with each dip made her whole mouth go dry—because another part of her body was incredibly wet.

Aurora caught a glimpse of herself in the mirror. She wasn't ugly. She knew that. But she wasn't what you called a show-stopper either.

She was checked out and flirted with, asked out by associates at work, had drinks sent over while out for dinner with friends. She was attractive. But she wasn't Shadley Taylor. She wasn't in Zak's league.

Never would be.

So she resigned herself to loving him from afar.

Fantasizing about him as she sweat her ass off and watched his ass tighten with each pop up from a squat.

She knew every tattoo on his arm.

Didn't know what they meant or the significance of them, but she knew them.

Knew the flowers on his right arm and the way they twisted down from his shoulder around and under his tricep to end just above his wrist. A peppering of scripted words she had never been close enough to read filled out the rest of that arm, along with Roman Numerals in big, dark block letters. He had two different sets of very realistic flowers on either shoulder—she knew they probably held significance—and more than once she caught herself tearing up as she stared at them.

It was harder to see what was on his left arm, but even from far away she could tell the work was beautiful. More writing, crashing waves, a lighthouse, a fish, footprints. It was all in there. It was all stunning.

"You almost done?"

She blinked the sweat from her eyes, grabbed her towel and wiped her face.

"You've been on here for like an hour." A muffled voice interrupted the music blasting through her earbuds. It was Shadley, and she was giving Aurora a very odd look. "These machines are for everyone, you know."

Aurora nodded. Her eyes flicked up to the clock on the wall, where sure enough, it was almost nine o'clock. "Yeah, sorry. Lost track of time. Been a long day."

Shadley smiled tightly, though the corners of her eyes didn't move. Was that Botox or just a fake smile? "Don't forget to wipe down your machine when you get off, please. I don't want to touch your sweat."

Don't forget to wipe down your machine ...

Aurora wanted to wipe down Shadley's fucking face. With her fist.

She slowed down, hopped off the elliptical and went over to the paper towel and spray bottle station so she could disinfect the machine for Shadley.

Why did the woman need *that* elliptical? There were like eight others.

Why did Shadley pick Aurora to kick off the machine? Yes, they were all occupied, but why didn't she go and flaunt her camel toe at one of the beefcakes down the row and ask them to give her a turn? Was it because she saw Aurora as an easy mark? A wounded gazelle on the Serengeti, the easiest person to bully off the machine, take down with her talons. Kill swiftly with one slice to the jugular with her bedazzled index finger.

With the pace of a snail in the snow, Aurora made her way back to the elliptical machine and wiped it down.

Shadley stood there, tapping her foot, her eyes focused on the row of televisions at the front of the gym above the mirrors. A few TVs had various news stations on: one, a Christmas comedy sketch special; another, sports; and the last had a cooking show where the Santa-hat-clad host was teaching some football player how to make something that Aurora could have sworn looked like lard pie but was more likely something festive and fattening like a French-Canadian Tourtière. It was Christmas, after all.

Shadley let out a huff and ran her manicured hand over her bottle-blonde hair, smoothing it back into its long, straight ponytail.

Aurora took her sweet time cleaning the machine, rolling her eyes and making a face of disgust when the woman's hot pink camel toe came into view as she bent over to wipe a few drops of sweat from the footholds.

"Can you speed up?" Shadley asked.

Aurora smiled sweetly. "I could, but I'm not going to. There are eight other machines, and yet you chose this one. There is no sign-up board, so technically, if I wanted to stay on this machine all day, I could. You don't *own* this machine. You don't *own* this gym. You pay your dues just like I do."

Shadley's face burned a bright pink beneath her bronzer, and her dark brown eyes turned fierce. "I could go and complain at the front desk."

Aurora tilted her head. "Okay." Then she hopped back up on to the same elliptical, turned it on again and resumed her workout.

Shadley let out an irritated growl. "You're a bitch."

Aurora shrugged, turned the music up on her phone and pointed to her earbuds. "What? I can't hear you."

She had to hide her smile for fear the woman in front of her might turn rabid and tear out her carotid artery with her Christmas-painted talons.

Aurora fought and argued all day long. Dealt with people slamming doors in her face and yelling at her on the phone more than she cared to count. Usually, by the end of the day, she had no more fight left in her, so she just rolled over and gave in, whether it be a person at the gym like Shadley or someone butting in line at the grocery store. She wasn't going to pick that hill to die on. She had bigger battles to fight, bigger fish to fry.

But not tonight. Something about the way Shadley was looking at her, speaking to her made Aurora see red. She wasn't the weakling of the pack. She wasn't a wounded gazelle on the savannah, the first to be picked off when the hyenas came scrounging. She would be one of the first to get away, one of the fastest in the herd.

Shadley was still flapping her lips, but Aurora couldn't hear her. The filthy rap in her ear was a welcome change from the shrill voice of Camel Toe Susan in front of her.

Aurora shook her head once again and pointed to her earbud. "Still can't hear you. Sorry."

Laser beams nearly shot out of the woman's eyes. Aurora dipped her head down to hide her smile. Stomping her foot, Shadley growled again, then turned and marched away.

Aurora snickered and turned away from where the other woman had retreated to, only to find HIM of all people watching her.

Her smile dropped instantly.

His didn't.

His grew bigger.

Her lips twitched as she debated whether to smile back. Now she just looked like she was having muscle spasms in her face.

His dark red eyebrow drew up on his freckled forehead, and he smiled even wider before shaking his head and glancing toward the front desk where, lo and behold, Shadley was making a complaint.

Ah, crap.

Aurora's gaze slipped from the flushed-face guy behind the desk and a pointing Shadley back to Zak. He was shaking his head again and rolling his eyes. He seemed to find all of this hilarious.

Was he not with Shadley?

Had he turned her down?

The person at the front desk who was handling Shadley's tirade glanced at Zak. Zak rolled his eyes again, shook his head and shrugged.

What was that about?

The employee behind the desk shook his head at Shadley, shrugged and made an apologetic face.

Shadley's head nearly exploded. She stormed off toward the changing room, steam retreating from her ears and possibly even her camel toe, the woman was that mad.

Aurora snickered again. Served the bitch right.

Ah, but where's your Christmas spirit?

Fuck Christmas spirit. Aurora had had a rough day at work, and all she wanted to do was jump on the elliptical at the gym, zone out and stare at Zak for ninety minutes. Was that too much to ask for? That was all she wanted for Christmas.

That was all she was probably going to get for Christmas.

She didn't have enough money to fly home to New Hampshire for the holidays, and her parents were struggling to make ends meet after her dad's heart attack this past spring and his now sudden retirement. She'd told them several times over the last few months that she didn't want them to waste their money and send her anything. She didn't need anything.

But of course, they hadn't listened, and a parcel had arrived in the mail not two days ago.

She didn't have a tree to put it under, so she bought a fake wreath at the dollar store and hung it on her wall, setting the parcel beneath it.

Merry Christmas!

So, yeah. Watching Zak bend and pick things up, flexing that ass of his, was her Christmas present to herself. And it was the only gift she was getting anybody this year, because things were tight—much like Zak's ass—but not nearly as nice.

Once again, in her own head, she'd zoned out completely.

Zak had gone back to his workout, and Aurora spaced out on the elliptical, reading the closed captioning on the cooking channel show and listening to the dirty, dirty rap music in her ear.

For some reason, she loved to listen rap music when she got her sweat on. And the dirtier the better. Maybe it was because the words helped fuel her fantasies about Zak, that he was doing to her what the lyrics of the song described.

Oh, if only.

It was Thursday night. She would head in to work for two more days—because Saturdays off were for bankers and firm partners, not first-year associates, aka mere peons—then have a much-deserved two days off, Christmas Eve and Christmas Day, only to burn the candle at both ends again come December 26th.

Two more days of work.

Those days off could not come fast enough. Mind you, she was only getting those days off because the firm itself was closed, not because she dared to take any vacation days, no way. She only hoped that Santa was kind to her and she didn't get a call from one of the partners with an emergency project that she had to do at home. She planned to spend those two days off in her bed with her vibrator and thoughts of Zak doing squats in her mind.

She was six months into her first-year associate position at her law firm, and already she was feeling burned out.

How did lawyers do it?

How did they work eighty-plus hours a week?

Their salaries are better than yours, so that cushions the blow of having no life. That's how.

Right. Money.

A lot of her colleagues would also respond with the answer *alcohol.* Too bad Aurora couldn't afford a bottle of wine from Trader Joe's to save her life at the moment. No, any spare change she had went straight to her parents—or her father's medical bills, to be more precise. Once she paid her rent, her utilities, her student loan payment and her food, she deposited the rest into her parents' bank account and hoped to God they had enough saved up that month to get her dad the heart medication he needed.

Life should not be lived with your fingers constantly crossed.

What was wrong with this world that lifesaving drugs were more expensive than a mortgage?

A tap on her shoulder had her bracing for another showdown with Shadley, only it wasn't Shadley at all. It was the guy from the front desk. "Just so you know, we close in about fifteen minutes."

Her eyes flew up to the clock. Holy crap, was it already nine forty-five?

She'd been pedaling the machine for another forty-five minutes and hadn't even clued in.

She really was exhausted.

No, you're burned the fuck out. You need sleep and lots of it.

Blinking, she nodded, yawned and slowed down her machine. "Right, thanks. I knew that."

He smiled and then took off to inform the next person.

She hopped down off the elliptical and scanned the gym for Zak. He was nowhere to be found.

Probably showering.

Oh God, Zak in the shower. *Yes, please.*

She needed a shower to cool off after that image.

Only she'd never waste the free hot water on a cold shower. Even if she lived on the surface of the sun.

Free hot water was a gift.

There was nothing quite like endless, free hot water. Well, it wasn't free. She'd paid a hefty lifetime membership for that hot water, so she was going to use it. Might as well save her own hot water bill at home.

Anywhere she could scrimp and save, she would.

She sprayed down her machine once again, wiping it clean of her sweat, then she headed to the changing room.

By the grace of God, Shadley was not in there. She must have left when Aurora was staring at Zak's butt. Which time?

She peeled out of her clothes, wrapped a towel around her and headed to the shower, ready to shut her eyes and let the water and soap wash away the disaster of a day—the disaster of her life.

BUY IT NOW —> https://books2read.com/CWTSD-SDS

ACKNOWLEDGMENTS

There are so many people to thank who help along the way. Publishing a book is definitely not a solo mission, that's for sure. First and foremost, my friend and editor Chris Kridler, you are a blessing, a gem and an all-around terrific person. Thank you for your honesty and hard work.

Thank you to Danielle Young, your suggestions on my plot were so helpful, and thank you to Dr. Felicia Kolonjari environment and atmospheric scientist from Environment Canada. Your insight into the future of our planet was as helpful as it was terrifying. Thank you. I'm freaking out a little, not going to lie.

Megan J. Parker-Squiers from EmCat Designs, your covers are awesome. I love these covers so much, you outdid yourself.

Author Jeanne St. James and Andi Babcock for beta-reading this book. Thank you so much for your feedback.

Author Ember Leigh, my author bestie, I love our bitch fests—they keep me sane.

My fabulous assistant, Megan MacPhail of Kiss My Smut, what would I do without you? You are amazing and I SO appreciate all your hard work, beautiful graphics and that you also beta-read this one for me. Thank you!!!

My parents, in-laws and brother, thank you for your unwavering support. The Small Human and the Tiny Human, you are the beats and beasts of my heart, the reason I breathe and the reason I drink. I love you both to infinity and beyond. And lastly, of course, the husband. You are my forever, my other half, the one who keeps me grounded and the only person I have honestly never grown sick of even when we did that six-month backpacking trip and spent every single day together. I never tired of you. Never needed a break. You are my person. I love you.

OTHER BOOKS BY WHITLEY COX

Love, Passion and Power: Part 1
The Dark and Damaged Hearts Series: Book 1
https://books2read.com/LPP1-DDH
Kendra and Justin

·

Love, Passion and Power: Part 2
The Dark and Damaged Hearts: Book 2
https://books2read.com/LPP2-DDH
Kendra and Justin

·

Sex, Heat and Hunger: Part 1
The Dark and Damaged Hearts Book 3
https://books2read.com/SHH1-DDH
Emma and James

·

Sex, Heat and Hunger: Part 2
The Dark and Damaged Hearts Book 4
https://books2read.com/SHH1-DDH
Emma and James

·

Hot & Filthy: The Honeymoon
The Dark and Damaged Hearts Book 4.5
https://books2read.com/HF-DDH
Emma and James

·

True, Deep and Forever: Part 1
The Dark and Damaged Hearts Book 5
https://books2read.com/TDF1-DDH
Amy and Garrett

·

True, Deep and Forever: Part 2
The Dark and Damaged Hearts Book 6
https://books2read.com/TDF2-DDH
Amy and Garrett

BOOK 4

•

Hard, Fast and Madly: Part 1
The Dark and Damaged Hearts Series Book 7
https://books2read.com/HFM1-DDH
Freya and Jacob

•

Hard, Fast and Madly: Part 2
The Dark and Damaged Hearts Series Book 8
https://books2read.com/HFM1-DDH
Freya and Jacob

•

Quick & Dirty
Book 1, A Quick Billionaires Novel
https://books2read.com/QDirty-QBS
Parker and Tate

•

Quick & Easy
Book 2, A Quick Billionaires Novella
https://books2read.com/QEasy-QBS
Heather and Gavin

•

Quick & Reckless
Book 3, A Quick Billionaires Novel
https://books2read.com/QReckless-QBS
Silver and Warren

•

Quick & Dangerous
Book 4, A Quick Billionaires Novel
https://books2read.com/QDangerous-QBS
Skyler and Roberto

•

Quick & Snowy
The Quick Billionaires, Book 5
https://books2read.com/QSnowy-QBS
Brier and Barnes

•

Doctor Smug
https://books2read.com/DoctorSmug
Daisy and Riley

•

Hot Dad
https://books2read.com/Hot-Dad
Harper and Sam
·

Snowed In & Set Up
https://books2read.com/SISU
Amber, Will, Juniper, Hunter, Rowen, Austin
·

Love to Hate You
https://books2read.com/Love2HateYou
Alex and Eli
·

Lust Abroad
https://books2read.com/Lust-Abroad
Piper and Derrick
·

Hired by the Single Dad
https://books2read.com/HBTSD-SDS
The Single Dads of Seattle, Book 1
Tori and Mark
·

Dancing with the Single Dad
https://books2read.com/DWTSD-SDS
The Single Dads of Seattle, Book 2
Violet and Adam
·

Saved by the Single Dad
https://books2read.com/SBTSD-SDS
The Single Dads of Seattle, Book 3
Paige and Mitch
·

Living with the Single Dad
https://books2read.com/LWTSD-SDS
The Single Dads of Seattle, Book 4
Isobel and Aaron
·

Christmas with the Single Dad
https://books2read.com/CWTSD-SDS
The Single Dads of Seattle, Book 5
Aurora and Zak

BOOK 4

·

New Year's with the Single Dad
https://books2read.com/NYWTSD-SDS
The Single Dads of Seattle, Book 6
Zara and Emmett

·

Valentine's with the Single Dad
https://books2read.com/VWTSD-SDS
The Single Dads of Seattle, Book 7
Lowenna and Mason

·

Neighbors with the Single Dad
https://books2read.com/NWTSD-SDS
The Single Dads of Seattle, Book 8
Eva and Scott

·

Flirting with the Single Dad
https://books2read.com/FWTSD-SDS
The Single Dads of Seattle, Book 9
Tessa and Atlas

·

Falling for the Single Dad
https://books2read.com/FFTSD-SDS
The Single Dads of Seattle, Book 10
Liam and Richelle

·

Hot for Teacher
https://books2read.com/HFT-SMS
The Single Moms of Seattle, Book1
Celeste and Max

·

Hot for a Cop
https://books2read.com/HFAC-SMS
The Single Moms of Seattle, Book 2
Lauren and Isaac

·

Hot for the Handyman
https://books2read.com/HTHM-SMS
The Single Moms of Seattle, Book 3
Bianca and Jack

•
Mr. Gray Sweatpants
A Single Moms of Seattle spin-off book
https://books2read.com/MrGraySweatpants
Casey and Leo
•
Hard Hart
https://books2read.com/HH-HB
The Harty Boys, Book 1
Krista and Brock
•
Lost Hart
The Harty Boys, Book 2
https://books2read.com/LH-HB
Stacey and Chase
•
Torn Hart
The Harty Boys, Book 3
https://books2read.com/THART-HB
Lydia and Rex
•
Dark Hart
The Harty Boys, Book 4
https://books2read.com/DH-HB
Pasha and Heath
•
Full Hart
The Harty Boys, Book 5
https://books2read.com/FH-HB
A Harty Boys Family Christmas
Joy and Grant
•
Not Over You
A Young Sisters Novel
https://books2read.com/not-over-you
Rayma and Jordan

BOOK 4

Snowed in with the Rancher
A Young Sisters Novel
https://books2read.com/snowed-in-rancher
Triss and Asher
March 4, 2023
·
Second Chance with the Rancher
A Young Sisters Novel
https://books2read.com/second-chance-rancher
Mieka and Nate
May 13, 2023
·
Done with You
A Young Sisters Novel
https://books2read.com/done-with-you
Oona and Aiden
October 13, 2023
·
Rock the Shores
A Cinnamon Bay Romance
https://books2read.com/Rocktheshores
Juliet and Evan
·
The Bastard Heir
Winter Harbor Heroes, Book 1
Co-written with Ember Leigh
https://books2read.com/the-bastard-heir
Harlow and Callum
·
The Asshole Heir
Winter Harbor Heroes, Book 2
Co-written with Ember Leigh
https://books2read.com/the-asshole-heir
Amaya and Carson

The Rebel Heir
Winter Harbor Heroes, Book 3
Co-written with Ember Leigh
https://books2read.com/the-rebel-heir
Lily and Colton
March 18, 2023

NATALIE SLOAN TITLES

Light the Fire
Revolution Inferno, Book 1
https://mybook.to/light-the-fire
Haina, Zane, Alaric and Jorik

•

Stoke the Flames
Revolution Inferno, Book 2
https://mybook.to/stoke-the-flames
Olia, Maxxon, Cypher and Alaric

•

Burn it Down
Revolution Inferno, Book 3
https://mybook.to/burn-it-down
Zosha, Knox, Shade and Tozer
June 3, 2023

ABOUT THE AUTHOR

A Canadian West Coast baby born and raised, Whitley is married to her high school sweetheart, and together they have two beautiful daughters and a fluffy dog. She spends her days making food that gets thrown on the floor, vacuuming Cheerios out from under the couch and making sure that the dog food doesn't end up in the air conditioner. But when nap time comes, and it's not quite wine o'clock, Whitley sits down, avoids the pile of laundry on the couch, and writes. A lover of all things decadent; wine, cheese, chocolate and spicy erotic romance, Whitley brings the humorous side of sex, the ridiculous side of relationships and the suspense of everyday life into her stories. With single dads, firefighters, Navy SEALs, mommy wars, body issues, threesomes, bondage and role-playing, Whitley's books have all the funny and fabulously filthy words you could hope for.

Website: WhitleyCox.com
Email: readers4wcox@gmail.com
Twitter: @WhitleyCoxBooks
Instagram: @CoxWhitley
TikTok: @AuthorWhitleyCox
Facebook : https://www.facebook.com/CoxWhitley/
Blog: https://whitleycox.com/fabulously-filthy-blog-page/

Exclusive Facebook Reader Group:
https://www.facebook.com/groups/234716323653592/
Booksprout: https://booksprout.co/author/994/whitley-cox
Bookbub: https://www.bookbub.com/authors/whitley-cox
Goodreads:
https://www.goodreads.com/author/show/16344419.Whitley_Cox
Subscribe to my newsletter here:
http://eepurl.com/ckh5yT

Treat yourself to awesome orgasms!
This one only ships to the US.

https://tracysdog.com/?sca_ref=1355619.ybw0YXuvPL

Treat yourself to awesome orgasms! This one ships to Canada!

https://thornandfeather.ca/?ref=734ThbSs

Made in United States
North Haven, CT
29 April 2024

51908442R00193